NEEDING TOMORROW

Book 2 in the New York Family Series

Written By:

CARRIE CROSS

Dedication

This book is dedicated to Eve Shulz. I will never forget the kindness she gave, the way she encouraged her students to live their dreams and the way she inspired me. I would not be the person I am today without having known her. She lives on in her students, her friends and her family.

Contents

Chapter One

In the last year friends became family through ups and downs that went against anything they had ever experienced before. Cassidy had found the love of her life and together they stood firm against the darkness at their door. It was during this time that Cassidy also overcame cancer and moved forward with her happiness.

It seemed like Ryan and Bridgette were on top of the world last year. They were engaged and had a child together. Joshua was the light of their lives. It was amazing how much having children could change a person, a couple.

It seemed as if everything was finally going to work in their favor. That was until one random Wednesday when Bridgette and Ryan were at work. Their lives had become happily mundane. However, their nanny decided that she wanted to enjoy their bathtub alone. The baby would be fine in his playpen for a while.

That was her first and last mistake as a nanny. In the time that it took for her to step into the tub little Joshua died. He choked to death on the piece of a toy that had broken off. The little plastic circle was not seen by his parents or his nanny. And his life may have been saved if his nanny would have been there to try to get it out of his mouth/throat in time.

Bridgette had been in a meeting when a call came in. She saw the look on her co-workers face and took the call on the spot. That was when she collapsed to the floor on her knees. The sounds of her screams echoed through the entire office. It was like she was suddenly under water and unable to feel, think or breathe properly.

Across town Ryan had been in a meeting with a client. The sound of his phone ringing was unusual so he picked up straight away. All he was told was that his wife collapsed after getting grave news. It was not until he reached his home and saw the look on his wife's face that he realized his son was gone.

There had been no need to say the words because the two parents simply knew. Joshua had been ripped from their lives. Each beat of their hearts felt hollow and mechanical.

There was no real life inside of it and they struggled to cope with what had happened.

It was a freak accident. An accident had taken something precious from Bridgette and Ryan. Joshua was gone. Somehow Ryan and Bridgette had managed to keep their relationship together. They had clung to one another in their sorrow and loss.

They had both moved forward with their lives. There were times that it was as if Joshua never existed. Bridgette was taking it outwardly the hardest. She had become almost robotic in her movements and her emotions had broken down. Ryan was all business and never wanted to discuss the accident with anyone at all.

There were days when it was like their son would toddle out and lift his arms to them both. The couple could almost feel him in their arms. There were other times that the loss of him almost consumed his mother. (Sometimes Ryan felt it as well.)

Several Months later so much had changed. There was a great deal of pain that happened. Everything had turned upside down. Not one member of the family had been spared from the darkness. Each person felt the loss of Joshua in their own way. Over time some clung together and others scattered apart to the wind.

That was before everything changed once again. The grief was tearing the couple apart. They knew that they were falling apart as individuals but never saw the break of their relationship coming.

Bridgette was sitting in the window seat watching the rain come down against the glass. The only light that was present was the light from the moon. The rain seemed to be perfect given her mood and the atmosphere in her home.

The new apartment felt as lonely as her heart and soul at that moment. All that she could think about was Ryan and how just a few days ago they had been about to get re-married. Everything had seemed so right with the world.

Both Bridgette and Ryan had been in love and everything was bright and sunny in their lives. That was before the loss of Joshua and when Ashley turned their lives upside down. The very name of that woman constricted Bridgette's heart made her feel like she was going to vomit. It was the same way when thinking of Ryan's name made her heart ache inside her chest.

All it took was one person coming into their story to change it all. The worst part was that Ryan had chosen Ashley over Bridgette. Even thinking about what happened made Bridgette feel sick to her stomach. She slowly pushed herself off the window seat and walked into her kitchen.

The light from the moon was enough to help guide her toward the island. She decided to open the fridge and pull out the orange juice. Then taking a glass from her cabinet she placed it on the island.

The sound of the orange juice being poured into the glass was almost shocking since the room had been so silent previously. Taking the glass into her hand Bridgette took a sip before forcing herself to drink the entire glass.

Bridgette didn't want to take care of herself. It was the last thing she cared about at that moment. The only thing that Bridgette could think about was the pain searing through her soul every moment she took in a breath. It wasn't fair. She and her best friend had been through so much over this last year.

Both the women had deserved so much better from life. Each woman deserved to have her happiness. As time moved forward it seemed like there was one tragic situation after another.

Bridgette had seen Cassidy fight for her life with cancer and lose her chance to become a mother naturally. She had been afraid that Cassie's ex Rufus would take them all out. Finally they were going to have their happy endings.

Cassie and Devante were happy together and moving forward with their adoption of a little one. At that moment Bridgette and Ryan were supposed to be happily married with a son. Now that was all a thing of the past and Bridgette could not seem to accept it.

This new reality went against everything she believed in and had hoped for. She felt her hands shaking and placed her empty glass into the sink and made her way into her new bedroom. Just a few days prior Bridgette had decorated the bedroom to suit her taste.

Cassidy had told her it was important to make the space feel like home. She and Devante had helped Bridgette get settled. Thankfully, they hadn't asked too many questions focusing on what she needed instead. It had helped her more than words could describe.

In this transition period Bridgette needed support but also the space to process. Each day was a step forward into the world she had never wanted for herself. This was the hand she had been dealt and she had to find her way through.

The bedroom was decorated with a French blue theme and felt like a peaceful retreat inside her penthouse. Devante had helped get her into the building and helped her find a new position at his company. It made her feel good to be able to pay her own way and have a home as a perk of the position.

It had never occurred to her that she would be Devante's personal assistant, but he seemed to have felt that she would be perfect for the role. At least until she found her footing. Cassidy knew that her friend could accomplish the job perfectly and had pushed her to do it. It was the best choice that she has made in a long time.

There was enough money to live on and to save up for her future. Her dream was to have a bakery upstate. And each week she was setting aside money for her dream. And in a couple of years she would be able to make big moves for her bakery and a new home of her own.

It would be nice to stand on her own two feet. In knowing that it was all on her own merit and not because she happened to be in love with someone who could afford it all for her. It wasn't like she was happy that Ryan had left her or the reasons behind it. Never that. But, she was happy that she still had the drive to care for herself and that she was showing him that he didn't break her. At the same time her heart was broken and sometimes she wondered if she would ever heal again.

The next day was going to be difficult for her because it would be the first time since the break up that she would have seen Ryan. It is going to be hard for her. At the same time Cassidy had helped her get some new clothes for her new position.

She would be a professional in the office and leave all of her feelings at home. In her safe space where she could fall apart in privacy. She would be damned if she let Ryan see the mess he made of her life. The loss of her son and the love of her life would be her private pain.

Getting into bed Bridgette wasn't thinking about her silky short pajamas or the way they felt against her skin. She was numb to everything but knew she needed to get some rest. Forcing herself to be responsible she sunk into her bed and curled up under the covers.

The sounds of the rain against her windows gave her comfort and between that and her exhaustion from all of her crying she fell into a deep sleep. There were no dreams that invaded her rest. It was just peace.

The alarm was loud and obnoxious to Bridgette's ears, and she wanted to kill it. Instead, she grumbled and sat up to press the button to silence the alarm. Then she made her way to the ladies room to do her business and then strip down to take a shower.

The warm water felt good against her skin, and she felt more alive than she had in a long while. After the shower she toweled off with her big fluffy aqua towels. She brushed her teeth and dried her hair/styled it.

The closet was filled with new outfits. Bridgette looked through them and decided to pick a cyan blue blouse and navy pencil skirt. She picked out a matching bra and panty set to wear underneath her clothes.

Then she found some navy blue pumps to match. To complete the look she found some silver jewelry to help her feel more confident. A bracelet her parents gave her when she was sixteen, a necklace from Cassidy and some earrings she purchased for herself when she moved to the city.

Bridgette felt more confident after a once over in her full length mirror. She smiled and took the elevator to the lobby. She was greeted with polite smiles from those she encountered and was pleased that her trip down kept her on schedule.

It pleased Bridgette that she had time to stop at the corner deli to get a bagel sandwich before work. She sat at a table alone enjoying her bagel and her coffee. Before leaving Bridgette picked up a coffee to go and was off.

It was easy to hail a cab and make her way to the office. Upon arrival, she smiled at the receptionist and was told to go straight up to Devante's office as she was early, and he would be eager to have her get started. The elevator ride to the office would have normally made her nervous.

Today it felt like she was on the way to her future, and she felt glimmers of happiness. The ding of the elevator to announce a stop and someone getting on the elevator did not take her attention away from her phone. She was checking emails and making sure she was prepared for what her new boss wanted from her this morning.

Then she caught the smell of smoke and spice and knew who she was sharing the elevator with. The first instinct in her soul was to look up and say something to him. The idea of hearing his voice was so powerful.

Instead Bridgette fought those feelings and instead opted to focus on her email and ignore him completely. There was the sound of someone clearing their throat, and she looked up as if she were just noticing someone else in the elevator carriage. For the briefest moment she felt like her heart would stop just looking at him in his gray suit.

The look of his hair tousled like it always tended to be was almost too much for her to handle. Ryan's evergreen gaze he leveled on her made her insides feel jittery and warm. There was nothing that Bridgette wanted to say to the man a few feet from her.

She simply nodded to him and went back to her phone. Ryan couldn't stand the fact that she barely acknowledged him in the elevator. He had cleared his throat hoping to hear her voice or have some sort of interaction with her. But, she had barely given him a slight nod of her head and went back to her phone.

"It is a lovely morning.", he said. She simply shrugged her shoulders not even looking up at the sound of his voice. He knew that things would be different between them. But he never imagined that she would be so indifferent to him.

The elevator dinged and the door opened. The second the door began to open Bridgette was ready to exit the elevator. Ryan simply stood back and watched her leave the elevator before leaving himself. All he could think was that she had never looked more lovely and that he missed her.

It was hard for him to walk to his office and not straight to her desk. Despite the urge to go to her desk he decided to be professional. The location of Devante's office being next to his only made it that much harder.

On a typical morning this would have been a relief. Ryan loved to get lost inside his work. This was clearly not a typical morning!

Once inside his office he picked up the phone dialing Devante and said, "What in the hell were you thinking in hiring her?!" His voice was more like a growl than a normally voiced statement. Devante laughed at him through the phone.

"You have an issue that is of a personal nature. I, on the other hand, needed to have a personal assistant. It just so happens that my soul mate knew someone who was qualified. Bridgette was in need of a new residence and a new job. So, I decided to help myself out and hire her. Which is none of your business.", Devante stated.

Ryan growled into the phone once more. Devante actually hung up on him. Ryan simply stared at the handle of the phone and blinked.

His best friend was not wrong but he hated the fact that he had so squarely put him in his place. It wasn't until there was a knock on his office door that he stopped stewing. He growled to have the person knocking come inside.

As he looked up he noticed his personal assistant Lorelei come inside his office. She smiled warmly at him and said, "This is going to be quite the long day, Sir. You have meetings all morning and then this afternoon is your long meeting with Mr. Salazar."

Ryan groaned and then looked up at her and said, "Thank you. Did you get the Simmons file?" She nodded and handed it to him. Then she waited to be dismissed. Ryan knew he was lucky to have someone so efficient and skilled as his personal assistant.

At that moment Ryan smiled warmly and said, "Thank you for everything Lorelei. Can you please work on the Richardson and Gilmore reports?" She nodded and went to her desk outside of the office. Ryan then started to read over the Simmons file and prepared for his first meeting in about ten minutes.

There was the distinct grinding of his teeth as he realized that Devante and thus Bridgette will be there in his meetings all day as well. There was no time to find a way in which to ditch his meetings. Ryan made his way into the conference room and seated himself to the side of the table.

In less than five minutes Devante and his personal assistant Bridgette came into the room. Devante took his seat at the head of the table and across from Ryan Bridgette took her seat. Lorelei took the seat beside Ryan and smiled warmly with everyone at the table.

The small group were waiting for Simmons and his personal assistant to arrive. It was silent as they waited a couple of minutes before their associates entered. The meeting began twelve minutes later.

Simmons and his assistant Roger came into the room and the meeting began. Devante took the lead on the meeting and Ryan stepped in when needed. Both Lorelei and Bridgette were taking notes on the meeting for their bosses.

Ryan was pleased that the meeting went so well. They now had the Simmons account on lock down. This should have made him very happy. Instead it was bittersweet and felt like an ache in his chest watching Bridgette speaking with Roger and Mr. Simmons.

There was nothing unprofessional about her conduct, and yet he felt jealous and sad watching them speak so warmly with her. It made his pulse bulge in his neck as he watched Mr. Simmons give Bridgette his card. The professional told her they would be in touch and Ryan saw red.

It was completely professional and yet it irked him. Just then the phone in his pocket buzzed, and he pulled it out and read the message waiting there. The message was from Ashley asking him how he was doing and if he wanted to get a drink after work.

It felt like too much to be so close to Bridgette and to get a text from Ashley at the same time. His friendship with Ashley had been the reason for his breaking off his engagement to Bridgette in the first place. Quickly racing to his office he closed the door behind him.

Once he was seated behind his desk he started to text Ashley back. He told her that he was having an awkward day although his meeting went well. Then he told her he would be delighted to have drinks after work in their old haunt down the street.

He would have offered Devante an invitation, but he knew Devante would have refused to spend time with Ashley. They had all been friends once but the fact that he and she had, in Devante's mind, screwed Bridgette over created disdain.

There was a knock on his door, and he grumbled for the person to enter. The sound of someone coming into the office made him look up. There stood the woman who haunted him. Bridgette stood straight and professional before him.

"To what do I owe this pleasure?", he asked. She kept her lips in a thin line for a few seconds before she said, "I have the Miller report for you. Mr. Salazar wanted you to have it quickly. He also said that you should have drinks tonight. Unless you were and I quote, "Otherwise occupied.""

The tone of her voice was very even and her gaze was more at the wall than his face. It was just as well that she was not looking at him because his face was bright red. He said, "I believe I will call him directly to respond.", he choked out.

She simply nodded and turned to leave. Before she could turn the knob on the door he said, "It is good to see you Bridgette." That was when she turned sharply and gave him a scathing glare.

"I am a personal assistant in this firm. I am not here to see you nor do I have the desire to go beyond my professional duty. Please keep your comments beyond my position here to yourself. I have no desire to hear them and it goes against our professional relationship.", she said with her voice like ice.

It made Ryan's entire body tense, and he instantly felt his body freeze. It was not until then that he considered what his actions had done to her or their interactions moving forward. Bridgette did not wait for him to respond as she turned back and left the room with great urgency.

Ryan considered what just happened and ran his hands over his face with a long-suffering sigh. It blew his mind that just last week they had been living in wedded bliss and everything had felt so perfect. Now she couldn't stand to be in the same room with him.

Did he make a mistake in putting his lifelong friendship before her? At that moment he just wasn't sure. The rest of the day was just as frustrating for him.

He sat in meeting after meeting with his personal assistant being the professional and to his dismay so was Bridgette. She ignored him unless it was professionally needed she acknowledged him. She was as polite as was expected but not an inch more.

14

It was wearing him down seeing her and admiring her from afar. All the while being shut out. Not that he could blame her. He'd broken off their engagement over his friendship with another woman. If the shoe had been on the other foot he would have been a lot less professional and polite.

Finally the end of the day and he didn't know he could feel so tired. It wasn't even a late night, and he felt weary to say the least. He'd called Devante and explained his plans for the night and offered he could join him and Ashley for drinks.

That went as well as he had predicted. Devante had said he would rather drop dead and be put into the ocean with cement shoes. It wasn't like he'd thought his friend would react differently. He just wished they could all simply move past all of the drama.

Ryan watched from the glass wall of his office as Devante made Bridgette laugh as the two walked to the elevator. He wondered if they would go out for drinks and if Cassidy would join them. All four of them used to do that after a long day.

It had been some of his fondest memories. Now he was on the outside of that social circle. It hurt, but he deserved it as it was his choice that made it transpire.

Gathering up some files to take home for this evening he put them into his briefcase. Then he was ready to leave the office and picked up his cellphone. Once in the elevator he checked his messages and saw that Ashley was early. He replied that he would meet her in a few minutes, and he was on his way.

Exactly seven minutes later he arrived at the little pub down the road. Ryan took a seat in the booth across from Ashley and smiled, greeting her warmly. She smiled in return and asked him about his day.

It was calming to hear her voice and have someone genuinely excited to see him. They talked about their days and then Ashley asked him how it was seeing Bridgette. It was like someone had poured ice water over his soul. He tensed and Ashley noticed.

Awkwardly she put her hair behind her ear and looked down saying, "I'm sorry for asking, Ry. I just knew it would be hard for you and wanted to be a pal." Ryan considered her words and then thankfully the waiter came and took their orders.

Then Ryan looked down at the table in front of him and said softly, "It hurt my heart to see her. Not because she was there or she was impolite. It was because she told me she wanted nothing to do with me outside of professional obligations. She was so icy and not at all like herself with me. And I know it is my fault that she feels this way. I am the one who broke off our engagement. And she is acting even more polite and kind than I would in her place."

Ashley considered his words and said, "I'm sorry that it is so painful and difficult. It may get better with time." Ryan nodded and figured that she was probably right.

Their meals and beers arrived and they ate in silence. Ashley seemed to want to ask questions, but she held back to spare Ryan's feelings. For his part Ryan just didn't want to think about Bridgette and the pain always in his chest.

After they had finished Ashley looked into Ryan's eyes and said, "I heard from Jake today. He asked to go for coffee and I told him I'd have to think about it." Ryan considered that and said, "You haven't seen him since the wedding right?" She nodded.

"Yes. I ran from our wedding, and yet he wants to talk to me anyway. And not in a chop off my head sort of way.", Ashley said. Ryan chuckled and said, "You two should meet. You can explain your side of things to him and perhaps you can both find some peace. Not all break-ups need to be so painful."

Once the words were out of his mouth he wished he could take them back. Ashley sort of winced but was too polite to make a comment in return. They sipped their alcoholic drinks, and he noticed she ordered a martini and it only left him missing Bridgette.

That was her drink of choice and so unlike Ashley. Ashley was known for her Moscow mules or scotch on the rocks. But, he didn't care enough to ask about the changes in her drinking habits.

He just continued to drink his whiskey. It wasn't until around nine in the evening that Ryan even checked his watch. He groaned and told Ashley he needed to head home to do some work. She said she would walk him to his car.

As the pair were walking to his car Ashley said, "I've been thinking. I think this entire thing happened for a reason. Jake and I. You with Bridgette. I think that it is the universe telling us something." Ryan stopped walking and turned to look at her as if she had eight heads.

"What the hell would the universe be telling us exactly? We are unworthy of love?",he asked in a snarky tone. The way his voice sounded made her wince for a second.

Ashley then came back to her senses and said, "No. I think it is telling us that we should give each other a try." Ryan's eyes became wide.

He looked her in the eye and said, "What?! We have been friends for most of our lives. We have never crossed that line. I have never seen you that way. Where is this coming from?!"

A moment passed before Ashley took a deep breath and said, "I've been in love with you for years. It is why I left Jake at the altar. And I think you feel the same way deep down because you left Bridgette for me. So... why not?"

Ryan shook his head and tried to clear his mind to be sure he was hearing her properly. Taking a breath he stepped backward to put space between himself and Ashley.

"The reason why not is that we are friends. I am friends with a great many people. Devante for example. However, you have never seen me considering dating him or having romantic feelings for him. I never would even if I found him to be desirable. I am not into my friends in that way.

Bridgette is the love of my life. I did not leave her "for you" I left her because of you. There is a difference.", he said with a sharp tone.

It took a few minutes before Ashley composed herself enough to speak. Ryan was tense and she was afraid to upset either of them further. At the same time she had to keep talking.

"That is not what you told either of us when it happened.", she said and then proceeded to walk to her car, get in and drive away. Ryan stood there sagging against his vehicle wondering how he got to this moment.

He'd never once thought of Ashley as anything more than his friend. She was not even his type, all things considered. If it was a matter of "being with" her or Bridgette in a romantic sense there was no contest.

Ryan would be with Bridgette each time. And yet there he was leaning on his car as if his legs were unable to hold him up. And he was painfully alone.

Not just because Ashley had left but because nobody understood what had happened from his perspective. It seems everyone thought he was picking a new romantic union with his friend over his fiancé. That would make him a total douche canoe. But, he hadn't done that.

In his mind he simply had to choose between a lifelong friendship and his relationship. It was unfair for anyone to ask him to make that choice in the first place. But, both women insisted upon it, and he had made a snap choice in the moment.

The choice to leave his fiancé was not his finest moment ever. However, he felt he had been given no real winning choices. At the moment he was wondering if he hadn't made a grave mistake.

Especially since Ashley has clearly gotten the wrong idea about the nature of his intentions and their relationship. It was unclear if their friendship could survive this miscommunication. And if it was so brittle to begin with, how could it have been worth losing Bridgette?

Ryan was clearly in a state and didn't think he could drive home. He called Devante at once. The second his friend picked up Ryan spilled his guts to his friend. Devante told him he would be there in ten minutes depending on traffic and to sit tight.

Ryan felt a little freer. His friend would arrive, and they would sort out this mess somehow. Things had to get better, right?

It took Devante about fifteen minutes to arrive at Ryan's car. The second he got out of his car he noticed just how drunk Ryan was and said, "Come on Buddy. We are going to my house, and we'll talk, get you some water and then put you to bed."

It was comical to see the fact that Ryan did not protest but instead got inside the back seat of Devante's car and laid down in the fetal position. Devante simply laughed and got behind the wheel of his car. He drove them to his penthouse.

Chapter Two

They arrived at the penthouse and the doorman arched a brow but let them in knowing Mr. Salazar well. Devante was holding Ryan up as they made their way into the elevator. This in Devante's mind was the definition of friendship.

On the way up to the penthouse Ryan said, "I really think I fucked things up this time! Ashley thinks I left Bridgette for her. She thinks we should "give it a shot". I don't want her like that. She is my -friend-. I left Bridgette because she told me it was Ashley or her. My lifelong friend or the woman I knew for like a year. I'm an idiot. She was more than that. Bridgette is everything!"

Rolling his eyes and shaking his head Devante said, "Let's get up to the penthouse and discuss this. I think I need a drink now!" They made their way inside the penthouse and were greeted by Cassidy in her little silk nightgown.

Devante's wife's hair was wavy down her back. He hated the fact that he was such a good friend for the moment. He wanted to take his wife to the bedroom and make her scream his name!

Instead, he looked into her eyes and said, "Ryan has had too much to drink and just now realizes his mistake. On top of that Ashley made a romantic move that he did not see coming. He's in a state."

Cassidy looked at Ryan and was a mixture of pitying him and wanting to take his head off. She thought better than to go forward with her feelings. Instead, she kissed her love and went back to the bedroom to read her latest regency period romance novel.

It was sometimes best to walk away. Devante sighed and knew that this kind gesture would cost him a romantic evening with his wife. He was sure that he would get an ear full about this in the morning. But, he knew he needed to be a good friend.

Ryan was sitting on the couch, next he looked up at Devante who was seated in a chair holding a glass of scotch.

There was tension in the room. It was clear that Devante was in deep thought.

"Ashley came into town several months ago and said we should get together for drinks. I thought nothing of it because she always did that. We always enjoyed drinks and catching up.", Ryan started.

Then he started to groan and continued, "Before I knew it she wanted to meet almost three times a week. That made Bridgette upset as she was never invited and Ashley pushed for more and more nights out. Bridgette said it was unfair to not introduce her to Ashley."

Taking a long swallow Ryan continued, "I decided to invite her one evening. However, the entire night was awkward and then we returned home. It was then that Bridgette said Ashley wanted more from me than friendship. I told her she was being jealous for no reason."

Devante sipped his glass and kept his thoughts to himself for the time being. Ryan carried on saying, "When my evenings with Ashley went to four times a week Bridgette had enough. She said that no woman would be comfortable seeing less and less of her fiancé."

It took Ryan a couple of seconds to get himself together. Then he carried on saying, "Bridgette felt that a woman would not be in favor of him spending so much time with another woman. Friend or more. In her mind it meant that Ashley clearly wanted more from me than my friendship. I told Bridgette that she was irrational."

Ryan had the sense to wince at the situation as he explained it further, "I told Bridgette she needed to stop being so jealous and start putting her time into something that mattered. That she should worry about being my wife and a productive person. I was condescending and rude to her."

Devante simply listened as Ryan went on," I went out with Ashley on a night I'd promised to take Bridgette out to dinner. And upon my arrival home she told me it was Ashley or her. I told her there was no way I could choose her over a lifelong friendship."

Taking one last sip of his scotch Devante sat up in his chair and narrowed his eyes at Ryan. Ryan swallowed and said, "I stormed out of the apartment and went down to the bar in my building for a drink. I'm not sure how but Ashley was still there. When Bridgette raced after me she saw me seated with Ashley."

At that moment Ryan went to the booze cart and got himself a brandy. He told Devante," Bridgette threw a drink in my face and said we were done. Then while I drank with Ashley she cleaned out her portion of our apartment."

Devante shook his head and murmured, "She called Cassidy. And they both cleaned out her portion of your apartment, and she moved in here for a few days. Until she was able to get her own place. She officially moved in last weekend…"

Taking a long drink from his glass Ryan hung his head low and said, "Thank you for caring for Bridgette. She needed someone and you were both there for her." Devante finished his drink and set his glass on the table roughly.

"We did not do it for your thanks. We are friends and she was treated unfairly. Of course we took her in.", Devante said.

This made Ryan start to cry and he said, "I hadn't spoken to her until today at the office. She made it clear she never wanted to speak to me on a personal level again. Only professionally."

Devante kept quiet before Ryan went on, "I hadn't even realized then that I'd made a mistake. I was too distracted by my having drinks with Ashley. Believing I was in the right."

Sipping his brandy Ryan continued, "Then Ashley came on to me and said we should be a couple. It was at that moment that I realized that Bridgette had been right all along. I lost the love of my life over a mistake. A huge fucking mistake."

Devante nodded and said, "What will you do now?" Ryan considered the question for a few moments staring into the fireplace. Ryan's entire body felt exhausted and he wished this was simply a nightmare he could wake from.

"I have no idea. I'm not sure there is anything that I can do. I'm still in love with her and I realize I've messed up our entire future together.", Ryan said. Placing his head in his hands he started to sob. It wasn't manly but there was no room for a filter at this point.

Devante nodded once more and said, "Perhaps treat her with dignity and respect in the workplace. Give it some time and then try to broker a peace between you." Ryan thought about that and simply nodded not sure what to say. Devante patted him on the shoulder and then got some blankets for him and set him up in the spare room.

They said goodnight and Ryan was alone in the guest bedroom. The bedroom was so quiet and lonely. Ryan felt like he had never been alone with his thoughts in quite this way before.

The only thing that he could remember was the devastated look on Bridgette's face when he chose Ashley's friendship over her. All he could think of was how beautiful she is even when she is sobbing or angry. The only thing that he could hear was her voice. For the first time since he was a small child he cried himself to sleep.

~~A Week Later~~

Ryan was seated behind his desk; working on some reports when he heard a knock at his door. He looked up from his work and noticed that Bridgette was standing before his desk. She was wearing a pinstripe skirt and ivory blouse. You could see her sexy lace bra through her top. Ryan tried to keep his face even.

"What is it that I can do for you today, Bridgette?" he said with a hint of wistfulness to his voice. She gave him a professional smile and she said, "I have the Billings file and Devante wants to schedule a lunch for this week. Also, we

26

need the budget for the Christmas party so that Lorelei and I can begin planning it," He took the file from her and smiled warmly at her.

"Thank you for the file. I can have lunch with Devante on Thursday afternoon at one. I will have the budget ready for you by Friday morning. Is there anything else?" She swallowed greatly affected from his smile.

Then she said softly, "That was all. I will leave you to your work, Sir." Ryan smiled and winked at her thanking her for her time. He then watched as she left the room.

Bridgette on the other hand was stunned by how Ryan was acting. It made her heart flutter in her chest to see him smiling at her and winking flirtatiously with her. At the same time it also reminded her that she needed to be strong and professional and not allow him to hurt her anymore. She would not allow herself to be his personal emotional punching bag.

The rest of her day went as well as could be expected. She sat in on a few meetings with Devante and took notes. Then she wrote up several reports and answered some emails.

It was around six when she realized that the day was over, and she had to rush to her apartment. She was having Cassidy over for a girls night with cocktails and junk food. As she was walking toward the elevator Bridgette heard a noise behind her.

Ryan was beside her in seconds and the smell of his cologne was overwhelming. She had to close her eyes to try to clear her head. Ryan was so close to her in the elevator that she could feel his breath on her neck.

"Have a hot date you are running off to?" he asked her. She nodded and said, "Yes! A very hot date. I am super excited." Ryan tried to hide his disappointment. He had hoped she would say she was just in a rush to feed a cat she got or meet with a friend for drinks.

The idea of her going out on a date with someone else made him hurt everywhere in his body. Ryan turned to look into Bridgette's eyes which were sparkling and said, "Have you known him long?" It was hard to keep the edge from his voice.

It was at that moment that Bridgette started to laugh and her eyes twinkled even more. He looked at her like she had grown several heads and said, "What is so damn funny?" She stopped laughing at his tone and saw the hurt in his eyes.

"I've got a date with Cassidy. We are having a dvd concert marathon. We are having snacks and wine. It will be amazing!", she said. The relief that washed over Ryan's face and body was obvious, and he laughed and said, "I am jealous! I miss those nights." She smiled warmly for the first time in his presence.

"Yeah, it is very special to be with Cassidy.", she said softly. There was an awkward silence for a few minutes and then Bridgette said, "I'm sure you have your fun planned for this evening." Ryan cocked his head to the side.

"I have no plans. I'm a single man with no prospects and my friends are all super mad at me for... reasons. So..." Bridgette shook her head and said, "I'm sure you can grab drinks with Ashley." There was venom in her voice, but she no longer cared to be polite.

Ryan shook his head and said, "No. She and I are not on speaking terms right now." Bridgette blinked at him, and then she couldn't help herself. She laughed hysterically until she hiccuped.

"You mean to tell me that you left me in favor of her and it was all for nothing! Perfect!" Ryan looked at her with his arms crossed over his chest.

"It is not funny, Bridgette. She came onto me and when I did not share her feelings she took off. A lifelong friendship over because she wanted inside my pants. Its pretty fucking painful to be honest with you. And I lost the one true thing that meant anything to me for that bullshit. Which hurts even more.", he said.

Bridgette was about to say something but the elevator dinged and the doors opened. The cool breeze rushed into the elevator car, and she walked out instead. She did not look back at him but just kept walking to her car.

He thought about running after her and better explaining things. But, he decided to go to the bar and grab a drink instead. He wasn't sure what he wanted from her. And until he sorted his shit out he couldn't drag her into his mess.

It was hard to become an adult and own your shit. It was going to take a long road to becoming the man that he wanted to be. He wanted to be worthy of Bridgette. Perhaps even more so than he had been before. Bridgette would also have a long and hard road. Ryan had no desire to cause her more pain or make her own journey harder. He really loved her and wanted the best for her. Even if it wasn't him.

~~At Cassidy and Devante's Penthouse~~

Cassidy texted Bridgette and asked her to come to their penthouse instead. There was some news that she needed to share with her. Bridgette had been quick to tell her okay and that she was on her way.

There was a mad dash as Cassidy went around the penthouse and started to light candles and made sure that she ordered Chinese take out for them. There were mixes to make different cocktails and mocktails. She was the best hostess. Even better than Bridgette herself.

The moment all of the items were set out Cassidy smiled to herself and set out the dvd's of concerts that she had been collecting since she was a teenager. In a few minutes the bell was ringing and Cassidy was happy to open it and let Bridgette inside. The girls ended up on the couch waiting for the Chinese to arrive.

They nibbled the snacks and drank some soda. They would have the wine later on. It was nice to watch videos and just be themselves. They felt relaxed and good just being themselves.

"So, there I was in the elevator with him! And he was trying to convince me that he and Ashley are no longer a thing. He said that she hit on him, and he turned her down. And then he said he had regrets about dumping me. I just walked the hell away. I am over it.", Bridgette said.

Cassidy shook her head. "The point you need to focus on is that he is a dumb-dumb. He did not realize that he loved you. And now he knows and he realizes what a bitch Ashley is. You need to decide how you feel about it all.", Cassidy said.

Bridgette simply nodded and took a sip of her sprite. Then the knock on the door had Cassidy up to get the Chinese delivery. But, standing there with the Chinese was Ryan. She looked from him to the food and back again.

"What the hell?!" she said. Ryan grinned and walked inside. He said, "I'm crashing the party ladies and Devante has decided to cut his night at the poker game short. We will all be having a nice time as friends. So, let's sit down at the table and eat. And then let's have some drinks!"

Bridgette stood up and shook her head at him, her eyes wide with shock.

Ryan simply smiled at her and placed the Chinese on the table. Before either woman could formulate her thoughts Ryan started taking plates and bowls out of the cabinets in the kitchen.

Cassidy followed him and took out some glasses and sodas from the fridge. Bridgette sat in a chair at the table. At that moment Cassidy simply shrugged. Bridgette decided she would envision kicking him and continue to be pleasant on the outside. Polite.

Everyone dished out their food and poured their drinks. Devante arrived sometime later and joined them. The friends all ate and chatted. It almost felt like it used to for a little while. However, there was an awkward elephant in the room.

Devante said, "So, Ryan... I hear that bitch Ashley had been telling our friends you were dating and now since she no longer speaks to you, they think you've broken up with her." Both Ryan and Bridgette both went rigid as he spoke.

Cassidy said, "Devante Salazar! That is so rude! That is Ryan's private life you are sharing here. Plus, I am sure BRidgette does not want to hear it. Furthermore, you should never speak that woman's name in this house. The way she was all over you before you tossed her skanky ass off of you was more than enough of her for a lifetime."

Devante laughed and said, "Babe, she was never my type and I never wanted her like that. She wishes she got into my pants. Her loss. And now the only woman in my pants is you!" Cassidy giggled and they kissed.

Ryan cleared his throat and said, "I was never "with" her. We were friends until she laid her hands on me. I turned her away from me and now she is pissed."

Bridgette looked at everyone in the room and then said in a small voice, "I was broken up with over a stupid skank who can't keep her hands to herself that you didn't even really want. I feel super great about myself now." Bridgette rolled her eyes.

She stood up and went into the spare bedroom slamming the door behind her. As soon as the door shut everyone jumped at the sound. Then Cassidy jumped up and followed Bridgette into the spare bedroom.

Meanwhile, Devante arched a brow at Ryan as if asking him to explain how he would fix this mess he had made. Ryan looked white in his face and said, "I really fucked up. I wish that I knew how to make it right."

Devante thought for a moment and said, "You can fix it by not crowding her. Let her heal and show her the real man you are. And then for the love of all that is holy do not fucked it up again."

He took the time to consider his friend's words and nodded while sipping his soda. Devante then lowered his voice saying, "I have something to tell you. Cassidy found out that we have a baby coming! The agency called us last week. I'm going to be a father!"

Ryan broke out into a complete grin and said, "Congratulations! Amazingly, your family is growing. I can't wait to spoil them as uncle Ryan if you'll let me."

Devante smiled and said, "Of course! You are my best friend even when you fuck up royally. But, ever do something stupid to hurt my family and I'll kill you."

Ryan laughed, and they finished their meals and then cleaned up. In the spare bedroom the girls were seated on the bed looking at each other. Bridgette looked like she was about to break into a million tiny bits all over the comforter.

"He left me in favor of a skanky bitch. And now he doesn't want her. I'm shattered, and he is seemingly sunny and happy.", she said. Cassidy said, "Sometimes men are stupid. He is just now seeing Ashley for the royal bitch that she is. Give it some time. Let yourself heal and always put yourself first. But, I have some good news for you!"

Bridgette arched her brow and said, "What good news is there in this shit storm?" Cassidy laughed and said, "I heard from the adoption agency and we matched! So, we are going to be parents!" Bridgette jumped off her seat and ran to her friend hugging her super tight.

"We are having a baby! OMG!", Bridgette exclaimed. Cassidy laughed and returned the hug. They continued to talk about colors for the nursery and baby shopping. Then they started talking about names that Cassidy could bring to Devante.

~~A Week Later~~

Cassidy looked at the wall and smiled warmly at Bridgette. The room smelled like fresh paint and the room was a light green color since they did not know the sex of the baby yet. Bridgette set down her roller and giggled at their progress.

"This kid is going to have a kick ass room!" Cassidy smiled at Bridgette's words. "I have to agree. I can't wait to bring the baby home to see these walls. I wonder if they will want the same color their entire childhood or beg me for different colors."

Bridgette smiled and said, "Well, if they want changes thank goodness we are painting geniuses." They both laughed. After cleaning up their supplies the ladies went to the kitchen for some salad for lunch. They chatted about the baby for most of the time.

Then Cassidy got serious and said, "Apparently, Ryan has cut off Ashley completely. She was so upset over it and the fact he didn't chase after her that she called Devante for help. He told her to fuck off. I know because he had it on speaker. It is a little hilarious at how pathetic she is becoming." Bridgette shrugged.

"Sometimes karma bites you in the ass. How is Ryan taking it? Having regrets about his treatment of her?", Bridgette said in a snarky tone. Cassidy tried to hide her smile at Bridgette's question. "Nope. His only regret is fucking this up with you.", she said. Bridgette ignored her and rolled her eyes.

"I say that for our hard work we should pop some popcorn, grab drinks and watch some Dawson's Creek on Netflix!" Cassidy laughed and said, "Do you remember when it was new? I was a Dawson girl. Who knew I would end up married to the exact opposite and be happier than I have ever been?!"

Bridgette grinned at her friend and said, "Yeah, I was -ALL- Pacey. I just liked that he was a rough around the edges good guy. And that face was carved by the Gods. Not to mention that butt…" The girls both laughed like teenagers and set up their feast for the show.

It only took them about ten minutes to set up and get comfy on the couch to watch the Pilot Episode. It took them back to a more innocent time in their lives. They commented on the way that the colors looked compared to television from today.

They chatted about how much the actors have changed over time. And how far they had come from how they thought and felt at that time. It was a nice time together as friends and Bridgette hadn't realized how much she needed it.

The truth was that she was lonely. She had her work, and she had her friends and that was basically her entire life now. She didn't feel inspired anymore.

It was like she had a weight around her heart and mind. She couldn't quite carry it on her own. So, days like today helped her feel a little more like herself. However, she couldn't help but wonder if Ryan ever felt that weight on his shoulders.

She wondered if he ever felt that sinking pain in his stomach and his chest. It was probably foolish to think of him at all. But, she couldn't help it.

The love she felt was not something she could turn off the way he had. Her love for Ryan was real and deep and even if the relationship was over. She was in pain because the love for him was still very much alive within her.

After they finished watching several episodes, went through their popcorn and ordered pizza Bridgette hugged her friend tight and thanked her for an amazing day. It has been a complete blast. Everyone had a good time and was able to relax.

She even hugged Devante which caught him off guard. She thanked him for making her best friend so very happy. He smiled and patted her on the shoulder.

They had insisted their driver bring her home. She sat quietly in the back of the car and looked out at the city as they drove past to her apartment. So many thoughts raced through her mind.

There was something so beautiful and electric about New York City at night. It made her long to pull herself back together and enjoy her life again. She wanted to go out and meet new people.

She wanted to have friendships, date men and feel alive again. It was at that moment that she decided she was done mourning the loss of what Ryan had taken from her. She would live to keep Joshua's memory alive. She would simply live. The second she arrived at her building she felt better.

It was as if something just awakened inside of her. She was practically skipping into her building and was restless in the elevator. Once she reached her floor she went to her door to unlock it when she heard her name. She turned to see a woman she had never expected to see at her home.

The woman who helped to tear her entire world apart. There she stood in all of her beautiful glory calling Bridgette's name. It made Bridgette's entire body tense and she was ready to fight this woman if needed and send her on her way.

"What are you doing here, Ashley?", she said the venom clearly in her voice. Ashley pretended that she did not notice Bridgette's tone and took a step forward. Bridgette took a step back and placed her hand up in a stop gesture. "Answer the question", she hissed.

Ashley stopped and rolled her eyes before saying, "I just want to speak with you. May I come in?" It took less than a moment for Bridgette to sigh heavily and say. "No, I would rather not have you in my home. If you need to speak to me you can always speak to me here."

Ashley looked uncomfortable not being in control of the situation but she stood tall and lifted her chin. "Very well. I want you to convince Ryan he should speak to me again.", she said in her tone even.

Bridgette looked at her as if she had taken leave of her senses and said, "No." Ashley considered the woman standing before her with pants on her clothes and her hair a total mess and sneered. The energy between the two women was volatile to say the least.

"I have known him for decades now. We have been best friends. I'm everything to him. But, for some reason he has lost sight of that. I blame you. Fix it.", she said through clenched teeth.

Bridgette started to laugh and said, "The fact that Ryan has such poor choices in best friends says a lot about him. Don't you think? I was a fantastic girlfriend and wife to him. He messed all of that good in his life up for your sake. Take that as a win for you. And whatever happens between you now is none of my business. I don't care what you want or need. I owe you nothing. I will do you no favors. Now leave before I have security, toss your ass out!"

Ashley turned bright red and said, "This isn't over, you low class bitch!" With that being said Ashley turned tail and left walking quickly. Bridgette breathed a sigh of relief as the she-witch left her vicinity. Unlocking her door and entering into her apartment gave her a real sense of calm.

She put her keys into the bowl on the entry table and checked her mail. She flickered the lights on and groaned at the bills she had to sit down and pay. Then she went into her kitchen and made herself a nice cup of cocoa.

After sitting at her island at her laptop paying her bills she made her way to the living room. She sat on her soft couch and left out a contented sigh. It felt like she had slain a dragon in telling Ashley off in her hallway. She set boundaries, she was honest, and she stood firm in the face of adversity. It had been a lovely day.

The chime of her cell phone rang, and she picked up her phone from the coffee table. She noticed it was an email from an ex of hers. She rolled her eyes. She had needed this text like a hole in the head.

It said, "Hey babe. I am wondering how you are doing? I heard about your upcoming divorce. Total bummer. I Want to make sure you are okay." She rolled her eyes even harder.

This was probably something that came with strings more so than his being worried about her welfare, but she decided to give him the benefit of the doubt. In a text back to him she thanked him for his concern, asked how he was and told him that she was doing very well.

Then she went back to Netflix and watched the movie Rebbecca. It was nice to just cuddle up on the couch with her blankets and watch something alone. She felt less lonely than she had been.

It seemed like slowly she was starting to get herself together. It did not take long before he texted back asking her to dinner. She smiled slightly and thought that since she was single she could accept.

At the same time he was an ex for a reason. So, she declined but thanked him for the offer. Then she made her way into her bedroom to take her pajamas out of the dresser. Then she went to the bathroom to change and brush her teeth. After she was finished she shut down all the lights and crawled into bed. It had been a long day.

In the dark Bridgette allowed herself to let go of all her fears, her hurts, her everything. She allowed herself to fully shut down. She was safe, home and had a great future in front of her. With a sweet sigh she fell into a deep and dreamless sleep.

~~The Next Morning, A Monday~~

The air was chilly and the leaves were falling. It was a beautiful day and Bridgette could not be happier that she woke up early and decided to walk to work. It is a special time of year for her, and she was amazed at how much nature you could still find in the concrete jungle that is NYC.

Stopping in her favorite little coffee shop down the street from her apartment she picked up a bagel sandwich and some coffee. She has become addicted to her coffee drinks ever since she moved to the city. Something new was bursting out of Bridgette. She smiled at people as they passed her on the sidewalk, she happily took her time walking to work, and she felt wonderful for it.

Perhaps she would make a habit of this. As the second the building where she worked came into focus she smiled. It was going to be an amazing day.

Her boss was a friend who understood her and allowed her to do her job her own way. They had found a good working relationship that suited them both. Everything was coming up roses for her.

The fact that her ex worked in her building, and she had to interact with him didn't even bother her today. Bridgette was a professional, and she knew she could handle anything that life sent her way. This new confidence was refreshing and helped her shoulders relax, her head to be held high and she felt like she was floating.

As she opened the door to the building and greeted the secretaries she was beaming. The only word that could describe her would have been radiant. Everyone seemed to have noticed the difference in her posture and could see the confidence rolling off her in waves.

There was positive chatter about her from the second she walked through the door. Some people assumed that it meant that she had met a new man and had moved on. And the idea of that seemed too small and ridiculous to her.

The minute she walked into the office and made her way to her desk Devante came out of his office and smiled at her. "Good Morning, Bridgette! Did you do something different to your hair?"

She simply smiled and laughed, "No. There was a change but it happened on the inside. I am so thankful my best friend has a man like you in her life. You care and take the time to notice everyone. Even your associates and co-workers."

He returned her smile and nodded his chin in her direction as if to say thank you. With that they hit the ground running and dived into their packed schedule for the day. At around eleven they entered the conference room and took their seats.

The client was arriving any moment when a commotion in the hallway caught their attention. Devante rose and went to check the hall to be sure it was safe. Bridgette couldn't help herself and craned her neck trying to get a view out of the windows in the conference room. But, she couldn't see much due to their frosted glass.

A moment later, sighing Devante returned and said, "Sorry about that. Security had to remove someone from Ryan's office and it got a little intense. Now he is as mad as a hornet and also late for this meeting. Thank goodness our client is also late this morning."

She simply nodded but refused to ask about it. She had come to realize that Ryan's life and issues were his own, and she need not care about it anymore. There was freedom in the indifference.

Bridgette decided to sit a little straighter in her chair and keep her new found confidence rolling into this meeting. She barely looked up when Ryan entered the conference room and took his seat. He was irked that she did not acknowledge him but tried to shake it off focusing on Devante.

"Thank you for the assistance out there. Since Lorelei will be out for a few days due to her broken ankle would it be alright if Bridgette helped us both out for a while?", he said. Devante turned to Bridgette and she simply shrugged.

He responded saying, "If Bridgette is alright with that. I assume you will compensate her for the extra work and time she will have to put in." Ryan gaped at his friend and ground out his words, "Of course! I would most definitely ensure she is taken care of in terms of the extra work. I'm an excellent employer."

Bridgette ignored him entirely and focused on her materials making sure she was ready to take notes when the meeting began. It was then that Devante announced he just received a text and their client was running late but on his way. Traffic was a beast this morning apparently.

She smiled warmly and said, "Thankfully, we have coffee and refreshments to help them calm when they arrive. And we will be able to get down to business after." Both men nodded.

Chapter Three

The next week in Bridgette's life could not have been more hectic. She had agreed to take over for Lorelei because she was a good person. And she wanted the office to be able to thrive in her absence.

The extra money would also be helpful. She was trying to save for the future and every penny counted. There were some things about this new arrangement that made for awkward moments. Mostly, for Ryan it would be seen.

That Monday he had to have Ashley forcefully removed from his office as she broke into it and was waiting for him when he arrived. I had only heard about it from Cassidy who was eager to share the information. Especially after I told her about the run in with Ashley in the hallway.

Ryan had been really mum about it. The security on the building was tighter now. She liked that safe feeling that came with it. It also ensured that she wouldn't have to see Ashley again.

That in itself made the entire security surge worth it in the end. She and Ryan had been totally professional and have actually worked well together. There were only a few times that Ryan seemed embarrassed by something or like he felt awkward around her.

It was almost cute. -Almost- She was not going down that road again. At the same time the way he had been so kind to her lately made her wonder if they could broker peace and become friends.

They would be in each other's lives since they were both Godparents to the baby Cassidy was adopting with her wonderful husband. And they were so close to both Devante and Cassidy. There would be cookouts, dinner parties and other functions when they would run into each other.

Perhaps friendship was possible to make it all less painful for them both. It was then her phone rang at her desk and jarred her from her thoughts. She picked it and did her professional greeting and was met by a familiar voice.

"Get Ryan on the line NOW." Ashley sneered into the phone. Bridgette could not help but smile as she said in a sweet/polite voice, "I'm sorry but that is impossible. He is in a meeting and can't be disturbed. Can I take a message?"

Instead of a response she was met with a dial tone which made her laugh out loud. That woman was crazy. Ryan walked out of his office and instantly felt alight with the humor of Bridgette's laugh.

He handed her some files and said, "What are you laughing with such glee in the office today?" She looked up at him, her eyes twinkling with mischief.

"Ashley called and demanded that I send her a call to you. I told her you were in a meeting and could not be disturbed. She hung up on me. And I couldn't help but think how crazy she is. I mean the hallway and now this. It's really kind of pathetic and childish."

Ryan's eyes narrowed and he said, "You did the right thing. But, the next time she calls please tell her that all calls are monitored and that she is not welcome to call or arrive here. As per my orders. And what the hell do you mean the hallway? She was in a hallway with you?!" It was at that moment that Bridgette felt frustrated and also she was blushing.

"A while ago I went home from Cassidy's house. We had a Dawson's Creek and pizza time after some snacks and painting the baby's room. I got home and there she was waiting outside my door. I have no idea how she knew where

I lived. Anyway, she was there and we had a big fight. Then she left. I have not seen her since."

Ryan looked her over and pinched the bridge of his nose. "What was the fight about?", he asked. That made Bridgette pause and she bit her lip.

There was a long pause, and then she said in a low voice since they were in the office, "She wanted me to convince you to let her back into your life. In her mind I owed it to her to fix things between you since in her mind I was the cause of your falling out. She said she was the love of your life and always had been. And that I'd fucked it all up. I told her that she was cracked. I told her that I owe her nothing and I wouldn't do it. She called me a bitch. I didn't mind because the feeling is mutual all things considered. I knew I didn't owe either of you a damn thing. I told her to work her shit out with you on her own and leave me out of it."

Bridgette licked her lips and held her head high making eye contact with him. He looked somewhere between horrified and embarrassed, and she almost felt sorry for him. However, he got himself into this mess, and he would need to figure his way out of it.

That made her a little sad and made her sigh. Just because something was the truth did not make it easy to accept. It only took a second for Ryan to register that she had sighed and she had a sort of sad look on her face. He lifted her chin with his finger and forced her gaze to meet his own.

"If she ever comes near you again please let me know, okay? It was my fault for trusting her. And it is my mess to

48

clean up. You owe nothing to anyone and never did. I'll find a way to make this right.", he said with conviction.

Bridgette was too weary to even consider arguing so she simply nodded to him. It was tearing Ryan's heart apart to see Bridgette thriving without him. It was hard to see the sadness in her eyes when she thought that nobody could see it there. And he wanted to fix it for her and selfishly for himself.

He was not a perfect man by any means and he was selfish. He'd taken for granted the one person who meant everything to him and he had discarded her like she didn't matter. She was all that mattered.

Ryan smiled softly at Bridgette and said, "Well, thank you for handling her both times. I will ensure she is no longer a problem for you. I think it is time I told her parents what she has been up to. She needs their money so they are the ones who best control her. Not that you needed to hear any of this. Although, in fairness her father is a big client for the firm."

She just nodded, unsure of what to say. Then he went back into his office to make some calls. Bridgette went back to her work and carried on until it was beyond closing time.

She barely remembered saying goodnight to Devante when he left earlier. She had been taking on extra hours to keep up with the work from her side of the fence and Lorelei's. The work was thrilling and she was honored to be doing it.

It was amazing money but taking a toll on her. She stood and arched her back trying to stretch. It had been a long day and before she became too exhausted she knew she needed to get home. It took her a few minutes to turn off her computer, pack up her things and make her way to the elevator.

Once she arrived at the elevator she realized she was not alone in waiting for its arrival. Ryan stood quietly at a polite distance and she was fighting the urge to speak to him. The ease between them had returned and she was so thankful for it.

At the same time it made her question her feelings and could lead her down a really dangerous road. In the end, against her better judgment Bridgette said, "It has been a long day today."

Ryan smiled and stepped closer, "Yes, it has. We still have the account by the way. Ashley's father was upset with her and not me. He told me that I'd best spend the rest of my life trying to make it up to you. And that our company has helped his business and he would never turn away from us. He was also concerned for his daughter's mental health. I told him that he should take care of her as he is her father. But, that she had broken the bonds of my friendship with her. He understood and agreed. So, the company will not suffer and neither should the rest of us."

Bridgette considered his words for a minute before saying, "He seems like a very fair man. That is good. Perhaps his love for his daughter will assist them in getting her the help she needs. At the same time I realize that must have been a difficult call to make. Are you okay?"

At her kindness Ryan cocked his head to the side and realized the depth of his idiocy. He had taken this magical woman for granted. It wasn't right. But, how does one fix something like that?

At the end of the day Ryan decided he needed advice from Devante. And a lot of luck to be able to make things right between himself and Bridgette. But, she was at least speaking to him and not ignoring him like she had been.

There had been progress but mostly from her end. She was being gracious and kind. Which was everything that she was underneath her skin. It was his turn to find a way to bridge the gap between them and do the work needed to fix what he had broken.

The elevator arrived and they both entered the car in silence. They both were going to the parking garage level. Ryan needed access to his car and she was meeting her driver there.

Devante had made having a personal driver part of her benefits for working for him. She suspected that was influenced by Cassidy but she did not complain. Once they arrived at the parking garage Ryan motioned for Bridgette to exit before him.

She did with a thankful nod and began walking toward the waiting car. Ryan started to walk toward his car and was nearly to his door when he heard a shriek coming from somewhere in the garage.

"You bastard! How could you do this to ME!?!", Ashley screamed at a high pitch. Then she was nearing him with some sort of weapon in her hand. Bridgette turned and watched in horror as the scene unfolded. Ryan managed to block Ashley and wrangle the knife from her hands. He wrapped his strong arms around Ashley to contain her.

Then he pulled out his phone and barked into it, "Your daughter just attacked me! I managed to get the weapon from her hand. I'm holding her quite literally right now. Please send someone to fetch her and get her some damn help. I do not want to humiliate anyone by having to call the police. I am getting sick of this, Charles."

There were things being said back and Ryan was nodding his head. "No, Charles, I can't put her on the phone. She is shrieking like a banshee and trying to kick me in my shins. You are lucky I got this call to you. Yes, that is correct. You do that. See you soon, Charles."

Ashley continued to scream and thrash against Ryan until she spent all of her energy and became limp in his arms. He rolled his eyes and sighed waiting for her father to come handle her.

Bridgette had been standing still watching everything unfold and felt almost sorry for the woman. She was clearly unwell and needed help. Mental health was something that should be taken seriously.

At the same time she had been worried about Ryan and his well being. But, it seems like he has it all under control now. So, she slid into her seat in the car and told the driver to take her home.

As Bridgette made her way home, Ryan was left to deal with the mess he had set into motion. Sometimes he wondered how in the world they all ended up in the places they had landed. Never in his wildest dreams did he consider that Ashley would lose her mind and attack him with a knife.

Never had he figured that she would misunderstand his feelings for her or their relationship. And at the moment he just wanted her to get help and get the hell out of his life. Beyond the fact he wanted her (a human being) to be alright that his feelings were non-existent for her.

It took around twenty minutes for Charles to arrive. He came with a limo and had a person in a white coat with him. I can only imagine it was a doctor of some sort to take Ashley to a facility to seek treatment. Charles got out of his limo and stalked toward them and lifted Ashley's chin.

"Baby, you said you were taking your medications and you had yourself under control. You have lied to me. And now I am having you committed to get the help that you need.", Charles said firmly.

Ashley shook her head, seeming too tired to speak. Charles stood firm and had the man in the white coat come to get her. She was lifted into his arms and taken to the limo.

Charles turned to Ryan and extended his hand for a shake. They shook hands as Charles said, "Thank you for taking care of her and for calling me. She has messed up an important friendship in her life. That is sad but her own doing. I wish you luck moving forward and will see you at our next meeting. You are a good man, Ryan." With that Charles got into his limo and sped off.

Ryan's shoulders finally fell and he let out a breath of relief. Ashley was finally someone else's problem. The only real concern he had now was how much of that Bridgette saw and if she was okay.

He'd gotten her address from HR in case he needed to save her from Ashley. At the moment all he cared about was reaching her apartment and explaining what happened and that she will be safe moving forward. So, he got into his car and sped toward her place.

At Bridgette's apartment she turned on the lights and went into her kitchen after dropping her things off in her coat closet. In the kitchen she pulled out some lemonade from the fridge and took out a glass. She poured her lemonade into the glass and returned it to the fridge. She took a nice long sip of the cool and refreshing liquid.

Then she sat on her couch and pulled up Gilmore Girls on Netflix. She enjoyed watching the show and the beautiful memories that it gave her. She was into her third episode when she heard a loud knock on her door.

That was odd. She hadn't been expecting anyone. Well, someone was here now so she might as well see who it is. She stood and walked to the door and opened it.

Looking out the peephole she noticed that it was Ryan waiting outside her door. She opened the door and looked at him confused. She had not given him her address.

"How do you know where I live?", she said instantly. Not waiting to explain or for an invitation he moved inside her apartment. Then waited for her to close the door behind them before he spoke.

"It was in your HR folder. I thought that I may need to rescue you from Ashley at some point after you explained the run in with her. But, that will no longer be an issue. I do want to discuss what you saw this afternoon and want to check in on you."

At his words she wrapped her arms around herself and then said, "Would you like a drink?" When he shook his head she nodded for him to take a seat on her couch. He did and she sat in the chair adjacent to him. There was an awkward silence so Bridgette decided to change it up.

"I was just getting into the car when Ashley started shrieking at the top of her lungs. I turned around just in time to see her going for you with a knife. My heart nearly stopped on the spot. But, you were so quick to calm her down and handle the situation that I wasn't there much longer. Once she collapsed against you, I knew you were safe.", she said.

Ryan nodded and responded saying, "Yes, it was not hard to disarm her and hold her still. I called her father and he came to get her. He is having her committed to a mental health facility. She was on medication and convinced him that things were fine. But, she has since stopped taking said medication and things are anything but. He is worried and disappointed. I understand. But, he is a good man and we have a good working relationship. He appreciated that I did not call the police on his daughter."

Bridgette nodded, not sure how to respond to that. It was awkward to discuss Ashley with Ryan after all that had happened. Ryan picked up on her situation and said, "I am thankful that it is over. She will no longer harass either of us. We can all move forward with our lives."

Bridgette smiled softly and said, "Yes. Although, I think I have been doing pretty well. Work has helped me a great deal. I have the Christmas party almost completely arranged."

He looked at her with a huge grin "If anyone can make Christmas amazing it is you! You are a Christmas addict.", he said. She simply smiled and nodded.

There was no use in denying the truth. The two of them smiled affectionately at one another and then Ryan sat forward and pushed her hair behind her ear. Bridgette winked at him and said, "It will be amazing. I can't wait until the night of the party and all of the magic that can happen."

Ryan then knew exactly how he was going to make things right between them. The grand gesture that he needed was being gifted to him. He stood up abruptly and smiled at her saying, "I am really glad that you are alright. I am happy things are working out for you. Believe it or not your happiness means a lot to me. I am so sorry for all that I have done to hurt you. But, I am in awe of the wonderfully strong and resilient woman who stands before me."

Ryan leaned forward and kissed her on the cheek ever so softly. It took a minute before Bridgette could focus again. All she felt was the warm tingles where he had kissed her cheek. But, as she gained back her senses she noticed he was walking toward her door.

The fact that he was leaving made her stomach drop and her heart ache. She wanted him to stay even after everything he had done to hurt her. Ryan turned abruptly and said, "I need to go. There are some things I need to handle. It was nice seeing you like this Bridgette! Until next time." And then he was gone.

Bridgette couldn't help but feel empty standing in her living room alone. But, she pushed herself to lock the door and go back to watching Gilmore Girls. Once she got to the episode where Rory comes home from Washington and gets upset about Jess making out with someone else she'd had enough for one night.

It was too close to her experience the past few weeks. She got up and started to turn off the lights in the living room and kitchen. Then she went into the bathroom and washed her face. Then she changed into her pajamas in an effort to relax for bedtime.

It made her happy to be in her bedroom and the prospect of some real sleep. Perhaps she would be safe from her sadness in her dreams. That thought was the last one she had before she drifted off into a deep sleep. Her dreams began soon after.

They were dreams of her with Ryan having a home inside the city and one outside of the city where they spent the holidays. The house was decorated for Christmas just how she liked it. And she was making Christmas dinner. Fires were roaring in the fireplaces and it all felt warm and cozy.

Then Ryan proposed to her again but this time it felt more real and more right somehow. She had said yes. They had their son and everything felt perfect. SeeBut, soon it was over and another dream began.

This time Ashley was coming after her telling her she would always have a hold over Ryan. That Ryan would always choose her over Bridgette. It made her wake up with tears rolling down her cheeks.

It was one thing to have a good dream but it was another to have her dreams invaded by the people who really hurt her and made her entire life fall apart. The dream that she had with Ashley had shaken her. It made her feel tempted to call Ryan and explain it and seek some comfort from him.

At the end of the day he was part of her heartbreak in the first place. Bridgette decided that this Friday she would go out and make new friends. This way she would have a wonderful new chance for support and something to take her mind off of everything.

A kind of peace washed over her as she realized that she didn't need Ryan to sort through her feelings. She did not need him to rescue her from her bad dreams or heartache. She was enough for herself and in that moment that revelation meant everything to her. Bridgette went back to sleep and had a perfectly peaceful and dreamless sleep from then on.

~~Nine Days Later~~

It was a Friday night and the club was packed with writhing bodies and people searching the crowd for their next hookup. Bridgette bit down on the straw of her drink and swayed to the music in front of the bar. She'd come out on her own and felt oddly safer standing by the bar just then.

This was the most liberating thing she had done in quite some time. It felt really good to be outside of the office and not to be at home in her pajamas. This was exactly what she needed.

A chance to meet new people and live a little again. She had noticed the way the men were checking her out and it sent a thrill up her spine. Maybe she wasn't as undesirable as she'd been feeling.

This night out was her chance to start over. She could be anyone that she wanted to be for the night. And maybe if she gained enough confidence she would feel more like herself. At least that was her hope.

When a woman felt desirable she could open her mind to new experiences. That was what she wanted. To be free from her grief and free from the pain. It was time to live again.

That is what her son would have wanted for her. That is what she wanted for herself. This would be a fantastic new beginning. And if she happened to get a new friend or an orgasm out of it... well she was game!

It was as she thought those things that a very tall, handsome and built blond man in a suit made his way over to her. The look in his eyes said that he wanted to wrap his body around her on the dance floor at the very least.

Chapter Four

She met his gaze and returned his lust filled stare. He stopped at the bar and played it cool as he ordered himself a drink. Then he turned to her with his drink in his hand and smirked at her.

"My name is Chris. What is yours beautiful?", he said. She looked him over slowly and then licked her lips before saying, "I'm Bridgette. Nice to meet you Chris". It was hard to hear one another over the music, but they made do.

Chris continued to look her up and down before asking her to dance. She accepted and they made their way onto the dance floor. The song "What Would Happen" by Meredith Brooks began to play and it seemed perfect for the moment.

Bridgette moved her curves along his body and made sure that her ass pressed up against his groin as she swayed to the music. Chris placed his hands on her hips and helped to pull her closer to his strong body.

As they danced Chris noticed that the other men in the club were all looking at Bridgette with lustful eyes and at him with envy. Something inside him sparked and he was excited to share this time with her. This woman could be someone special if for the night or longer.

This only made him even more excited to be there with her and to feel her body pressed up against his. He knew that he would be taking her home with him tonight. At the same time he was lost in thoughts of taking her home she was thinking about how much she wanted to have her wicked way with him.

She was a single woman and she had needs. It had been weeks since she had sex and it had been lackluster the last time. Ryan was distracted and basically humored her.

It was basically like making love to a fish. But, she quickly shook that thought away and focused on Chris and how damn sexy he is. Bridgette wanted to go home with him and straddle his lap and ride him until he cried out in pleasure and said her name.

After the song ended Bridgette looked up into Chris' eyes and said, "Take me home with you." His eyes lit up with desire and happiness. He simply nodded and took her hand in his. She felt shocks run through her body as her small hand fit so well in his larger one.

This was not what she was used to but she couldn't help but feel excited about it. Chris took her out of the parking garage and opened the door of his sports car for her. Then she slid inside feeling the leather against the backs of her legs and closed her eyes. Of course even his car would be sexy.

Chris slid into the car with ease and started the engine. It purred as they started toward his place. He had an apartment not far from the club.

She winked at him when he turned to look at her as he drove toward his place. She squirmed in her seat and the short skirt she had on rode up on her thighs. This was going to be a really good night for both of them!

They arrived at his building and he parked in the garage and clicked the elevator button to take them to the top floor. She arched her brow and he said, "It is my building. Only the best for my digs." She rolled her eyes and shrugged.

Money did not impress her in the way it seemed to influence other women. As they arrived on his floor Decon placed his hand on her lower back and guided her inside his penthouse. It was even more extravagant than Devante's place.

It was very open and yet very masculine at the same time. The penthouse smelt woodsy and spicy. The lines were clean but there were knick-knacks all over the place on his shelves. There were also a lot of books.

There was no doubt that it was a beautiful place. Looking up into Chris' eyes she focused completely on him. Fuck his apartment! All she cared about was him.

The place wasn't hers and what he had meant nothing to her. She needed to get that tie off him. To unbutton that white shirt of his. To peel off those pants and free his cock that she wanted to wrap her lips around.

Chris kissed Bridgette deeply sliding his tongue along hers as he growled against her mouth. She pressed her body against his deepening kiss. Then his hands were on her everywhere as if he wanted her naked before they'd even reached his door.

This was perfect in Bridgette's mind because she wanted him just as much. She untied his tie and threw it to the floor without a second thought. She unbuttoned the buttons on his shirt without breaking their kiss. She moaned into his mouth.

Then her hands were at his waist unbuckling his belt and tossing it aside with his shirt and tie. Looking into her eyes Chris pulled away from their kiss and licked his lips breathing heavily with need. Bridgette started to pull down his pants noticing he was only left with boxer briefs.

She admired the bulge in his pants and licked her lips with desire in her eyes. Without a second thought she relieves him of his boxer briefs and sinks to her knees. The intention behind her actions were clear and only made their lust pulse more intensely.

The next thing Bridgette knew Chris' hands were wrapping her hair in his grip and pulling her toward his thick hard cock. She moaned, opening up her mouth to take him inside her wet warm mouth. Chris moaned his eyes rolling back into his head as he felt Bridgette's velvety mouth on his cock.

Then she pulled away and licked his cock up and down teasing the tip before taking him back into her mouth. She looked up into his eyes and winked at him. The naughty minx knew just how to turn him on.

He needed no more encouragement and began to fuck her face in earnest. It made them both moan and she was squirming as her panties became wetter and wetter. The way in which Bridgette was worshiping his cock made Chris growl in desire and need for release.

He felt himself getting closer to cumming and said, "Fuck baby... I am going to cum down your throat! Take it all, baby girl!" And she happily moaned as she did so. Looking up into his eyes and showing her pleasure that came from pleasing his cock.

There is little time for either of them to recover before Chris was pulling Bridgette up from the floor and kissing her deeply. Then he picked her up, never breaking the kiss and takes her to his bedroom.

Once they arrived in the room he laid her gently on the bed and looked at her with darkened eyes. The lust reflected there is unmistakable. Bridgette writhed with need on top of his cool sheets.

As Chris undressed her and the coolness hit her skin she knew what it felt like to be both hot inside and cool outside. As Chris touched her body with his hands, his mouth, his tongue she moaned in complete abandon.

Flipping Bridgette over so her elbows propped her body up as her ass was in the air Chris ran his hand over her ass softly and then with no warning he spanked her hard. She let out a little whimper/cry and licked her lips feeling her wetness dripping down her thighs. Chris grinned and spanked her other cheek harder and saw how she responded.

That ass of hers was wiggling in need for more. Chris gave her more spankings until she could only hear the sounds of his slaps against her ass. Her moans like music to his ears.

After about twenty he stopped and placed his dick at her entrance and said, "Do you want me to fuck this cunt baby?" She growled in response, and he laughed, spanking her once more before thrusting all the way inside her wet cunt.

The feeling of him filling her was almost shocking with how intense her entire body felt. She cried out in pleasure, in pain and in pure joy! She had never felt so full in all of her previous experiences.

Chris was hitting the most delicious parts of her body with his hard cock. And he was anything but gentle. He'd wound her hair around his hand and pulled her up to kiss her as he fucked her body.

It felt so deep, so all consuming and almost maddening. She was fighting the urge to cum from the start and it only grew as he continued to pound her hard. Then Chris did the most unexpected thing by grabbing her throat and squeezing.

He growled in her ear, "I want to feel you cum on my cock! Cum hard, little one!" That was all it took for her body to surrender to his demand, and she fell over the cliff of arousal. She came harder than she ever had before. Her entire body was quaking from the inside out.

Her breath was labored. And she collapsed onto the bed as she felt him grip her hips and pull her roughly back into him. Never stopping his assault of her pussy as she fucked her hard and then came deeply inside her.

Panting he leaned over her placing a kiss and a bite on her shoulder/neck area. Then he pulled away and went to the bathroom. Bridgette was so overwhelmed by emotions and so spent that she stayed limp on the bed.

When Chris returned he had a warm towel in his hand and told her to lay on her back and spread her legs for him. She did so without hesitation, and he cleaned her with such a gentleness it almost took her breath away.

Once he finished he tossed the towel into the bathroom and came back in all his naked glory to the bed. He nibbled her lips and teased her mouth with his tongue. In that moment there was only the two of them,

Chris looked deeply into her eyes and said, "I'm so happy you decided to dance with me." She smiled in return and said in a breathy voice, "How could I resist? You tick all my boxes."

He chuckled and moved hair from over her shoulder and said, "You are one surprise after another. I like you already. Stay the night?" She nodded, and they both went under the covers of her large bed.

As she was falling asleep she heard his voice in her ear saying, "I'll look over you and care for you, little one. Rest." And for the first time in a very long time she had a dreamless sleep that was nothing but peaceful.

~~The Next Day~~

The sun was streaming through the windows in Chris' bedroom and Bridgette strained to get her bearings. She remembered that she was in Chris' penthouse and that they had come there after the club. And then like a tidal wave of desire the memories of their night together came back to her.

She couldn't remember a time she was so turned on or felt so safe with someone. Who was this man and why did he do these things to her? It was something she knew she wanted to explore.

Stretching Bridgette reached for him. That was when she noticed he was not in bed and on his pillow was a note. She lifted it and grinned at what it said.

> *"Bridgette, thank you for the best evening I have had in a very long time. I have to go to work and you looked too peaceful to wake up. Feel free to take your time getting up and help yourself to breakfast from my kitchen. Make yourself at home and then let yourself out. My door automatically locks when you close the door. I hope to hear from you soon, sweetheart."*

It was then that she noticed he'd left her his phone number and signed it with kisses. Perhaps he was just as enamored with her as she was with him. Getting up she padded to the kitchen completely naked and searched for something for breakfast.

She found some bagels and toasted one for herself and spread some cream cheese on it. It pleased her that he had similar tastes in food. She liked the idea of them having things in common with one another.

After finishing her breakfast she put away her dish into the dishwasher and went to the bathroom and took a warm and luxurious shower. The warm water felt good against her sore body. She felt like she had run a marathon last night. At the same time she felt alive and needy. It did not take long for her to touch herself.

Bridgette was leaning against the wall of the shower with her leg raised, spreading wide to get better access to her clit. She rubbed it and closed her eyes thinking of Chris and what it would be like to fuck him in the shower. But, what took her over the edge was remembering how he had told her to cum and how he called her little one.

The way his voice sounded so rough, needy, masculine made her shiver and feel so aroused. She felt in those moments like she belonged with him and to him. It made her feel vulnerable and safe at the same time. After her shower she went to the bedroom and changed into her clothes from last night.

It was then she picked up her phone and saw several missed calls and texts from Ryan. After they had broken up she changed her number. It made Bridgette wondered how he got her new one. She decided to read his texts anyway.

They were all asking her where she was. He'd gone to her place, but she wasn't home, and he was concerned for her well-being. Shooting him a text she said that she was alive and well.

The text went on to say that she went out the night before and met a new friend. And she stayed at their place due to the late hour. It wasn't exactly a lie. But, what he didn't know would not hurt him either.

Before putting her phone into her bag she texted Cassidy that she was alright and that she had a lot to tell her when they had lunch later in the day. Then she rushed toward the office. She was two hours late for work!

That was a first for her. But, she figured that Devante would forgive her this one time. She finger combed her hair and slipped on her shoes. Then she left to hail a cab to the office.

In the taxi she sent Devante a text telling him she was on her way and that she was deeply sorry for her being so tardy to work. He returned her text quickly saying that he was simply glad she was alright. Then she slipped her phone back into her bag and rode to the office.

She was overdressed for the day and looked like she was ready for the club. But, that didn't matter. It was more important she was there and did her work. It took about twenty minutes to reach her place of employment.

Upon arrival, she paid the taxi driver and gathered her things walking into the building. There were definite looks from others she took in her state of dress. But, she just held her head high and walked into the building as she owned it. She nodded to the receptionists and went to the elevator, her heels clacking on the floor behind her.

In the elevator she leaned against the wall of the car for a moment when her phone buzzed in her bag. She lifted it out and saw a text from Ryan simply saying to be in his office as soon as she arrived to meet him in his office. She texted back in affirmative and sighed.

This was going to be a very awkward conversation to have before coffee. But, she would be honest with him and professional. He was an associate and not her ex here at their professional place of work.

Bridgette softly knocked on his door and waited for his greeting before she pushed the door open. She stepped inside and met his gaze walking with confidence to the chair in front of his desk. She sat and said, "You wanted to see me?"

The look on his face was somewhere between desire and utter shock as he looked her over. His gaze finally landed back to hers, and he cleared his throat. "Yes, I wanted to discuss what the hell happened last night," he said. This simply made her arch her brow and look at him as if he'd asked her something in another language.

"I fail to see where that is any of your business. We are at work, and we are associates within the company. That is the extent of our relationship.", she said softly.

This made him arch a brow at her and look into her eyes, "We both know that isn't the truth. We have been so much more since the day we met. So, I take it you went to that club to find a fuck buddy for the night. Did you think a good fuck would erase me from your heart? I could have saved you the time. This is not over between us no matter how many times you fuck a random asshole."

The gasp that came from her throat was the only sound in the room. She couldn't believe that Ryan had spoken to her in such a crude fashion. But, beyond that how had he known where she was or what she had done? Was he having her watched?! That was a clear line crossed that she could and would not abide by.

"How the fuck do you know what I was doing last night?! Did you follow me?!", she shrieked. He pinched the bridge of his nose and nodded. "I wanted to be sure that you were safe after the incident with Ashley. I had no idea you would go on the prowl!"

Bridgette looked deeply into his eyes, her voice coming out like a flow of venom, "Call them off NOW! And we are done with this conversation. I answer to Devante when it comes to my attendance, and we've had our conversation about it. There is nothing for you and I to say to one another."

Ryan noticed that she was shaking; she was so mad at him, and he could relate. He was planning the grand gesture to get her back, and she was off fucking some random guy she'd met at a bar! It wasn't until the door slammed shut did he notice she'd left. He was too lost in his rage at being too late. Or was he?

Devante was in his office and arched a brow when she entered. A large sigh escaped from between her lips as she sat in the chair in front of his desk. She knew she needed to speak honestly and get her professional life back on track.

"I am very sorry for not calling in that I would be so late. It was inconsiderate and rude. I will not be late again or act in this reckless manner. This job means a lot to me." Bridgette said.

He nodded and said, "Also, please take more care in your attire. We may have a riot during some of our meetings over that dress. But, we will soldier through." She smiled warmly at him and thanked him for his understanding. That was when Devante completely shocked her with his words.

"Ryan was setting up things to get you back. He had come up with a plan to make it happen and was trying to work it out. When you weren't home he lost it and was worried about you. I know he fucked you over and you owe him nothing. But, his heart is on the line too. Also, the man that you went home with last night is a problem.", he said.

There was a long pause before he continued, "Not because you went home with him. You are an adult who can make her own choices. It is a problem because of who he is. Christopher Ciccone is Ryan's rival in business and I suppose mine also. I have a more friendly relationship with him than Ryan. Ryan does not get along with him. At all."

Bridgette simply blinked at the information and she flushed. "Do you think that Chris knew who I was last night? Is this some pissing match between him and Ryan? And more importantly does Ryan know who it was I went home with?", she asked in shock.

It was hard to believe that she could have been set up. Last night was supposed to be her moment of freedom. Instead it is turning out to be a complete and total nightmare.

Bridgette knew that she loved Ryan. She might love Ryan for the rest of her life. At the same time she knew they would never be right for one another. It would never be the same. She was ready to move on.

Devante shook his head and said, "I have no idea what Chris' intentions were last night. It would give me pause if I were you. And no Ryan does not know who it was. I had his security team tell him it was a random guy from the club. Because to you that is what he was."

There was an awkward silence in the room before Bridgette stood and smoothed her skirt. She thanked Devante for the information and told him she would prepare for their next meeting and see him in the conference room. The rest of the day went by like any other day despite all of the confusion within her and the tension between her and Ryan.

Chapter Five

T he elevator was taking its sweet time as Bridgette stood waiting for it to arrive. She had stayed late again to catch up on the work that she missed this morning. She also made some final touches to the Christmas party.

It did not take long before she noticed Ryan was standing off to her left waiting for the elevator as well. As the doors to the elevator opened she stepped forward, and he followed.

They punched in their stops on the console and waited as the elevator took off. Ryan leaned against the wall of the car and looked longingly at Bridgette. She looked at him and licked her lips before she spoke.

"I've discovered some information from Devante. Apparently, there is a problem with the person I went home with last night. And I feel that I owe you my honesty on this if we are ever going to be friends again." Bridgette said.

At her words Ryan arched a brow. She continued, "I went into the club and was thinking about meeting a new friend or friends. I was not set on getting laid if that is what you are thinking. But, I was sipping my drink and this very attractive man approached me. And the idea of dancing with him made me excited so I said yes. I am a single woman and there was nothing wrong with it. It was harmless until he placed his hands on my hips…"

Once she trailed off Ryan said in a raw growl, "Spare me the details, please." She simply nodded and went on. "I had no idea who he was. As far as I knew he was a random man from a club. And we just so happened to go back to his place. But you and Devante both know him in terms of business. And so that complicates things."

Ryan shook his head and sighed, "Is he a client and is pulling his account because of it?" She shook her head and said, "No. It is worse than that." Ryan couldn't imagine what could be worse but had a sinking feeling Bridgette was about to tell him.

"It was Christopher Ciccone." she said in a low voice. Ryan stiffened and his eyes went wide in total shock. It was as if someone just poured ice water over his soul.

He looked deeply into her eyes and ground out, "What the fuck, Bridgette?! His motives for getting YOU into his bed were less than honorable. I can tell you this because I know him."

She looked down, tears pooling in her eyes and said, "Devante said it was suspect, but he did not know Chris' motivations. And I have yet to speak to him so I have no idea if it was on purpose for him to seek me out or if I was just a hot girl in a club with him."

Ryan shook his head and growled, "You will NOT speak to him again. His motivations mean nothing. It ends now!" At Ryan's roar she lifted her head and looked into his eyes.

"I'm an adult woman. I have the right to go home with any man that I choose as I'm single. And that is your own doing. I am sorry that I happened to meet someone you dislike. But, until he and I sort this out I'm not convinced he is the enemy. And you have no say in this. This is my personal life.", she said.

Ryan flinched at her words because they were true, but they stung nonetheless. It was then that the elevator doors opened and Ryan simply slumped his shoulders and walked toward his car. Meanwhile, Bridgette went toward the car waiting for her like clockwork. She looked back at him sadly and slid into the car on her way back to her apartment.

The ride was long to her way of thinking but in reality it was the same amount of time it always took. The rain drizzling down her window reminded her of the tears she wished she could shed. She'd hurt Ryan without meaning to, and she had the best sex of her life with a man who may or may not be trying to take him down. Was she just a pawn?

Taking out her phone she texted Chris and asked him if he would meet her at his place at eight sharp. He texted back and told her it was perfect for him, and he couldn't wait to see her. With a sigh she let her head lean back against the weather of her seat.

It was going to be a long night in which she was unsure she was going to come out unscathed. Bridgette tried not to over think on her way into her apartment. She placed her bag and keys on her entry table and went straight to her bedroom to strip off the dress from last night and relieve herself of the heels.

Then she changed into a pair of tight jeans and a sweater. She placed her hair into a ponytail and applied some makeup to complete her look. She would wear some flats when she went to leave.

Making her way into the kitchen she sighed, taking out her pitcher of lemonade and poured herself a glass. Sipping it she decided to make herself some dinner. Perhaps it would be better to go into this with a full stomach.

Also, the act of cooking would take her mind off of everything that was happening in her life. She decided to make herself some spaghetti with onions and peppers. It was nothing fancy but it was something to fill her stomach and a meal that she enjoyed very much.

An hour later she put her bowl down on the coffee table and sighed happily. She was fed and feeling more relaxed. It was nice to be in her sanctuary. It felt like she was home and safe from all that could harm her here.

The anxiety was not flowing through her body as it had been previously. But, it was still there. There was a sinking feeling in her stomach when she thought about Ryan's reaction to knowing it was Chris she had been with. And the same feeling when she thought about the things she would need to discuss with Chris tonight.

Looking at the clock she realized she needed to call the car to take her to Chris' place. She sent the text for the car and started making her way down to the lobby of her building. It was especially cold tonight, and she had bundled up in mittens and a warm coat.

The car arrived right as she stepped into the cold night, and she slid inside and gave the driver the address. The ride there was filled with too much thinking. It felt like she was on the way to her very own execution.

Upon arrival at Chris' place she slid her phone into her bag and went inside to begin the elevator ride to Chris's place. Once the doors opened she saw him wearing nothing but tight jeans, his body glistening from his shower and his feet bare. She tried not to feel aroused but the second she saw him her thighs were covered with moisture.

This man did things to her body that was new to her, and she couldn't deny she loved it. Holding the door open he motioned for her to come in. Neither of them said a word.

There was a smirk on his lips at the sight of her. She returned his smile, the arousal in her eyes saying all that needed to be said. Their body language made it clear that they were both still attracted to one another.

It sent a thrill through them both knowing they shared this mutual need. The air was electric and it almost made Bridgette forget why she came over in the first place. Closing her eyes and sighing she looked deeply into his rules.

Bridgette licked her lips and then said, "May we sit?" as she gestured toward his seating area in the living room. He nodded and she took a seat. He decided to sit on a chair as she chose the sofa.

"I take it that this is not a simple desire to see me again?", he said a little mischief in his voice. Bridgette swallowed and said, "There is that. But, there is also more." He nodded and offered her a drink. She declined and played with the hem of her sweater.

It did not take a rocket scientist to figure out that she was upset about something. Chris searched her features and said, "Did I do something wrong last night? Are you upset with me over it?"

She shook her head and said, "Last night was perfect for me. The best sexual experience I've ever had to date. But, this morning when I arrived at work I discovered that you have a connection to my life. And I have to ask you... did you know of this connection before you came up to me at the club?"

Chris took a long wig of his drink and then placed it down on his glass coffee table. His entire attention was on Bridgette as he said, "I saw a woman in the club who was beautiful and I wanted to get to know her better. What is this connection between us? What am I missing here?" Nervously Bridgette licked her lips again and then took the bottom lip between her teeth.

"I am the ex wife of a business associate of yours. I am also the personal assistant to Devante Salazar. It was Devante who thought I should be cautious of your intentions and pointed out your issues with Ryan. Ryan and I were married. But, he broke my heart and it ended."

At the news Chris raked his hand through his hair. "I really had no idea. Does this change things between us?", he said in a low voice.

That seriously made Bridgette consider the situation and in doing so she tilted her head to the side and bit her lip. Chris looked at her noticing her actions and couldn't help but feel attracted to her.

The way she moved, the way she spoke. Of course she was Ryan's ex. He would have fallen for her quickly and wanted to make her his own. It amazed him that it had seemingly been a vanilla relationship. He had known Ryan a long time and was very aware that his tastes ran more toward a D/s kind of relationship.

"I had an amazing time last night. I would like to continue to get to know you better. Unless my former relationship with Ryan is a problem. The relationship we have now is strictly professional at my request. I work for Devante so I suppose I work for your opposition in business. Is that an issue?", she asked.

Chris smiled widely and said, "Not at all. Devante and I get along very well. We've been business associates for quite a while. And Ryan and I go back even longer. Until our falling out we were actually quite close. The situation is only as awkward as we make it. It seems to me that we are both single and free to explore our feelings here. I would like that.", he said.

At his words Bridgette's shoulders sank in relief, and she beamed a smile at him that made him both feel happy and hard all at once. They sat in silence for a moment. It was then Chris that asked her if she would like a tour of his penthouse with all of the lights on.

She accepted and he held out his hand for her. She took his hand, and they explored every nook and cranny of his home. As soon as they finished their tour they sat back down on the couch in the living room area, and he pulled her close to him.

They spent the rest of the evening cuddling on the couch and talking about themselves. Bridgette learned that Chris was one of eight children and his best friend's name is Decon. Bridgette told him all about her friendship with Cassidy, and then she brushed over her relationship with

CARRIE CROSS

Ryan. They talked about childhoods and favorite colors, ice creams and favorite holidays.

At around ten they decided to have some snacks, and they talked about how she was planning the company Christmas party. Bridgette was having such a good time that she even asked him to come with her as her plus one. He accepted but said it may be controversial if he came with her.

She'd only smiled and kissed him in return. She wasn't worried about controversy. After their snacking they watched some Netflix and before long Bridgette was yawning and looked at the clock.

"Shoot! I should be getting back home. I need to be up early for work tomorrow. Thank you for meeting with me. I'll text when I get home to let you know I'm alright. And we'll get together this weekend?", she said.

Chris smiled and winked at her and said, "Mmm. I look forward to that text!" At the door Chris leaned down and kissed her softly on the lips and smiled in return. It felt really good to be spending time with him.

She had come unsure of what would happen next. Now Bridgette felt relieved that she was not a pawn in a game between two men she admired and liked. There was a sense of peace that washed over for her.

At the same time she would be lying if she didn't admit that she felt nervous deep in her stomach over how Ryan would react to her getting closer to Chris. He saw him as a

84

threat somehow. There was so much she did not know about their falling out.

The falling out between the men was something that is in their shared past. It was not something she felt comfortable prying into. Bridgette just hoped they would keep it away from her. All she wanted was peace and to be happy. And for their happiness as well.

As the car pulled up to her building she noticed a man in a long coat leaning against the building smoking a cigarette. She didn't think anything of it when she got out of the car and began to walk inside. But, the man put his cigarette out and caught her elbow.

She turned into him stunned, and he leaned down and kissed her. At first, she stiffened, shocked by the action but soon she sunk into the taste of him. He pulled away and tipped her chin up to look into his eyes. This man was a complete stranger, and she just kissed him back!

The mystery man said in a low gravelly voice, "You are beautiful." She felt an electric shock down her spine at the sound of his words. Her panties were damp, and she felt light-headed from the kiss.

The man leaned down and whispered in her ear, "Let's go inside. I will introduce myself, and we will see where that leaves us." She shivered with want at the sound of his voice, but she also stiffened.

It occurred to her that she just met this man and now he wanted to come into her home. Was that safe? At that moment she didn't care. She was going to let him come upstairs to her apartment and if he wanted he could take her panties off with his teeth. Whoa! Where did that thought come from?

Bridgette nodded and took her keys out of her purse to be ready to open the door. They went inside the elevator and looked at each other with heated gazes. Once the door opened they made their way to her apartment.

As she was unlocking her front door she felt his breath on her neck and the heat of his body close to her own. There was something magnetic about him. It was crazy that she could have this kind of connection with someone.

Bridgette didn't even know his name! All of it made her question herself for a second. Then the feel of him so close to her wiped away any doubts she may have had. She was single and it felt right so she was going to live her life to the fullest.

Inside the apartment she tossed her purse and her keys on the entry table and turned to look into his eyes. The handsome man's eyes locked with her, and she could barely control her breathing. She just knew that he was going to take her, and she couldn't be happier.

How he stalked toward her and the heat in his eyes was setting her on fire. She could do nothing else but lock her gaze on him and lick her lips in anticipation. The moment that the man reached her he pulled her roughly into his arms and kissed her with fierce passion and claimed her mouth as his own. She had never felt quite like this before.

Sparks were flying all over her body, and she melted into his embrace. The man gave a moan that was like a groan low and husky into her mouth. There was no time to think or doubt her actions because his hands were everywhere.

It was wild and passionate. Nothing had ever felt so untamed as he felt in that moment. She felt free, he felt untamed and together they were wild.

His mouth left her own before finding its way to her neck. Bridgette moaned and pushed her head back exposing her neck for his pleasure or maybe her own. There was the titillating sensation of his teeth raking their way down her neck and nibbling at her tender flesh.

She couldn't help but gasp in surprise and pleasure. His rough and large hands pulled her skirt up. Before she could blink her panties were sliding down her legs. Bridgette was melting with desire for this stranger.

All she could do was spread her legs wider to assist in his actions. His tongue darted out to pleasure her neck and collar bone. The way his rough hands felt on her thighs made her moan and helped to make the moisture pool between her legs.

It took mere moments before his hands were cupping her sex, and she was arching against his hard body panting for more. His deep chuckle made her hum with need. No man had done so little and yet turned her on so very much.

The heel of his hand teasing her clit as she pants the word please to him. His grin was wide, and he murmured against her skin "Your wish is my command Princess." before biting down on her sensitive shoulder.

The mixture of his hands on her most private place and the bite make her shake with pleasure, and she starts to drip in need of more. There were two swift beats of her heart before his hand left her heat, and she was about to groan at the loss. But, before she would he swiftly picked her up into his arms and carried her to her bedroom.

Laying her down on her bed as if she weighed nothing and was precious she was exposed from the waist down. The man's gaze was fixed on her entire body and there was an intense heat reflected in the pools of his eyes. Bridgette couldn't believe she was there and didn't hesitate to lower her dress exposing her breasts to give him a better view. Her eyes never left his own as she did so.

This was about the fire between the both of them and the raw need they shared. In return he started to slowly strip off his clothes. The shirt comes off first, and then he makes his way down to his belt.

Bridgette's eyes following his every move; her eyes on fire with lust. Then he sets the belt to the side and pulls his pants down revealing black boxer briefs. She licks her lips as he begins to pull his boxer briefs off and exposes his long and thick cock for her greedy gaze.

Bridgette's mouth waters and his eyes dance with mischief at her reaction to seeing him naked before her. This man was raw, dangerous, powerful and all male. She needed him to be rough and hard with her.

In the next moment he's crawling onto the bed and over her body ripping clothes from her body. Not caring how much it would cost to replace. He could buy her another one.

Right now getting her naked was his only goal. And Bridgette did not care at all as the scraps of the outfit she so carefully picked out landed on the floor. All she could think of was her burning need for this man to sink himself deep into her and ride her raw.

Next her bra fell away in the same fashion, and she looked into his sparkling eyes and said, "I guess we're even now." He chuckled and said, "Oh no baby… we won't be even until I'm balls deep inside your sexy little body." Bridgette shivered against his body and never took her gaze off of his as he moved to line his cock up with her entrance.

She bit her lip and tried to hold back her groan of pleasure feeling his heat so close to her own. But, he heard it and it spurred him forward. He thrust hard, rough and deep inside of her. The sensation made them both moan in pleasure at the same moment.

This was going to be a long night of raw and hot fucking. They also both knew it would not be the last time that they had sex together. This was the beginning of something even if they had no idea of what that was.

Each thrust was more rough and harder. It made Bridgette hang on to him and move her body with him going along for the ride. Their sex was steamy.

Her legs wrapped around his body encouraging him to go deeper and harder within her. His strong arms surrounded her body like a cage of sexiness. This was by far the most intense and rough sex she had ever had in her life. And she wanted more!

Their eyes locked making it feel even more intense and hot as they moved together with a need undefined. Before Bridgette could properly realize what was happening he was pulling from her. Then he was turning her over on her stomach and pulling her hips up so her ass was up and her face was down.

Without a moment of warning he thrust hard inside her sweet hot heat. Once inside her again he began to pound himself within her with each hard thrust of his hips. She felt full and taken.

It was glorious and she never wanted it to end. Gripping the sheets and moaning her pleasure and slight pain that was delicious and not at all a deterrent. The sounds of their bodies pounding against one another the only sounds in the room as her breath caught with the force of his thrusts.

Neither caring how much noise they made just as long as they kept moving forward. Bridgette's breasts swaying with the force of his thrusts and his hands coming down from her hips to her breasts to squeeze them as he fucked her roughly. She had never felt so feminine and desired before.

This was more than sex. It was on another level and she wanted it, reveled in it and found a new part of her sexuality inside of it. On a moan Bridgette said, "Oh fuck! I am getting so close! Please...."

His hands left her breasts and went back to her hips as he increased his thrusts and growled that she could cum if she said his name. Then he revealed that his name was Decon. As her orgasm exploded through her all she could think of was the pleasure and his name.

She screamed his name as she shook from head to toe in the most pleasure she'd ever felt in her life. It set off Deacon's own orgasm, and he growled her name as he exploded deep within her body. They stayed connected in place panting for a few moments with no sounds except their breathing.

Once he gathered himself Decon slowly pulled away from Bridgette and went to the bathroom without a word. He returned with a damp and warm cloth. Decon tapped her hip to signal her to lay on her back, and then he cleaned her up between her thighs with a gentleness that shocked her.

She had never expected this kind of treatment from anyone but especially not someone who had so thoroughly fucked her just moments ago. She caught her breath and smiled at him. Then feeling a little cheeky she extended her hand and said, "Well, you know my name is Bridgette. But, it is a pleasure to meet you Decon."

Then her smile faded, and she looked at him with wide eyes. It was then she remembered where she had heard that name before. It couldn't be?! Could it?!

Chapter Six

"Are you... are you Chris' best friend Decon?!", she said in complete and total shock. Suddenly she felt the need to cover herself with the bed sheet. He cleaned off his cock with the cloth and tossed it into her hamper.

Then he slowly looked into her eyes and said, "Yes, he is my best friend. No, he would not be upset that we just had the best sex of our lives. We share women. We are a package deal. He knows I came here tonight to talk to you. He didn't know we would have sex because I didn't even know that would happen. I didn't plan on that."

Bridgette sat up her nakedness not a thought on her mind and looked into his eyes. It was time for her to ask some hard questions and get some answers. If he wanted a triad could she be a part of it?

"You want to have a triad relationship with Chris and another woman?", she asked. Decon smiled at her and said, "Well, Chris and I are straight so… we want to share our woman. But, yes… we would be like our own triad I suppose. We aren't big on labels."

She thought about that for a moment and was not upset by it. She was more curious than anything if she was being honest with herself. Bridgette's mind was whirling at a mile a minute with thought after thought.

"Why didn't Chris tell me this when I met him?", she asked. Decon came to sit beside her on the bed and smiled kindly. The air between them crackled with an intense emotional surge.

"I think he liked you and didn't want to freak you out too much. I mean you already knew he had history with your ex. That would be enough in itself to send you away.", he said thoughtfully.

Bridgette looked at him and cocked her head to the side waiting for him to continue. Decon winked at her and continued, "He wanted you to like him before he sprung something else on you. Plus, he knew I needed to meet you and see if we had chemistry too."

There was a moment of silence as Bridgette bit her lip. It was taking a minute to process all of the information coming her way. Decon allowed her the space and time to be able to come to terms with everything.

"We certainly have chemistry. But, I'm not sure that I'm right for you both. Not because I am against the kind of relationship that you both want. I'm just not sure that it is me or that I am ready for that kind of commitment to one person let alone two people.", she said.

Decon smiled and nodded. "That is okay. Why don't we take it one step at a time?", he said in a calm and understanding tone. Bridgette agreed. Then she realized they were both seated on her bed naked casually chatting.

She blushed, stood and went to her dresser and took out some yoga pants and a tee shirt from her drawers. She next finds a pair of panties that match and puts them on before getting dressed in the clothes.

Decon winks at her and says, "Taylor Swift fan huh?" She looks down at her Reputation Era tee and nods. "Yes, I am. Problem?"

He shakes his head and says, "I actually like her music." Bridgette smiles and knows they will at the very least be friends for life based on that statement and somehow Decon has the same thought. Decon goes about getting dressed, and they make their way into her kitchen. She makes them some breakfast, and they chat about their lives and find they have a lot in common.

There is a knock at the door and Bridgette scampers off to open the door in a wonderful mood and when she opens the door Chris is on the other side. She opens the door wide and invites him in for breakfast. Noticing Decon there he greets him and takes a seat.

"I take it your conversation went well...", Chris says. Bridgette blushes and Decon grins. "We did not talk at all last night. I did not know his name until I came, and he asked me to scream it. We talked this morning.:, Bridgette said.

Chris smiled warmly and said, "Well, that is most unexpected but good." Decon smiled and said, "I think so too. But, we aren't rushing anything. Just because we have amazing sex doesn't mean Bridgette wants to commit to one person let alone two. And we aren't going to rush or push her. This is her life. And at the very least we can all be friends. And help each other out in the orgasm department if need be."

Bridgette flushed and said, "Yes, that is all true but you don't have to be quite so blunt about it D." Chris only smiled and winked at them both. This was going far better than any of them could have hoped.

After breakfast was finished they decided to meet for dinner to see what a night out as a threesome would feel like. After the men left Bridgette went to change for work. Then she smiled to herself and thought about how her life had changed so much in such a short amount of time.

It was then she noticed the time and cursed under her breath. She was seriously late for work and needed to get her ass in gear! Once she was in her tight pencil skirt and professional blouse with a blazer she slid on her heels and was thankful she already had her pantyhose and underwear on.

This would be a nice outfit for her date tonight as well. With that she hailed a cab and was off to the office. Once she arrived everyone looked at her like she had three heads or something. Did she look that different?

Could the amazing sex with Decon have changed her that much or was she being fired or something? That was when Ryan stepped out of his office and crooked his finger at her and said, "Bridgette, my office."

She set her things down at her desk and then made her way inside his office with haste. It was strange because even the idea of losing her job did not bother her this morning. She knew her worth and knew that somehow she would find something else if she needed to.

At the same time she was curious why everyone was giving her off looks. Bridgette was also curious why Ryan wanted to see her. Devante was her boss and he had not contacted her or seemed upset with her.

"Yes?", she said casually. He had his back to her at first but turned and narrowed his eyes on her. It seemed as if he was trying to contain his temper before he spoke.

"It has come to my attention that you've been late a few times recently. In addition to that you've been seen around town with Chris and Decon. This would mean nothing except for the reputation of the firm. They are rivals of ours in business. And they are in a complicated and taboo kind of romantic relationship situation. Should you join them in such a thing and the press caught wind of it… it could reflect badly on the company.", he said in a firm and even tone.

Bridgette did not know if she was angry or if she was just stunned. She knew her personal life was not now or had ever been tabloid worthy. She also knew this was more personal than professional. If it had been a company issue Devante would be speaking to her.

He sat on the edge of his desk and looked down on her from his perch. Bridgette sat up straight in her chair and looked him in the eye and said, "It seems to me that you have some unfavorable and taboo sexual habits you have kept to yourself. If those were to leak to the press that would reflect badly on the company but I doubt you are lectured about that."

Ryan eyed her but kept his mouth shut. There was no sense arguing with her when she was right on that point. It pained him to know that she was probably about to make some more good points. Could he argue? Was this even a professional problem or just a personal one based on his broken heart.

"It is how you met Chris and Decon, right? At the sex club? My sex life is none of your business nor does it reflect on this company in any way, shape or form. I do not appreciate discussing gossip about my life with anyone.", she stated with anger in her voice.

She went on to say, "I owe you no explanations nor do I need to defend myself against gossip. As for being tardy... yes I have. However, I have also stayed late to compensate for the time and will work hard to make sure it does not happen again. Was there something else, Sir?"

At the tone she used to say Sir he flinched. He looked away and swallowed before saying, "No, that was all. I will see you in the conference room in five minutes for the first meeting with Devante."

She simply nodded and left to attend to her things at her desk and to prepare for the meeting. It really made her frustrated that Ryan was making life harder on her. It was no longer simply about their personal life. This was bleeding into her professional life and she was not going to stand for it.

There was a coldness between Bridgette and Ryan all day. Devante and the other employees all noticed the change between them. At lunch Devante convinced Ryan to go with him to a local bistro.

They arrived and were seated toward the back. They put in their orders and then Devante said, "What the hell is going on with you and Bridgette? There are ice clusters all over the office." Ryan sighed and his shoulders slumped.

"I've been having her followed. She is having a relationship with Chris and Decon. I was not prepared for her to move on so quickly and not with them." Ryan said. Then he took a deep breath before moving on.

"I told her that there was gossip about it and it could reflect badly on the company. She put me squarely in my place about her love life and my place in it. Apparently, she knows how I met Chris and Decon. That I kept parts of myself from her. Which does not help her impression of me.", Ryan stated.

Devante simply shakes his head. Then he steepled his fingers and looked at his friend across the table. It was time for him to speak as a friend and a business partner.

"Either be completely honest with her and let her make up her mind from there or simply let her go. You can't continue on this way for either of you.", he said. Ryan nodded sadly.

"I'm afraid that if she knows everything she will tell me to "fuck off" for good. A part of me thinks I deserve that at this point. But, at the same time it is killing me thinking of her with Chris and Decon. They are good people outside of being assholes in business. I know they would never hurt her. But, damn it… she is mine!", he said in frustration.

Devante shook his head and said, "She was yours. Now, she belongs to herself. And she is trying to find where she belongs. She is discovering herself and her sexuality. Maybe they will help her and that will lead her back to you. And maybe she is meant for them. Either way… it is out of your hands."

Ryan hated when his friend was right. It was hard to realize that this aspect of his life was truly out of his hands. All he could do was focus on himself, his life and his career.

Being the confident man that he was, Devante strolled to his office with a grin on his face. He felt like he provided his friend with good advice, and he had a date with his lovely wife that evening. Life could not be better.

Ryan on the other hand returned to the office with a scowl and sank to his seat with a hiss. He was unhappy because the chances of getting Bridgette back were slim at this point, and he had nobody to blame but himself. He picked up his phone with a scowl and barked for Bridgette to come to his office at her earliest convenience.

It took exactly seventeen minutes and twenty-six seconds before she knocked on his door. Ryan swallowed before he told her to enter the office. Bridgette walked into the room with her classy grace with that undercurrent of raw sexuality that she possessed.

Ryan had a hard time keeping himself in control. But, he sat straight and looked her in the eye as she took her seat and licked his lips. He was going to need to make things right for both of their sakes.

"I've asked you here for a personal reason. I wanted to apologize this morning. And I wanted to invite you for drinks after work this evening. The purpose for the drinks would be to properly apologize and to explain some things I have withheld for far too long.", he said cautiously.

When she did not respond he continued. "I expect nothing to come from the conversation or from you. It is entirely so you know everything and can make up your mind from there.", he expressed emotion clearly in his voice.

It shocked him that his voice remained even and did not shake once. Bridgette arched her brow and listened to him entirely. Once he finished she folded her hands in her lap and looked him in the eye.

"I am sorry but I must decline. I have a previous engagement tonight. I would like to discuss this matter with you another time however. What does your calendar look like for the rest of this week?", she said calmly.

It did not miss Bridgette's attention that he looked disappointed that she would not meet him that night. At the same time he seemed to relax when she said she would meet him later in the week. It was a moment before Ryan looked through his calendar and said, "I am available for dinner on Thursday. Does that work for you?"

Bridgette nodded and said, "Yes, that gives me time to prepare, and I am free that evening. I look forward to learning the truth. Until then let's keep things between us professional from here on out, okay?" Ryan simply nodded his agreement.

The rest of the work day is like any other day. Everyone in the office does their best work and all of the clients are happy with the work being done. The Christmas party is this coming Sunday and the entire office is buzzing about it.

Bridgette discretely asked for an extra ticket for the event so that she could ask Decon could accompany her as well as Chris. It would be nice to have them both with her for the party. She felt like after Thursday night she would need the added support in facing Ryan at such a private/public event like that.

Speaking of those very handsome and magical men she grinned as she thought of them. Then she finished up her work and packed up her briefcase. Once she completed her task she made her way to the elevator.

Bridgette smiled at Devante as they rode down to the parking garage. Their cars were waiting beside one another, and they wished each other well and went off to their respective dates. Things were finally looking up for them both!

The moment her car arrives at her apartment Bridgette takes a deep breath and smiles. She hadn't intended on changing but at the last minute she wants to look special and fresh for her men. So, she scampered up to her apartment and changed into a silver dress that is short with a low neckline.

She finds strappy heels and fixes her makeup to be smokey and seductive with red lips. Everything comes together so well she feels a little slutty and giddy at the same time. Bridgette makes her way down to the lobby of her building and smiles at her doorman as she walks to her car.

Everyone is looking at her in a new way. She is being looked at as a desirable woman. As she slides into the car her cellphone in her purse begins to ring.

She pulls it out and answers as the door closes and her driver enters the car to take them to the restaurant. The call is from Cassidy letting her know that she wants to have a girls night sometime in the new year, and she can't wait to see her at the party this weekend. Bridgette tells her she is excited too and then hangs up happily.

It takes just about twenty minutes to arrive at the restaurant. Once the car comes to a stop the butterflies in her stomach start to flutter. They increase as the door opens and not only is it Chris but also Decon standing there waiting for her.

Bridgette smiles at them both and slides with grace out of the car. But, once she is standing before them in the light they both have an intake of breath and curse under their breath. She looks at them worried that she made a mistake in her wardrobe. But, they simply grin at her and kiss her gently.

Their lips on her skin gives Bridgette a sense of calm, and she feels like a princess being escorted into the finest restaurant in town by both of them. They have the best table in a secluded section of the establishment.

They were seated and Decon leaned in close to Bridgette and said, "Slide your panties off and hand them to me under the table." She looked at him with an arched brow but slowly shimmied out of her panties and handed them to him. He smiled and placed them in his pocket. Chris winked at her from her other side and she felt so comfortable caged between them.

Their waitress tried to flirt with them but neither man acknowledged her advances. They simply ordered their meals and a glass of wine for the table. She placed her order last and couldn't help but frown at the woman's back as she went to put in their order.

Both men chuckled at her unhappiness with the waitress, and she grumbled about unprofessionalism. The conversation shifted to their days and their mutual happiness at sharing their meals together. When the food arrived they still continued their conversation between bites.

Bridgette looked a little nervous when she turned to Decon and said, "I already asked Chris because I didn't know you yet... but will you come with us to my Christmas party? I can't imagine going without you there too."

The smile that crossed Deacon's face made him light up and look even more handsome than he normally looked. Bridgette licked her lips and said, "Does that mean you'll come?" He nodded and leaned in to kiss her passionately, not caring who saw him do it.

The kiss made Bridgette moan and sink into his body. Chris cleared his throat and said, "If you don't stop that I am going to drag her into the bathroom and have my way with her. And I would much rather wait and have us all go back to my place after dinner."

Decon chuckled as he pulled away reluctantly. Bridgette's cheeks were bright red, and she looked at Chris with her eyes wide. He grinned and said, "Yes, baby... we have plans for you tonight."

The rest of the meal went with general conversation and Bridgette squirming in her seat. Each movement she made just made her remember time and time again she was without her panties. This made both men wink at her and made her even more excited for their plans for the evening.

It didn't matter that she had no idea what those plans were. She just knew they involved both of them and that was enough for her. After the meal had finished Deacon went to settle the check and Chris stood taking her hand and helped her out of their booth.

Then with his hand at the small of her back led her out into the cool night air. She shivered, and he placed a jacket around her shoulders and helped her into his car, sending her car home. Then Decon joined them inside the car for the ride to Chris' home.

The drive to the penthouse was quiet. All three of them had their minds on what would transpire once they arrived at their destination. As the car came to a stop they each released a breath and smiled at each other. They exited the car carefully and made their way up to Chris' penthouse.

Once inside the men took off their blazers and Bridgette took off her borrowed jacket. Then they all looked at each other in a moment of silence. It did not take long before Chris moved forward like a puma; taking Bridgette into his arms kissing her deeply. He growled into her mouth.

His passion for her was clear and alive between them. Then before she could register what was happening she felt Decon behind her unzipping her dress. There was a pulse racing between each of them as they were consumed with desire.

They stumbled happily into the bedroom. Once inside the bedroom Chris breaks the kiss and helps lift Bridgette's dress off of her. Next he sent signals to Decon. Decon went to a dresser and started to gather some items from inside.

Bridgette was so lust drunk that she hadn't even realized she was naked. All she focused on was Chris and the way his mouth made love to her own. Then Decon joined them and whispered in her ear, "Do you trust us, princess?"

She nodded, but he asked again and told her to use her words. In a breathy voice she said, "Yes". Decon took her into his arms and placed her on Chris's bed.

Chris then took her wrist and began to place it into a leather cuff with a soft inside.

Once she was secured he put a rope through the O ring connected to it and tied it securely to the bedpost. Then he repeated the process with her other wrist. Once that was complete she felt Decon doing the same process but with her ankles until she was spread eagle on the bed.

She was naked and open for their view. Bridgette's heart was racing with excitement and it showed between her thighs. Chris and Decon looked to one another and with a nod they both stepped closer each one coming forward from a different side of her body.

Chris took her right side and before she could blink his mouth was coming down over her breast. His hands were over her stomach teasing her flesh. Before long Deacon's mouth was over her other breast.

Next his hands were on her thighs teasing her and making her yearn for him to touch her in her most private of places. Then she felt them both pull away from her. As her eyes open she notices them both standing at the foot of the bed taking off their clothes.

It is hard for Bridgette to decide where to focus her eyes as they are both so attractive. She yearns to drink them both in with her lust filled eyes. After the men have stripped themselves of their clothes Decon picks up a flogger and teases her torso and sides gently.

This makes Bridgette arch against the touch and squirm against her bonds in need of more. A grin passes over Decon's features as he flicks the ends of the flogger over her body with more force. It does not hurt but instead opens her flesh up to delicious sensations that awaken her desire.

Chris leans down and swallows her moans with his kiss and Decon continues to flog her body, section by section. When the flogger hits Bridgette's hot heat she arches and cries out against Chris's mouth. Both men grin and love how responsive she is. Chris broke their kiss and picked up a pair of nipple clamps and placed them on her sensitive nipples.

She moaned in pleasure and pain as they went on her breasts. The way that they pinched her nipples was new but exciting. It was something she never dreamed of before and she knew on some level it was so good because they had aroused her.

Decon placed his hand on her sensitive clit at the same time. She was awash in sensation and couldn't believe she was in bed with two sexy men. It felt so good to allow them to be having their way with her. Once the clamps were secure the men nodded to each other and started to untie the ropes.

They had her untied quickly and they moved her body. She wason her hands and knees. Chris slides on to the bed beneath her, and they position her to straddle his lap. She grins down at him and licks her lips. He strokes her cheek and leans up to kiss her biting her lip before he pulls away.

The way his hands felt on her body made Bridgette moan. Chris groaned as he lowered her down onto his hard cock and locked eyes with her. Then he whispered in her ear, "Lean forward and let us fill you, baby."

Before she could think about what was happening she felt Decon behind her. He was teasing her with his finger, the cold feeling of lube between her cheeks. The way his finger felt over her tight hole and how his fingers felt pushing past her ring. OOO!

It was painful and new, and she wanted more of it. He played with her ass with his fingers encouraging her to begin moving on Chris' cock. It felt so good and she wanted more.

When she began begging for more Decon grinned and pulled his fingers out of her delightful ass and smacked it playfully. The next thing Bridgette knew there was more lube being poured onto her asshole, and then she felt Decon's hard cock up against her. His hands gripped her hips, and she bit her lip as he thrust forward.

She cried out never feeling so full or so much pain all at once. Bridgette could feel her tight hole being stretched by Deacon's hard cock, and she wanted more. It was then that Chris told her to hang on as he began to fuck up into her body. Then Decon began to fuck forward into her ass.

As they moved inside her in perfect rhythm she could only moan in pleasure and delicious pain. The moment they knew that Bridgette was loving the way their fucking felt the men held nothing back. Her men fucked her hard and in tandem. She held on them and surrendered to their sexual delights and gave in to sensation.

It was the best sex she had ever had in her life. It was raw, it was rough and it was intense. And before long she was not even sure the sounds she was uttering was a language anymore. The men didn't seem to notice or care as they continued to pound into her body and search for their orgasms as well.

It was Bridgette who came first. The sensation of her tight little cunt restricting around his hard cock made Chris cum next. And then once her tight hole tightened around his cock Decon lost his fight and came hard crying out her name.

They disengaged and ended up laying in a pile of limbs on Chris' bed panting and smiling. Bridgette started to laugh and said, "Is it always that good?" The men laughed and

Chris said, "No, baby. It can be good but it's never been that good before you."

Decon just nodded and pulled her close to him from behind. Chris pulled her front close to him. Sandwiched between them felt perfect.

It didn't take long until the three of them fell asleep. They stayed that way for a few hours until Decon woke up and slipped out of bed. He padded to the kitchen and took a seat at the island. He started to eat an apple.

It was going to suck when Bridgette left them, but he had a feeling she was going to. As much as the sex was amazing something told him deep down that she wasn't meant to be theirs. That fact hurt, and he wished he could make it go away, but he knew it was true, and he had to accept it. It didn't shock him when Chris joined him and started a pot of coffee a half hour later.

"You know she isn't meant to be ours right? We are her lily pad, man.", Deacon said. Chris turned around with the hurt Decon felt written all over his face and nodded.

"Yeah, I hate it man. She should be ours. We deserve her a hell of a lot more than he does.", Chris said. Decon simply nodded and accepted the cup of coffee from his friend.

They talked a little bit more before they heard Bridgette start to stir in the bedroom. They'd decided to let her come to them this morning. Bridgette awakened alone in bed and smiled at how deliciously sore she was feeling. She picked up her discarded dress and slid into it and padded into the kitchen.

"Good Morning!", she said cheerfully. The men both smiled and nodded over their coffee mugs. Chris offered her some coffee and she accepted.

Then they all sat down for waffles. They talked generally like nothing mind-blowing had happened the night before. The silence was driving Bridgette mad, and so she broke it by saying, "So...tonight I am meeting with Ryan to discuss things. He said he is telling me everything. And then I can do whatever I want with the information."

Chris put down his cup and nodded. Decon looked into her eyes and said, "Are you going to take him back?" She shook her head.

"I am hearing him out because he owes me the truth. All of it. He held back parts of himself from me during our relationship and that wasn't fair to me. I deserved to know. And he should never have left me for that bitch. I deserved better than that.", she stated.

They both nodded in agreement. After a beat of silence she continued, "I'm happy that I have met the both of you and that I have learned about myself sexually. I am glad to be friends with you both. It has been magical and I still want us to go to the holiday party on Sunday. I am selfish and I will need your support. Especially after tonight's revelations."

They both agreed, and then they went to get dressed for work. After both men were dressed for work they took

Bridgette home to get ready for her day. They waited in their car and took her to work before going to their office.

It made her feel fresh, new and special to be dropped off by them. With her head held high she walked into the building and took the elevator up to her floor. She ignored the gossip around her.

Bridgette was a professional, on time for her job, and she had no time for gossip or other people's opinions. She was single, and she could be seen with whomever she chooses. Plus, she deserved to have wicked nights like last night.

That made a grin appear on her lips and her eyes lit up. She was positively glowing as she walked into her office and made her way to her desk. Everyone noticed the new sway to her hips and the glow on her cheeks.

The man seated in his office looking at her through the glass and scowling noticed most of all. Ryan couldn't believe she had allowed them to drop her off so boldly this morning. And now she is coming into her place of work... his place of work like this!

He wanted to punch something. Hard. But, no he would keep his composure and carry on as they agreed. Professional. Until tonight. It was the night in which he would tell her everything and pray she would find her way back to him somehow.

Bridgette sat down at her desk and started straight into her work. She was working on some reports and keeping her mind focused. There was no room to be nervous about the night ahead of her or thoughts of the night before.

She went straight into her professional mode. Everyone in the office was more focused on her personal life than she was. At noon, she broke for lunch and decided to stay in and eat at the little café in the building.

Bridgette had a salad and ice tea and watched the people walking by on the sidewalk. The hustle and bustle of the city calmed her nerves and made her feel like she was a part of it somehow. She felt like she belonged and loved it here. This was her city, and she was proud of her accomplishments.

The job was going well despite her personal conflicts. She was overcoming her past and rising to the occasion. The rest of the afternoon passed in regular professionalism and hard work.

It wasn't until everyone else started to finish up for the day that she noticed it was time to pack up her things and end her work. Bridgette had been getting into the zone and was even ahead of her deadlines lately. Devante had been proud of her accomplishments and offered her a raise. But, now she needed to focus on the man in the office behind the glass that was about to rock her entire world.

Chapter Seven

R yan tried to keep his nerves in check as he took the elevator down to the parking garage. He'd driven himself today as he wanted as much alone time with Bridgette as possible. She was waiting for him beside his car, and she looked serious and yet a little nervous as well.

That made him relax a little. Ryan walked up to the car with a renewed sense of confidence and smirked at Bridgette. "Hello, Bridgette.", Ryan said.

At his words she turned from her position leaning against his car and faced him. She stuttered a little and said, "Hello, Ryan." in a little bit more of a breathy voice than intended. He smiled warmly at her and winked. She frowned and said crisply, "Shall we go?"

He noticed she was quick to put her hand on the door handle, and he chuckled. "Sure, babe. Let's roll. We are going to my place so we can have privacy. At the same time you are free to leave at any time. I have a driver on stand-by." Ryan responded.

They both got into the car once he unlocked it, and they sat in silence the entire drive to his penthouse. Once they arrived he pulled into his parking space in the parking garage and turned off the car.

They exited the car in silence before he said, "This isn't a death sentence you know. I had dinner catered in. I have drinks prepared by an amazing bartender on loan from an amazing bar in town. It will be a nice evening on that score at least. And you will walk away with your answers no matter what that means in the end for us."

That stopped Bridgette in her tracks, and she looked him in the eye and cocked her head to the side. "We will see. I am not going to assume anything. Whatever happens, happens.", she said.

Ryan placed his hand on the small of her back and started to lead her into the building. Within the next moment she moved out of his grasp and turned on him. Bridgette had no intention of letting him lead her anywhere. She had to set boundaries.

"I can make my own way. I will simply follow you. After you" she said, gesturing him forward. He wanted to object, but he bit his tongue and did as instructed. This was not the time to push her.

Once inside the elevator they awkwardly took the journey to his floor and were greeted by his butler. It seems that he had gone all out for her this evening. Bridgette was not impressed by these gestures as his money and luxury had never been her idea of romance or happiness.

She hadn't loved him for those reasons. As they entered the penthouse she took off her blazer and handed it to the butler along with her coat. He was kind enough to take her purse and briefcase as well.

Ryan gestured toward the table which was set elegantly complete with lit candles. Bridgette sat down primly and took her napkin and placed it in her lap and noticed that they were being served instantly. The meal was her favorite Italian dish from a restaurant downtown. She looked at him and arched her brow.

"Only the best for you.", he said simply. She wanted to laugh at that notion but instead decided to let it go and enjoy the meal. The wine was wonderful and complimented the meal wonderfully.

As they ate, their conversation was general and polite. There was a crackling tension under the surface, but they tried to ignore it to enjoy the meal together. Once they finished the meal there was an uncomfortable silence.

"I owe you the truth, and so I will share it with you. I should have given it to you from the start. That is something I will regret for the rest of my life. ", Ryan stated.

She simply nodded and gestured toward the couch. They moved to the living room area and took a seat. Ryan sat in the arm chair and Bridgette sat on the couch clutching a pillow for comfort.

Ryan took a breath and began to explain that when he was eighteen he was dared to go into a new club. He went into the club and learned a lot about BDSM and sex in general. He became a member sometime later.

It was there he discovered that he was a Dominant and loved to explore certain fantasies and fetishes. For a time he had many consensual purely sexual relationships with submissives he met at the club. Ryan became known for his skills and sexual prowess.

That was where he met Chris and Deacon who also shared similar skills. There had not been a time he had been in love with one of his submissives. That all changed when he met Bridgette he fell in love.

He didn't know how to explain himself to her and was afraid to lose her. In his mind he could keep those parts of himself separate or at least keep that one side of himself silent. It was stupid and childish, he told her.

Bridgette sat up and asked, "Was Ashley one of your submissives?" Ryan stiffened and nodded. Bridgette looked up at the ceiling and said, "Well, that makes a little more sense then."

After a moment of silence he went on. Ryan went on to explain that he had known Ashley his entire life. And when she had asked him to help her to explore her sexuality he'd agreed.

He thought he was helping her out and getting laid as a win-win. But when she wanted more, and he didn't feel it he was torn. Ryan had tried to make it work at first but eventually they broke up.

Until he messed up and chose her over Bridgette which in his mind was his most horrible regret of his life. As it cost him his relationship with her. There was real remorse in his tone and in his eyes.

Bridgette sat up straight and looked Ryan in the eye and said, "Thank you for telling me the truth. I believe I owe you the truth as well. I have taken this time as a single person to explore my sexuality. And I have come to learn that I believe I am a submissive. It is a shame that you weren't open with me in the first place. Maybe we could have been right for each other after all."

At her words he winced and looked at her with hurt in his eyes. It made her pause to see the hurt in his eyes. She was trying to be open and honest with him and hadn't meant to be vindictive with him.

The truth had been hard to hear and it felt like a knee-jerk reaction to lash out at him but in all honesty she wasn't even really upset with him. Strangely she understood his situation. But she wasn't sure if she would have fucked up in the way he had if she'd been in his shoes.

At the same time he had hurt her, and she felt entitled to at least some of her hurt and anger. Looking into his eyes she cocked her head and said, "I didn't mean to be a bitch. I am hurt and angry. I feel like I have the right to be. But, I hadn't set out to be hurtful on purpose." He nodded and licked his lips.

"I haven't heard from Ashley since her father took her away and I intend to keep it that way. I haven't been to my BDSM club since we met. And I am not fucking anyone else." he said before taking a breath

"I'm still in love with you. But, I don't deserve you and I know you have moved on. I don't like it and I will never like it. You are the one for me, baby. But, I will respect your choices and wait until this thing between you and those chuckle fucks is done.", Ryan said.

She laughed when he called her two men chuckle fucks. She knew he was trying to save face and that he respected her choice in men. And that he respected them.

She looked into his eyes and said, "Thank you. I would like to be friends when this is all over. Do you think we can do that?"

All he did was nod. She went to say something else but stopped. This was the start of real healing for the future. It was good.

That was when their gazes locked and he said, "I will always be here, Bridgette. I will be here to catch you when you fall, to watch over you when the shadows come in and love you even if from afar. You will always have me any way in which you want me."

There was a lump in her throat so this time she simply nodded. They sat in silence for a few minutes, and then he asked if she wanted something to drink. It was nice to have a little break in the tension.

She shook her head and said, "I should probably get home. Thank you for talking with me. As much as the truth hurts and is hard to digest I have to say that having honesty between us does make things better. I know in time this will all heal. I just need some time."

He nodded and walked her to the door. It was hard for him not to kiss her goodbye. She smiled warmly at him and kissed his cheek before leaving.

The way her kiss lingered on his cheek made him feel warm. There was one thing for certain. He was going to work on earning her love back and this time he would never let her go.

Once Bridgette arrived at her home she took off her shoes. She placed her keys in the little bowl she kept on her entry table. She sighed and suddenly felt so exhausted.

Nothing had gone the way she had expected it to. She'd expected to fight with Ryan or feel completely broken and although the truth was hurtful she felt good. She felt like it was a step toward healing and moving forward with her life.

That was a comforting thought and without thinking twice she walked into her bathroom and disrobed. Turning on the water she made sure to set it to steaming and left naked to go set out her clothes for after her shower.

A silk and sexy nightgown that only came to just above her knees. She loved it because it was crimson red with lace around the low neckline. Sometimes a woman just needed a sexy outfit to make her feel special.

It made her feel sexy and had a matching robe in case someone came unexpectedly, or she wanted to be a tease. And tonight she paired it with a silky pair of black panties. Smiling to herself she set out her favorite cream to rub on her arms and legs after the shower and her perfume for good measure. Why not feel good for herself?

After that was completed Bridgette made her way into the bathroom and stepped into the shower. The water ran over her body in a delightful way that made her moan with pleasure. It felt like she was alive for the first time since Ryan had broken her down.

She knew it was the combination of the wonderful sex with Decon and Chris, the professional success at work and the complete truth between her and Ryan. All of those wonderful connections and situations were allowing her to move forward. She was awake and alive again; she would never be taken down again. She was far too strong for that.

At least that was how she felt standing naked under the warm spray of the shower. Sometime later after she'd completed her night ritual after her shower she smiled to herself and ordered a pizza. She deserved to be pampered even if it was just her alone at home.

Let someone else cook dinner tonight, and then she would curl up in bed with a book and rest well. She didn't need to be in bed with a man or men every night. She did not need someone every second. She could be very happy in her own company.

There was a knock at the door, and she rushed to get her pizza. But, instead of the pizza delivery guy Decon and Chris stood there with grins on their faces. She cocked her head to the side and said, "How did you know I'd be home?"

They looked at each other and then at her and shrugged asking if they could come in. She opened the door for them and paid the delivery man who had arrived during their shrug fest. She offered them pizza and they accepted. She got some plates out, and they all sat down around her island and ate in silence.

After dinner she grinned and said, "I shouldn't have ordered pizza. I had dinner at Ryan's but… he unsettled me. And pizza was comfort food."

They were quiet for a minute and then Chris sat forward and said, "Oh yeah? What did he serve? He's a shit chef so I am sure he ordered in."

She laughed and said, "Yes, he knows better than to try to cook for me. I'd make him choke it all down himself. He had my favorite restaurant cater my favorites and included wine. Candles and all. People would have thought it was a special occasion or a date."

There was a stiffening to both men's bodies before they forced themselves to relax. She shrugged and said, "The food was good." The men looked tense and a little worried.

She looked them both in the eye and said, "I told him after a dinner of silence that it was time he came clean. He did. About it all and I would be a liar if I did not say that it was painful."

After a breath she continued. "It made me angry too. Because he never considered my feelings or choices. He was worried about losing what he wanted." She looked into their eyes and went on.

"That is fucked up of him. I told him so. But, I'm not as hurt as I thought that I would be. Probably because I'm not sure what I would have done in his shoes. ", she said. Taking a sip of her drink she paused.

"I can't judge him 100% just because I got my feelings hurt. I told him that in time I'd like to be friends. But, I also told him that he and I were clearly over. And he said things…

but I believe I have a friend for life. And that for me is what he is and will be.", she finished.

Decon leaned forward and said, "We know him, babe. He is in love with you and he is waiting for us to fuck up so he can step in. He will always be in the shadows waiting for you to change your mind on him."

Then he continued after a moment, "Believe me when I tell you he will work his ass off to earn the right to deserve a place at your side. We've known him a long time. This isn't over between you two."

Chris simply nodded in agreement. Bridgette wrapped her arms around herself and shook her head. Things in her mind were 100% over between her and Ryan. She wanted to move on with her life.

"I will never allow him to hurt like he did again. I was a blind fool. I may have some understanding and sympathy but I'm not going to open myself to him again. He set fire to the house, not me and now it's gone." Bridgette said.

The men looked at her and considered the way she held herself and the tears she was holding back. They knew that Ryan and Bridgette were far from over. And they understood clearly that she wasn't ready to accept it yet.

As her friends they would support her from this moment and beyond her realizing that Ryan is the man for her. And until then if she wants they will give her love, respect and a very good time in bed. They will always be her friends but she will leave them. And they didn't hate her for it.

They understood her and themselves. They would meet their woman someday. It would just hurt when she walked away because they had wanted it to be her.

They changed the conversation to happier topics like the upcoming holiday and the party coming up that weekend. She was so pleased that both men would be going with her to the company party. It would make the event fun.

Both men had promised her some personal fun after the party back at Deacon's place. Bridgette was so excited to see Decon's place. The experience will be something new in many ways. Just thinking about it had her wet between her thighs.

That night they simply stayed for some crappy television shows as an excuse to relax and be together. It made her happy to open up to them without pressure. It helped them all get closer to each other and feel more comfortable.

For the first time in a long time she was feeling genuinely happy for where she was in her life. And it wasn't simply because she had a man or men in her life. It was the combination of having friends, an active life, a job she loved and a sense of herself again.

As the rays of light broke through the blinds in her bedroom she stretched like a contented kitten. It was a fresh day and thankfully the last day of her work week. She loved her new career but lately they have had some heavy caseloads, and she was working super hard.

It would be nice to veg out this weekend and just be a bum until the Christmas party. The sounds of Godsmack filled her apartment as she shook her ass singing along and got dressed for the day. She decided to wear a provocative but professional outfit today.

It would be nice to be more herself and not worry about any of the men in her life. She was dressing for herself as her hips shook to "Voodoo". About twenty minutes later she grabbed her briefcase and keys and ran down to meet her car service.

Once she slid into the back seat her phone started to ring, and she looked at it confused. It was an unidentified number, but she picked up and said, "Hello, who is this calling?", in her most professional and even voice.

The man on the other end laughed and said, "So, formal and even. Good job Bridgette. My name is not needed. Just know I am watching."

Before she could ask any questions or make a comment he had hung up on her. The first thought that she'd had was to call Ryan, but she knew that she needed to rely on herself. It would be wrong to run to him every time she had a problem.

Plus, considering their strained relationship right now she did not want to burden it further with this. Instead she called Devante's cell and when he picked up she said, "Can we have a personal meeting today? I know you are slammed all day. Perhaps we could stay late today? I know this is sudden but I could have a big problem and be in over my head."

The silence on the phone let her know that he was considering what she had said. He finally spoke after a minute and said, "I will rearrange my schedule. Come straight to my office when you get in. We'll sort it out. I take it that you don't want Ryan involved."

She sighed softly and said, "That is correct." He simply grunted in acknowledgment and hung up. The car ride seemed to take forever that morning and her happiness she had been feeling since leaving Ryan's house was fading.

The last thing she needed in her life was an unexpected and kind of scary complication. Once they arrived at her employment building she thanked her driver and told him she looked forward to seeing him this afternoon. Then she made her way inside and to the elevator.

Somehow she couldn't shake the feeling of being watched. The words the man had told her washed over her like cold rain on her soul. Had she been followed?

Was she being watched and if so for how long? Suddenly she felt less safe than she had in a very long time. It would be so nice if this was simply a nightmare and that she could wake up soon.

The second the elevator doors opened she rushed straight to Devante's office without taking off her coat and setting her things down first. She knew he wouldn't mind. The main focus was to talk to him and see what he thought before she went into a complete panic.

This could just be a silly prank or something. Devante was seated behind his desk, his back straight and his hands steepled before him. Bridgette came in, closing the door behind her and took a seat.

The nervousness was rolling off of her in waves, and she saw him recognize this quickly. Devante casually sat back into his chair looking at her. This gave her time to gather herself and prepare to explain everything to him so they could calmly find a way forward.

Once Bridgette had calmed down she looked Devante in the eye and said, "I've been working on making my life better. I finally felt like I was healing and moving forward positively. Then on my way to the office this morning a call came in."

Taking a moment she swallowed hard. The nerves were jumping off her like waves. Devante was starting to worry about what was happening and how he can help.

"The number was not displayed and my gut told me to answer professionally, even. I did that and it was picked up on by the man on the line. I'd never heard his voice before.", she said, shaking now.

Devante arched his brow and said, "Go on." Bridgette fussed with the hem of her skirt and said softly, "He told me that he noticed my professional and even tone. Then he said his name was not needed when I asked who was calling. Then he simply said he was watching."

Bridgette looked her friend in the eye and said, "The call disconnected before I could ask any other questions or comment. No calls or anything since. I do feel like I am being watched. That could be paranoia."

The last part came out in a fearful gasp of words. The terror was starting to bubble up to the surface. Bridgette could not remember a time when she had felt so vulnerable.

Devante leaned forward and said, "We will trace the call. We will put someone on you to ensure your safety and discreetly look into this matter. I take my employee's safety seriously. ", he said seriously.

"You are also family. So, this will be handled swiftly. You have my word. However, due to your need for details on you I have to discuss it with Ryan." he stated grimly.

As she went to protest he held up his palm to stop her. He knew that this news was upsetting. At the same time it was his responsibility to care for his people in the best way possible.

"Ryan is part owner of this business. He has the right to know when an employee has a threat against them. I will remind him to remain professional. However, I would also mention this briskly to your men." he stated calmly.

"They will want to know. And not from Ryan because if you don't get to them first he will insert himself between you. Not to hurt you. To protect you.", he stated. At Bridgette's wide eyes he chuckled.

"Ryan is in love with you. He won't be worried about pissing you off if it means keeping you safe. But, I will attempt to handle him. You handle Chris and Deacon.", he said with a sigh.

"Please ask them to come to the office for a meeting please. Clear my calendar as we will be busy working on this all day. Thank you.", Devante said matter of factly.

Bridgette nodded and grabbed her briefcase and made her way to put her coat and case away. Then she started on her tasks for the day. The phone rang twice and went to voicemail for Chris so she tried to get Decon. He picked up on the second ring.

"I need you to remain calm and keep in mind that I'm a big girl…" she started. At her words he growled and said, "What the fuck is going on, babe?" She swallowed and informed him about the call, the meeting with Devante and his request for Decon and Chris in the office all day. Once she was finished she heard silence and waited for his response.

"We will be there in a half hour. Tell him to clear a conference room. And tell him that I will deal with Ryan. He is going to be a dick about this and I won't have him taking pot shots at Chris." Deacon growled at the last part.

Quickly Bridgette said she would relay the message and hung up. Then she hurried to her messaging application on her computer and told Devante the message from Decon. Devante said it was no problem and that he would handle it.

Chapter Eight

Bridgette went to work on some reports and got lost in her work. That was until she heard a flurry of activity and some women gasping. She bit her lip and tried not to smile.

Yes, Decon and Chris were very attractive and forceful. It would be quite a shock to see them together walking into the office on a mission. At the same time she also felt a twinge of jealousy. They were her men. At least for the moment!

Standing she went to greet them and escort them to the conference room as was her job. Once she met them they both looked her over from head to toe with heat in their eyes. She blushed and looked at them with open lust and desire.

They winked at her and told her to lead the way. She did and once they had arrived she went to leave. Before she could leave Devante said in a rich and stern voice, "Stay. This involves you and we need your view on this matter. Take a seat here beside me."

She did as she was told and now they were waiting on Ryan. He had no idea what he was stepping into. It was less than three minutes when a scowling Ryan entered the conference room.

His focus on Devante as he said, "You know asshole if you wanted to bond you could have waited until after I'd had my coffee. What the fuck is so important..."

The words stopped and his gaze narrowed when he noticed Chris, Decon, and Bridgette around the table. Everyone was looking at him, and he felt like a bomb was about to be dropped on him. It did not improve his mood.

He looked from each person to the next one landing on Bridgette and said, "What the fuck is going on here?!" Bridgette jumped at the sound of his thunderous roar. She looked up into his eyes with tears of her own.

Before Ryan could have a second to regret his anger that looked like it was toward her, Decon stepped in. It was apparent just by the look on his face you could tell that Decon would scold Ryan. And for once Ryan knew he deserved it.

"Sit the fuck down and you will be filled in. But, quit taking it out on Bridgette. We all know you are just hurt and scared. Fucking shut your trap.", Decon said in a growl.

Ryan clenched his jaw and hands and sat down and looked at Devante. Devante stood, drawing their attention to him. He had a way of commanding attention and silence from people when he stood or spoke.

"This morning Bridgette came to my office for a meeting. She was very unsettled after a most unexpected and startling phone call from an unlisted number. It would seem she is being watched in some way. ", he started in a clear and calm tone.

"The extent of this we are not clear on yet. I promised her my protection as her boss and as her brother in this life we have all chosen for ourselves. I understand that this is not something one person can handle. This is a family matter.", he continued.

"Despite our differences or conflicts, all of the people in this room are family now. We have to formulate a plan as a family. That is why I have asked you here today." Devante finished.

It was then that Ryan shot up out of his seat and started to pace and said, "I can call in contacts I have, and we can put people everywhere she goes. And on her personally of course..."

Devante lifted his hand to stop him. As the unofficial leader of the meeting and of the family he had to be the voice of reason. He understood Ryan's feelings but knew they had to be logical and smart to handle this.

"No. You are not taking point on this. I am. The reason you are here is that we are partners, and she is our employee. You deserve to know what is happening. You deserve to be in on security here at the office and the concerns for our employees. Beyond that you have no say here.", Devante said calmly.

The look on his face relayed that Ryan did not like what Devante said or the tone in which he used to communicate it. He looked at his friend with a glare and then turned his attention to Bridgette who looked guilty. So, she had asked Devante not to involve him in this.

Chris spoke for the first time, his voice calm and focused as she said, "At the end of the day our focus needs to be on keeping Bridgette safe. While she is here in your building that falls to Devante and Ryan and you will do your very best. Decon and I can add security to our homes and when she is with us."

He took a breath because he knew that even though he was being logical he needed to keep himself in check. Part of him wanted to echo Ryan's sentiments. As long as Bridgette was their girl they would care for her as such. And even after she would always be their friend, their family.

"This leaves when she is alone in question. Devante, I am sure since you are family you will agree with Decon and me that we would like her to have personal security during this time. Ryan as her friend I am sure you want nothing but her safety as well. We are all on the same team here.", Chris stated calmly.

Ryan looked at him not caring to hide his disdain for this situation or the other men in the room. He wanted to handle this situation on his own. This was bullshit and everyone in the room knew it. He was best suited to protect her, and he was her… damn it he was in love with her!

Taking a deep breath Ryan calmed himself which took great effort. He sat up in his seat and decided to act professionally. He could be calm and act accordingly.

In a clear and powerful voice he usually reserved for the boardroom he said, "The security in our building will be increased especially on this floor as the top members of our company work here. This will make sense and will not cause alarm to the general employee population. It also makes sense since an employee on this floor was threatened. We shall keep her name out of the information provided to employees."

He took a pause to sip some water set up on the conference table. Then he continued, "We take everyone under advisement when making these kinds of calls. And we have no idea if this is isolated to just Bridgette or company-wide yet. I take it that Decon will be using his contacts to trace the call and get us more information about motivations, names, time frame, etc."

Decon simply nodded. Chris leaned forward and his gaze locked with Ryan's saying, "I have added additional security to my workplace, home, and have someone who was former FBI willing to shadow Bridgette. Decon has done his security upgrades for his office and his home as well. We also called Bridgette's building and Devante secured more security for her there."

At those words that Ryan simply grunted he'd heard him. He then turned to Devante and said, "The party needs to have more security. Bridgette is known as one of our rising stars and can't miss the event. We need to be sure that she and everyone else is heavily protected. Can you make arrangements?"

Devante nodded and started texting someone about it straight away. Bridgette looked at them all making plans about her life without her and cleared her throat. She could not stand for these men excluding her.

"I realize I'm not powerful or rich like the rest of you. But, this is happening to me. I would like to have some say in my life moving forward.", she said, staying as calm as she could.

The men looked at her. They were all quiet as they tried to formulate the correct responses to her statement. None of them wanted to offend her but they also wanted to do everything in their power to protect her.

"I know that you feel that way. It is understandable but there is little you can do.", Devante said. Ryan looked into her eyes and the hurt she'd wanted to exclude him was clear.

She bit her lip and didn't look away saying, "I never meant to be a bother. I just wanted to be sure I was not in a panic over nothing. It could have been a prank. I never meant for it to become all of this. I had just started to feel like myself again… and I just wanted to be me and be happy…" the last of her words trailing off.

Ryan rounded the table and crouched down to take her hands into his own. It was not even a second thought. He needed to touch her, talk to her.

Looking into her eyes he said, "We will figure out what is going on and get you back to that happy place okay? I think you should consider staying with Chris or Decon for a while. You will be safer that way."

He had love and worry reflected in his eyes, "We don't know if you have cameras at your place and how safe we can make it. It will be better to be with someone else. Maybe you three could hunker down somewhere else that is safe. Unknown. It is up to you. Just, please be safe."

It wasn't until he finished speaking and their eyes met that the flood gates of her emotions released, and she broke down. There was nothing but soul-wrenching sobs coming from her body. Ryan took her into his arms and held her tight as she cried. Decon and Chris nodded to one another.

Devante watched with an arched brow but said nothing at all. After a few minutes, Bridgette stopped crying and looked up into Ryan's eyes, and said, "I…I'm so sorry. I didn't mean to get your shirt so wet. It just all came at me at once. I didn't expect this to happen."

He stroked her hair lovingly and said, "It is okay baby. I'll be your tissue anytime you need." She laughed and quickly stood up when she realized she'd been in his lap, in his arms. Bridgette smoothed out her skirt and looked around the room.

Decon smiled at her and said, "So, who wants to stay at an AirBNB and have a new adventure together?" Chris chuckled and said, "I'm game if the lady in our life agrees." Bridgette turned bright red and simply nodded.

That agreed upon; the men started to make arrangements including having other people secure her apartment and back her things. The rest of the day was spent with the men making phone calls and arrangements.

Information came in steadily. Apparently the call was from a burner phone in the city. That meant there was no record of who purchased it and no way to trace it to anyone.

It also seemed that her entire house had been bugged and filled with cameras. The feed was set to go to a place routed overseas through proxy servers but then the trail got lost. They were having people working on it.

It was unsettling to know that someone had been watching her living her life. Someone had watched her eat, sleep, shower, dress… it made her entire body feel frozen and icy. Wrapping her arms around herself she looked up to notice Ryan watching her.

He came closer and offered her some coffee and said, "Drink up. It will help warm you up and feel better. We'll get you through this safely. We will find the bastard doing this and stop them." She nodded and gave him a brittle smile. She believed him.

The way Ryan and Bridgette were interacting was not unnoticed by the other men in the room. Chris and Decon knew that after Sunday they would need to sit down with her and have that really painful conversation and let things go. But, before they did they would all enjoy Sunday as a way to have a happy memory to remember their time together.

Devante on the other hand was curious about the entire scene. He noticed that Decon and Chris were not shocked at all. They'd expected her to still be in love with Ryan. And they knew she would end up with him in the end.

Maybe he had previously misjudged these men. The only two people oblivious to what was happening seemed to be the two parties directly involved in the situation. Ryan got up and kissed Bridgette's cheek before nodding to the men and leaving to do some work in his office before his heart made him do stupid things.

It was at that time that Devante cleared his throat and said, "Well, gentleman I think we have everything handled. Thank you for clearing your time. I take it we'll be seeing you on Sunday at the party?" The men nodded.

Bridgette said, "They have agreed to be my dashing dates. I've been looking forward to having them with me on the dance floor." Everyone smiled and then men took her hands and kissed them before giving her soft kisses and promising to call her soon.

Then they left to return to their work. Bridgette left the conference room and made her way back to her desk on shaky legs. Once seated Bridgette went back to her work with trembling fingers trying to act like it was a normal day.

Her phone beeped and when she checked her text messages Cassidy had sent her three. All of them telling her to call her and informing her she was pissed that the first call she made was to her husband and not her. Bridgette smiled and texted back that she knew that the baby was about to come into their lives and Cassidy needed to focus on that.

This was not Cassidy's problem. Plus, she should be glad Bridgette went to her new big brother. Cassidy made her promise to come to dinner soon and told her they finally had the date when the baby was coming and that she had to be there. She was Godmother after all.

At the end of the day, Cassidy still couldn't shake her unsettled feelings. Everything felt off and strange to her. Her nerves were raw and on edge, and she was confused about her feelings.

The sex with Chris and Decon was amazing, and she wouldn't trade their easy friendship for the world. At the same time, even she could admit she still had feelings for Ryan and it was keeping her from feeling something more for both of the men in her life.

Could they tell? Was she hurting them by having this affair with them? As she sat in the car on the way home her thoughts started to drift toward different things.

It was crystal clear to her that she loved the city and loved her job. Bridgette felt at home in so many ways. At the same time she was so conflicted on the road ahead of her in her personal life. She was about to become a Godmother soon. She was not getting any younger either.

Did she want to get married and have a family of her own? Yes, she did. But somehow in her mind and heart, she knew it wouldn't be with Chris and Deacon.

Not because of the menage aspect of things. She did not care what others thought about her or her relationships. She just couldn't close her eyes and picture that life with them.

Late at night when she was alone with her private thoughts she would close her eyes and imagine Ryan and the children they could have. All of her emotions felt upside down, and she felt like she was in an emotional salad spinner. No matter how much she loved her city and her job she felt like everyone around her would be safer and better if she left.

This new problem was about her and now everyone else was suffering financially and emotionally. Extra security and being on eggshells. The second she arrived at her building she thanked her driver and hurried to her apartment.

Once inside she wrapped her arms around herself and leaned against the door. It was then that she came up with a plan. She would call out tonight before bed. She would pack and then take a taxi to the bank. She would withdraw all of her savings and take a taxi to the airport.

Then using a part of the savings she would get a ticket one way to a place far away and once there buy a cheap car. She'd start over and save everyone the pain of having her in their life. It was too much for her to fully process emotionally so she shut herself down into survival mode and started packing a bag.

All she needed was a couple of outfits, her ID for the plane, and her checkbook. She would have to leave everything else behind. The only three things she would bring with her were a picture of her with Cassidy and Devante on their wedding day, a picture of her baby and a picture of Ryan and her from when they first met in the OC.

It pained her to not have a picture of her and Chris and Decon. At least she still had her memories of them. Taking a few deep breaths she hurried to pack and get to the bank before they closed.

After she called her cab she started downstairs and smiled at the doorman. She told him she was going to Cassidy's place. He smiled and hoped she had a good time.

He'd even opened the door to her taxi for her like a gentleman. She hated to lie to him, but she couldn't afford to leave a trail. Once she arrived at her bank the manager asked her if she was in danger and that was why she was emptying her account.

She told him simply that she was going on a trip and needed the funds for travel. He'd smiled and loved that she kept her checking account open and only took her savings.

Once that hurdle had passed she left the bank and headed to the airport.

The choice to leave her phone at home and to get a new one at the airport was easily made. She would add the important contacts she'd written down in it later. She made sure her phone was prepaid and not easily traceable.

Upon reaching the airport she made her phone purchase and then made her way to the ticket counter. She asked them when the next flights were leaving and where they were going. They had a cheap flight to Nevada.

She'd never been there before and knew it was not somewhere they would look for her. Bridgette purchased a ticket there and waited for them to call her flight. In the waiting area, Bridgette sat her leg bouncing up and down as she waited to be called.

There was a nervous energy rushing through her body. She forced herself to stop moving her leg and to take a deep breath. The more nervous she acted the more suspicious she would seem.Bridgette needed to blend in and not be remembered.

As a result Bridgette tried to focus on starting over somewhere else and having a new life. She would go to Nevada and see what she could find. Maybe she was always meant to start over and live there.

Her only regret was the hurt Cassidy would feel at her loss. But, this was to protect Cassidy and the baby. To save them all.

As she boarded the plane she felt like she was being watched and she forced nausea away. She was just nervous and paranoid. Taking her seat she shut her new phone off and placed her bag in the overhead compartment. She was traveling light.

The less she had with her the easier it would be to become a ghost. The flight was unremarkable and she was thankful for it. Once she arrived in Nevada she took a cab to the cheapest car dealership she could find and purchased a used car that ran well.

It was a simple car over ten years old but would suit her purposes. Once she secured her car she went apartment hunting. She had to find somewhere that was nice but would take cash and not ask too many questions.

That was going to be difficult, but she had a feeling she would find someone who would understand the need to start over. After looking with no success for several hours she finds a cheap motel and gets a room for a few days.

That would let her look for work and for a place to stay while having a place to crash until it all worked out. Taking one of her three burner phones out of her purse she called Cassidy. It rang twice and then she picked up.

"Hello?", Cassidy said. It sounded like she had been crying. "Cass? It's me.", Bridgette said into the phone. There was an intake of breath on the line and then her friend screeched in her ear.

"OMG! Are you okay? Where are you? Nobody could find you. They looked everywhere. The men are losing their shit and so have I!" Cassidy said. Bridgette closed her eyes and pinched the bridge of her nose with her free hand.

"I'm okay. I can't tell you where I am. I left because it is not safe for you if I stay. None of you would be safe. Someone is after me and not all of you. I can't place you in danger or have you waste money on extra security because of me. I'm in the wind. I'll be fine. You all need to move on with your lives.", she said.

Cassidy released a pained sob and said, "You can't mean that. You can't do this to me... to all of us. We love you, asshat!"

Bridgette smiled and laughed "I'm an asshat. But, your asshat. I need to go now, babe. Tell Ryan I'll never forget the good times. Tell Chris and Declan they saved me. And tell your husband he is the best brother in the world. And tell my Godchild that I will love them forever. And as for you... I love you, bitch. Forever." Then she hung up before Cassidy could reply.

She went to the alley and stomped on the burner phone and chucked it away. One down. Then she returned to her cheap room and locked the door. She wondered how much protection the door would provide if an asshole wanted to get into her room.

Then she decided she would sleep lightly in the bathtub. Nobody would expect her to be hiding in the bathroom. There were pros and cons to this idea.

An extra door to lock and a shower curtain to hide behind. But, also trapped if someone found her. She would have to fight her way out.

Limited options meant that she had to hope her plan would work out. She took some things off the bed and set up her bathtub bed and shivered. The new start of her life was a rocky one.

The tears started to fall before her butt hit the tub's base. She cried herself into sleep. The next morning she forced herself up out of the tub and emptied it of her pillows and blanket.

Then she placed her bag behind the toilet and took a shower. Once she finished that she changed into a new outfit and got ready to take her purse and look for a job somewhere and a place to live. She hoped she would have better luck than she had the previous day.

She ended up going to a diner and talked to the waitress in her fifties. During that conversation she found out they needed someone to take over the night shift. Bridgette was able to fill out an application and was told by the woman named Elise.

The conversation between the women was friendly. Elise shared that the owner would contact her soon. After finishing her coffee she asked Elise if she knew somewhere she could rent a room or small apartment with cash.

The woman said that she did. Bridgette wrote the address down and went to go check it out. It was just after one in the afternoon when she finished signing the lease to a little studio apartment a block from the diner. The older man Mr. Jinkins was more than willing to help her out.

The apartment was clean, if not a little small and older. But, she did not need anything extravagant. The price was right, and she was close to the diner.

The rest of the afternoon was spent checking out of the motel and walking back to the diner for dinner. She moved a few things to her new apartment beforehand. She felt accomplished to have found a place to stay so easy.

Before she went to leave the diner Elise stopped her and said that the boss wanted to see her in his office. She nodded and followed her down the hall in the back of the building. Once they arrived outside the door Elise left her to knock.

A deep man's voice told her to come in. When she opened the door a handsome man in his forties looked up from his work and she gasped softly. He was beautiful with grass-green eyes and black hair graying a little at his temples.

This man was stunning like a retired model or something. There was a smirk on his face as she looked him over, and he said, "Am I checking you out for the job, or are you checking me out, babe?"

Bridgette started to flush a pink shade with embarrassment. He chuckled and pointed to the chair to indicate she should take a seat. She did and tried to keep her nervousness at bay.

He looked at her with kind eyes and said, "My name is James. I own the diner and four others on the West Coast. This one is my first and my home base if you will. I also have other investments and businesses. But, I like to stay hands-on. Elise tells me you need a job and would be perfect for our night shift."

It took a moment for her to calm down. Then Bridgette looked at him and licked her lips before saying, "I have been a personal assistant for quite a while now. That was before…I had to leave my home and am starting over from scratch. I need the work. I've never waited tables before, but I am willing to learn and work hard."

James; gaze softens and he says, "Well, I admire your honesty and dedication. I have an opening at another one of my businesses that may be more suited to your skills. I need a personal assistant at my main gig. I'll write down the address and I expect to see you there on Monday morning. That will give you a long weekend to get your things together. I am sure you will feel the salary is generous as are the benefits. I have a feeling you'd like cash instead of a paper trail. That is no problem."

She nodded and bit her lip. James stands and hands her an envelope.

"Think of this as a sign-on bonus. This way you can pick up some clothes for the office. And get some groceries and settle in." She looked up at him in shock with tears in her eyes.

"Thank you", she whispered. He smiled kindly and waved her off. She stood and went to leave when he said, "I'd like to take my number from my card inside the envelope and call me tonight. I want to make sure you get home okay and are safe."

She simply nodded thinking that was kind and a little creepy. But, she decided to go with kind and simply nodded in agreement and went back to the diner. She decided to treat herself to some dessert to celebrate her new job.

Elise smiled at her and said she hoped she would stop in from time to time. Bridgette promised that she would and enjoyed her apple pie a la mode. The ladies chatted and then Bridgette walked home.

It was nice to have a car but the walk back and forth from her place and the diner was nice. As she got home she smiled at herself. Everything was working out for her. And thank goodness she was out of the creepy motel she had stayed in when she first arrived. She sat down and made a list of all the items she needed to pick up at the store tomorrow.

New bedding, some outfits for work, some new shoes for work, groceries, toiletries, and something to decorate the apartment to make it feel a little more like her own. The weekend passed in a flurry of activity. Bridgette purchased what she needed and started to clean her apartment. She cleaned the fridge first and filled it up with healthy food.

Then she made her bed in the new bedding set she picked up at the store along with some new sheets. Then she set up her bathroom with a new shower curtain and her toiletries. Once that was done she hung up her artwork on command strips.

She looked at the Brooklyn Bridge and smiled warmly. It was a way to have some home with her even being here. Weirdly, the painting gave her comfort.

Sunday night she smiled as she thought about Friday night. When she had called James like she promised he told her she did well. Then as they hung up he called her baby girl.

Normally that would have been super weird or sound cheesy from someone else. But from James, it sounded normal and kind of hot. Ugh, she groaned and gave herself a mental shake.

There was no room in her life for lusting after her boss. Bridgette was curled up in bed reading a book on her kindle when there was a knock on her door. She froze for a moment and went to look through the peephole to see who it was.

She had a baseball bat under her bed that she grabbed on her way to the door. She sighed in relief when she saw James on the other side of the door. Then she opened the door and looked at him confused.

"How do you know where I live?" He chuckled and asked her to invite him in. Then he simply told her that he knew some people and had his ways. She shrugged and asked him if he wanted something to drink. He declined and sat at her small table in the kitchen area.

"The reason that I came over tonight was to make sure you were doing okay here. Do you have everything that you need?", James said. Bridgette nodded and said, "Yes, I do. Thank you for your kindness and concern."

He smiles at her, and she almost can't breathe for a moment. He was so handsome, and then she noticed his nose had been broken. It was such an imperfection that could have made another man look less handsome. But, for some reason it made James look more handsome.

The corners of his eyes crinkled with pleasure as she looked at him. She returned the smile he had given her and said, "Is there anything special I should bring tomorrow? Coffee or something for you. I know I'll probably be in HR doing paperwork all morning. But, I could come early and drop it off for you..." she said.

He grinned and said, "Tomorrow just worry about yourself. We will discuss your duties and find our balance with time. I appreciate your wanting to make sure I am taken care of though. It has been a long time since anyone cared if I had my morning coffee."

There was a tone of mischief in his voice, and she simply smiled. After a few more moments of chit-chat, he excused himself. He knew the hour was late and they both needed sleep for the following day. James waited outside her door until he heard her locks click into place.

Bridgette hadn't felt so cared for in a while now. It wasn't about sex or someone needing her. It was about someone wanting her to be okay and that was all. Kindness. Bridgette made her way back to bed and sunk under her covers with her kindle.

She was reading the latest book by Mia Knight. It made her happy to think that maybe somehow someday she could have an epic love story like the ones Mia wrote about. Unconventional but real and solid. Sighing softly she turned out the little lamp on her bedside table and closed her eyes.

Saying a silent prayer that everyone back home was okay, she closed her eyes. And in her secret thoughts, she prayed that whoever was spying on her was gone. That she was safe and getting the fresh start she was working hard to achieve. After those thoughts, she drifted off to a peaceful and dreamless sleep.

Chapter Nine

I t was annoying to hear the beeps from her alarm clock at 5 AM on Monday morning. But, Bridgette tried her best to be a morning person and push through it. The smell of her favorite shampoo seemed to help her perk up and get ready for the day. She had picked up some outfits for work and looked through them quickly.

Bridgette felt that for her first day she should wear her gray pencil skirt with a matching blazer and a pale pink blouse. Her underwear was lacy and pale pink as well. She felt both sexy and professional.

That would leave a lasting impression at work. After she had dressed Bridgette took her time with her hair and make-up. She wanted to look as good as possible.

It was important to make a positive impression with her co-workers. After she was finished getting ready she grabbed a protein shake and hit the road. The drive to the office should only take ten minutes, but she wanted to arrive early.

As she pulled into the parking garage of the large skyscraper she wondered what she did to deserve this amazing opportunity. Parking she checked herself in the mirror and then grabbed her bag and started to walk into the building, her heels clacking on the concrete as she walked. She smiled to herself and took the elevator to her floor.

Once she arrived a kind woman and a cranky-looking woman were sharing the space behind a large desk. The cranky woman looked at her as if she was scum on her lake while the nice woman winked as she spoke on the phone.

"My name is Nancy. How may I help you?", said the cranky one with a terse tone that made Bridgette straighten.

"I'm Bridgette and I'm expected. I am the new personal assistant…" she said. Nancy's eyes narrowed and she said, "Mr. O'Ryan is expecting you. If you'll follow me I will show you to his office."

Standing Nancy smoothed her tight red skirt and started to sashay her way down the hallway to a large set of twin doors that looked expensive and modern. She knocked and then opened the doors and waited for Bridgette to follow her.

Bridgette did so and Nancy said, "The new hire is here, Mr. O'Ryan." The way Nancy's voice was now as smooth as honey made Bridgette arch a brow.

In the next instant, James was on his feet greeting Bridgette and dismissing Nancy. Before leaving Nancy glared at Bridgette and went back to her desk. Bridgette ignored her and sat in the chair in front of her boss' desk.

James smiled at her and said, "I wanted to just touch base with you before you go down to HR." At her nod he continued to speak, "In the morning I like to have a Starbucks caramel latte. After that, I would like all of the paperwork and messages I need to handle before I look at my emails and prepare for meetings. Those things should be laid out on your desk first for you to pass on."

Bridgette made some mental notes and smiled warmly, "That is perfectly fine, Sir. I am excited to get to it! Today I have to do paperwork in HR. After that should I come up and work on the schedule for the week?"

He nodded to her in agreement, and she thanked him for the opportunity. After she had left to go to HR James smiled to himself. She was very skilled it seemed.

Hiring her was a good choice and this would work out nicely. There was not a lot of time to daydream because his phone started to ring. There was a strange number on the caller ID so he picked up and said, "O'Ryan here..."

There was a brief pause and then a man said, "Hello. I am from a firm in New York City and have a rather awkward and sensitive question for you. One of our employees is missing. We suspect she is on the run from a stalker. Her name is Bridgette, and we know that you were looking for someone to be your personal assistant. She would not have happened to have applied would she?"

James stiffened in his chair and decided to deflect to give himself some time to understand Bridgette and her motives before talking about her. He said, "There have been several applicants. I am still looking for someone qualified for the position. If I notice one of my applicants matches your girl I will contact you. May I ask who I am speaking with?"

"My name is Ryan. I'm the co-owner of the firm, and we are all very worried about her.", he said. James said firmly, "Thank you for calling Ryan. I will keep an eye out for her."

They both hung up and James growled and said, "Fuck!" Then he tried to ignore the situation and focus on his work. He would speak to Bridgette over lunch.

Meanwhile, Bridgette was in HR with a nice woman named Cynthia who was wearing a ton of makeup and smelled like the perfume counter at a fancy department store. There were many things that she needed to fill out. But, since she was paid in cash it was less paperwork than when she worked for Ryan and Devante.

Her heart ached at the memories of her working with them. She missed them so much. But, this was for the best. A fresh start.

The paperwork only took an hour, and then she made her way upstairs. She made her way to her new desk and sat down beginning to sort out the schedule for the week. It seemed that James was about to have a meeting with his board of directors in ten minutes.

It was his last meeting before lunch. She took her pen and pad and went to the conference room. She made sure that the files needed were placed on the table along with a notepad and pen.

Then she went to the Starbucks in the building and purchased James a coffee placing it on the conference table. The meeting was about to begin when James entered and smiled at how Bridgette had set up the conference room. There were danishes and coffee available for his board of directors.

She even went above and beyond and got him his Starbucks. As she took her seat to his side he smiled broadly at her. She was ready to take notes. The board entered and the meeting began.

It was a long two-hour meeting but Bridgette never shied away from her duties and everyone in the room was impressed with her silent work. She seemed to blush when she was introduced formally to everyone. It was quite charming and everyone seemed pleased except Jeremy.

But, few things made Jeremy happy these days. After the meeting, Bridgette went to begin transcribing the meeting into a report. James went to his office and noticed Jeremy was on his heels.

The door shut crisply behind the men and Jeremy said, "What the fuck man? A beautiful woman as your personal assistant. I thought you were casual sex and never went after the girls here."

James arched a brow at his little brother from another mother and said, "I hired her because she is beyond qualified and she was down on her luck. I needed someone in this role, and she happens to have experience."

Jeremy arched his brow and said, "Sure, bro." James sighed and said, "She is just someone I am showing kindness, you ass. Stop making it salacious."

Eying his brother Jeremy said, "Well, according to Nancy you want much more than that. It is the hot gossip of the office now. You know how Nancy fawns over you. There may be a problem between her and your girl."

James sighed and said, "Firstly, she is not my girl, and if there is a problem between my staff members I will handle it. I am shocked you even showed up today."

Jeremy grinned and said, "I had to check out the new girl. Think she would go to dinner with me?" James literally growled at his brother and said in a low voice, "You leave my assistant alone. She is on the run and scared. She doesn't need your bullshit."

Jeremy laughed and winked at James before leaving his office. Jeremy stopped at Bridgette's desk and sat on the edge where there was a space and grinned at her.

She looked up and arched her brow saying, "Is there something I can do for you, Sir?" He smirked and winked at her and said, "If not for my bro maybe. But, as it stands now… I just wanted to give you a heads up that Nancy has it out for you. Workplace gossip is all over the place, and she is catty with friends. Thick skin, babes."

Before she could wrap her head around his words or respond he was gone to his own office down the hall. There was something strange about what he said, and she couldn't figure it out. She wasn't dating anyone so nothing was stopping him from asking her out.

Not that she wanted him to. She was still bruised by Ryan and trying to move forward with Chris and Decon. The loss of them in her life was harder than she thought it would be.

Also, who was his brother? The news about Nancy was not unexpected as she'd suspected it already. But, she also knew she was qualified for the job and did not need to justify herself to anyone. She could handle catty women.

Shaking her head Bridgette decided not to let any of her encounters with Jeremy rattle her. Instead, Bridgette dove into her work and made sure she had her emails completed, and forwarded important messages to James. She also ensured that their schedule was updated as changes happened with clients scheduling a new meeting or having to cancel.

Thankfully, there were more appointments and only one rescheduling. It appeared that this business was quite popular and profitable. At around noon she was finishing up an email to an investor who wanted to have a meeting about an upcoming charity event when James came out of his office and stood in front of her desk. She finished and looked up at him with a smile.

"What can I do for you, Mr. O'Ryan?" The moment their eyes met James' eyes sparkled with mischief, and he said, "Call me James."

She shook her head and said, "Respectfully, I think it would be better to remain professional during work hours. I don't want to start on the wrong foot here with my co-workers." He grinned and said, "Fair enough. I would like to take you to lunch and get you caught up on the upcoming charity event."

Bridgette bit her lip and considered this new development. It would be wise to get up to speed and there was no room in the schedule for a formal meeting. At the same time, she knew if Nancy saw her leaving with James it would be an issue.

She cocked her head to the side and looked up at him and said, "Alright. But, we leave separately. I do not want to start with more gossip than is normal for a new hire. I did not get this job because of something inappropriate between us and I won't have that rumor started." James was both impressed and amused by her thinking process and nodded his agreement.

"I will be down in the parking garage. We can take my car. I'll go down and you come about ten minutes after. I'll handle the rest."

Giving him the most brilliant smile he'd ever seen she said, "That is agreeable. Please tell me we will get real food. If I have one more salad I'll turn into a rabbit!"

He chuckled and leaned down near her ear and said in a low voice, "I'll feed you something, substantial baby. And you'll never be a rabbit to me... a kitten maybe." Before she had time to respond he was leaving for the parking garage whistling.

It took Bridgette a few moments to power down her computer and gather her things. She would of course not accept James purchasing her meal so she needed her purse. With a sway in her hips and a smile, she made her way past the front desk to the elevator around nine minutes later.

Nancy said, "Some people can't be professional. They need to wear tight clothes to show how desperate they are to get laid. They sleep their way to the top." There was a sneer in her tone and Bridgette chuckled at the words as she passed by the desk.

"Have a lovely afternoon, ladies. I'm off for lunch. Do you want me to bring you something?", Bridgette said. Both women looked at her in shock and simply shook their heads.

Her smile was warm and friendly when she said, "Okay! Be back in about an hour. My cell is on if you need me. The work phone that HR gave me. I emailed everyone the number in case there is an issue."

Feeling like a rockstar Bridgette made her way down to meet James in the parking garage. The ride in the elevator seemed to take forever and for the first time, Bridgette felt nervous. It was a working lunch and yet the idea of sharing a meal with James made her tummy do a flip.

It wasn't fair that her hormones were smitten with her boss. She had enough drama back in New York and couldn't afford to get involved with anyone. Not that James would consider starting a relationship with her.

He was simply a kind man who wanted to help her out. She was his employee for crying out loud! Moving out of the elevator with confidence and newfound clarity she made her way to where James was leaning against a classic 1977 corvette that was cherry red with tan interior. She grinned, impressed by his choice of car.

"That is a beautiful car. You are lucky you don't live in a place with snow or you'd be unable to drive it this time of year.", she said. Once the words had left her mouth she cringed. It made her think of how she left before the company Christmas party.

It would be Christmas soon, and she would spend it all alone. It was almost too much emotion to process. Noticing her reaction to the mention of snow James discovered she had left a state that had snow and that she was running from some painful things.

He wanted to help her but had no idea how to accomplish that without knowing more information. He forced himself to grin and said, "This is the love of my life. This car has been with me for many years now. Ready to ride?" She nodded and slid into his car with a grace that took his breath away.

He wanted her in his car more often. As James drove them toward the diner she smiled. It would be nice to see Elise and tell her all about her first day so far. Bridgette would also be happy to eat some real food.

She wanted a big cheeseburger with tons of ketchup and fries with ranch. Bridgette turned to James and said, "I'm smitten with your businesses. They pay for me work I love, feed me, and have given me a new friend in Elise. If you tell me you own a shoe store I may just drop to my knees and beg to be yours forever!"

They both laughed. James winked and said, "I run two malls in town. There are shoe stores in them so…" Bridgette literally shook her head in shock. "You know how to make a girl wish you weren't her boss, haha"

James grinned at her and said, "I've never wanted to date an employee before. I would say you are safe but… who knows!" Bridgette eyed him and said, "Well, wants and actions are different things. So, what do you eat for lunch normally?" James noticed her change in subject and let it go so as not to make her bolt from the car or something.

"I normally go to my diner and have a nice meal. I change it up every now and again. I have to say I have never had our salads although they are popular.", James said. With a laugh, Bridgette said, "Well, maybe you should try them to see why they are so popular. I for one want a huge unhealthy cheeseburger with tons of ketchup and fries with ranch on the side. My diet is blown today!"

He laughed and said, "You are a sexy woman no matter what you eat. You don't need to be on a diet." Bridgette simply smiled warmly and reached out to squeeze his hand.

They arrived, and he parked in the back of the building near the side door to the diner. He took her hand when they stood beside the car and led her inside. Bridgette had never seen the back of the diner before, and she chuckled when he took her to his office.

"Just can't stop working can you, boss?" The mischief in her eyes made him smile, and he said, "Nope. We are eating here before we go to visit with Elise. I'd much rather share the time with you alone to discuss the event."

There was a moment of silence before Bridgette said, "What exactly is the event for?" James sat behind his desk and looked at her saying, "My company is sponsoring a charity gala to help raise funds for the local women's shelter."

Bridgette smiled and said, "That is a wonderful cause. What can I do to be of help?" They then began discussing themes, colors, vendors, and the guest list. The time flew and when Elise joined them she had the boss' usual and a juicy burger and fries for Bridgette.

The only thing she forgot was a drink for Bridgette who asked for a vanilla milkshake. Laughing at her enthusiasm over her burger, fries, and shake Elise went to fetch the tasty drink. Once they finished their meals sometime later they made their way out to the diner itself and sat at the counter.

Bridgette loved the old-school 50's diner vibe and the cool stools they had to sit on. Elise caught her up on things, and she told Elise all about her day. When she was explaining the weird situation with Jeremy coming to her desk she noticed James stiffen beside her. He'd been sending emails on his phone but he'd stopped to look at her.

"Jeremy is my brother from another mother. My younger and much more charming brother if we are being honest. He and I both work for the firm that you now work for. He isn't involved in my dinners.", James told her.

Taking a sip of her shake, Bridgette nodded and wondered why Jeremy thought there was something between her and James. She held her musing to herself and carried on speaking about her day. Elise was grinning like a fool when she'd heard about what happened with Nancy as Bridgette left for lunch.

James chuckled beside her and offered her a high five at how she handled herself. Noticing the time James sighed and suggested they make their way back to the office. Bridgette hugged Elise and picked up her things to pay for lunch when James shook his head.

"This was a working lunch. It is on me. Now, let's hit the road and get back before Nancy has us married off or something weird.", he said Then James put on his aviator sunglasses and started to lead her to the car. Bridgette leaned her head against the seat after sliding in and smiled warmly.

"That was amazing. I am pregnant with a food baby but so worth it!" James looked her over with a heat in his eyes and said, "You still look just as beautiful as you did before lunch."

The car started and they drove back to the office. This time James told her to make her way up before him. This way she could settle in without the women making a fuss or thinking she was with him.

Bridgette smiled and thanked him for lunch before making her way to the elevator. James watched her walk and had to adjust his pants. He'd been excited since the moment she slid into her seat before they'd left.

The woman was making him feel like a pervert and not even caring. This was going to be a rough road in having to behave himself. She wasn't interested and was trying to start over.

It would be bad to make moves on her. She was his employee. And yet… no he shook his head. About fifteen minutes later he made his way up to his office.

The look on Nancy's face when he walked through the door really bothered him. She looked eager and excited to see him in a way that went beyond the employee and employer relationship. He would have to talk with her in HR on Friday.

He made a note to ask Bridgette to set up the meeting. This was going to be a problem if he did not take care of it quickly. Walking into his office he noticed that Bridgette wasn't at her desk.

Then when he looked through the doorway he noticed her bent over to pick something up as she faxed things. The look of her ass in her tight skirt was enough to make him moan. He was tempted to come up behind her and help her personally get what she needed.

Good grief! His brother may be right about his feelings for her. She was broken, and he wanted to help her heal, and he wanted her like he hadn't wanted someone in a long time. But, there was so much in the way of a relationship with her.

Her new career as his assistant, the fact she was keeping things from him, and his issues. And yet there she was... lighting up his world. They needed to talk. He'd find the time to get everything on the table and see what happens from there. Soon.

At four in the afternoon, he asked Bridgette to please add a meeting with Stacey from HR and Nancy to his schedule for Friday morning. She had not asked questions and made it a point to get it on the books for first thing after his emails and usual morning routine. The rest of the afternoon went smoothly as they worked at their respective desks.

It wasn't until he looked up and noticed it was seven in the evening already that he stood and stretched. James had not worked so efficiently and smoothly in years. It felt like he and Bridgette were a well-oiled machine getting the job done.

This made him smile and feel proud of his choice in hiring her. At her desk, she was busy typing up a report when he came up behind her and leaned down toward her ear saying, "It's time to quit for the day, kitten. Since I kept you so late, come have dinner with me. We can talk about your first day."

Startled Bridgette jumped and then looked at him and said, "Uh… is that wise Mr. O'Ryan?" He grinned and said, "Yes, it is. That way I can be James again and get the real scoop on what my assistant thinks of my company and me."

She couldn't hide her smile as she nodded and said a weak "Okay." Then they were gathering their things and getting prepared to leave. The only person still working was Nancy. They agreed she would follow him so he would leave first.

As James started to walk past the desk Nancy called out to him. He turned and went to her desk asking what she needed. She leaned forward and her ample breasts were suddenly on display. He wanted to roll his eyes and sigh but instead, he ignored her attempts to seduce him.

"I thought we might go get a drink, Sir," she said. He looked at her and shook his head, "I don't do drinks with my employees. Thank you for the offer though. You are doing very well here Nancy. We are lucky to have you on the team."

She nodded and said, "If you change your mind here is my number." Then she slid her hand over his arm and placed a slip of paper in his palm. He shook his head and went to the elevator.

Friday could not get here soon enough for him. He wanted to button this up and move on from it.

About fifteen minutes or so after James left Bridgette started to make her way to the elevator.

She ignored Nancy until she got to the elevator and turned to say, "Have a lovely night Nancy! Thank you for making my first day interesting"

Nancy was silently seething when the elevator doors closed, and she descended to the parking garage. At her car, Bridgette slid into the driver's seat and took a deep breath. The first day had gone better than she expected it to.

She smiled when she opened her eyes and there in front of her car was James. He came over and she put her window down. There was a sexy smile on his face when she looked up at him.

He said, "I'll get in my car and you can follow me. We'll talk about your day and have some dinner. Sounds good?" She simply nodded and he went to his car.

It took about twenty minutes until James stopped his car in a driveway. Their rundown of her first day would be at his home. This both thrilled her and made her nervous. She pulled in behind his car and got out to follow him inside.

James smiled at her and flipped on the light while tossing his keys into the bowl on the entry table. Bridgette was in awe of how lovely his home was. It had marble floors and countertops with beautiful artwork that made it feel elegant and simple at the same time.

It was warm and beautiful. She arched her brow at him and he said, "When I moved here from California I had a designer come in. I wanted this to be my home for the rest of my life. So, I had them build it the way I wanted it to be for when I found the love of my life and potentially started a family. But, it has just been me here since it was built. My wife and I split up once I arrived and was still in a condo. She is still in that condo from what I hear. Although, we don't speak anymore so she could have moved."

Bridgette nodded and tried to hide her shock that he had been married previously. She herself was engaged once. So, she had no room to judge him for having a life before they met. Or at all seeing as how he was simply her boss.

James was in the kitchen when she walked in and sat on a chair in front of his large island. He smiled at her and said, "I love to cook. Do you mind if we eat in?"

She smiled softly and said, "I am a decent cook for some dishes but not super handy in the kitchen. I look forward to eating one of your meals. I will compare it to the diner of course."

He laughed and said, "My meal will be delicious but may fall short of the diner's food." As James cooked their meal which she found out was lasagna and fresh garden salad they talked. She felt like she should tell him something personal since he explained his house and previous relationship.

"I'm originally from the East Coast. I'd never been this far west until I moved here. I just picked a place and flew here. It was an impulse decision. I have no regrets though.

I'm falling in love with Nevada. I had a relationship back there. I was madly in love and engaged. I thought we would have this fairy tale wedding and life would be perfect. But, he chose a former lover over me. He wrecked me. I'd just started to move on and recover. I was finding my happiness again. But, things changed and I left.", Bridgette said.

James listened and leaned against the island looking at her while he poured them some wine.

"That sounds rough. Do you still love him?", he dared ask.

"Ryan was so much to me for so long. I couldn't imagine a second of my life without him. I was consumed by him and the way I left when I was with him. I guess you could say it was the first time I'd ever been in love. But, now... I don't hate him or blame him anymore. We'd had a heart-to-heart before I left. I love him and think a part of me always will. But, I'm over him."

James tried to hide his reaction to hearing the name, Ryan. That was the man who had called asking after Bridgette. It may be over for her but not for him. He wondered if Ryan was the reason she ran. Bridgette smiled and sipped her wine.

"Ryan was never abusive or anything. I'm not running from him if that is what you are thinking. We were on good terms when I left. He is probably freaking out with my other friends that I left. I called my best friend to let her know that I was okay on a burner phone. But, I didn't call anyone else. She will let everyone know the news. And nobody can find me.", she said.

The heat in her cheeks and tears that pooled in her eyes shocked her. She hadn't meant to share so much with him. Taking her hands into his own James looked at her with a gentle friendly look on his face.

"I won't tell a soul. Thank you for sharing with me. You can always talk to me. Are you wanted by the police or something? Is there something I can do to help you?", he asked.

She shook her head and said, "Oh no! It is nothing like that at all. I've never been arrested or committed a crime or anything. I was being stalked by someone. My friends wrapped themselves around me. They hired security and went all out to protect everyone in our friend circle. But, it was me they wanted. They spied on me with cameras and stuff. It wasn't safe for my friends. So... I ran."

Chapter Ten

T he news shocked James. She left because she wanted to shelter her friends and keep herself safe in one swift motion. This changed how he saw everything now.

She was not a battered woman on the run. Not a criminal in over her head. She was a victim trying to survive on her own. It took guts to do what she did, and he admired that. James came around the island and lifted her chin to meet his gaze.

"I admire your courage to leave everything behind in the hopes of sparing your friends. But, you do realize it makes you more vulnerable. What if someone tailed you here? This is serious.", he said.

She shook her head and said, "I've used cash, burners and have not left a paper trail. I think I have been doing everything right. Maybe being a little too high profile with the job with you. Considering it is what I did back home. But... I could always find another job or state if I get made." The sound of disgust that he made sent shivers down Bridgette's spine.

"I have some contacts who can look into this for you, kitten. I'd feel better knowing you are safe. I also want to put better locks on your door. Tonight we'll make that happen. Also, I need to tell you that I got a strange call this morning about you. So, you may have been made already.", James said.

Bridgette's spine went ramrod straight, and she quivered. The fear in her eyes made James' heartache for her.

"The man was named Ryan. He said that someone with your qualifications could be looking for a job. That his employee Bridgette had run from a stalker. He seemed worried. At the time I thought it was due to concern for an employee. But, now... he's your former fiancé right?", James asked.

Bridgette nodded and looked at him with tears in her eyes. "If the good guys can find me, so can the bad ones. I have to leave..."

James moved to block her against the counter and said softly, "No, kitten. You need to trust me to take care of you. There is no reason to run and always look over your shoulder. It is just you and I. I can keep you safe and can take care of myself. Do you trust me?"

Bridgette thought about it and bit her lip "I'm not sure that I should be considering we just met. I mean I barely know you. But... I do."

He smiled and kissed her cheek, "Good girl. You will learn that I am honest and trustworthy. I have the power and ability to protect you. But, you need to let me call Ryan and explain that to him. And that I have you safely here."

At that moment Bridgette looked very unsure of that and James pulled her close against him and whispered in her ear, "He needs to quit looking for you. If he does he will lead them straight to your door. Once he knows you are safe he can move forward, kitten. We can keep you safe."

She simply nodded, and he went to take the food out of the oven. They ate in silence before she said softly, "Thank you for being so kind to me. I never meant to become a burden to you. I left to free everyone from that burden and look where I am now. In the same space except there is one of you instead of a circle of people."

He shook his head and said, "Kitten, stop that right now. You are never a burden to anyone who cares for you. It will all be okay. And my motivations are not entirely selfless."

The tension between them was an elemental thing, and she bit her lip before asking, "How come?" He sighed softly and ran his hand through his hair before saying, "I have never been so drawn to a woman before. Not even my ex. I am beyond attracted to you and want to keep you safe and happy. I'm selfish. I want you here in Nevada."

Bridgette swallowed and said softly, "But, I'm your employee and not nearly as beautiful as Nancy..." At her words, he crowded her space and placed his hands on her shoulders locking eyes with her.

"You are beautiful to me. I don't want another woman. I want you. Even though it is wrong because I'm your boss and we are so new to each other.", he growled.

Before she could respond or grasp his words his lips were on her own daring her to open her lips for a crushing and passionate assault. There was tenderness and desire in his kiss and as she let a moan escape he slid his tongue against hers. It had been so long since someone had held her like this and she had never felt so alive or desired before.

Not even with Chris and Decon. James growled as he separated them and took a step back looking deeply into her eyes. She smiled softly and stepped forward, taking his face into her hands and kissing him passionately.

It was glorious to feel her lips against his and breathe her in. At the same time, he knew this was not the time to take her to his bedroom. They had time to explore what was between them.

Even if it may give him a wicked case of blue balls she was well worth the sacrifice. And so he pulled away and looked into her eyes bringing his forehead to hers.

"We have time, kitten. It's killing me not taking you to my bedroom and making it our bedroom. But, we have time to explore this and right now you need to know you are safe with me. Not that we got caught in the heat of the moment.", James said in a hoarse voice.

Bridgette was practically panting with need and couldn't seem to find the words. She licked her lips since her mouth had become a desert, and she looked into his eyes. His smile warmed her soul and he said, "Move in with me. I'll take care of you and we can explore this. You'll be safe here."

She shook her head and said, "Not yet. I need to get myself stable first. It is too soon that I've been on my own again. I need some time. We can change the locks and I can call you when I'm home so you know that I'm okay and I feel less alone."

It took almost all of his energy to nod and agree to her terms. He wanted what was best for her over his desires. And she hadn't said it would never happen.

Just that she needed some time and had proposed ways to keep her safe. It was fair. At the same time, it created a sinking feeling in his stomach.

"I've decided we need to change the plan a little. I'll call Ryan in the morning and tell him your applied but left suddenly. He will think you are in the wind again. And his efforts to find you will take him and the stalkers in the wrong direction. Then we can work on protecting you and you living your life here. To really sell it you should use a burner and call your best friend again. If she thinks you are still on the run it is confirmation of my statements to Ryan. It keeps the trail cold.", James said.

Bridgette nodded and swallowed. "They are good people. I hate lying to them but it protects them and it keeps me safe too." James nodded and moved a stray section of hair from her lovely face and leaned forward to kiss her.

"Well, let's finish up here and get you home before it is too late.", he said. She nodded and then before he could turn to clear the dishes she was wrapping herself around him and kissing him deeply. He wrapped his arms around her and held her tightly against him.

This was more wonderful than he could have imagined. Having her come to him and be so open in her affection. When Bridgette pulled back to look into his eyes he was lost.

He knew somehow this woman was going to forever change his life. And he didn't care what that meant. All that mattered was that she was here with him at this moment. She smiled at him and blushed a little.

"I'm so happy we met. It feels like you were always meant to be in my life.", she whispered into the space between them. He grinned and leaned down to whisper in her ear, "I feel the same way, kitten."

He pulled away reluctantly and went to put the dishes in the dishwasher. She asked if she could help, and he said she already had. This domestic scene felt right to them and Bridgette almost regretted her stubborn need to be independent. She wanted to stay here with him and explore what it was between them.

Looking into his eyes while seated on a chair at the island she said softly, "Thank you for everything. My life may have been a complete shit show and you are giving me something normal. Stable. I appreciate that."

He smiled at her and walked over cupping his hand on her face and leaned down to kiss her softly. When James pulled away Bridgette opened her eyes and grinned saying, "You make it hard for a girl to go home after a night like this."

He smirked and said, "Good. You are always welcome here. Think of this as your second home." She looked into his eyes with tears of her own and said, "Do you really think I am safer here? Or do you just want to explore whatever this is between us?"

The expression on James' face became serious, and he said, "Your safety comes first. I feel like this house has better security since I have an alarm system that is state of the art and also I'm here, and I am licensed with firearms. I do not keep them where anyone can be hurt accidentally. But, I know how to protect you and myself from harm if need be." At his words, Bridgette physically relaxed and gave him a shy smile.

"Would it be okay if I stayed here tonight? As a trial run. And if it feels okay and safe can I move my stuff in? I don't have much... I mean if you have a spare room or...", she asked shyly.

James smiled as she trailed off and he said, "I have several nice guest rooms if you feel more comfortable. But, all you have to do is ask and I would gladly share my room with you, kitten."

At her blush, he said, "No strings attached. Just me holding you if it gets scary. I won't ever force myself on you or push you into something that you aren't okay with. We go at your pace."

Bridgette smiled bright and said, "Thank you for that. I appreciate it. All of it. It means so much to me. Can I stay with you for the night?"

He nodded and tucked her hair behind her ear gently saying, "Since you don't have your pajamas why don't you use one of my shirts? It will be a bit big on you but comfortable."

She simply nodded and followed him up the staircase and into the master bedroom and admired the size, decor, and attached bathroom. He looked a little shy as he said, "I built this house with the intention I'd meet someone special, and we'd share our lives here. I have room for family to visit, potential family yet to be created and all the things I thought a wife should have in her home. It was wishful thinking but I've come to feel very at home here. And I hope that you will too."

Bridgette smiled shyly and nodded as he handed her a button-down shirt of his from his drawer. She kissed his cheek and then went into the bathroom to change. When she came out he told her to put her clothes in the hamper.

They would sort out her wardrobe in the morning. She felt happy about her clothes being in his hamper and sharing this space with him. It felt right and safe. Bridgette looked up and smiled softly as she saw James already in bed.

Her brow arched when she noticed that his chest was bare, and she wondered if he had something under the blanket. A red flush flamed her cheeks as she imagined what was under the blanket on the bed. James couldn't help but grin seeing the look on her face.

He had a pretty good idea what sort of thoughts she was having about him. He simply patted the other side of the bed and said, "Come join me, kitten. We have a big day tomorrow."

It was as if his words shook Bridgette from the trance she had been in. She made her way to the bed and carefully lifted the blanket to allow herself the space to get beneath them. She looked up into James' eyes as she moved to face him in the bed.

The flush on her cheeks wouldn't go away and this only made him smile kindly at her. He leaned forward and gave her a chaste kiss and turned out the light. Bridgette did not know if she was thankful for the reprieve or disappointed because she wanted more with James.

The next morning sunlight filled the bedroom and James opened his eyes with a smile. As he looked over he was pleased to see a sleeping Bridgette in his bed. They had only kissed a few times and yet just having her here with him felt right.

He almost felt bad for this Ryan person who was looking for her. He must have loved her and fucked up badly for her to leave him. But, his loss would be James' gain as he would never hurt this beautiful creature beside him.

It was like sleeping beauty awakening from her slumber when Bridgette's eyes opened slowly. She smiled warmly at James and said, "Good Morning."

He returned her smile and said, "Morning, kitten. Did you sleep well?" She blushed a little and nodded, not trusting her voice. She had dreams about James that were very firmly adult, and she was not ready to share those with him now… or ever.

James chuckled and said, "Sometimes I wish I could read your mind. But, alas I am stuck with what you feel like sharing. And that is okay too!" James started to get out of bed and Bridgette flushed even more seeing him in his boxer briefs.

He looked more attractive than she imagined he would. He started pulling fresh clothes out of drawers and he closed and turned to her and said, "Like what you see, kitten?"

She nodded and flushed even more. He came toward the bed leaning down to kiss her and whispered in her ear

"I'm glad you like what I have to offer. But, we need to get dressed and get to the office, kitten. And if you keep looking at me like that we may never leave this room."

At his very erotic threat, she scampered off to take a shower and knew he would find her some clothes to wear in the meantime. His chuckle followed her as she heard him starting to get dressed. After her shower, she returned to the bedroom to find it empty but on the bed, there was a clean work suit in her size waiting for her.

There were even underthings. She grinned and wondered how he managed to get those things here so quickly. But, shrugging her shoulders she started to change into them. It felt nice to be in clean clothes and after her shower, she felt rejuvenated.

In the kitchen she found James seated at the island sipping some coffee and reading over some email on his phone. He looked up when he heard her and smiled warmly looking at her change in clothes.

"I'm glad that everything fits. Come and have some fruit and yogurt before we leave for the office.", he said. Bridgette sat down and started to put some yogurt in the bowl left out for her and some fruit on the little plate in front of her.

As she ate she smiled at how tasty it was and how much she was enjoying James' company. It felt right to be here and share these simple moments with him. After she finished he smiled at her and said, "Well, we should start going now. Do you want to go together or have my driver take you? Either way is fine with me. I figured I would give you the option since Nancy has been less than friendly so far."

Bridgette stiffened and looked at him with her head cocked to the side and said, "Could your driver take me? Just because I would rather not start office gossip. I know eventually, we need to tell them. But, I'd like them to know me and see how hard I work before they make judgments about me."

James nodded and smiled warmly at her, "Okay, kitten. I figured you would say that. I like that you feel like this is going somewhere so down the road we'll need to share that there is something between us. Makes me happy."

She wrapped her arms around him and gave him a long and passionate kiss before scampering off to be taken to work. He grinned and headed for his car to drive in. Bridgette smiled as she arrived first at the office. She thanked the driver who had said his name was Miles for driving her.

He simply smiled and said he would be on call for when she was finished with work. She made her way through the lobby and made her way up to the elevator. As soon as the door opened she was greeted by the scowl on Nancy's face.

"Well, you managed to arrive and look professional.", she sneered. Bridgette gave her a sunny smile and said, "My workday begins in ten minutes as per my contract. I'm actually early. But, now you are delaying me from starting. But, I know you are only concerned for the company with which we are both employed."

Nancy huffed as Bridgette walked by and went straight to her desk. She placed her briefcase down and began working on emails. Twenty or so minutes later James walked into the office.

Nancy hurried around her desk and greeted him. She asked him if he wanted anything, and he said firmly, "I have an assistant for that. Thank you anyway." James went straight to his office and started to work on his emails.

It was not even five minutes later that Bridgette knocked and said, "Your coffee, Sir." He smiled thankfully and picked up his cup to take a sip. It pleased him that she had made the perfect cup of coffee.

Before he could say a word she was back at her desk working hard. Their relationship in the office was flawless and it pleased him to have his company in such good hands. Nancy kept finding excuses to come into James' office through the day, and he couldn't wait for Friday to come.

She was like a gnat in his ear and could not take a hint. He had never been interested in her as anything more than an employee and at the same time, she was getting so lost in her obsession over him that she was slacking on her duties. At the end of the day, Nancy was at her desk and was finishing up her work.

Bridgette ended up walking past to leave early. It was James' suggestion so they did not leave at the same time. Nancy hurried from behind her desk and grabbed Bridgette's arm. She leaned in close and sneered, "Have you fucked your way to the top yet, slut? You better back off before you get hurt."

Bridgette looked at her like she was insane and pulled her arm back. Turning to Nancy she said loudly, "I have never fucked my way to the top for anyone I have ever worked for. I'm not a slut in the slightest, not that my personal life is any of your business. And I would consider that to be a threat. Threats mean a trip to HR and a formal complaint."

Nancy blanched and looked at her with a fire in her eyes. Bridgette leaned in close and said, "And for the record… I would not go around threatening people smarter than you. It usually ends badly for you."

In the office, you couldn't hear a pin drop. It was so silent as Bridgette walked away all she heard were her heels on the floor. She went directly down to the floor with HR and made a formal complaint.

Then she made her way down to the car waiting for her. As soon as she was seated in the car she had her cell buzz. She smiled because the only one who knew her number was James.

She picked up and heard, "Kitten, you handled her so well. Meet me at your place so we can pack you up and settle up with the landlord. Then we can go home and have some Chinese take out."

Bridgette grinned and said, "You are an amazing man. You know a girl could fall for someone so great."

James was grinning not that she could see him. He told her he'd see her soon and hung up. Then he dialed Ryan's number.

The second that Ryan picked up James took a deep breath and said, "Ryan? This is James. You had called me to inquire about someone named Bridgette." Before he could say another word Ryan started speaking in a rush.

"Have you found her? Is she okay? Where are you right now? Where is she?", Ryan said hurriedly. James cleared his throat and said, "That is the thing she did to apply to work for me. But, she wasn't suited to the position she applied for. I decided to give her a position she was right for. But, then you contacted me about her. She kind of freaked out at first when I confronted her. But, then she explained what happened. You need to stop searching for her as you are leaving a trail. If you can find her, so can the stalker. She is safe, but she is not going back to New York. She can't contact anyone back there. She is settling in where she is. She wanted me to tell you that she is okay and to move on. All of you. She misses you all and loves y'all, but she's got to protect herself and all of you."

Ryan sighed heavily and said, "That does sound like her. But, we are doing well in our business. We have the means to protect her here. She needs to come back home."

James was firm when he said, "The lady has shared her wishes with you. Twice now. The first was when she called her best friend and now through me. I think it is time you respect them." Ryan cursed under his breath and hung up without a goodbye. James almost chuckled at the younger man's frustration.

It was about a half-hour later when he arrived at Bridgette's place. He knocked on the door and beamed at her when she opened the door. She pulled him inside and kissed him hard.

He melted into her kiss and wrapped his arms around her enjoying the kiss. After what felt like a few moments he pulled back and said, "What did I do to deserve this?"

She smiled warmly at him and said, "I am just really happy to see you. I have everything almost packed up. Can you help me load the car?" James went straight to work.

After he put her box into the car he helped her to pack her bag and then went to the office to settle up with her landlord. Once they were all packed up and ready to roll James smiled as she got into the car with his driver and went home.

He followed her in his car. The cell rang in his pocket but James ignored it so that he could focus on getting home to his woman. It felt so nice to know that he had someone special at home waiting for him.

He would help her move into their room and then order dinner. Wow, it blew his mind that his room had become their room. It felt so right that he didn't even second guess it.

Chapter Eleven

The phone would not stop running even as he pulled into his driveway, and so he picked it up once he turned the car off. "This is James.", he said into his phone.

Ryan's voice rumbled as he said, "Is she with you? I need to know that. I know you have the means to keep her safe. Just tell me. I know the line is not secure but I need to know... please."

James looked at Bridgette getting out of the car with her bag over her shoulder. She turned to smile at him, and he said into the phone, "Yes. She is with me. Please leave her in peace to heal. I will protect her with my life."

Then it was James' turn to hang up on Ryan. Bridgette hurried into the house and took her bag to the bedroom placing it on their bed. She had flutters in her stomach just thinking of the bed as being theirs.

It was so healing to be here with James and letting herself be so open to their blossoming relationship. That was when she decided to put her things away. In the middle of putting her things in the drawers and closet. James walked into the bedroom with her box and smiled at her kissing her forehead.

"You are almost all moved in. We should probably buy you some more toiletries. Anything you need just give me a list and I will have someone get it for you.", James said.

Bridgette smiled warmly and said, "You know we could both do the shopping. It could be an adventure, Mr. Serious." He grinned at her and said, "I have other things I would rather do with you." Bridgette blushed and kissed him softly.

After they finished in the bedroom they went downstairs and Bridgette picked out a movie for them to watch as James ordered dinner. They sat down with the movie ready to be played when James sighed and said, "We need to talk about a few things first, kitten." Bridgette looked at him with worry in her eyes and it melted something inside of James.

He stroked her cheek and said softly, "This Nancy thing is not okay. She is spending less time focused on her job and is fixating on me. It was never something I have encouraged or wanted.

We have our meeting on Friday with HR. And they have your complaint. I may have to fire her, and she may put her anger on you instead of on me. I know legally I have done nothing wrong and I have no reason to be upset about this. No blowback on me could harm me. But, you are more sensitive and since dislikes you she may come at you. I will protect you as much as I can but I want you prepared for her venom."

Bridgette nodded and said, "I have handled women who have been unprofessional and cruel at work before. I'm prepared and I already discussed my concerns with HR, and they have it all on file. So, should she step out of line I am covered. There were witnesses to the way she treats me. I'll be fine. I appreciate your worrying over me though."

There was an awkward silence before James looked at her even more seriously than he had been. Bridgette looked even more worried before he spoke.

"This afternoon I called Ryan. We spoke twice actually. I was honest with him, and he was honest with me. He knows you are here with me and knows I can protect you should you need it. He's letting go.", James said with honesty and compassion in his tone and facial expression.

Bridgette nodded tears pooling in her eyes. "Thank you for talking to him, for being here for me, and for being you.", she said in response. Bridgette placed her hand in James' and kissed him softly.

James sat there for a moment simply looking at her and said, "It is okay to be upset, Bridgette. You loved him and a part of you always will. You have sacrificed a lot to be here. For the people you love and for yourself. It is okay to be sad. It is okay to cry. I will be here with you every step of the way."

He pulled her onto his lap and kissed her cheeks as she started to sob against his shoulder.

"I'll never see them again. I love them so much, and they are just gone from my life. It... it hurts so much!" she said between sobs. James rubbed her back and said, "I know kitten. Let it all out."

It was wonderful to just cry and get out all of her feelings of love, loss, and change. James held Bridgette as long as she needed and as her tears started to stop, and she calmed down his used the pad of his fingers to wipe away her tears. He kissed her cheeks and forehead before softly kissing her lips. Bridgette buried into his chest and felt so safe and content in his arms.

~~

The next several days went very well at work. Nancy was seemingly on her best behavior and everything at the office was professional and normal. At home the couple enjoyed themselves getting to know each other, taking turns making dinner, and having a good time together.

They were falling more and more in love. It felt idyllic and wonderful and not once did they worry about anything. Then on Friday morning, Bridgette woke up with a sudden rush of anxiety. She sat up in bed and watched James sleeping soundly and was amazed at how someone older than her could look so childlike in his sleep.

But, then he opened his eyes and looked worried at her. She said, "I woke up anxious today. I have no idea what is happening. I just feel like something is going to happen that we haven't expected and it will be bad. I can't explain it."

James took her hand into hers and said softly, "We will face whatever comes together okay? I know that this meeting with Nancy will be a big deal. But, once it is over we can breathe and just be. And as for anything else we have each other to lean on."

Bridgette smiled and agreed with him. James stood up in his boxer briefs and offered her his hand. "Come on, beautiful kitten. Let's take a shower together." Bridgette was really happy at the thought of sharing her morning shower with James.

They went into the bathroom and he slowly took off the shirt of his that she was wearing. As he unbuttoned it with ease she watched his hands feeling her skin heat at the slight way he touched her in the process. Then once the shirt was gone from her body she was left in only a pair of panties.

She felt so vulnerable and exposed and yet she was on fire with heat from within. There was a need for this man to explore her. And so when he placed his hands at her hips and began to move her panties down her legs she shivered with desire.

As she stood naked before him James was in awe of her beauty. It was not just her physical appearance but the light that seemed to shine from within her. She was blossoming before his very eyes.

Leaning down to whisper into her ear he said, "You are beautiful. Thank you for sharing yourself with me this way, kitten."

The feeling of his breath on her skin and his words made her body flush with an instant need for more of him. She reached out and ran her fingers over his bare chest enjoying the way he felt. Then she began to run her hands lower on his body until she reached his boxer briefs.

She looked up at him with a naughty grin and then began to pull them down. James arched a brow but let her explore his body. It made him very excited to feel her hands on him.

Bridgette pulled his boxer briefs completely off and admired his frame. James was built for sinful thoughts and actions. She couldn't help her grin as she looked him over and then winked at him when she met his eyes.

Then before he could react to her she sank to her knees keeping eye contact and wrapped her lips around his hard cock. His eyes rolled in the back of his head as she worked her mouth over him pleasurably. Bridgette felt so happy to be pleasuring James and hearing his moans and grunts.

It made her feel empowered and also turned on. The sensation of Bridgette's tongue over his cock made James moan and press further into her mouth. Bridgette took him deeper, and they both moaned as she explored his cock.

The way that James's fingers felt in her hair encouraged her to move forward and continue. As she continued to move her mouth over him at a rapid but measured pace he felt himself getting close.

"That's it kitten! I'm so close..." Before he could finish he made eye contact with her again and came deep in her throat. James was really happy to see his woman swallow his cum and look so serene as she looked up at him. Bridgette was so aroused and wanted to have him touch her.

As she stood up James wrapped himself around her and then lifted her into his arms and they both entered the shower standing in the back as she leaned down and put the water on. They kissed with her in his arms as the water grew warm. At the feel of warmer water, James lowered her down to her feet.

The couple stood pressed against one another as James took a sponge and started to lather body wash over Bridgette's body. She felt so alive and aroused by his movements even though none of his actions were sexual in nature. All he had to do was touch her or look at her, and she was set aflame with desire.

Bridgette giggled and took the sponge from James' hands and started to wash him. If the noises he made were any indication he was just as aroused by her ministrations over his body. After they finished washing each other they locked eyes and kissed passionately.

Then before either of them knew it James had Bridgette pushed up against the shower wall. They were kissing and then her legs were around his waist, and he was teasingly moving around her entrance. Bridgette whimpered and said breathily "Please...more."

It was as if she was speaking to his heart and his cock at the same time. James kissed her sweetly and then when she was least expecting it slammed himself into her warm sheath. Bridgette held on to him, her nails digging into his back as she arched to meet him and moaned her pleasure.

They moved together and James made sure to follow her cues in how fast he moved within her and how hard. They were both pleased when she begged him to go faster and harder. Their lovemaking became frenzied, and she kept panting her needs and wants.

Bridgette moaned into his ear as she held on to him tight and said, "Oh James! Fuck me!" The man did not have to be told twice. He started to move as hard and fast as he could in that position and when he felt her body wrap around his hardness he looked into her eyes, and she cried out her release.

This set him off into his own, and he growled her name into her ear. They both stayed still in the shower for a little while until the water felt cold, and they disengaged and went to dry off. Neither one of them had ever been late for work because of a sexy shower experience, and they were quite pleased to share that first.

After toweling off and sharing a quick kiss they rushed into the bedroom to get dressed for work. There was no longer any anxiety within either of them as they rushed to their cars and were well on their way to work. This would not be a typical Friday at all!

~~

It was around nine in the morning when Bridgette arrived at the office. Nancy was sneering as always but said nothing to her. She must have been given the notice to see HR this afternoon.

The other women and men in the office greeted her with kindness and smiles. She felt at home here and the walk to her desk with her coffee in hand made her feel happy. She was a professional and the work they did here was really good.

Everyone was wonderful except for Nancy and she wished the woman would lighten up and realize they were all players for the same team. Setting her coffee down she booted up her computer and put her things away like normal. The morning was off to a quiet and productive start as she began answering emails and working really hard on her spreadsheets and scheduling.

It wasn't until a half-hour later when James walked in that the day turned sideways. Nancy greeted him at the elevator with coffee for him. She hadn't made it the way he liked and he arched a brow at her and thanked her for the coffee but said he would rather it come from his assistant at his desk.

Nancy proceeded to follow him into his office and shut the door behind them. Bridgette wanted to burst through the door and cause a scene but she forced herself to stay put. She focused on her work and tried not to hear any words coming from the closed office.

She needed to maintain her professionalism at the office. But, it was very hard when the love of her life was in there with a she-devil! James sat in his seat and looked at Nancy with an arched brow.

"Why did you follow me into my office and close the door, Nancy?" She sauntered to the front of his desk and bent down so he could see her exposed breasts from under her shirt. He rolled his eyes and repeated his question.

She said, "I know that woman out there is trying to say that I have accosted her in the hallway. I know she has it out for me. I want us to discuss it, Sir."

James simply raised his hand to stop her and said, "There was a report given to HR. This is a matter for HR and you have an appointment with them this afternoon. Everything you have to say can be said then. Not in my office. Not without my consent and not in a locked room. Now, please excuse yourself and get back to work, Nancy."

This woman was not someone who took it very well. Nancy took a seat before his desk and said, "What does this woman seem to have that I don't?" Her voice was filled with venom when she said the word woman and she looked like she was ready to explode.

James signed and said, "We will not discuss any of my employees including you here in this office. Please leave my office before I have security remove you." Nancy looked at him with fire in her eyes and sighed before standing up slowly and sauntering out of the office.

The sway of her hips and her full red lips did not get overlooked by anyone in the office. Including Bridgette herself. James sighed as he leaned back in his chair and opened up his messenger system for everyone in the office to communicate and started typing.

He told Bridgette he needed to see her once she was done with her emailing. She told him that she would be delighted to meet with him for a meeting. It was very formal and he cringed. She was upset over the encounter with Nancy, and he wanted to keep it professional at work for her sake.

At the same time, she needed to be reassured nothing was happening. He groaned and started in on his emails. He knew she would be in eventually, but he had to be patient and professional.

After half an hour he called her line and waited for her to answer. When she answered it was in a professional tone, and she answered as she would any other business call. He was proud of her and upset all at once because he wanted her to be less formal with him.

Even if that was unfair it was what he was feeling in the moment. Bridgette said, "How may I help you, Sir?" There was nothing in her tone to suggest that she was upset but he knew in his heart that she was.

James said, "Please come to my office. There is a matter we need to discuss and then I have a meeting and would like you to cover some of my emails."

After a beat, Bridgette said, "I will be there in a moment, Sir." Both of them hang up and a few moments later there is a knock at his office door. It only took a couple of seconds before Bridgette opened the door and entered the office. She closed the door and looked at him.

Taking a seat she had a pad in her hands and was ready to take notes. James looked at her and smiled at her and said, "I want to begin by stating that I did not ask Nancy to come into my office. She invited herself and closed the door after her. I told her we would not discuss a thing until we meet with HR. She did not want to leave or let it go. I made it clear to her that nothing would happen. She left."

Bridgette looked into his eyes and said, "I'm aware of how Nancy works. There is no need to discuss this with me here or outside of this room. I appreciate the fact that you care."

James nodded and then asked her to send some emails and explained who they needed to go to and the content that needs to be within them. She took notes and then thanked him and went to leave. Before she could open the door he said, "Bridgette?"

She turned around and he smiled at her and said, "Thank you for doing such a good job." Bridgette gave him a wide smile and then went to her desk and continued her work. They both worked through lunch and planned on a bigger dinner for them.

Bridgette is busy working on the emails as requested and once she is finished plans on working on her regular workload. James walks past her and makes his way toward the elevator. It is his time to go to HR and have a pre-meeting with them before Nancy goes down to the office.

James takes a seat in front of MaryAnn Lind who is their head of HR. He explains what has been happening for months and why he has never made a formal complaint. He gives dates, times, and explicit detail on everything. Some people witnessed the behavior as well.

MaryAnn is appalled because it sounds like sexual harassment toward the boss! She takes notes, makes sure that James files a complaint that details all he has told her. And for good measure, she has been recording it vocally. They are now prepared to discuss things with Nancy.

There was a knock on the door and Mary Ann said, "Come in!" The door opened and Nancy walked in. She looked shocked to see James seated in front of Mary Ann's desk.

Mary Ann directed Nancy to take a seat in the empty one beside James. A couple of moments passed in silence before Mary Ann took a deep breath and said, "Nancy, it seems that there have been several complaints lodged against you over the last six months. The first one came from a co-worker who was concerned you were becoming romantically obsessed with James. Then three others lodged the same complaint but it was not taken seriously."

As the words settled in Nancy went to open her mouth when Mary Ann cut her off and said, "That was a mistake. It seems that we now have witness statements, complaints, and more evidence that points to this being true. These actions could be considered sexual harassment which is against company policy and in the contract you signed when you were hired. Also, your work seems to be suffering. This is not a new problem. This is an over six months long problem."

Mary Ann stared at Nancy and waited for her response. Nancy took a deep breath and looked toward James and when he did not give her an expression or jump to her rescue she slumped in her seat. Then she looked toward Mary Ann and said, "I wanted to be more to James than his employee. I thought if I kept trying he would give in. I knew he had not been with someone for my entire time working here. And I felt he wasn't gay so that I had a chance. I didn't realize other people noticed or that my job was suffering as a result."

After having spoken she looked at the floor and flushed feeling for the first time the shame of her actions. MaryAnn sat forward and said, "Aside from these other complaints we have a recent complaint from one of our new hires. She claims you have gripped her arm, gotten in her face and accused her of false charges, and threatened her person. Is that correct?"

Nancy had fire and anger in her eyes and through gritted teeth said, "Technically..." James arched a brow and looked toward Mary Ann. A moment went by before Mary Ann said, "These are all violations of our company policy and your contract. I am sorry, but we will have to let you go, Nancy. If you had come to me sooner or you had behaved yourself in the first place it would not have ended this way."

Nancy sat straight up and looked into Mary Ann's eyes, her own blazing and said, "You can't be serious?!" James sat up straight in his chair and said casually, "There are policies in place to protect every employee from harassment and sexual harassment. You read over that contract with our HR department and you signed it correctly?" Nancy simply nodded.

James went on and said, "And you have admitted here in the recorded meeting that you have broken that agreement. The very one that you signed with HR." Nancy turned to glare at James and said, "This is all a trick to punish me because you are screwing your assistant!"

Mary Ann arched a brow at Nancy and said, "No, Nancy this has to do with your breaking your employee contract. James is not firing you although he could. Instead, I am firing you for your admitted behavior. Based on your reaction you still have not realized the error in your actions. Clear out your desk before the end of the day. Your final check will be mailed to you as soon as possible."

Nancy screamed and marched out of the room. James looked at Mary Ann and said, "One last thing since I am here in your office. We have a strict employee dating policy that states you have to express your relationship and sign that it will not harm your position. I would like to put on record that I am in a romantic relationship with Bridgette. I am willing to fill out the paperwork as is policy and I believe she will be willing as well. Please make an appointment for her to fill the forms out. I can do it now if you have the time."

Mary Ann looked at him with her head cocked to the side and placed the paperwork before him. "I am happy for you, boss. I will get this filed and have her come down to fill out her forms before the end of the day today."

He smiled and saluted and made his way back to his office. Bridgette was working on her final report when a message popped up on her screen from HR asking her to fill out some new paperwork. She replied that she would be down once she finished her report.

After going to HR she would be able to go home. The work completed Bridgette stood up and stretched. She was so glad that she was able to accomplish more work than she thought she would for the day.

This meant she was ahead of her schedule for next week. This would help everyone in other departments as well as move the meetings for next week along a lot more smoothly. She was very proud of her hard work and dedication to the job.

It was funny but no matter how happy she had been to work for Devante and Ryan she was never as content as she was here with James and her new co-workers. Making her way toward the elevator she pulled out her phone and shot off a text to Elise inviting her to dinner on Sunday night after her shift at the diner. Bridgette wanted to make something special for her friend and she knew James wouldn't mind the company.

As she walked past the front desk in the lobby area she heard a snarl of "bitch" as she walked past. She had no idea where it came from or why nor did she care. She knew who she was and nobody was going to shake her confidence. As soon as she arrived on the HR floor she made her way to Mary Ann.

It made her a little nervous that the head of the HR department wanted to speak to her. But, she did not let it stop her from walking into the office confidently. MaryAnn asked her to be seated and presented her with some forms to sign.

She explained they were to declare her relationship with James to keep from any unwanted gossip and/or legal issues. She said James had already signed his copies. Bridgette did not think twice to sign the papers after hearing that and having read them herself.

It felt like a weight being lifted off her shoulders. The paperwork only took about ten minutes, and then she was back in the elevator making her way toward the parking garage. Upon her arrival on the parking garage level, she felt a hand grip her arm and spin her around.

Before she could figure out what was happening someone was punching her in the face and trying to drag her to the ground. She started to fight back on instinct and cry out for help. Her screams echoed in the parking garage.

It did not take long for Bridgette to be pulled to the ground and then the kicking started. Her ribs and stomach were on fire. It seemed like she would not get any relief. It took a few more minutes of a brutal beating until voices were heard. Bridgette barely heard them, her ears were ringing, and she was bleeding from her head and into her mouth.

Even though her eyes were swollen she noticed that the person who was beating her ran away. She saw the shoes and knew who it was. But, she could barely move her mouth without wanting to scream. She figured her jaw was broken in some way.

James thought his heart would explode with pain as he took in the sight before him. Bridgette was broken on the ground bleeding and whimpering. He had seen grown men come back from war and look like they were in better shape than she did.

He ran to her and tried to gently lift her into his arms. Everyone else from the elevator was calling 911 and rushing around trying to find a way to help Bridgette. It seems that Bridgette has become beloved by his employees.

There were sirens in the background but nobody seemed to notice them. Everyone was focused on Bridgette who was shivering even though she lost consciousness. James held her and told her, "Come on kitten. You need to hang on. The ambulance is coming!"

But, it seemed like it would never arrive so he picked her up and placed her in the backseat of his car, and had his driver take them to the hospital. It seemed like the car was moving at the slowest pace and James yelled from the back where he cradled the love of his life in his arms.

"Go faster damn it! She is barely breathing!" Then he looked down at her and whispered in her ear, "You are scaring me here, kitten. Please hang on for me. We are almost there. Please hang on. I need you." But, there was no response and he felt like he was losing the most important person in his life.

James felt like a complete and total failure. He promised her, and he promised her friends back home that he would protect her. And now look at where they were.

At the same time, he knew his life would be incomplete and meaningless without her in it. He was not a religious man but he prayed that somehow she would survive so he could make it up to her. The car stopped and the door burst open.

There was a stretcher waiting for them, and he handed Bridgette off to them and barked that she needed to be seen as soon as possible, and he wanted updates. That she was his fiancé. Not one person questioned him or the lack of a ring on her finger.

They knew James by reputation and knew not to question his word. They set to working on Bridgette and he went to sit in the waiting area. It was breaking his heart not to be with her.

He wanted to hold her hand and tell her they would make it better. There was a sinking in James' stomach when he realized he had to call Ryan with the news. Her friends and family deserved to know.

At the same time, he knew that hot head kid would be on a plane to kick his ass for letting this happen. But, he was a man of honor and had to do the right thing. So, he took out his cell and made the call.

Chapter Twelve

I t rang three times and then the man himself picked up. "Ryan, this is James. Something has happened. I need you to be calm although once you hear what I have to say I have a feeling you'll be on a plane."

Ryan was silent for a second, and then he barked into the phone "What the fuck did you do?!" James took a breath and said, "I was finishing up with some paperwork in my office. Bridgette left before me after going to HR. And when she reached the parking lot someone jumped her. I didn't get to the parking garage until the dipshit ran away. But, it's bad... they just took her in to assess her injuries but... it's really bad. I held her and rushed her to the hospital but it's too soon to know anything yet."

Ryan screamed that James was an asshole who should have done better to protect Bridgette. Then he said he was going to tell everyone the news and then James had better prepare for the entire posse as he called them to arrive. Before James could respond Ryan had hung up on him.

James sighed and said, "Well, it will be an awkward family reunion. Knowing my girl she will want me to put them up at our place. But, if that is what I need to do to make her happy and move forward that is what we'll do."

He called and got his people to clean the spare rooms and ordered extra security and had his best friend get started on looking into what happened in the parking garage. He would find the bastards who did this to her and make sure that they pay. It was four hours later when someone came out to speak to him about Bridgette.

They told him that she had four broken ribs, her lung had collapsed but they were able to fix it, her jaw was broken and she had two black and blue eyes, they were keeping her overnight to check for internal injuries but so far there are no signs. And they want to be sure she did not have a concussion.

He prayed that she would make it out of this alright but was thankful it was not worse. He knew that her entire body would be bruised and sore for a long while. But, she had hope in moving forward and healing. And James would be damn sure that they were there every step of the way.

An hour after that they said that he could go visit her.

She was starting to come around. The police wanted to interview her, and he said they could only if he was with them. They agreed and promised not to stress or strain her. The police stood on the side of the room and let James go inside first. He sat beside her bed.

"Kitten, I'm here...", he said. Bridgette opened her eyes and looked at him and tried to speak but couldn't. She had a pen and paper and wrote, "Hey Handsome. You are really here.".

He smiled warmly at her and said, "I will always be here for you. These lovely police people want to ask you some questions. I will hold your hand the entire time as you write out your answers." She tried to nod and winced.

The police asked her questions and she wrote her answers for them as best as she could. They discovered that from the shoes she saw when she was on the ground she thinks her assailant was Nancy. She said she did not see very much and walked them through what had happened.

The police thanked her for her help and left to search for Nancy. They wanted to question her. The moment they had left Bridgette looked into James' eyes and wrote down.

"Thank you for talking to me. I couldn't talk but I heard you. I need you too. I will never leave you. And while I'm on a roll... I love you. And as soon as the jaw is healed I will speak the words to you." Her eyes were smiling and it was enough for him.

James smiled and said, "I love you too, kitten." It took a couple of minutes before he sighed and looked up at the ceiling and at her arched brow, he knew he had to come clean with Bridgette.

Taking her hand gently into his own he said, "When you were taken away, and they were working on you... I felt like I had to call Ryan. So, I did and he yelled at me for not protecting you. Nothing he said was anything I wasn't already feeling. And then he said the entire posse was coming. I assume they will be arriving soon. I've already called for the staff to make up their rooms at our house. I will take them in and care for whoever shows up. I will make sure they are all safe and alright. I've also beefed up security, and I am looking into finding Nancy. We will fix it all and handle it all, kitten. You just heal and focus on yourself."

Bridgette wished she could frown. She wrote "They need to see me first. No matter what time it is. They will never accept you or our relationship otherwise. They need to know I'll heal and that I trust you. They need to know you are mine and I'm yours."

James grinned and said, "Yes, kitten. We will do it your way. Whatever you want." After he said that she wrote that she wanted him to have a cot in her room and she would cause hell if anyone denied that wish. He chuckled and told her that he believed it and pulled out his phone to make it happen.

After the arrangements were made and the cot came into the room Bridgette started to relax. Then James' cell started to ring and he groaned and showed her the caller ID.

She wished she could laugh and wrote, "Answer him since I can't."

James groaned and picked up saying, "James," Ryan said in a rude tone, "We have arrived. We are outside the hospital and say that we can't come into the room unless you say it's okay. So, may we please have access to our girl."

He counted to ten and tried not to explode and looked at Bridgette who gave him a look in her eyes that said 'I am so sorry.' James said to Ryan, "Yes, please come through. She wants to see you all. Listen, she needs you to be calm and read what she writes. And don't crowd her."

Ryan grunted and agreed. Then footsteps sounded outside of the door and it slammed open after a few minutes. In a rush of movement Ryan, Chris, Decon, Devante, and Cassidy holding a baby rushed inside the room making it cramped.

Bridgette would have laughed out loud if she could have. There was her New York City family in the flesh and they came in like they needed to defend her from evil. It felt so good to see their faces again.

Bridgette locked eyes with Cassidy first and tried to sit up to see the baby. That was all the encouragement that Cassidy needed to rush to her and show her the bundle of joy. "Meet your Godson Jackson!"

Bridgette wrote on her pad, "He is the most handsome little man to ever grace us with his smile." Cassidy wiped a tear and said, "I love you. I'm so mad you left us but I understand why. I'm so sorry that bitch hurt you! I swear to God if she crosses my path I'll take a bitch down New York Style!"

It did not take long for Bridgette to smile with her eyes and write, "We'll do it together!" Cassidy laughed and hugged her gently. Then she turned her attention on James and said "I'm this badass bitch's best friend. If she loves you which I'm thinking she does by the way she is looking at you… that means you are family. So, welcome to the family, James!"

James smiled and said, "Thank you, Cassidy. It is wonderful to meet you and your son there. He is a cute fella." Nodding her approval Cassidy stepped back and let her husband come close next.

Devante took Bridgette's hands into his own and squeezed them. His eyes were sad and relieved all at once. "You claim me as your brother and then you leave me. Don't ever scare me like that again! I'm so glad you are healing. I am so sorry this happened to you. We've missed you so much."

Bridgette pulled away to write, "I'm sorry, bro. I was scared and trying to spare you all. I messed up. But, it all worked out because it got me here. It means I've met James and that makes all the difference. I love him. I love my life here. And once I am healed we can put all of this behind us."

Devante smiled and said, "That is our girl! We love you, Bridgette." That was when he turned to shake James' hand and said, "Welcome to this crazy family. If you hurt her we will have no trouble disposing of you."

Bridgette smacked Devante's shoulder, and he chuckled as did James. Then James looked at everyone in the room and said, "If I hurt her I would gladly accept your punishment." That was when Chris stepped forward and looked into Bridgette's eyes and said, "Hey. We missed you and lost our minds when you left. You stood us up for the company party."

She smiled with her eyes and wrote, "I guess I did. I never meant to hurt either of you. I never expected my life to change so fast. You both mean so much to me. We are this strange little family..." Chris chuckled and agreed with her.

He hugged her gently and she returned the hug as best as she could. Then Chris turned his attention to James. "This woman is precious to us. She is family and always will be. If you fail to keep her safe and keep her happy we will step in."

James grinned and said he would have it no other way. Decon stepped up next and hugged Bridgette so tight and yet so gentle. She wrote quickly to him after he stepped back a bit. "Hey, stranger. I really missed you. I'm sorry for all the pain I've caused. My heart was always in the right place. We are family and always will be. I promise never to disappear again okay? And please make sure Ryan does not kill James. I've finally found my soulmate and do not want any deaths in this room."

She winked at Decon and he laughed. Then she turned the page so nobody else could see what she wrote on the legal pad. Decon shook James' hand and said, "This one is special. Never let her go and try to forgive the rest of us who loved her first and lost her. Realize we broke in losing our chance with her but healed in knowing she still cares for us like family."

James simply nodded and looked at her with questions in his eyes. She winked at him, and he relaxed knowing it would all be okay in the end. Bridgette locked eyes with Ryan and she softened her gaze instantly.

He held her gaze and looked her over before rushing forward. He wrapped himself around her trying to be careful of her injuries. When Ryan placed his forehead on hers he said, "I was so scared I'd lost you. Never run again okay? I can live with you leaving, I can handle your moving on... I just need you whole and happy."

She couldn't stop the tears that flowed down her face, and she nodded to agree. Then she pulled away to write to him.

"You can't get rid of me that easily, Ry. I'll always be in your life and you in mine. But, you have to back off on James. He is a good man, and he's the one. I have never been so sure of anything in my entire life. Trust me. I love you, always.", she said.

He nodded and said, "I love you too. And I promise that I will try. For you." James watched them and felt pride at how well she was handling these interactions. Ryan turned and reluctantly let go of Bridgette and faced James.

"This woman is everything. Never hurt her or I will be back in an instant to take her for myself. She is more than you can possibly realize yet. But, she has chosen you and I will respect that, I will accept you into our family but one wrong step and you are finished.", Ryan said.

James nodded and extended his hand for a shake. The room was tense as Ryan hesitated to take it and shocked everyone by taking James in for a manly hug. The light in Bridgette's eyes couldn't be put into words as she beamed seeing everyone she loved in the same room.

She started to write to James, "Welcome to the family, Sir. I love you. Now, get my family home and tucked in, and then hurry back to me. I can't sleep safely without you."

James accepted her words and kissed her gently on the head before saying, "I love you too, kitten. I will take care of everyone and get them settled into our home. Then I will come back to you. I can't sleep safely without you either."

The next moments were a flurry of goodbyes and hugs. Then James led everyone out of the room and into the hall. He told them all to come with him in his SUVs.

They transferred their luggage and loaded it into the cars. Once they were on the road they were amazed at James and Bridgette's home. It was beautiful and so perfect for her.

Even Ryan commented on the fact it was like something Bridgette would have dreamed up. That filled James with a sense of pride. It took about an hour and a half to get home and have everyone settled.

They even had a crib for the baby. Cassidy and her husband Devante had thanked him for getting all they needed ahead of time. He simply said, "It was no trouble. You all have a room here so you can come and visit. We are family." James made sure that everyone had eaten and knew where things were.

He checked into the security and once he felt like everything was in place he raced back to his love.

~~

James walked into Bridgette's room and grinned when his girl opened her eyes and looked deeply into his own.

"I've settled everyone in at home. The baby even has his own crib and they have all the supplies they will need. I've asked them to stay until you come home. This will give you some more time with them. All of them can work remotely so it isn't a problem. ", he said.

Then he kissed her softly on her cheek. She wrote to him, "What did I ever do to deserve you?" He chuckled and said, "You were born, kitten. That was all you needed to do to be here. I'm yours. Always have been just didn't know it yet."

She wrote, "I'm yours too, Sir. Always." He gently cuddled her in his arms and then told her it was bedtime and got on the uncomfy cot. At that moment it was the best thing in the world. It kept him by her side. Where they both belonged.

It did not take very long before Bridgette was asleep and having peaceful dreams of getting married to James. How her family supported them with love as it happened. James was having dreams of finding justice for his girl so they could move forward. Both were in deep states of sleep for hours.

~~

A week later Bridgette was writing furiously at James. "Get me out of here! I am over it. I want to go home. I want to be in our bed and sleep beside you for real. NOW!" He couldn't help but laugh at the spark in her eyes as she demanded things.

There she was healing from a horrible beating and she was stubborn and ornery about getting back to their home. He loved her with all of his soul. He said, "We will take you home when the doctor says it is wise. Not a second before that. Be patient"

There was a fire in her gaze and she wrote, "No. I will not sit on my ass here wasting a bed that could go to someone in need. Take me home!" A nurse comes in and checks on Bridgette's dressings and her vitals.

Then she smiles warmly at her and says, "Ms. Bridgette we know you want to go home. Your doctor said you can go home if you follow his directions and have someone care for you around the clock until your ribs heal and your jaw is healed. You will need to come in for bi-weekly visits to monitor you. You need a live-in nurse in the meantime."

Bridgette beamed! She wrote, "You are an angel" to the nurse who smiled and winked at her. The second the words were from the nurse's mouth James was on the phone making arrangements and also telling the crew back at home.

Everyone was falling in love with Nevada and coming together as a family. After about an hour the doctor came in and looked over Bridgette one last time and then sent her home. The list of directions for her was huge and she wished her jaw was better so she could frown and throw a fit.

Instead, she focused on the fact she could go home. Her family was waiting for her at the house and she was ready to hold her Godson. Most of all she wanted to cozy up to James in their bed as they fell asleep and wake up the next morning with him beside her.

The entire office at work was pulling for her and stepping up to cover her workload. They all came to visit her over the last few days. It seems like they care about her and couldn't wait until she came back to work.

This warms her heart and makes her feel like she has made a home here in Nevada. Around four in the afternoon the paperwork was completed and Bridgette's things have all been packed and ready for her journey home.

In the car, she turned to James and held his hand before writing "Thank you for putting up with me. I know I am a royal pain in the ass. I just need to be home with you to heal."

He smiled and kissed her hand. "I know, kitten. I am happy you are coming home. I will be happiest when your jaw is better and I can hear your beautiful voice once again."

She nodded in agreement. Their driver was happily driving them home and occasionally asking if she was okay and being kind. As they pulled up to the house she saw a "Welcome Home" banner hanging from the porch.

She smiled at her friends as they all stood waiting for her. Even little Jackson in his father's arms. There were tears in her eyes as she took in her family. She leans over and hugs James for making it possible and then leaps from the car (as much as she could in her condition) and hurries toward her people.

The second she was on the porch Cassidy was hugging her gently and leading her inside where a feast was waiting for her. The men followed them in and sat down to enjoy everything. James grumbled as they left him to bring her things inside.

After placing her things in their room he joined everyone at the table to have an early dinner and talk. Bridgette was not talking but writing like a fiend. Everyone seemed to be having a really good time.

Cassidy was a mother hen making sure that Bridgette had her pain medication on time. Then she made sure that her son was content. James was quite amused as he watched her handle his staff, her best friend, and her son with efficiency.

After everyone was settled in for the night several hours after their meal James picked up Bridgette and kissed her softly. He turned to the room of her family and said, "If you will excuse us. Someone needs her beauty sleep."

The mirth in her eyes as she curled herself into his arms made everyone relax except for Ryan. He was still having a hard time accepting Bridgette with someone else. But, he nodded to James before they all retreated to their rooms.

The second that James settled Bridgette down on the bed she looked at him and winked. She wrote "As soon as my jaw is better and the rest of my body you are mine, Sir. I mean I will climb you like a tree!"

He chuckled and said, "I have never wanted a woman to come through with something as much as that." She nodded and started to get into the perfect cuddle position when his cell rang.

She arched her brow and he said, "Hang on kitten. I need to take this and then our cuddles can commence!" She gestured for him to get lost, and he laughed leaving to take his call. The second he picked up the phone his best friend Kyle said, "This was Nancy who beat the shit out of your girl. Seems she has a history of this behavior but because her parents are all high and mighty it has been covered up. Currently, she is in their house under lock and key so the cops can't find her. But, we have. You need to use all your connections if you are getting justice for your girl. Also, we are closer to finding out who is stalking her. No connection to Nancy though." James sighed.

He said, "Good. We will move forward on Nancy and keep working on the stalker situation." After James hung up he sat down on the couch and sighed heavily. None of the next steps forward would be easy. He was going to need all the help he could get.

As if on cue Ryan walked in and sat down across from him and said, "Tell me" James told him the news and what they were up against and Ryan nodded before saying, "We have the resources between all of us. And there is nothing we wouldn't do for Bridgette. We will all get through this. I think we need to gather all of the evidence and work with a lawyer to make sure it is airtight against Nancy. And once we have that handled we can focus on the stalker."

James responded with, "But, you all are from New York how can we do this long distance." Ryan grinned and said, "There is a new branch of our offices opening in Nevada. We are overseeing it getting started. While we do that we can also be working on helping Bridgette's problems. Nobody needs to know or think anything suspicious. That is if you will continue to let us stay here."

James grinned and said, "Family is always welcome for as long as you want. Thank you for this. That woman is the love of my life and I would give anything for her." Ryan nodded and said, "I'm starting to see that."

The men decided to have some scotch and discuss the upcoming months. Ryan was frustrated that he couldn't help but like James. He wanted to hate him for replacing him in Bridgette's heart. But, this man was right for her.

Beyond that James was a good person and a good friend. Even knowing what Ryan once was to Bridgette. At around midnight Ryan excused himself to get some sleep and James turned down all the lights and made his way upstairs to his bedroom.

The moment he opened the door he took in the sight of Bridgette sitting up looking at him. She wrote furiously saying "Where were you?! I've been worried but not enough to move. And this romance novel is really good."

James smiled and leaned against the door frame and said, "Missing me, kitten?" She tossed a pillow at him and wrote, "I love you. But, you suck!" James chuckled and closed the door and started to get undressed.

Once he was in nothing but boxer shorts he made his way to the bed. He lifted the covers back and sank into the bed. Bridgette moved in to cuddle with him and nuzzled him as best as she could with her jaw.

He whispered against her hair, 'I was downstairs talking with Ryan. The entire family will be staying here for a while. They are helping with our problems and also launching their own branches of their companies here in Nevada."

The light in her eyes was beautiful as she beamed at him. Bridgette winked at him and wrote, "It will be nice to have my family here." James agreed and said, "I love you, Bridgette." She wrote, "I love you too, James." With that, they curled close to each other and cuddled to sleep.

Chapter Thirteen

It was about a month or so later when the doctors decided to take the wire off her jaw. The entire process was strange and weird for Bridgette. She had always been so healthy that this entire experience has been weird.

She hadn't been to the doctor so much in her entire life before her assault. And now here she was having metal taken out of her so she could use her now healed jaw. It wasn't without pain or discomfort but it was so much better than it had been.

The doctor told her to take it easy and stick to soft foods at first. And then work her way up to harder things and talk as normal. She was just glad she could smile again and say a few things.

James held her hand through the entire thing and made her feel safe, supported, and powerful through it all. He was like an angel in her nightmare and she was so happy he was in her life. Over the last month, they had been working on building a case against Nancy.

Between the interviews with staff at work and the police reports, it was looking very good. Bridgette's testimony they took down about the shoes Nancy was wearing that day and how she had seen them earlier in the day and then as Nancy ran from the scene of the crime was compelling. She had even remembered what the seams had looked like.

In a day they would be bringing the charges to the District Attorney. It made Bridgette nervous because apparently, Nancy was from a wealthy and political family in the area. But, she was no stranger to being obsessive and violent.

There was a paper trail that her family had tried to keep hidden. Kyle, Chris, and Decon were able to uncover it and it would be presented in the case. As well as the complaints against her from HR before and after Bridgette had been hired.

Their lawyer Manny seems to believe that the case is air-tight and that the DA will want to pursue charges against her. That will mean a trial and she would have to testify. It was a little scary but since she had done nothing wrong and was not hiding anything it should be pretty straightforward.

As James took her hand and took her out of the doctor's office he said, "So beautiful how does it feel to be able to talk again?" She smiled and said, "It feels good. I need to go easy and it is sore. But, if it gets really bad then I go ahead and take some medication."

James nodded and beamed. It gave him great joy to hear the sound of her voice. They went for some lunch at the diner and Bridgette ended up having her favorite cream of wheat. It was heaven to her and James finished his meal quickly just so he could watch her eat.

It made him happy to see her healing and so content as she did it. After their lunch, the couple made their way back to their home to meet with everyone including Manny before the charges were presented the next day. As everyone sat around the table Bridgette looked around and soaked in all of the love and compassion of those around the table.

Before they could begin she stood and said, "Thank you all for being here for me. I could never have come this far without any of you. I know things are just getting started but I believe we can overcome all of our challenges."

Cassidy rose and said, "I think I can speak for everyone in this room when I say it is an honor to be a part of this. We will get justice for you and for everyone that woman has harmed. And we feel honored that you wanted us by your side as you have healed. You inspire us with your strength, and we will always be here for you."

Everyone nodded in agreement and the meeting began. Manny took the lead as he understood the legal process and what would come next. He tried to prepare them for any cross-examination that may come during the trial. And that a good defense lawyer would try to use things against Bridgette in court.

There was nothing about her life that would be out of bounds. Bridgette squared her shoulders and said, "I understand. I have nothing to hide. As long as I am given adequate time to explain my choices nobody will judge me. And if they do it will be irrelevant to the case."

Manny smiled and said, "Yes. That is the perfect attitude." The rest of the meeting went well. After everyone had a nice dinner and tried to accept the changes coming their way.

It was hard to imagine that their private lives may be made public record. But, each of them wasn't ashamed of their lives or who they were. They could handle anything and would stay firm as a unit moving forward.

But, as prepared as they felt they also knew that curves in the road could come out of nowhere and things could get rocky for each of them coming up.

The next day Manny went to his meeting with the District Attorney and the man was eager to move forward. It seems he had heard rumblings that the last DA was paid off to keep Nancy out of jail and bury the evidence. With the evidence they had collected he felt confident they could garner a conviction.

This was both good and bad news. It meant that the trial would be high profile and they would all be exposed. But, sometimes you have to ride the wave to obtain justice.

The next several days consisted of being asked to interview about their statements to the police and their claims against Nancy. Everyone was happy to help in any way they could. Bridgette did the best she could while still healing her jaw. All of her medical records relating to the assault were obtained by the District Attorney and they had sensitive conversations about how her sex life in New York, her choice to leave and even the fact she was being stalked would all be topics that they would have to speak about on the record.

If they were open about these things and prepared they couldn't be taken off guard during the trial. They even discussed how James had filed the paperwork for their relationship as had she. Nothing was out of bounds.

Bridgette felt exposed and at the same time she had nothing to be ashamed of or to hide. This would invade their privacy for this period but it was worth it for justice. In the end, they could go back to their private lives once it was over.

~~

The next month flew by quickly as the District Attorney moved forward with the case. It was his biggest and most high-profile case to date. The Mayor wanted this to move quickly and with vigor.

It was a re-election year and he said he wanted justice to help him win. The District Attorney humored him and was honored to move forward with the case at a more rapid pace.

Bridgette for the most part focused on her recovery and getting back to work. She was pleased that when she returned the staff had thrown her a welcome back party at lunch. There was even cake!

Then they filled her in on all the words she had missed and got her up to speed. Because they had done so much extra work while she was away it didn't feel overwhelming and she was so thankful to them.

The media had been interested in Bridgette and her life because of the case.

She had issued a statement asking for privacy. But, they followed her to and from work. There were lies told in the newspapers and magazines. But, everyone who knew her would never believe them.

As much as life changed she was herself at her core. James and his security tried to protect her from the press as much as possible. It was a learning curve for them all.

Thankfully, it was not like New York or any other larger city. There was press but it was manageable. But, the biggest change in her life was a happy one. She was having a wonderful time getting to know her Godson and spending time with her family.

There were even whispers from Devante himself that they may just set down roots in Nevada and stay close by. Things in Bridgette's life were on a distinct upswing until Friday morning when she arrived at work. There was an envelope with her name on it left on her desk.

She asked the head of the mail department about it and he told her that it was waiting with the other mail this morning. She frowned and wondered what it was. Before opening it she called James' line and waited for him to pick up.

The second that James picked up and said, "Hey kitten. What can I do for you?" She hesitated to tell him but then explained the envelope. James told her to wait for him before opening it.

The next thing Bridgette knew four beefy-looking security men and James were next to her desk scowling at the envelope. The head of security Rick looked at it and said, "I will open it. It is safer that way in case it's rigged somehow. I will wear gloves in case there is a substance on it."

Bridgette looked at him with an arched brow and James simply nodded. Rick pulled some gloves from his pocket and lifted the envelope and opened it. The second he started to read the contents of the letter he scowled and told James to get some gloves on.

James picked up the letter once he had the gloves over his hands. He growled at the letter and looked to Rick.

"Call the District Attorney and the local police. We need this on record., James gritted out between clenched teeth. The second after the words were out of his mouth James gave the letter to Rick and tossed his gloves. James took Bridgette into his arms and kissed her hair.

"We will handle this, kitten. Please don't worry.", he said. There was a fury building inside of Bridgette. She was frustrated that she was being handled.

Bridgette wiggled out from James' grasp and turned on him and the security team left and said, "I am sick and tired of being handled. I am a grown woman and I can handle knowing what is going on. So, someone better start talking to me about what has happened to make the need for security to be so tight and I want to know the contents of the letter."

The way she stood like a furious storm with her hands on her hips. James tried not to show that even when she was pissed at him she was the most beautiful woman he had ever seen. He was in love with her and supposed he had to let her make her own choices with her life.

With a sigh, he said, "There have been threats, kitten. We wanted to make sure that you were taken care of. And the letter said that you would be dead before the case ever goes to trial."

She looked even angrier, her eyes were fired when she said, "I'm not going to be intimidated into letting Nancy get away with this. I'm going to thrive."

It did not shock anyone in the room to hear her words and see that they were completely true. James lifted his hands in surrender and said, "You are in control of your life, kitten. We are but your humble servants wanting to serve you."

She laughed at him and said, "I highly doubt that. But, I want more say and to be involved in choices made. I want you to tell me about threats. This is my life on the line here."

Everyone agreed and the security men all went back to their posts. James and Bridgette went back to work for the afternoon. It was around six by the time they had finished their work. James sat on the edge of Bridgette's desk and waited for her to power down her computer. He loved watching her pack up her things for the day.

There was nothing she did that didn't interest him. After a few moments, she placed her hand in his and suggested they get going. They walked hand in hand toward the elevator. All of the employees including Mallory who replaced Nancy at the front desk smiled and waved as they walked past.

There was harmony at the office these days and everyone was thankful. Productivity was way up, and they were all proud of their work. As they rode the elevator down to the parking garage James kissed her and held her close.

They felt like they were in their world and almost missed hearing the ding when they landed on their floor. The doors opened and they reluctantly pulled away from each other and made their way to the car. Their driver wasn't behind the wheel as always and James was pulling out his cell to call him immediately.

They heard the ring coming from close by. Never letting go of her hand James went to find the phone. After looking for several minutes they came across their driver laying face down on the floor. His phone was in his hand ringing, but he wasn't even moving.

James hurried to call 911 and then bent down to check for a pulse. It was faint but still there and he let the paramedics know. Then he gripped Bridgette's hand and took her to the car and locked her inside.

He told her to wait there since she would be safe. James looked around to see if someone was lying in wait to harm them. He never put his phone down and was connected to 911.

The operator told James that the police and ambulance were on the way and trying to get to a safe place in care the assailant was still there. However, he could see nobody but himself and Bridgette in the car. There were a few moments of silence as James tried to figure out what to do next.

There was suddenly a noise, and he realized it was coming from the car. He ran, dropping the phone and racing to the car. He opened the door and pulled a confused Bridgette out of the car just before it exploded.

The impact of the explosion forced them both to the ground. James took the brunt of the impact from the explosion. The explosion rocked the entire building, destroyed the car, and threw shrapnel all over. James forced himself to stand up and looked over Bridgette.

She looked okay and said, "I'm okay, I'm okay!" He nodded and looked for his phone but it was destroyed after the explosion. But, there were sirens in the distance.

All of a sudden James collapsed and Bridgette shouted to him. He couldn't hear anything but her voice and couldn't seem to open his eyes. He felt like he was underwater and sinking fast.

Bridgette ran to the road where the first responders were coming in. She shouted that they needed help quickly!

The paramedics went straight to James and took care of him while the firefighters tried to put out the flaming car. There were a few extra EMTs who went to check on their driver. Everyone was rushing around like chickens with their heads cut off. Bridgette just held herself and tried to hold in her tears as she took in everything happening around her.

A police officer came up to Bridgette and asked her a few questions. They handed her a blanket and she told them to call the District Attorney. Then she asked if she could use a phone and she called everyone at the house.

She told them to come to the hospital as quickly as they could. Bridgette caught up to the ambulance and got inside. She was riding along with James. She held herself close as she felt like if she let go she would fall apart into a million pieces.

They worked on James, and she watched feeling in a haze. It seemed like the ambulance was going so slow. Upon reaching the hospital James was whisked away behind closed doors to be worked on. They took Bridgette to the waiting room and seated her in the corner.

It was mostly private, and they promised to inform her family where she was as soon as they arrived. Bridgette felt cold and alone in the chair and no matter what she did... she couldn't make it better.

It was a half-hour later when she heard familiar voices. She looked up and saw Cassidy. Devante was holding Jackson and she ran to Cassidy and fell apart. Her cries were heard all over the hospital, and she didn't care if anyone or everyone heard it.

Ryan moved Cassidy back and took Bridgette into his arms and held her close. Then he picked her up and sat her on his lap.

"It will be okay, baby. James is a fighter and he loves you so much. There is nothing on this earth that he would let come between you. Are these injuries okay? Ryan said." She cried into his chest and nodded a little.

He smiled softly and stroked her hair saying, "Good. Now you let it all out. I can take it." And so she fell apart on his lap as everyone else took a seat to wait for news.

Bridgette fell asleep once all of her tears had fallen. Ryan held her close and made sure she was warm and safe. Cassidy held her son and rested her head on her husband's shoulder.

Chris and Declan paced around the room wanting to hear some news. They went for coffee runs a few times. It had been five hours when someone came to talk to them. Bridgette was still sleeping in Ryan's lap so he gently woke her. She jumped up out of his lap and winced a little from the pain. She'd been hit by some things during the explosion and was sore.

The nurse asked if James' family was there and she stood tall and said, "I'm his fiancé." Everyone nodded and the nurse flushed and said, "James has some severe burns and cuts on his back and leg. There was a blow to his head so we want to keep an eye on that. He has not regained consciousness since he arrived. We believe that is due to the impact of that blow. His surgery to repair some of the damage done internally from his fall was a success. He will be with us for at least two weeks. Perhaps more. We are just waiting for him to wake up."

Bridgette looked the nurse in the eye and said, "Take me to him." She agreed saying just one at a time could visit with him. Everyone nodded and took their seats once more to wait.

The walk to James' room seemed like it was going to take forever. The nurse stopped in front of a closed door and said, "There are bandages and since he has not woken up and his lungs took a beating he is hooked up to some machines. Be prepared."

Then the nurse opened the door and Bridgette walked inside with her. The first thing that came to Bridgette's mind was "He looks so small." At the same time, she moved forward and sat beside James' bedside.

She took his hands in hers and looked at him and said, "You have to come back to me, baby. I need you. You protected me so well. But, I need you for more than your protection. You are the love of my life, come back to me."

The nurse had left them alone, and she started to weep softly. It was so painful to see James laying there so helpless. He was a powerful man and to see him sidelined in this way was heartbreaking.

She was so exhausted from everything that happened that she fell asleep slumped over his bedside holding her lover's hand. A few hours later the nurse came in and since there had been a shift change this nurse was not as quiet as the last. Bridgette woke up with a start and looked around confused.

The nurse looked at her and said, "You should go somewhere else to sleep. This is his room to recover and not yours." in a snooty tone. Bridgette's eyes glared at the woman, and she said in a sweet-sounding voice, "Your job is to make sure his vitals are stable and if not fetch a doctor. Not give me advice and how to handle my time with my fiancé. Finish your work and leave."

The woman made a shocked noise and held her hand over her heart and mumbled before leaving the room. There was a slight movement under her hand and she looked up to see James' eyes open. She cried softly when he said, "That's my girl. Protecting me and us even here."

She hit the call button to get someone to come and evaluate him. Then he leaned in and kissed him softly on the lips.

"I love you so much James." Bridgette said, her voice filled with emotion. He winked at her and said, "I know baby. We make quite the pair. First you and now me in the hospital. Think they will start giving us a discount for coming in so much?"

He tried to laugh but winced as he did. His entire body hurt to some extent and he was struggling to keep his pain level a secret from Bridgette. He didn't want her to worry about how banged up he was.

Hands-on her hips Bridgette looked at him and said, "Oh no you don't! You need to be honest with your pain levels so we can get you what you need. No macho crap here, Mister."

James rolled his eyes and grunted at her. She held her ground and eventually he said he probably needed more pain medication. So, Bridgette went off to find someone since they still had not arrived to look him over.

Not five minutes later the doctor and some other staff were in his room looking him over and teaching him how to self-administer his medication. The nasty nurse from earlier was also removed from his case. She had made sure to file a formal complaint and have her removed. James would only have the best care. Especially on her watch.

As the day progressed James slept most of the time and eventually Ryan came inside the hospital room. He looked at how thin and tired Bridgette looked and said, "Hey lady. I think you need to come with me and grab some food. After we have some food and you rest a little." Bridgette looked up and frowned.

"I can't leave him.", she said softly. Ryan shook his head and ran his fingers through his hair.

"Baby, there is no reason to suffer along with him. He wouldn't want you to starve. Please come with me. We will have our phones and they can call us the second that he needs you. We'll leave Chris and Dec in here with him. You know they'll watch over him.", Ryan told her.

She reluctantly nodded and went with him. Chris and Decon stayed with James and watched him rest. It amazed them that he was doing as well as he was given what happened to him.

The men started to talk about their plans for the week and checked their phones for updates on what happened at the parking garage. It was looking like Nancy's father Richard Crest hired someone to handle his little problem and take out the driver, James and Bridgette in one go. But, the driver was trained to fight and the hired help wasn't able to handle him.

In the end, the driver died trying to stop him from harming James and Bridgette. The man they hired was inexperienced and botched it up. They messed up in hiring someone and leaving a paper trail.

The District Attorney was already gathering that evidence to add to his already filed case and will bring charges against Richard Crest as soon as it is all buttoned up. It all seemed too easy and that was really pissing Decon off and he shared his thoughts with Chris. They both wanted to keep digging to see if there was more of the story than just the hit placed on their family.

Sometime later Ryan came back with Bridgette who looked a little better. This entire experience had taken a toll on her. They all sat in silence when Bridgette spoke, "I'm glad Devante took the baby and Cassidy home. I don't want Jackson to get weird hospital vibes. And they were wrecked. We will call and update them as we know more."

She looked over toward Chris and Decon and said, "You two should go get some rest too. I know you are working your normal jobs and working on this nonsense we are going through. You need rest before you burn out. Ryan will stay with me until I send him home to rest too."

The men eyed her and then reluctantly nodded knowing it was useless to argue with her, and they did need the rest to do their jobs well. Each man hugged and kissed her cheek before leaving the room. Ryan took the seat next to her and said, "We are all here for you and James. We will get through this."

Bridgette simply nodded and kept her eyes focused on James. He was her entire world and she just got him in her life. They needed more time. She realized he knew that and felt the same way and that is why he was fighting so hard to heal.

The rest of the day passed quickly and around ten that night Bridgette was sleeping at James' bedside again. Ryan looked at her and smiled with peaceful happiness. No matter how much it hurt him he knew she was where she belonged.

There was a slight noise and he looked up to see James looking back at him. Ryan smiled at the man and said, "Two things, man. One, damn it is good to see you breathing. You had us scared for a while there. And second… She looks so peaceful here where she belongs. She has not left your side for more than an hour and was under great pressure from us to eat and handle her business." James smiled warmly and looked down at her sleepy head.

"She is my warrior. Even when she doesn't realize that she is. I'm a very lucky man to have her by my side. I'm glad to be here. Do we know who shot our driver and blew up the car?", James asked.

Ryan stiffened and said, "We can discuss it once you are better. Right now you need to get better for her sake." James ground his teeth and said, "I want to be briefed tomorrow. With Bridgette by my side. We agreed that she can be let into information related to her life and have a say in how we walk forward. I will not break my word to her."

Ryan looked uncomfortable but he nodded. He told James he would be back tomorrow and take care of their girl. James simply nodded at the same and stroked Bridgette's hair. She was so exhausted that she slept through it all.

Chapter Fourteen

Three days later James ground his teeth and looked at the love of his life with clenched fists. "They said I can go home. I'm cleared. I do not need an around-the-clock nurse. The love of my life by my side and our family is all the help I'll need." he said.

She stood before him with her hands on her hips and said, "You are a stubborn man. Fine. But, you get wheeled to the car!" James tried to stay angry with Bridgette but he couldn't.

She was his little tornado and he loved her to pieces. It would be rough on them, compromising sometimes since they were both stubborn. But, their life would be happy and beautiful.

Once this entire Nancy situation was behind them he was asking her to marry him. Bridgette cocked her head to the side and said, "What are you planning now?"

He chuckled and replied, "I'm just deciding the rest of our life. No big deal." She laughed and said, "That is not fair. We should do that together, Sir."

The air between them crackled and she went forward to kiss him. He placed his hand on the back of her neck deepening the kiss. And that was the exact moment that their family arrived. There were cheers and hoots of happiness. The couple turned and smiled. Bridgette had a blush on her cheeks.

"It seems that our chariot has arrived, kitten," James said. Everyone started to ask him how he was and the guys helped him up out of bed and into the wheelchair for transport. He could not have been happier that they were springing him out of the hospital.

They needed to have that meeting as a family about what happened and how to proceed.

~~

A couple of hours later the entire family was around the large table in the dining room. They were having dinner after their meeting so Cassidy kept popping out to the kitchen to watch their food. At the head of the table was Ryan.

It took several minutes for him to set the groundwork on what they learned after the attack and who found out what information. Chris and Decon added in information here and there. Devante sat silent as he was taking this all in fresh with Cassidy, Bridgette, and James.

After they finished their explanation James said, "Where is the District Attorney in his case against the father?" Ryan sighed and said, "They are still waiting for some forensics to come back from the lab. Once they have that handled they plan on moving forward with charges. The trial starts in three weeks for Nancy. They also wanted to put you all in witness protection. Instead, we convinced them to let our teams handle it."

Devante looked grim as he said, "We need to add more men here at the house. I hate to say this as I know we all value our independence, but we need to hunker down until the trial is over."

Everyone was quiet until James said, "Yeah, I will work from home and Bridgette will do the same. We will have extra security at our offices to protect our employees. Time to settle in."

Bridgette looked at him with sadness in her eyes and said, "I love you. We'll get through this."

Cassidy came into the room and smiled at her family and said, "This just means we have more time to bond. We are a family and we will handle this together. A united front."

Everyone cheered and went into the kitchen to start bringing in bowls, silverware, and glasses so they could start to chow down. It felt wonderful to have so much love and support. James and Bridgette were happily overwhelmed by everyone coming to their aid. The baked ziti and fresh garlic bread didn't hurt the situation either!

~~

Over the next few days, everyone fell into a rhythm. Cassidy and Devante worked from their bedroom and in the mornings Cassidy had breakfast set for everyone. Chris and Decon set up their office in James' den.

They worked hard to keep things moving forward. Ryan set up temporarily in the dining room. He could easily set up his workstation and take it down before dinner. Everyone sort of had lunch at their stations.

James and Bridgette worked from their bedroom which already had a desk setup. Everything was working well until the District Attorney called and said that some of the evidence from the car explosion was missing. This set the men in the house into action, and they had people on the ground at the lab, at the police station, and at the scene asking questions and digging to find what happened.

They also shared the information and proof they already had connecting Richard to the crime. The District Attorney had a case without those items, but they really sealed the deal. It had everyone scrambling and made the man who set these things in motion look more guilty.

He was now tampering with two Federal Investigations. Everyone was on edge to see what was coming next. So far there was evidence tampering, an assassination attempt, and who knows what else they haven't discovered yet.

The trial was starting in two weeks at this point and Bridgette was the one who was the calmest. She had lived through enough to know that staying calm was key in moving forward through rough things. It was a matter of keeping herself together and ready for whatever came next.

She had enjoyed spending time with Cassidy and ordering some new clothes for the trial. They wanted everyone to look their best and present their united front. Elise was only too happy to babysit during court hours during the trial. She was being overpaid for it and she said that they were spoiling her by letting her earn a living, savings, and play with Jackson.

Elise had become like a grandma to him. They were one big really happy family. It made their lives feel better and easier. And yet... the storm was coming.

Bridgette was seated at the window in her bedroom looking out over the property when James walked in. He noticed the far-away look on her face and wished he could read her mind. It took him several minutes of watching her before he cleared his throat and walked toward her saying, "Hey kitten."

She turned and looked into his eyes, hers a reflection of love and happiness to see him. And yet she also looked haunted. James crouched down in front of her and said, "Kitten... talk to me. What is going on?"

After a few beats, Bridgette sighed and said, "I'm trying to prepare for whatever comes our way. But, there is no idea what a wild card like this Richard person is. It is hard to come up with the proper defenses." He smiled at her and took her hands into his own.

"We will be ready for whatever he sends our way. We have security teams and systems. We have each other and our family. We are all smart and on guard. We will make it through.", he said.

Bridgette simply smiled and kissed him passionately and whispered, "Has the doctor given your permission to get naked with me yet?" She giggled and he said, "Yes, want to start right now or wait for tonight?"

James winked at his woman and she said, "Tonight" in a husky voice. They kissed again and James pulled away reluctantly and said, "We better stop before I can't control myself. You have a way of making me crazy, kitten."

She beamed at him and told him that it went both ways. Deciding it was best to cool themselves off they started talking about work to help him get out of "the mood". It seemed to work, and they accomplished a great deal in the next few hours.

Everyone at the house loved their work and their offices. But, there was a cozy feeling working from home. They were productive and yet found more time to be with each other and feel safe in their little bubble.

The meal that night was roast beef with all of the sides you'd expect to accompany it. They feasted happily and shared stories of their lives before they met and precious memories together. After everyone put their dishes in the dishwasher and cleaned up the dining room and kitchen they sat around the fireplace and talked some more.

It was around nine when Cassidy excused herself to put the baby down and get some rest. Devante followed about forty-five minutes later. The men were all talking about work stories and crazy college hijinks when they heard a noise from the back of the house.

James looked at the man and nodded. They had created a plan of who would go where they should be under attack. Weapons were strategically placed around the home and men knew their posts.

In silence, they made their way to those locations with their weapons. James looked at Bridgette and told her to go to Cassidy and take her into their bathroom with Jackson and lock the door. They weren't to come out no matter what they happened to hear. She nodded and went upstairs.

The moment she knocked on the door Devante was up and had a weapon in hand. She nodded to him and then followed what she had agreed to. This was the beginning of the storm.

James and Ryan took charge by going straight into the danger. James was on the right and Ryan on the left. Both had weapons and ammunition on them in case it got ugly. James slowly opened the back door and stepped out onto the porch Ryan at his side.

There was silence at first, but then they heard a moan. It was coming from Ryan's side of the house. He looked at James and nodded that way. James responded to his understanding with a nod and went his own way.

Ryan was stealthy in his movements and when he came to the edge of the house he found two guards shot to death and one bleeding out. The guard looked at him and said, "More men. They are coming!" Before Ryan could process more shots were coming his way.

It was like they were surrounded and maybe they were. The worst part was that it was night. Everything around them was in low light or complete darkness. James cursed low as he started to return fire from his side of the house.

He knew they were in a rough space if their men could be taken out so easily. He'd found four men dead from their security team. Using his cell he texted his personal security to call the police, send more men and let them know where everyone was.

Then he continued to shoot toward the sounds of the bullets coming toward him. Occasionally, he would hear a grunt and knew he hit someone. It was clear to both Ryan and James that they needed to get inside and try to cover the windows and barricade as much as possible until help arrived.

They managed to get inside and close the door. They were joined by Devante, Chris, and Decon. Everyone moved furniture in front of the windows and doors at the rear of the house. This was where they were being invaded.

Then men returned fire on their attackers and Chris and Deacon went to fortify the front of the house in case they came in from there. Once everything seemed to be as safe as possible they continued to fight it out with their attackers. The sound of sirens and a text from their head of security alerted them that help was indeed on the way.

Devante said he would handle them once they arrived. It took only five minutes more before there were police there, ambulances, and their full security team. Ryan handled filling them in with Devante. Meanwhile, Chris and Deacon went to the back to make sure the threat had left them.

Then James went upstairs to check on the women and Jackson. They were shaken up but not injured in any way. Devante came up and told them that it was safe to return downstairs. So, they made their way to the kitchen.

It took around an hour or more to secure the scene and process everything. The family gave interviews to the police and then once everything was complete they set out to board up and clean up from the shoot-out. An hour after all of those things had been accomplished they started to settle in the kitchen.

The toll of the night weighing on each member of the family. James was shocked when a call came to his cell. It was the District Attorney personally asking if they were alright.

James filled him in and the man promised to see justice was served for them all. Bridgette was getting coffee for everyone when she noticed Ryan looked pale and was leaning against the island. She set the mugs down and went to him in a hurry.

He looked at her and said, "Don't worry babe. I'll be fine." That was when she noticed he was bleeding from his abdomen. She looked to her family at the table and shouted.

Everyone turned quickly and as Devante rushed forward Ryan collapsed into a heap on the floor. Devante checked his pulse and screamed to have someone call 911. He said that Ryan had been shot and it looked bad.

Chris and Deacon looked shocked into place as they stared at the virile Ryan looking ashen and small on the floor. James was on the phone with 911 and security faster than he'd ever dialed before. An ambulance was on its way but Ryan was so still and barely speaking.

There was so much blood soaking through his clothes. Cassidy hurried upstairs to tend to Jackson and get out of the way. Devante stayed cradling Ryan in his arms. Bridgette was on her knees in front of them, her hands touching Ryan's face as tears streamed down her own.

James was outside waving in the ambulance and police. The EMTs raced to Ryan and told Bridgette and Devante to leave him so they could work. Devante took Bridgette into his arms and held her like the brother he was and said soothing words into her hair as he watched.

The EMTs were trying to save Ryan's life but even they looked ashen and afraid. Devante told them he and Bridgette were going in the ambulance. They simply nodded.

James went to check on Cassidy and then once he knew she was okay he told Chris and Decon to stay and guard the house. To keep Cassidy and Jackson safe. He would call with the news. Then he rushed to his car and drove to the hospital just fifteen minutes behind the ambulance.

Everyone knew it would be a long night but nobody expected this. James seethed as he drove to the hospital. The police were clueless and not much help right now.

The District Attorney was doing everything right, but they were still under attack. There had to be a better way. All of his prayers and good wishes were that Ryan would recover.

They did not sign up to lose a member of their family. And if he didn't make it, heaven help those people! He would go to hell to send them where they belong and get justice. This was super personal.

As the ambulance pulled into its bay the EMTs rushed Devante and Bridgette out of the way and told them to ask at the desk where to wait. Then they got Ryan out of the ambulance and hurried into the back. Both of them waited in the chairs provided near the Emergency Room and neither realized they were shivering.

They just clung to each other and waited. Time seemed to stand still as they waited for news of Ryan's condition. James came into the waiting room in a rush and the second that Bridgette saw him she lunged into his arms and broke down.

He wrapped his arms around her and held her tight. Over her head, he looked at Devante and nodded. The man gave a weak smile and then said, "We haven't heard anything yet."

James sat beside Devante and pulled his love into his lap. Her head went to his shoulder, and he stroked her hair. They waited for what seemed like forever for someone to come and talk to them.

After an hour had passed Devante went to the desk and asked if there was any word and to please inform them as soon as possible as updates came in. The woman was so charmed by Devante she didn't even ask if they were his family. She offered to go check on Ryan personally.

Bridgette scoffed against James' neck and started to explain all of the laws that woman was breaking and how it could cost her job. Few people knew that Bridgette was once a caretaker and had to learn a lot about HIPPA and other important legal sides to Healthcare. Devante and James just shrugged and went on with their waiting.

The woman Wendy finally returned and said that Ryan was in rough shape. They had lost him three times on the table but were able to get him stable. They are taking him into surgery now as the bullet hit some vital organs.

She told them that it was critical at this moment, and she would find out more when she was able. They thanked her and followed a nurse who took them to the waiting room outside of the surgery wing. James is the kind man that called the house and told Decon their latest update and where they were waiting.

Deacon said that he and Chris made dinner for Cassidy and that everything was calm and quiet. But, they had extra security come in just in case, and they boarded up the damaged windows. They would have a repair person come the next morning.

It seemed like the hours dragged on. Bridgette fell asleep in James' arms, and he held her close. Devante started to pace and curse in Spanish. Hour after hour just ticked on by as they sat in the waiting room.

It was around seven in the morning before someone came down to fetch them. Devante stood and James gently woke Bridgette up. As Bridgette woke she noticed the nurse and stood up straight.

They all looked at the nurse who looked grim. She said, "Please follow me. The doctor would like to talk to you and let you have some time with him." The little group of three made their way through the halls following the nurse who had introduced herself as Maria.

The doctor greeted them outside of Ryan's room and said, "The surgery was touch and go. We had lost him twice in addition to three times they lost him in the Emergency Room. That did a lot of damage to his body. We ran some tests and it would appear that Ryan's injuries were more severe than we realized. He is not responding as he should, and we have reason to believe that he's not going to recover."

A sob ripped from Bridgette's soul as her legs gave out, and she collapsed right there on the hospital floor. James bent down to pick her up and hold her close to his own eyes close to tears. Devante looked hard and mean as he turned on the doctor and said, "Are you telling me you want us to take him off the machines? There is no hope at all?"

The doctor simply nodded and Devante cursed under his breath. The doctor sighed and said, "I am so sorry about this. If you know the number for any of his closest family and friends I would call them. He may not make it until the end of the day at this rate."

Devante took out his phone and called his wife and told her the news and asked her to have Elise watch the baby. She told him that she, Chris, and Decon would make their way to the hospital now. Then he took Bridgette's hand in his and helped give her strength. With her love and her brother on either side of her… they all moved forward into Ryan's room.

There were tubes all over the place and beeps from the machines. Ryan looked ashen and small in the bed. Bridgette moved with speed to sit beside his bed and hold his hand. It felt cold so she tried to warm him with her hands.

She looked at him and said, "Hey Ry. You were so brave last night. You saved us from the bad guys… but you need to keep fighting. I'm not ready for you to leave me. We just got back to a good place. We are family."

The tears flowed down her cheeks and said, went on, "I love you, Ry. You are so special." Devante took a seat on the other side of the bed. He held his friend's other hand and spoke to him in Spanish.

Ryan had joked he needed to know both languages to properly understand Devante. But, none of his words of love, friendship, and brotherhood stirred his friend. All of their love isn't changing his condition like in books and the movies.

Devante looked brokenly at James who stood behind Bridgette and said, "It's real isn't it?" James nodded at his friend. Tears were flowing down Devante's face as he looked back at Ryan.

Chris, Decon, Devante, Cassidy, Bridgette, and James were seated around Ryan's bed. They took turns talking to him. Asking for forgiveness, telling him that he was loved and even some jokes were said. Maria came in and asked them if they were ready.

It was soft and filled with compassion. Everyone left their places except Bridgette and Devante. Everyone else left the room having said their goodbyes. Bridgette and Devante wanted to be there with him until the end.

The doctor came in and explained what was about to happen. Then they turned off the machines and took out the breathing tube. Bridgette and Devante held Ryan's hand. Bridgette looked at Ryan and said, "I love you. I will always love you. But, you need to let go. It's okay to move on. We know you are tired."

Devante looked at his friend and said, "I love you, brother. I will always remember you and so will my son. Your legacy will remain. It is okay to leave this world. We will see you in the next one."

It was as if Ryan had heard them. He stopped breathing and was gone just as Devante finished speaking. Bridgette broke down and cried over Ryan's body. Devante sat back in his chair still holding Ryan's hand and cried softly.

They had really lost their best friend, their brother. He was gone. James came in sometime later and picked Bridgette up and said, "Let's go, baby. They need to take care of him. We've made all the arrangements."

Devante stood and said, "I will pay for it on my own. I owe this to my brother. We will give him a proper send-off." James nodded and they walked to the waiting room.

None of their family had a dry eye. Devante went to his wife and held her close. The end of Ryan's life had an impact on each and every one of them. They set to work on his funeral arrangements. They would be having them back in New York. Everything he had worked for would not be in vain. And they also all vowed they would find his killer and get some justice for him.

Chapter Fifteen

Life after Ryan was going to be the hardest thing that anyone in their circle would ever have to face. In the days following his death, everyone worked hard to keep his legacy alive. They hired a private jet to take them to New York City for the services.

They also had Ryan's body moved privately. They arrived and made their way to Devante and Cassidy's place. Everyone stayed for dinner, and then they all went to their homes. Bridgette and James stayed with the couple.

The next morning everyone was quiet and withdrawn. At around eleven they would be having their last goodbye to Ryan. Cassidy was up early and made sure her son was fed and ready for his babysitter.

Devante made his way into the kitchen looking dapper in a black suit. Cassidy looked at him and her breath was taken away. She was so in love with him and proud he was her husband. And even through her sadness, she was thankful for what she has.

Sadly, Devante kissed his son on his head and then kissed his wife. They ate in silence. After an hour their buzzer sounded and Chris and Decon came up.

Cassidy got them some coffee and the men sat in the living room and told stories about Ryan. Chris and Decon looked so handsome in their suits. Sometime later James and Bridgette came out.

They were also dressed for the service. The time went by so slowly and yet fast as they waited for the limos to arrive. The family planned to be the first there.

~~

A few hours later they were in their limos on the way to the service. Chris and Declan were in their own limo and the rest of the family were in the other. It only took them forty-five minutes to arrive at the service. There were flowers and pictures of Ryan everywhere.

They went inside and took their seats in the front row and looked at his casket. It seemed so surreal. Bridgette could not believe that Ryan was really gone. It felt so wrong that he would never hug her again, she would never hear his voice...

Bridgette sat in the front row looking at his navy casket with silver details and shook her head. This was all wrong. He was supposed to get older and expand his business, fall in love and get married, and have children.

She wanted to share their lives as friends, as family. And now his life was just abruptly over. All Bridgette felt was numb as she heard the melodic music playing low in the background and the hum of the voices discussing memories of Ryan.

Ex-girlfriends were saying how they would miss their chances to get back together with him and how he'd loved them most of all. People were gossiping about why she was considered family and in the front row. And then there were those sharks discussing his money and wondering about his will.

As if his will meant anything to anyone who knew and loved Ryan. He was a force of nature and so special. He died to protect her and their family together.

That meant more than anything he would have done with his will. She wanted to scream at those people and kick them all out of the service. But, the pastor was about to speak, followed by each member of her family.

This was about Ryan... her Ryan. And not about the petty people in the background. It just so happened that Bridgette was the last person to speak.

She stood on shaking legs and made her way to the podium. She sighed and stood straight remembering this was for Ryan. He needed her to be strong for him.

Looking out into the crowd she saw her family who were giving her looks of support. And she knew she had to do this for all of them.

"Ryan will always be larger than life to me. I met him and instantly fell in love with his handsome face, winning smile, and sense of humor. What girl wouldn't? Our love story was not a lifelong romance. And I can honestly say what we had, in the end, is eternal. It went beyond romance, beyond lust, and fell into a place of magic. We were special to each other. We were family. I know that so many people in this room know what it is like to have Ryan gaze at you and smile. But, a select few know what it was to be his family. The family he built and chose. We are all here tonight to say goodbye to him. But, Ryan will never be gone because he lives in our memories. He lives in our actions that would make him proud. Because he made us so proud to know him. Ryan was more than a label. He was someone who risked his life for me and our family. He is our hero. He is eternal and so is our love for him. You've each been given a glass... Please raise it and toast for the man with whom we love and will always remember! Your memory and legacy live on Ry. I love you."

There was not a dry eye in the house. Everyone was toasting Ryan and remembering him. She smiled softly and looked at James with tears in her eyes and went to him. He took her in his arms and held her close, kissing her hair.

The rest of the service went fine. After a few hours, everyone left and just the family was left. They would go with Ryan to his final resting place. He wanted to be buried in New York so they made it happen.

After the burial, they all went back to Devante and Cassidy's place. It was late, and they had finished some Chinese take-out when Chris and Declan said they wanted to crash on the couches. Nobody could object.

It was best to stay together. And so they all sat up in the living room telling stories about Ryan and how much they were going to miss him. It was like nothing else mattered. None of their problems existed. Just Ryan and their family.

Everyone crashed in their designated places to sleep and the house was quiet. Even baby Jackson seemed to find a night of peaceful sleep. They needed this peace. And after all, they had been through the rest. Their tears and mourning had taken a toll on them. It was like this peaceful night was a gift from Ryan. And they treasured it.

~~

Three weeks later they sat in a courtroom in Nevada. The trial was finally starting. (It has been postponed due to new evidence and Ryan's death.) James and Bridgette sat on the aisle in the front row on the prosecution's side of the courtroom.

Beside them were Cassidy and Devante and lastly Chris and Declan. They took up the entire row of seats. Each of them felt they owed it to Ryan to show up every day and stay strong to see justice served.

This was no longer about the assault that Nancy had committed. It was a united front against all of their enemies. The trial for Nancy was just the beginning.

The District Attorney was going second in presenting his case. This made everyone sit on pins and needles waiting for the Defense to plead their case. The Defense attorney table was filled with three lawyers. The lead lawyer was named Zeke Tenneson, next in line was Patricia Stevens and the last lawyer was Fredrick Olsen.

Zeke stood before the court with his expensive brown suit and said, "We are here today to find the truth. And we will be taking the time to prove to you that the truth is that my client Nancy is innocent of all charges against her. The story is simple. Two women in the workplace. One is established and experienced and the other is new with less experience and becomes jealous of a woman she sees as her rival. Then the lies begin."

Bridgette stiffened in her seat and bit her lip. James squeezed his woman's hand. They continue to listen as the defense tries to paint Bridgette out to be a vindictive and jealous woman who pinned false allegations on Nancy.

They painted James as a sex fiend who sexually harassed his employees and inspired them to fight over him. These were all words with nothing to back it up except for Nancy's eventual testimony later on in the trial. The District Attorney started to look over at them and give them comfort that he saw this coming and was prepared.

It took three days for the Defense to lay out their case but they had very little evidence aside from Nancy's word and reputation in the community. It was finally time for the Prosecution to shine! The District Attorney greeted the judge and jury warmly.

Then he started his presentation by saying "There are two kinds of people that we will explore during our time together. Some live their lives in the truth and those who cover up their misdeeds look like the first group of people. We will see both sides of the coin during our time together. The Defense wants you to believe that Nancy is an honest and upstanding citizen. But, that is not quite the entire truth. You see, since the year 1997 she has had over a dozen formal complaints written about her from employers, co-workers, and even some classmates and teachers."

He looked over at the Defense counsel and said, "Nancy and her family have tried to hide and suppress those facts from the general public. They tried to use their money and position in the community to assist them. And for a time they had been successful. However, we have copies of these documents. We will present them and speak to witnesses from these events. But, we are not here to assassinate Nancy's reputation. We simply plan to show her behavior over time.

The pattern of how she works and how her actions are then covered by those around her."

The DA then turned his attention toward Bridgette.

"We will show you that this woman sitting before you was not only attacked but harassed and brutalized by Nancy's actions. We will show you forensic information, crime scene photos, testimony from the victim and others around the assault. There is nothing but the truth and evidence here, folks. And we look forward to sharing it all with you over the coming days.", he said.

Then the DA smiled warmly at the jury and nodded to the judge and took a seat. Then he began presenting evidence to support his claims, and they were off to the races. The next week was filled with submitted evidence to the court, having experts explain what the forensic data meant, the witness testimonies that connect evidence to Nancy and create a pattern of behavior.

On the very last day of the testimonies, she is asked to take the stand. Bridgette made sure to wear her best outfit that made her look both professional and relatable. It was how she normally dressed really, but she felt like herself but more confident in it. Bridgette took the stand and was sworn in. She adjusted herself in her seat and looked to the DA and waited for him to address her.

The first thing that he asked her was her name, her date of birth and to explain her story before coming to Nevada. She told him all of the answers being careful not to address touchy subjects. He then asked her about her relationship with Ryan.

She was honest but not overly informative as the details of their relationship were not important. She made it clear they dated, became engaged, broke up but remained close friends. More like family in the end. She had been close to crying but held it in as best as she could to get through the questions.

The District Attorney then started to ask her about her relationship with Chris and Declan. She was honest about their having a relationship between them and that they parted ways as friends. More like family and they were still close.

Then he asked about her reasons for coming to Nevada and her first few days. She was honest as having it all on record can count as evidence in her case against her stalker once they catch them. The next set of questions had to do with her being hired for James' company and what her time there has been like. She explained that the first day Nancy was snide with her, but she did not feel like it was a big deal at first.

Bridgette went on to explain that she tried her best to handle Nancy's comments and threats on her own. But, after a while, she felt that she needed to involve HR to protect herself and also let them know about Nancy's behavior. In the end, she stated that she was unaware of James' plans in how he was going to handle Nancy.

All she knew was that he had requested a meeting with Nancy and HR for the Friday of that week. Then the DA had to ask about her intimate relationship with James. She explained it began as a friendship and developed into more. But, they decided not to mix business with pleasure.

They never discussed work at home, and they kept things private until the Nancy situation became out of control when James said he thought they should add the information of their relationship to HR. To protect them both professionally and establish their honesty.

The jury seemed to be understanding and the DA was proud of her honesty like she had been prepared for by her lawyers. But, at the same time, her testimony did not seem staged or rehearsed. Then it was time for the defense to cross-examine her.

Zeke stood before her and greeted Bridgette politely. She responded in kind but mentally prepared herself for him to try to rip her apart. Zeke said, "Bridgette, you said that you left New York because of a stalker. Has the police ever found this person or is there evidence of this alleged stalking?"

She explained how she discovered her stalker, the evidence collected, and that currently, it was an ongoing investigation both with the police and her private security team. Then he asked her about her relationship with Chris and Declan. He asked her if she felt having a romantic relationship with two men was morally bankrupt.

She sat up straight, looked him in the eye, and said firmly, "I have no shame in any of my relationships. Each person has to decide what makes them happy and what works for them in their life. At the time we felt that we were a good match for each other. In the end, we took different paths. I have no regrets on loving either of them or the time we spent together."

Zeke thought for a moment and then said, "Did you cheat on Ryan with those two men? He seemed very distraught after your break up and during your time with them" Bridgette sat with her hands delicately in her lap and said, "Neither Ryan nor I ever cheated on one another. We had some issues that could not be fixed within our romantic relationship so we moved on."

It did not take long for Zeke to become frustrated at her answers. So he changed tactics and said, "Is there a reason why you leap from relationship to relationship?" The implication that she is unstable and not committed to her relationships was clear.

It was also clear he was trying to slut-shame her. With a sweet and genuine smile, she said, "I have always been open and honest with the people I am in a relationship with. Before our differences were known I was going to marry Ryan. I honestly believed we would be a couple forever. After it ended I was broken and I met Chris and Decon. They helped me to heal, and we were happy while we were. Sometimes relationships are not able to work out. I am now in a committed and happy relationship. All of my relationships have been healthy and happy for as long as they lasted."

The District Attorney stepped in and objected to Zeke's questions as he tried to further slut-shame her. The judge was in the Prosecution's favor on this line of questioning.

Zeke then turned his attention to her having a romantic relationship with her boss.

She answered honestly that there were sparks between them before she started working for him. But, at the time she had to put her work before her feelings. Until everything changed between them in a way that was acceptable for them personally and professionally.

Then he asked if she was sleeping with James before or after he gave her a bump up from working in a diner to being his personal assistant. She was honest and explained that she had wanted any job she could find to survive. But, upon speaking with James he asked her about her work history.

She was honest that she used to be a personal assistant, but she could not provide evidence as she was on the run. He chose to give her a chance for which she was thankful. And quickly they found a way to make it work and everyone seemed impressed with her skills.

Her co-workers were included in that. It was at that time that Zeke said he had no further questions for her, and she could step down. Bridgette was so confused about why he asked those questions.

It seemed to work more in their favor than in the defense's favor. At least she had done her duty, was strong for Ryan's memory, and told the truth. They next called upon Nancy to take the stand.

Zeke was taking the lead and questioning her first. Nancy was dressed for the trial in much more conservative and innocent-looking clothing. The exact opposite of what she always wore to work. Which was one of the District Attorney's key pieces of evidence.

Nancy took her seat and was sworn in. Zeke asked her the same questions that the DA had asked Bridgette. She answered her name honestly and birthday. But, she embellished her experiences at work and being hired. She made it out to be like James had started flirting with her and hinting at a relationship together.

Then she went on to say that his attention was taken by a slutty new woman who he hired based on her assets. Zeke encouraged her to speak her mind, and she basically made it like James and Bridgette were cheating, and they were depraved people who broke her heart. When it was his turn the District Attorney asked if James had ever asked Nancy out.

She said, "No, but it was implied." When he questioned her on if they had ever gone out together outside of the office she could give no examples other than times where most of the staff were also invited. Then when he asked her if she had ever been kissed by James she said no but that it had been clear he wanted to.

The District Attorney said that it seemed to him she assumed a great deal and did not have an actual relationship with James. This sent Nancy off into a tantrum for the ages. She stood up and started shouting that he was a liar, that Bridgette was a dirty slut who took James from her, and that James would always belong to her.

The judge told her to control herself, or she would be held in contempt of court. Even her lawyers tried to calm her down, but she wouldn't stop until security dragged her from the courtroom kicking and screaming like a madwoman. The court was sent into a recess and after the judge said given the circumstances and since witness testimony was complete he would like to move on to closing statements next week.

Everyone agreed and they left the courtroom for the weekend. The moment that the family stepped out of the courtroom they were engulfed with attention from reporters and cameras. They said they had no comment on what happened in the courtroom.

Everyone thought because the case was being televised that it gave them the right to harass everyone involved. But, thanks to their security team they all made it safely to the car. Upon arriving at the house everyone went to change and Cassidy relieved Elise. But, I asked her to stay for dinner with them.

This has become their routine. Everyone was thrilled to be in comfortable clothes and seated around the table. Tonight they ordered pizza to spare them all the task of cooking a meal.

They filled Elise in on what happened in court, and she was flabbergasted at Nancy's behavior. It would have been comical if not for the serious subject matter.

Elise shook her head and said, "As if Mister James would be swayed by someone's beauty to the point he'd let his business suffer. No, he finds good people and gives them the chance to shine for them and the company. And he has never had eyes for anyone but our Bridgette in a very long time."

Everyone agreed and tried to enjoy their meal. Cassidy and Devante went to their suite to help clean up Jackson who wore most of his dinner on his person. They enjoyed bathing him and spending time as a little family. And they needed it after a long week in the courtroom.

Chris and Deacon went out to a bar to unwind and have some fun as a stress relief. Elise said she needed to get home and spend some time with her cat Buttons. That meant that Bridgette and James were left all alone in the living room.

They curled on the couch and avoided watching news shows. The couple decided instead to watch movies and talk all evening long. It was around midnight when James carried a sleepy Bridgette up to the bed and tucked her in.

Chapter Sixteen

The house seemed peaceful and like a sanctuary for them all. Especially, since they had fixed the damage from the night of the attack and kept things simple while they mourned and healed from everything. It was four in the morning when Chris and Decon came home.

They tried to be quiet but everyone heard them. They had a mighty nice time last night. Once they were in their rooms they quieted down and the rest of the household fell back to sleep.

The weekend passed by nicely with everyone working from home and gathering for their dinner as usual. They never took away Ryan's chair and it almost felt like his spirit was with them. The healing was a process and sometimes at night when they went to bed they felt a little afraid that a repeat attack would happen.

Sometimes they woke up and it felt like it was all a dream and Ryan would walk in any moment and tease them about something silly. In the end, the house stayed quiet and Ryan was actually gone. But, they moved forward and focused on their work, their family, and little Jackson was a balm for their hurts.

Saturday night they had a package arrive. It was more of an envelope with paperwork inside. Devante opened it and read it to everyone. Ryan had left an iron-clad will, and they wanted them to be at the reading.

The lawyer was willing to fly out to Nevada to be with them. It was as if the thought of Ryan's will tore open healing wounds, and they all went silent. Each member of the family dealt with their grief in the best way they could. Devante said he would call the man in the morning and set something up for after the trial.

Everyone nodded, and then they went about their days as normally as possible. The rest of the weekend flew by and it was Monday morning before they knew it. So, it was back to Elise coming to care for Jackson.

And the entire family getting in their best clothes for the trial. Another day in court where this time it would be the Defense rests its case. Then the DA would rest his case, and they would wait to hear back from the jury. The last few weeks had been tough on them but there was an ending in sight.

The hope is that the jury will see their side of things and favor Nancy for the pain and suffering she has caused so many people. Especially the pain and suffering she caused both James and Bridgette. But, you never knew with a mixed jury who would see things in what way.

The best they could do was to trust the truth, the evidence, and the District Attorney. The Defense harps on about how unfortunate it is that people would ever paint Nancy in a negative light. Her wealthy family gives to charities, they hold fundraisers and balls, they have an upstanding reputation in their community.

Why would she ever lie or go to such lengths? He even tries to tear apart the evidence against her which spans well over a decade. The lawyers for the Defense end up sounding just as mad as their client did in court after her testimony.

The District Attorney presents a solid conclusion to his case. He has evidence, he has a testimony, and he has common sense to bring it all together. He reminds the jury that they are not there to villainize Nancy.

They are there to see justice done for the crimes committed. It was time to wait for the verdict to come in. The jury was now in their special room debating over evidence and what they would decide.

Everyone kept their phones on as they sat in the living room at home waiting. Nobody was out of their court clothes just in case they needed to rush down to the courthouse. They would continue to live as if they were on call to the court until the verdict was read in front of them.

Jackson proved to be a welcome distraction as everyone played with him and showered him with love. It helped them to move forward and not live on pins and needles. It would take three days for the jury to conclude.

The call came in around noon on the fourth day. Everyone scrambled to the courthouse. Elise stayed with Jackson as she was now his full-time Nanny.

James had hired someone else he trusted to run his diner. All was well with their little world so far. The hope was that the verdict would come in and give them the justice they craved.

Arriving at the courthouse each member of the family was harassed by the press as they made their way inside as a unit. Once inside they took their seats and waited for the judge to come in and the jury. After everyone was settled into their seats the judge asked if the jury had reached a verdict.

Their spokesperson said yes. The judge was given the verdict and accepted it. Then the spokesperson stood and said, "We the jury find the defendant guilty of all charges."

There were gasps and a scream from the courtroom but for Bridgette, it was as if time had stood still. Justice was being served after all they had been through. Her physical body was back to normal but her mental health and emotional health had suffered far worse. And now it was on public record she told the truth, and she deserved justice.

Meanwhile, on the other side of the courtroom, Nancy was throwing a fit and screaming that her Daddy was going to hurt them. She was livid and said that this was bullshit, and she would never see jail time. The judge told her to be quiet for she would be sent a hefty fine in addition to her jail time. But, she kept on screaming until security took her away to her jail cell.

The judge said the following day he would hold the hearing to discuss her sentence in full. The family decided to have take-out come to the house and stay in their pajamas and celebrate this step in the process. The delivery man came with their Indian food and everyone tucked in and enjoyed the meal together.

Then they toasted with a bottle of champagne from Ryan's collection that he left them. Devante said, "Once the sentencing is done we can meet with that lawyer. Then we can move on to the second trial in a few months."

Everyone was quiet and then Bridgette said, "Ryan would want his final wishes carried out. So, we will make sure that it all works out for the best." There were many nods of agreement and a sense of sadness followed.

It would have been so much better to celebrate with Ryan than having to remember him. At the same time, Devante raised his glass and said, "To justice and to Ryan!" Everyone repeated his words and toasted.

The next day they were back in court and Nancy seemed sedated. The judge looked at her firmly and said, "It seems from the evidence presented that you are used to getting your way. You are used to doing misdeeds and allowing others to cover for you. But, a jury of your peers have found you guilty and now it is time to accept the consequences of your actions. Under the law and based on your crimes the highest sentence I can give you is twenty years in prison. And that is exactly what I am sentencing you to. I hereby sentence you to twenty years in prison for the crimes you've been found guilty of."

Nancy looked half asleep. Her lawyers looked like tops about to explode with rage. And Nancy's parents looked angry and vengeful.

The judge looked directly at all of them and said, "And nobody should become vigilantes over this verdict. If you do, you will end up in court and will suffer a fate similar to Nancy's. Then he dismissed the court, closed the case, and wished everyone well.

Nancy's trial was finally over! And they had gotten some justice. But, the storms were not over, and they weren't in the clear yet. They still had the appointment with the lawyer and Richard's trial ahead of them.

~~

A week passed since the trial for Nancy ended. Bridgette and Devante were in the kitchen sipping on some coffee. It was an hour until they were due to meet with the lawyer at James' offices.

James was in the shower and Cassidy was fussing over her son and getting him dressed. Elise was just arriving and Chris let her in. Decon was reading in the living room waiting for the time to pass for them to leave.

The time seemed to fly by as everyone finished their breakfast. Then they touched up their looks and everyone was ready to get into the car to drive to the lawyer meeting. The SUV fit everyone because it had a third seat in the back. James drove and security followed behind them.

As they pulled into the parking garage of James' offices the security team went first to ensure it was safe. Then James and Bridgette led the way into the offices. The staff were all there working hard but happily greeted them all.

James led the way into the conference room and asked if anyone wanted coffee or something else to drink. The lawyer asked for a coffee with creamer and sugar. Then once he was sorted everyone took their seats and were ready to hear the lawyer out.

The lawyer stood before them and said, "I met Ryan when he was in his teens. He was an ambitious young man and asked me for some legal advice on starting his own company. We became fast friends and I always handled the legal side of his affairs for the most part. His personal ones especially and sometimes he would ask me to consult on his business affairs. A little while after his greatest mistake in life, letting Miss Bridgette go, he came to me and wanted to update his will. I told him he may want to wait until he was less emotional and more level-headed."

Then the man took a sip of his coffee and carried on.

"In the end, he decided to move forward with the changes. He wanted it made clear that Devante continues with the business and running the day-to-day. He wanted it ironclad that his friend was the owner of the company and continued their dream. He wanted his half of the shares to go to Miss Bridgette. That way she would always be taken care of and had a part of the family business to herself. He wanted her to also have 90% of his personal wealth and belongings. The other 10% would go to his estranged brother Rory in the hopes that he would carry on their family name and make something of himself, for himself."

At the looks of confusion on their faces, he said, "Rory has not been in Ryan's life for many years now. They have been estranged since just after I met Ryan. On and off they had spoken but never for long or with a good outcome. Rory has some issues he needs to deal with and Ryan wouldn't let him in unless he handled them."

Bridgette sat up and said, "Why would Ryan leave me so much? We were estranged at the time. And wouldn't he have fixed it once I left, and we'd both moved forward?"

The man smiled kindly and said, "Ryan told me in no uncertain terms every step of the way during that period it was what his wishes were. And that he could not die without knowing that it was ironclad."

There was one final thing the lawyer needed to say, and he pulled out his briefcase and opened it. Inside he found envelopes with each person's name on them. Even James. He placed them on the table and said, "These are Ryan's letters to each of you. He wanted you to have them in the event of his death. I know nothing about the contents inside them. That is between you and Ryan."

Each member of the family picked up their letter and tucked it away. The only one who couldn't was Bridgette who held it to her chest. The envelope even smelled of Ryan's aftershave, and she felt tears run down her face at the scent.

The lawyer patted her hand and then said his goodbyes and left to return to his hotel. He would go back to New York in the morning. James helped Bridgette up and held her close as they walked to the car. No words were needed as they got into the car.

The drive back to the house was very quiet. Once the family arrived at their home everyone went to their rooms. Devante sat down in the chair beside the window in the bedroom she shared with Cassidy and looked at the letter.

Before he could focus on it fully his wife was by his side and placed a glass of scotch in his hand. She kissed his cheek and said, "I figured that you would need this. I'll give you the privacy to read your letter. I'm taking Jackson to the living room to play while I make dinner. Elise is helping me make a new dish!"

He smiled and kissed her softly before watching her leave. The moment that the door clicked shut he sighed. It was time to read the letter from Ryan.

As he broke the seal and the scent of his friend invaded his space he closed his eyes. It was almost like Ryan was beside him. Opening the letter he started to read.

"Dear Devante,

If you are reading this letter that means I didn't survive the storms that are circling around all of us. I've decided to be prepared for anything ever since we arrived in Nevada. My girl has moved on and found her bliss. And I am so happy for her because she deserves to be loved the way that she needs to be. I'm still hurting because her "happily ever after" is with someone else. At the same time, I support and love her. Always.

That is something I need your help with. I am leaving her my shares of our business and 90% of my assets. I'm leaving her most of my things. I want you to have all my bachelor pad stuff. The childhood stuff should go to my brother Rory. But, everything else is Bridgette's to do as she pleases. You probably know all of these things already. But, I want you to help her with her side of the business and her finances.

I won't be there to help her through this and I hope that you will see her through the business side of things. I also hope that you will help her with the loss of me. This is going to break part of her spirit because my girl feels so deeply. She is going to second guess everything she ever said to be both good and bad. I need you to let her know that it is all okay. She was honest at the moment and I have no regrets.

We are all a family and she and I are so much more now than we ever were before. I need her to realize my love for her is eternal and that you'll all move on.

As for me... please take care of yourself. There is no room for regrets, my friend. Everything was good between us in our relationship, man. Our friendship was more of a brotherhood. We are the best of friends and always will be. There is nobody I trust more to keep our legacy moving forward and with our shared vision for the business. I want Jackson to be proud of us both and all we created.

Please take care of your little family. Make sure that Cassie and Jackson know how much I loved them. And if you add to that family of yours I expect you to tell those kids how much uncle Ryan rocked! If you don't I swear I will haunt your ass, man.

I love you. I know men don't often share those words with one other. But, it is how I feel. I would never have been happy in this life without you by my side, brother. You were and always will be more of a brother to me than even Rory. I appreciate that more than my words can say. Try not to miss me too much okay? But, smile when I come up and keep our stories alive with the kids. I know it is a big ask but look after Bridgette and her family. I know that she has James, and he is a great guy. But, she will always need family by her side. Be the brother to her that you always have been for me. And although I like James and accept him into our family... keep an eye out on him! Don't fail to give him shit. And remember I'm always with you all, every step of the way!

Goodbye, for now, bro! See you on the flip side!

~Ry

PS- There better be some hot chicks up in heaven! I think I at least deserve some female attention for all I've been through. Think of me on a cloud with a cocktail and a babe on my arm. Just don't tell the girls that. ;)"

Devante could not help the tears that began to fall as he finished the letter. It was as if Ryan had spoken the words to him. He broke down and cried as if the news were fresh of his passing.

He felt the sense of loss more strongly than he ever had before. Ryan was really gone and he'd left him a letter to help him cope. But, it only made him miss him more.

It wasn't fair that his brother was killed over this insane woman's bullshit. The things driving Devante forward now were his strong need for justice for Ryan and his promise to keep Ryan's memory alive. Their business was thriving and the expansion to Nevada was coming together like a dream. And yet all he wanted was his friend back.

He would give anything for the chance to go back and save Ryan's life. With a heavy heart and a sigh, he stood up and stretched his legs. He placed the letter in the desk drawer with his other personal items. And then went to find his wife.

She was always a balm to his soul even on the most difficult of days. She was his soul mate in every sense of the word. As he descended the stairs he saw Cassidy holding their son. She was whispering softly into his ear.

Somehow he just knew she was telling him about his uncle Ryan for which he got his middle name. As he joined his family and held them close his wife met his eyes. The love he found there went beyond words and he was so thankful for her being in his life.

Cassidy handed their son to her husband and stood stretching. She asked him if he would be okay watching the baby while she went upstairs for some privacy. Devante knew instantly that she wanted a chance to read her own letter from Ryan.

He nodded his emotions creating a lump in his throat. She leaned down and kissed her husband on the lips softly and went to their room. Taking a seat on the bed Cassidy opened the letter from Ryan and began to read...

"Dear Cassie,

Well, if you are reading this I've passed away somehow. I always had a feeling that I would die young. I just had no idea it would be so soon. I had hoped to meet the woman of my dreams and have a family before that happened. But, life is a funny thing. I met the woman of my dreams and found out I am not the man of hers.

I have no ill will toward Bridgette. I will love her for eternity in a way that goes beyond lovers. She feels it for me, too. We are more. That is why I need you to be there for her. Remind her how much I loved her and how at peace I am with how it turned out. Despite the hurt that I feel. That is all on me and nothing she needs to feel bad about.

I approve of James. I think that he is everything she needs and I want her to move forward. I'll be there with her every step of the way as her own personal cheering section. Although, please spare us all and don't imagine me in a cheerleader uniform!

Devante is and always will be my brother. I love him in a way I never thought I could love someone. And then there he was. The brother I never had (even in my brother) and always wanted. I cherish my time with him and all of our memories. He is going to need you now more than ever before. Losing me is going to be hard on him. Please let him know that I love him and will always be there for him. Even now. I'm looking down on you all.

Please tell Jackson about his uncle Ryan. Keep my memory alive in our family that way. And with any other little ones that may come along. I suspect you will add to your family over time. Watch over the next generation in the way only you can, Cassie.

There was never a woman more suited for my brother than you are. You are so special and beautiful inside and out. I love you as if you were my sister. I am going to miss out on so many things but I want you all to live fully and in my own way I will be there with you.

Be brave, love as fiercely as you always have, and don't be afraid to move forward. I'll be here in your memories. Keep that

*man of yours on track so he keeps our legacy
alive and running and so your children can
after we are all gone.*

I love you, Sis.

*Love,
Ryan*

*PS- Maybe keep some of those stories about
me for when Jackson is a bit older okay? I've
been a bad boy! -winks-"*

Tears were streaming down her face as she read the letter and after she finished it she pulled out her tissues. It took her a solid five minutes to compose herself. The letter made it all feel so fresh and real.

It was so final now that Ryan was gone from her life. And yet his sense of humor and love radiated from the page and into her heart. After Cassidy got herself together she went downstairs to help Elise finish dinner.

Elise being the kind woman she is, opened her arms for Cassidy the moment she saw her. They embraced and Elise rubbed her back and said, "Your Ryan was a wonderful person. I know you are all in a world of pain. But, it will become more manageable with time. And he is alive within your memories of him."

Cassidy smiled and nodded before drying her tears and jumping into their tasks in the kitchen. Meanwhile, down the hall sitting on his bed, Chris opened up his letter from Ryan and wondered what he would say to him.

They had gone from friends to enemies and landed on being family. The second he pulled the letter from the envelope he wanted to put it back. It felt too hard to read the letter.

This kind of pain was something that Chris was not used to feeling. It felt worse than their broken friendship had ever felt. This was so final.

But, taking a deep breath he opened the letter and started to read it...

"Dear Chris,

We have been through so much in the time we have known each other. We've been good friends, enemies and now here we are as brothers. I never would have guessed it would take the mutual love of a woman to bring us back together. Then again... she is not just any woman. Bridgette is the kind of woman that can build bridges nobody else would think of building. She can bring hearts together as easily as she can bring minds together. She is in a word... a miracle.

I'm not thrilled you slept with the love of my life. I'm a man after all and I hate the idea of her with anyone else. But, I accept it without anger because I know she needs you and Declan. I broke her spirit, and she needed you both to help bring her back to herself. And for that, I will be forever thankful to you both.

I am even thankful to James for being the love of her life. He gives to her all of the things I always wished that I could and never quite could provide. She and I have something now that transcends being lovers. It is eternal. However, since if you are reading this I am no longer able to look out for her and be there for her I need you to promise that you will.

Be her brother and care for her in how a brother would. Help her get past my death, celebrate her wedding day, be there when her children are born and whatever else comes her way. I know this is a lot to ask but I trust my brothers to see this through for me.

Chris, forgive yourself for what happened between us. I have forgiven you and feel like our slate is clean. I love you, man. I will always be with you in your memories and in a more spiritual sense. Not to get all mushy on you. Just want you to know I will always have your back.

Be good to yourself, thrive in business, and find the love of yours and Declan's life! Go get that girl and love her fully. And never let stupidity keep you three apart. Learn from my mistakes and love as deeply as I have loved Bridgette. I have no regrets there.

Keep my memory alive by telling the next generation stories about me. But, keep it age-appropriate for where they are at. I had some wild times and need them to be adults before that gets out!

See you on the flip side, brother!

~Ry"

Chris could not help the tears that came to his eyes as he read the letter. Ryan was open and honest with him about everything. It felt like he had been chatting with him over a beer like old times more than him saying his final goodbye. And yet that is what this letter was.

This was his way of saying a final goodbye. After taking a few minutes to compose himself Chris decided to take a shower. That was when he heard Decon go into his room in their suite.

He knew that his friend would be opening his own letter and having a personal moment with Ryan as he had. The final goodbye to their friendship and the start of something different.

~~Sometime later...~~

Decon sat down on a chair in the corner of his bedroom and opened the envelope. It smelled like Ryan and that made it almost easier to open the letter. It was like Ryan was visiting with him one last time.

This was something Decon hadn't realized that he needed all along. The letter was in his hands as he started to read...

"Dear Dec,

> *I suppose if you are reading this I'm dead. That really sucks! I was hoping we would have a bonfire with just the dudes. I wanted us to chill like we used to and catch up. We have become brothers and it was high time we celebrated that. But, instead, you have had to sit through my death, my funeral, and the fall out from my life being over. That is a total bummer, man.*

> *I wish I could have sat down with you and told you just how much you mean to me. I wish I could have done it with Chris too. I love you both as brothers and valued our time together. It sucks it took you doing what I couldn't do with my girl for it to happen though. Yes, yes... she is with James and I accept it and him. I will always see her as my girl.*

Bridgette is our miracle, bro. I know you are still in love with her and feel the same hurt that I do over how things have turned out. She is a once-in-a-lifetime girl and that makes losing her all the more tragic. But, we were not her happy ending. She has found that, and we need to be happy for her.

I know this sounds crazy and impossible but someday you and Chris are going to find the woman meant for you. Maybe I'll send her your way! ;) That would be sweet! Anyway... you will meet her and you will feel complete in the same way that Bridgette does with James. Life will go on with time and healing. I promise.

On that note, I need you to be a brother to my girl. Be there through all of the ups and downs that life throws her way. Yes, even losing me. This is the time for you all to bond as a family. Yes, even James. Try not to be too hard on him. He is new to all of us and it is a lot to take on. Bridgette is his happily ever after and he deserves that.

Also, when the time comes for you and Chris to become parents... please keep my memory alive with your kids. Tell your love about me too! Make me a part of your family for all the days of your lives just as you were for mine. I'll always be your

*brother in heaven. And we will be together
again someday... but make it a long long
time from now, dude. You have a lot of shit
to do still.*

I love you, dude.

~Ry"

Decon laughed, cried, and ended up feeling peaceful after reading the letter from Ryan. He felt hope for the first time since Ryan had died. There was the peace that everything would be okay and a sense of hope for their futures.

Someday, they would think about Ryan and laugh at his silliness and keep his tired jokes alive for the next generation. Ryan was gone from this world, and yet he lived on through them. Decon changed clothes and started to go downstairs.

Dinner was starting to smell good, and he wanted to help set the table. He was a member of this family and would help out where he could. Plus, as promised he needed to find it in his heart to let James in. He needed to accept him and his relationship with Bridgette for all of their happiness.

James and Bridgette decided that they would read their letters privately and sometime after dinner. Instead, they sat in the living room with Devante and Chris as they played with Jackson. It felt good to be surrounded by family and feel a sense of calm.

One of the two trials they faced was over, and they had won. There was hope that they would win the second and that they could all find peace and move forward.

Chapter Seventeen

It was around midnight when Cassidy and Devante called it a night. Before Elise had left for the day she put Jackson to bed so the adults could sit and talk by the fireplace. About forty minutes later Chris and Decon called it a night.

It seemed like they were eager to go to their suite and discuss their letters from Ryan. Bridgette turned to James and said, "Why don't I take a warm bubble bath and you can get into bed and finish that novel you started?"

James smiled and agreed that was a good idea. He helped Bridgette set up her bubble bath complete with vanilla-scented candles. Then he left her to her privacy and went to the bedroom.

At that moment James decided that he would rather read his letter from Ryan. So, he pulled the envelope out and opened it. Taking the letter into his hands he began to read...

"Dear James,

We are family and yet very new to each other. It may puzzle you as to why you get a letter from me in the event of my death. But, for me, this is a no-brainer, man.

The love of my life has been Bridgette. She will always be the love of my life. The way I feel about her is absolute and timeless. It is eternal. It goes beyond lovers. We are family and always will be. And as her happily ever after you are a part of that family. I want you to know that I accept your place in her heart and her life. I accept you in our family.

I know you don't need that from me. You would be here no matter what because you are hers. Our girl would have nothing different. But, she is also yours and that leaves you with a hefty responsibility. You need to take care of her and make her happy for the rest of her life. That means marriage,

298

*children, and the entire bit. You are now
her everything. Do not let her down or help
me. I will come down to earth and drag you
into hell.*

*That being said, she has three brothers
in our family who have been instructed to
accept you, keep an eye on you, and make
sure you do your job with her. So, you are
most welcome to set that up, pal! :)*

*I also want to thank you. Thank you
for being the man that Bridgette always
wanted and needed. I would be a liar if I
said I didn't wish it were me. But, if it had
to be anyone else I would have wanted it to
be you.*

*Just please be understanding as she
grieves my loss, tell her we were beyond good
and she has nothing to feel sorry for, and
for the love of all that is holy please tell the
next generation about me. Keep me alive in
the memories. Her children deserve to know
about uncle Ryan. Your children do.*

*You were becoming my brother as I
wrote this. And I am proud to say we knew
each other. My heart may hurt because I
am not the man for her. But, it is also full
because you are.*

*Until we meet again... and probably
fight over her...*

~Ryan"

James was a little shocked at the way he felt reading the letter. He never felt so accepted, so sad over the loss of someone or so determined to keep those promises to Ryan. It was a new set of emotions he had not been expecting to feel from the letter. And yet there he was.

Quickly he tucked the letter away and went back to his novel. The last thing he wanted was Bridgette to come out and see him emotional or his letter from Ryan. It was special between the two men. And it would stay that way.

~~

Meanwhile, in the bathroom, Bridgette was taking off her clothes and sighed happily as she sunk into the warm water and bubbles. The scent from the candles helped her feel more relaxed. She closed her eyes and bit her lip.

The last thing she wanted was to read Ryan's letter. It felt like the second she read it this nightmare would become real. At the same time, she knew that she had to take that step to move on with her life.

But, a life without Ryan felt so incomplete and broken. How would she ever really move on without him by her side? He was her person in so many ways.

They relied on each other and needed one another in ways that defied a label. It was simply eternal. That word kept coming to her mind whenever she thought of him. Taking a deep breath and holding the letter to her chest she took in Ryan's scent one last time.

Then she tore open the letter to read it…

"My Beloved Bridgette,

You are and will always be the love of my life. You are my miracle girl. My girl. And you always will be. I have no regrets about our life, loving you, or the place you hold in my life/heart. There is nothing at all for you to feel down about. You should remember our life together with great happiness and love.

This letter has been the hardest to write. It is the last one that I am working on. I hate that my writing means that I am no longer with you. I need you to know that leaving you wasn't my choice and I tried as hard as I could to stay with you. We are eternal. No label or boundary applies to us. We are family.

I need you to know that I accept James in your life. I think that you have chosen a great person to share your life with. He is a part of our family now and I couldn't be happier. This means that you both have something special. I know for a fact that where I am I'll always keep my eyes on you. I'll always be there when you need me or want me there. Just close your eyes and I'm there, baby.

You'll be able to share your worst and best moments in your life. I will be right by your side when you and James get married. I will be there when your babies are born. I will be there for every precious moment.

Thank you so much for always loving me. It was the most worthwhile time in my life. I have never been happier than I have been with you. Please keep my memory alive in the memories you share with your family moving forward.

Now the harder parts... My brother Rory and I have been estranged for a very long time now. But, I am leaving him a portion of my things (childhood stuff) and a part of my assets. I want him to have a chance to get his shit together and make a fresh start for himself. If he fails to do that and needs help, give it to him. But, have James help you decide. My brother is not very responsible and can be manipulative. Don't let him steamroll right over you.

I hate writing this letter to you. Each word is the truth, but I am crying as I write it. I hate thinking of leaving you behind. I wanted you to be in my life for all of it and I am so thankful you were with me for the rest of it. I know you held my hand as I died. I know you never left me. I am so sorry that I left you, baby. It wasn't my choice.

If I could change it somehow I would. I would give anything to be with you and for you. Please try not to miss me. Know why, baby? I am always with you no matter what. No need to miss me.

Someday when you join me in heaven... I'll fight James for my turn to be with you again! ;) He and I both know it will be a showdown on a cloud. I'd really love that chance with you. But, more than anything I'd like the chance to see your smiling face. So, smile for me sweet girl. Love with all of your heart. Keep me close to you always. And make beautiful babies!

See you when it is time... but make sure to be an old lady when that happens. The world can only handle losing one of us this early. And keep your brothers close okay? Especially Devante...

I love you with all my heart and soul!

Love Always,
Ry"

Tears were racing down her face all through the letter. She knew this was her final goodbye with Ryan. At the same time, she felt a sense of peace like he was with her.

There was a smile on her face and a sparkle in her eye. Bridgette took a long time in which to relax and enjoy her luxurious bath. She remembered a time when she shared a bath like this with Ryan and how much fun they had splashing each other until they ended up making love.

It was like magic and she almost felt like she was with him at that moment again. There was a lovely warm feeling in her soul when she remembered Ryan. It made him feel alive to her in a special way.

Bridgette stood up and got out of the tub being careful to step on the mat. She dried off with her towel and placed a pretty white robe around her body. James looked up at her with love and understanding in his eyes as she came to their bed.

"I love you, James. I will always love him too. I will always miss him. But, our future is our own, and we will live it to the fullest.", she said. James smiled at her and patted the bed for her to get under the covers with him.

He set down his book and turned to take her into his arms. Their kiss was soft and then became more passionate. Reluctantly James pulled away from the kiss and kissed his woman's forehead.

The love in Bridgette's eyes for him set James' heart alight with happiness. There was never any doubt that they would move forward as a couple. But, at that moment he realized that she was his soulmate.

The plan to marry her felt even more special and important. They settled in for the night. Bridgette has dreams of Ryan and her happy memories of their time together. James had dreams of Bridgette and how their life could be. It felt like Ryan was guiding them forward and James was so thankful to him that he gave them his blessing.

~~

The next few months moved by fairly quickly. The security team kept them safe. Chris and Declan had completed the transition of expanding their business to Nevada. They had proper offices and made new contacts in the area.

Their offices in New York were running smoothly. The next thing on their list was to find their place. That way they could start keeping an eye out for the love of their life.

Devante had completed his set up of his expansion to the area before the guys. The business back in New York was thriving and the expansion was also doing very well. He was working hard to make Ryan proud of their business.

He even renamed it in Ryan and His honor. It was their joint creation and would always be. Cassidy was starting to look at homes in Nevada for them. They decided to have homes in both states.

This way they could return to New York when business came to them. The house in Nevada would be their home base. They wanted a place of their own to raise their family.

Once the second trial was over they wanted to move to a new place. Also, they wanted to expand their family. James and Bridgette returned to the office and have been getting back into their routine.

Their business was thriving and the replacement for Nancy was a joy to have on staff. As a couple, they were also thriving. James wanted to talk to her about their future in a few days.

He decided that he wanted her to walk into the courtroom with his ring on her finger. It was time to move forward and heal. Everyone promised to be around the table for dinner. It was an important time in their lives.

Each member of the family was moving forward in their own way. Once they were all seated at the table Chris said, "Decon and I are really glad we expanded our business to be here in Nevada. It is going better than we expected it to. There is a condo across town we are thinking of buying. This way we won't cramp your style. We know this will always be our home. But, we need to stretch out for our future."

Bridgette beamed at them and said, "I want you to look at the things in Ryan's place and take something for your new pad. This way a part of him will always be with you both in your home."

The men were choked up but nodded. Devante beamed at the idea and said, "We should all do that! It will be an amazing way to keep his legacy alive."

Cassidy perked up and said, "We are looking at houses to help expand our family. But, we feel the same way about this house. It will always be our home. We will visit often. In addition to the new house, we are keeping our place in New York too. We are so blessed to have the ability to have successful businesses and warm and welcoming homes."

It took only a moment for Bridgette to look at her friend and say, "And with the new house you will be able to expand your family!" Cassidy grinned and said, "It is on our mind. But, we want to get settled and have the trial behind us." Everyone nodded and continued to talk about their futures.

The meal was delightful and they were all feeling confident moving forward with the trial against Richard. This case was going to take the hardest toll on them all. This was the man who ordered their home to be attacked, the man who caused Ryan's death, and the man who tried to destroy them.

At the same time, they had the District Attorney's support and a ton of evidence to help prove their case. After their meal, everyone decided to turn in early and lay out their clothes for the next morning. The trial was set to start and it was going to be a long climb to reach success. Everyone wanted to be at their best to face the road ahead of them.

~~

Sunlight was creeping into their bedroom when Bridgette woke up and stretched her arms. James was seated beside her watching her with a smile on his face.

He looked deeply into her eyes and said, "My life was empty and cold before you stepped into it. You have given me sunshine and love beyond measure. I can't imagine spending a day without you by my side. This relationship is for the rest of my life. Will you be my wife? I love you, Bridgette."

The look of love and shock on both her face and in her eyes told James all he needed to know. He grinned and waited for her to say something. She looked deeply into his eyes and said, "Yes, I will marry you!"

She pounced him with a warm hug and a deep soul-stirring kiss. He took the ring he had purchased for her long ago and slipped it on her finger. She grinned at the beautiful marquis-shaped diamond ring. It was perfect for her.

They kissed and cuddled some more in bed. Then they each went to their spaces in the closet and took out their clothes for court. They admired each other as they dressed. Then they kissed a little more on their way downstairs for breakfast and coffee.

The rest of their family had gathered downstairs already. Bridgette walked in and said excitedly, "We are engaged!" Cassidy jumped up out of her chair and squealed!

NEEDING TOMORROW

She was so happy for her best friend. Devante and the fellas all looked at James giving him the stern brother's face. Elise started to cry with happiness. And Jackson was enjoying his breakfast and did not care at all about the announcement.

All in all, congratulations were shared and everyone had some happiness to bring with them to the courtroom. The ride to the courthouse was short and they were escorted into the building with minimal fuss since they arrived so early. They filed into their row with Chris first, Decon next, Devante and Cassidy beside them, and lastly Bridgette and James on the aisle.

The judge took his seat and the jury followed. The Defense were the same lawyers as Nancy had in her trial. Richard was wearing an expensive pinstriped suit.

The District Attorney was prepared and ready for the trial to begin. Everyone was prepared for the legal battle to begin. The Defense was starting to present their case to the jury.

Zeke stood up and began his opening statement. "This case is about the truth. We are all presenting evidence to try to expose the truth. We will prove to you that Richard is a good person, an upstanding person, and a family man. The prosecution will try to convince you that this man sitting before you has committed terrible crimes, hired men to commit terrible crimes and that he has harassed an entire family. But, in the end, the truth will see the light of day."

Moving with confidence Zeke took his seat and looked smug as he glanced over toward Bridgette and James. James

309

took his fiance's hand and kissed it making sure her ring was seen by everyone. They were a united front and nothing and nobody was going to ruin their happiness or future. The District Attorney stood and greeted the jury with a kind smile.

"It is honestly what was said in the Defense's opening statement when the truth and the search for the truth was mentioned. At the same time, we have differing views on what the truth really is. We have evidence, expert, and witness testimony to prove that Richard is accountable for his actions and crimes. We will show you that the man was not how he carved his image. This man before you is someone who went above and beyond for his daughter with no boundaries. He could have been helping his daughter. But, instead, he went against the law to cover her crimes and his own. This is not to demonetize him. This is to show that he was responsible for his actions and needs to be punished for them. Justice needs to be served."

After giving Bridgette and James a nod the DA took his seat. The judge explained to the jury that they would start with the Defense providing evidence and testimony later in the day. And that they would spend the next three to four days showcasing their side of things.

Chapter Eighteen

The Defense was presenting their case by trying to convince the jury that an honest man was being accused of false allegations. They had friends and business partners of Richard's on the stand. Everyone seemed to paint a picture of an upstanding man and citizen.

There was very little evidence to show their case. This went on for several days. As they sat there and waited through the testimony everyone had to work hard to keep their faces blank. There were times when they all wanted to roll their eyes and laugh at how absurd the descriptions of Richard were.

In the end, they all kept their cool and moved forward with the trial. On the last day of the week, the Prosecution were able to present their case for the first time. They would have time to go into the next week as well.

But, that first day they presented a great deal of forensic evidence from the crime scene from the attack on the family home. They presented computer evidence from several hired goons that lead back to Richard. At the same time, they presented experts that have discussed the evidence in detail.

The DA spent time asking questions so that it all made sense to the jury. They took apart each piece of evidence part by part. It was going to take into next week to be able to get all of the evidence sorted through since there was so much. At least they were off to a solid start.

~~

The weekend passed by without anything major happening. The family passed the time catching up on work that they fell behind on during the week. Sunday night they all tried to unwind for another week of the trial.

~~

Monday morning each member of the family met down in the kitchen for breakfast. After they finished their meal everyone put the finishing touches on their clothes for court. Then they made their way to the car for their ride to the courthouse.

As they pulled up to the courthouse they noticed the press were gathered and ready by the time they showed up. The press were in front of the building in force and security had to help each member through the crowd to get inside the courthouse. Everyone took their seats and prepared for the DA to continue with presenting the case.

All of Monday was presenting more evidence and having experts explain it. The Defense did not question or object to any of those items. Bridgette and James held hands during the entire day of evidence. Devante and Cassidy did the same. They kept their mouths shut and their faces blank.

Tuesday they finished presenting more evidence to the jury. The next day was filled with evidence from Nancy's trial and why it was relevant to this trial. The defense just sat there through it all and said not a word.

Thursday they started with witness testimony. It took them until the end of Friday to get to Decon and Chris' testimony. They were questioned on their work in security and the information they uncovered and how they found it.

They were also asked about their previous experience testifying in other cases. (Without details of those cases.) It was late afternoon on Friday when Devante was asked to take the stand. The District Attorney wanted to hear Devante's story of the attack at the house, his role in the events, and about Ryan's shooting and the experience of losing him to violence like that.

The testimony was honest and raw and the jury seemed to be moved. The defense did not want to cross-examine anyone that testified. It was scheduled that Monday morning James and Bridgette would take the stand.

~~

The weekend went well as Declan and Chris announced that they found the perfect condo and purchased it. They would move in after the trial and expected everyone to help them move in. Everyone readily agreed. Then everyone caught up on some work and of course, had their family dinner times.

~~

Monday morning the family made their way through the press to get inside the courthouse. They were shocked by how many outlets seemed interested in this trial. There were easily more people than were at Nancy's trial.

They all took their seats and waited for the court session to begin. James was called to the stand first and was sworn in. The DA asked him about the attack on the house. James was asked about how he and Ryan conducted themselves during the attack.

He was asked about once they realized Ryan had been shot and what happened after. The detail in which he shared the events of that night made everyone stiffen and feel emotional. It was as if everyone were reliving it or living it for the first time.

The DA went on to ask him about the attack in the parking garage and what happened after that. There was no detail that he had forgotten or missed out on sharing. At the end of his testimony, there was a clear picture of Richard's misdeeds.

It was not until later when they had Bridgette on the stand that it all came together. She explained the events of the attack on the parking garage that took the life of their driver. The next line of questioning was about the night that Ryan was killed.

She told things from her perspective. The moments when she discussed Ryan bleeding out in front of her, the ride to the hospital, and his death she fell apart. They took a moment to have her blow her nose and compose herself.

The moment that Bridgette completed her testimony they decided to take a break for the day and would reconvene the next day for the defense to present their final statement. The day after it would be the prosecution would provide their closing statement.

The rest of the week went exactly as a normal trial would. The defense said their peace and then the prosecution went ahead and said theirs. The jury was then tasked with choosing if Richard was guilty of the crimes presented or if he was innocent.

Everyone was on pins and needles waiting for the jury to come back with their verdict. The family stayed close to each other and focused on Jackson and each other while they waited. It was on Friday afternoon around lunch when they were called back to the courthouse for the verdict.

The moment that everyone was settled into the courtroom the judge looked at the verdict. Then the spokesperson for the jury read the verdict to the court.

"We the jury find the defendant guilty of all charges against him including but not limited to the murder for hire." The entire room erupted. The press went crazy, Richard shot up and screamed bullshit and then his lawyers looked red and upset.

The family looked at each other and nodded. They stayed cool until they got home. The judge asked for order in his court and said that Monday morning he would sentence Richard.

He thanked the jury for their service. Then he dismissed the room. Richard screamed threats to the family as they left. But, none of them paid him any mind.

They wanted to go home and let their emotions out. The family thanked the DA and then shuffled into the car to go to the house. The fight to get around the press was difficult but their security did a great job.

The second the door closed in the car they all cheered. They have finally gotten justice for Ryan. Each member of the family shuffled into the house.

They opened Ryan's favorite wine and toasted him. Devante said, "We did it, Ry. They found him guilty and his henchman too. They are going to pay for what they did to you." Bridgette burst into tears and said, "Ryan is finally free to move on." James took her into his arms and held her close.

Everyone shed some tears and then they all went to start dinner. After their family dinner, everyone went to their own rooms to unwind. The last thing left was to be there for the sentencing of Richard.

Then they would move Chris and Declan into their condo. They would then move forward with all of their plans and goals. Bridgette wanted them to start looking for Rory once the trial is all over. This way they can explain that they got justice for Ryan.

~~

The weekend went really well. Everyone went back to their routine of working from home and catching up. Then they also shared meals and had a good time as a family unit. They planned BBQs and family events throughout the next few months.

Cassidy made sure to get some alone time with Bridgette to start to discuss wedding plans. In the end, Bridgette really wanted to have a fall wedding. They started playing on Pinterest to get some fresh ideas and a color scheme.

They occasionally asked James for his input and he basically said the wedding was her thing and he would plan their honeymoon. That was all the ladies needed to hear! It seemed like the wedding planning and work took up most of their time. The men started to discuss bachelor party ideas and Devante gave some honeymoon suggestions. It was a time of healing and happiness.

~~

Monday came before everyone knew it. They were seated back in the courtroom and waiting for everyone to settle down. The judge came to take his seat and explained the sentencing process.

Then he looked Richard in the eye and said, "It is one thing to love your child and provide them aid when they need it. It is another to break the law, hire people to attack others, and to mastermind an assault on a family in their own home. Due to your actions, two lives were lost. Based on these charges you were found guilty of. I am giving you life in prison without the possibility of parole. You will live out your days considering your actions and remembering the lives you took. The families that you harmed for some misplaced sense of protection for your child and yourself. And if I hear one more threat toward anyone else in my courtroom from you there will be consequences. Are we clear?"

Richard ignored the judge and turned to sneer at Bridgette and James. They simply looked ahead at the judge. The judge then dismissed the court and Richard was taken away.

His lawyers looked like losers. And the District Attorney went to discuss the verdict with the press. The family needed to be taken out with heavy security to get past all of the press.

The moment they arrived at their home everyone felt weary. So, they just went to their own rooms and relaxed until dinner. They ordered Chinese and enjoyed the meal together. Their last meal with everyone under the same roof. It was beautiful to spend the time talking about Ryan and their happy memories.

~~

The next morning everyone was up bright and early. They kissed Jackson goodbye and left him with Elise. It was time to move Chris and Declan into their condo. All of their things were in a storage unit, they rented a moving truck, and they'd packed up their things from the house.

They had even had someone pick up the thing they had wanted from Ryan's place and had it shipped. They picked a coffee table that he used to place his beers on and drink with them. Everyone agreed they should have it. In the end, that table was the first item to be placed inside their condo.

In a way, it felt like Ryan was there with them. And so everyone picked up boxes and moved them inside their condo. They had sub sandwiches for lunch and planned on ordering a pizza for dinner.

Everyone was going to hang out at their place and help them unpack. Even when they moved on with their life they would always move together as a family. There was a lot of laughter and happiness all day long as Chris and Decon made their way into their future.

Bridgette took them aside and told them that they better plan on spending Christmas at their house. And she expected invites to cookouts at their place. They all agreed and hugged each other. It felt good to be settling into their lives.

This was a fresh start and the lives that Ryan wanted for them. And the lives that they had wanted for themselves. Chris and Decon knew that this would be their forever home with the love of their life. So, they kept the decor minimal so she could make it how she wanted it.

They had not even met her yet but they wanted to make sure when they did she could find a place with them. This was a home for all three of them and not just Chris and Decon.

At about ten, both couples wished Decon and Chris well and started for home. Once they got home Devante and Cassidy went to check on Jackson and get some rest themselves. They spent their time before bed looking at houses online and whispering plans of the future.

James took a seat on the couch and looked over at Bridgette seated in a chair and said, "Soon we will have this place to ourselves. I think you should re-decorate it the way you like. This way it feels like my home and a little more like your home too. What do you think?"

She simply smiled and said, "I would only make some minor changes. I really love our home. You did a great job with it." James thanked her and they sipped some wine. Around midnight the couple made their way to bed and fell asleep as soon as their heads hit the pillow.

It was all finally behind them. The storm had past and they could move forward with their lives. Each member of the family had peaceful and happy dreams that night.

~~

The following three months were hectic for everyone. Devante and Cassidy found their dream home in Nevada two weeks after the trial had ended and moved in a month later. They were decorating and making it into their home little by little.

Jackson loved his new house and the new puppy his parents had given him. Decon and Chris were loving their condo and the family came by to visit on weekends. Their company was doing well and they managed to find Ryan's brother Rory.

They gave the information to Bridgette who wanted to reach out to him herself. She had and was waiting on a response from him. James' company expanded to have offices in New York and Bridgette decided that they would keep Ryan's place for Rory if he wanted it.

They also were doing well in their home office. The diner was thriving as were James' other businesses. The wedding planning was moving ahead. They planned on an October wedding.

~~October of that year.~~

Bridgette stood in her wedding gown holding hands with James as they said their vows. The beautiful colors of dark purple and orange tones really set the tone for their wedding. Cassidy stood as maid of honor and her husband Devante was the best man.

In the front row were Chris and Decon giving thumbs up gestures to James. The wedding was private and small but filled with laughter, happiness, and above all else love. The wedding and reception were held at a cabin in Colorado.

It has always been Bridgette's dream to have a cabin wedding. James was really happy with his wife's choice of wedding venue. As they danced their first dance Bridgette whispered, "I guess you are stuck with me, husband."

He grinned and pulled her closer and nipped at her ear saying, "Good." They gazed into each other's eyes and got lost in the moment. All around the couple people were chatting, talking, and watching the happiness as the couple danced together.

There was nothing but joy. This was exactly what the couple had wanted for their special day. James picked up his wife after two hours at their reception and said, "I'll be taking my wife now. We have some important things to do… like catch a plane and start our honeymoon!"

Bridgette gaped at her husband and said, "What?!" Everyone laughed as he took her out of the building and loaded her and her bag into the car. They were at the airport thirty minutes later.

A private plane took them to their honeymoon destination. At their villa, he set her down still in her wedding gown and kissed his wife. She kissed him back and told him he was crazy. He simply grinned and showed her their bedroom.

It was a lovely room but Bridgette had very little time to admire it because her husband distracted her. James began to undress his wife slowly making them both heat from the passion between them. As soon as the dress was off of her body she was left in some very sexy wedding-inspired white lingerie.

James kissed her and told her she was the most beautiful woman he had ever seen. Then he laid her down on the bed and began to pull down her pair of white panties. He removed them with his teasing nipping at her thighs as he did so.

Bridgette moaned and arched her back as he started to use his magical tongue on her most private place. James used long swipes of his tongue teasing his wife and making her squirm on his mouth. Periodically he took his time to suck on her love button and made her go crazy.

Then once he was satisfied she was in a frenzy for him he slowly pulled away never losing eye contact with her. James took his time in taking his pants off. The moment he was exposed and hard for her time stood still.

He moved with the grace of a puma as he slid over her body and placed his hardness against her opening. She felt so hot and wet around him as he pushed forward. Bridgette cried out in pleasure and bucked up against him. She begged him for more and he gave it to her.

They soared on the wings of pleasure as James moved forward in and out of his wife. They moved in tandem and pleasure radiated between them. Bridgette looked deeply into her husband's eyes and told him how much she loved him.

He responded with the same. And then he picked up the face moving within her. Before either of them knew it Bridgette was bucking against him quickly and cumming hard on his cock. James was crying out his own release and growled her name.

After their lovemaking session, they stayed wrapped in a tight embrace.

"Thank you for making my first time as a married woman magical," Bridgette said. James grinned and kissed his wife with soft warmth.

"I love you, wife." She giggled and licked his neck saying, "I love you too, husband." They ended up talking about their wedding and reception until they fell asleep.

Chapter Nineteen

It took two weeks on their honeymoon for both James and Bridgette to announce to each other that they wanted to go home. They flew on James' private jet back to Nevada. They arrived home late in the night and James picked up his bride and walked her across the threshold.

It was romantic and wonderful to be home. Elise had spoiled them by leaving some frozen meals for the couple. They worked as a team to heat up the meal and set the table.

They had a romantic meal complete with candles. After the meal, they curled up in bed together and made love until they were exhausted.

~~

The next morning James went downstairs to check for their newspaper. The paper was waiting on the porch as the security team pretended not to be there. But, there was something else along with the paper.

It was an envelope addressed to Bridgette only there was no return address on it or even her full name. It simply said "Bridgette" on it. The second he was back inside he called Decon and Chris. Decon answered the phone and sounded half asleep.

"Hey man. It is James. We just got in late last night. I went to grab the paper and there is a strange envelope that just says "Bridgette" on the front. I haven't shown it to her yet. She is still asleep.", James said.

After a few moments, Decon became more clear and started to ask some questions about the envelope. In the men, both men agreed that Chris and Dec would come over in twenty minutes and fingerprint it. Then they would open it and see what they were dealing with.

The second Bridgette woke up they would update her on the situation. It took fifteen minutes for the men to arrive and Bridgette was still sleeping. The men sat down at the table when Chris said, "I think we should wake up Bridgette.

This could be the stalker back, and she should know what is happening. She can help us decide our next moves."

They all nodded in agreement and James went to wake up his wife. Walking up the stairs James entered his bedroom to find his wife missing. It was only when he heard a flush from their bathroom that he could breathe again. Bridgette walked out in her adorable pajamas and smiled warmly at him.

"You are up early. What is the occasion?" That was when James' expression changed from happiness to concern. "Kitten, we need you downstairs. Chris and Dec are here. We need to talk about something that ended up on our porch this morning."

The expression on Bridgette's face was one of complete and total fear. She looked into his eyes and said, "Is it the stalker?" James took her in his arms and said honestly, "We aren't sure yet. But, if it is, we will find them. There are no more trials or funerals left. We are all back to business and Chris and Dec happen to be in the business to help with these kinds of situations."

She simply nodded and grabbed her robe to be able to go downstairs and face the facts as they unraveled. In the kitchen, Chris was getting himself some coffee and offered some to Bridgette. She shook her head and Dec took her hands in his own and said, "This could be nothing. But, either way, we will handle this as a family."

The men all looked grim but Bridgette smiled a little. Chris was sipping on his coffee as Decon took gloves out of his pocket. He put them on and proceeded to take fingerprints from the envelope.

After taking the fingerprints off the envelope Decon opened it and took out the letter inside it. He read it silently...

"Bridgette,

> *My love, how could you betray me this way? I've loved you since before Ryan ever got his disgusting hands on you. I followed you to Nevada and gave you some time to set your life straight and wait for me. But, you let that buffoon James touch you and you betrayed me by marrying him. You will pay for doing this to me. You will hurt like I am hurting."*

Deacon said, "There is no signature on it. But, it is the stalker back again. We are hopeful we can pull some prints." Chris offered, "We will find this cockroach and make them pay for what they've done and are doing for you."

James nodded to them and turned to his wife, "This will all work out. But, we need to beef up security. If they got to our porch they could come inside or attack like the last one. We need to be prepared." Pinching the bridge of her nose and sighing heavily Bridgette said, "Yes, we need to be safe and prepared. I am just so upset that this is all starting up. We finally had peace in our lives."

Everyone understood where she was coming from. It seemed like the second that they let their guard down something bad had happened again. At the same time, the men wanted to move forward and they knew they could even with tighter security and the process of finding the stalker.

James smiled at Bridgette and said, "I know it isn't exactly like we planned. But, I want to move forward with decorating this place. I want to work on getting you in your new office and decorating it for you. We'll be busy but it will help move things along before we find the stalker."

Bridgette smiled and winked at her husband. Their two brothers looked at them strangely and tried to figure out what that wink meant. Both men came up empty and they shrugged. They said their goodbyes and went on their way.

~~December of that year.~~

Bridgette was pleased when her husband came home with their Christmas tree. She had set up the artificial trees around their home. Bridgette was completely over the top when it came to Christmas.

She was decorating the artificial trees on her own. But, the entire family was coming over for dinner and decorating the tree after dinner. It took a little while for James to get the tree into their living room and position it properly.

It was a very large tree since the room was so large. The look on Bridgette's face was serene as she saw the tree. Her eyes were twinkling as she looked at James.

"That is the perfect tree, husband. I can't wait until we decorate it with everyone!" The entire house smelled of pine and spice. Bridgette had been baking and cooking up a storm for everyone.

It was going to be one of her special Christmas-themed nights for the family. She gave Cassidy Thanksgiving and Halloween. Summer holidays were all Chris and Dec.

But, Christmas belongs exclusively to his wife. James shook his head as he watched her prance around their home with glee. It didn't take long until their doorbell rang and he answered the door as his wife turned on Christmas music.

Decon and Chris came in laughing at how over the top Bridgette was about Christmas. They came with wine and some bread that looked like it came straight from the bakery. James thanked them and told them to head into the living room.

He took the items they gave him over to his wife in the kitchen and caught a quick kiss. Sometime later Cassidy and Devante arrived with little Jackson bundled up in his mother's arms. They were followed by Elise who had some sort of pie in her hands.

Bridgette waved them all in and James' wife came out of the kitchen just in time and greeted our guests and relieved Elise of the pie. Then she asked the women to follow her to the kitchen once their coats were off. The woman discussed the things Bridgette had baked and cooked for them and new twists that they may use for actual Christmas and Christmas Eve.

The men all sat down with beers and looked at the tree in wonder. James laughed and said, "My wife is insane about Christmas. This is the one we are decorating tonight. We have to lug all of the totes down from the attic. We will get a workout for sure. And the Christmas music is non-stop until New Year!"

The men laugh and say "Yup!" in unison. This was not their first rodeo with Bridgette and her Christmas ways. Jackson was given to his father who showed him the tree and explained to him what a man's role in tree trimming was.

The others sat and laughed at the expressions on the little one's face. The ladies came in with refreshments sometime later and told the men it was time!

Taking their cue the men worked their way to the attic and began bringing down Christmas decorations for the tree. There were many different boxes. Some from James's life, Bridgette's life, Ryan's decorations, and even some brand new ones to add to the tree. Each member of the family had taken at least one special decoration from their collection to add to the tree as well.

As the Christmas music played and the fire roared in the fireplace they began singing and decorating. Everyone was having a blast. Jackson (with some assistance from his father) put his first ornaments on the tree. The look of wonder on his face was priceless.

As they added decorations from Ryan's box to the tree they told stories about him and the ones they had memories of. The night was passing by quickly when there was a loud knock at the door. Bridgette was glowing as she went to answer the door and then they could hear a faint conversation before she came back into the room.

Bridgette was followed in by a younger man who looked part confused, part pissed off and part wasn't trusting. She turned to her family and said, "This is Ryan's brother Rory. I asked him to come to trim the tree with us and share in our dinner tonight. He agreed to come for Ryan since we are honoring him on our tree."

Everyone stood there stunned except for Jackson who was chattering away to himself. Rory looked a little shy and unsure of himself for a moment.

Bridgette turned to him and said, "Rory, this is our family. This handsome devil is my husband, James. To his left is Chris and beside him is Decon. Holding the handsome Jackson is Devante.

And Devante's wife is beside him, that is Cassidy. And our lovely Elise is last of all."

It took a moment for Rory to get all the names and faces correctly. But, since he had been writing with Bridgette and speaking on the phone so much lately he knew some of them pretty well. It took only a few moments for her family to shover Rory with love and he went straight to Ryan's box.

He started placing things on the tree and sharing the stories of Ryan and their childhood. It took twenty minutes before they all felt like Rory had always been a part of their family. Even with his rough around the edges attitude and youthfulness. He became their younger brother and they would defend him at all costs.

As they sat down to dinner Rory asked if he could help so they set him to work on setting the table along with Devante. It seemed that both men had a report that was a little different than the rest of the group. They were cracking jokes and fast friends.

As soon as the table was set everyone sat down to share a meal and a lot of love. All in all, there was a lot of happiness around their table. They had a new member of the family, the tree was decorated and they shared delicious holiday treats.

They also gave tribute to Ryan and saved him a seat at the table. It was their tradition so he would always be honored. Rory seemed very moved by all of how this family kept his brother's memory alive.

It was astounding to him that these people had so readily and easily accepted him into their homes and lives. It would have been nice if it had been because of something he did. But, he knew that everyone had to start somewhere and apparently his ground zero was being Ryan's little brother.

And the older he became the more proud he was to be Ryan's kid brother. Sometime later...The night was a success and Bridgette felt very proud of herself. She said her final goodbyes to the last of their guests and made her way into the kitchen to clean up.

After that, she went into the living room and watched the Christmas tree. James came up from behind Bridgette and wrapped his arms around her. They couldn't help but admire the lights and decorations on their magical tree.

They stayed that way for a while until James nibbled her ear and said, "Come to bed, wife." She giggled and agreed to go to bed with her husband. They needed some alone time after having so many people over to their home.

In the time since the first letter had arrived with their morning paper, the stalker had only sent three others. They all said the same things. But, so far every trail they have gone down has been a dead end. Bridgette had taken the approach that until he was in her face she wasn't going to worry over it.

She trusted her brothers and her husband in terms of finding the man and for keeping her safe. Bridgette made her way upstairs and went into her bathroom to change into a satin nightgown. She knew that her husband would appreciate her in this choice of satin and lace.

The color of the nightgown was crimson red. She giggled and made her hair look mussed and sexy and then came out to wow her husband.

"I'm impressed with how you worked so hard to get Rory here with us. You have a way with people…." James' words stopped when he saw his wife. She was a stunning beauty inside and out. But, she was sexy too. Bridgette grinned at her husband and gave him a sexy smirk.

"It was an amazing experience for us all. And now we have a younger brother. But… I would much rather talk about you and I… and getting naked!" James did not need to be told twice and he swept his wife off her feet and set her on their bed.

His hands were all over her and pushing up her nightgown over her thighs. Then without warning, he leaned down and nibbled her leg and thighs teasingly. Bridgette couldn't help but gasp and make the sexiest little sounds he did so.

She squirmed and looked at him, her eyes filled with fire and need. James then started to take his expert tongue over the lips of her pussy teasing her. As she gasped and writhed with need he pushed his tongue into her folds and teased her clit. He continued this pattern over and over until his wife came on his tongue.

There was little time before James was over her body and kissed her passionately. Bridgette was still on her orgasmic high when he plunged deep inside her depths and made her cry out in pleasure and with the shock of it. She was so sensitive and ready for him.

Arching her body to meet his Bridgette moaned his name and pleaded with him to continue to thrust in and out of her. Taking his needs from her and soaring to new heights of pleasure together. They continued to move in unison exploring each other with their hands, with their mouths, and riding the waves of pleasure as they came. It felt so freeing to be able to explore each other and try new things as a team.

Neither of them had ever felt such heights of pleasure or desire in their lives. It just solidified their bond. The couple continued to make love until they were breathless and exhausted from their adventurous exploration. Bridgette and James curled up in bed together and kissed until they both fell asleep.

There was a sense of peacefulness that fell over the entire house as the couple slept. That is a false sense of security that many people sink into as they let their guard down. Two of their security guards were fighting for their lives.

They were shot close range with a gun that had a silencer. As James and Bridgette slept peacefully there was violence on their back porch. The stalker made his way beyond their alarm system and slipped inside of the house from the back door. He stood right where Ryan had died and grinned.

That was when he left his love letter/threat to Bridgette on their kitchen table. Then he made his way silently up the stairs and peeked in on the couple. It took all of his strength to keep his rage intact as he saw the woman of his dreams sleeping with another man.

He wanted to murder James for touching what was his and rail at her and torture her for her betraying him. Instead, he watched them for a few minutes and then forced himself to go back down the stairs. He left a special gift under the tree and then made his way out in the same way he entered the house.

~~

The next morning Bridgette woke up with a start. She couldn't remember what she was dreaming about. The fact that her heart was racing and alarm raced through her veins made her believe that it was a bad dream.

Looking over at the space beside her she smiled softly and watched her husband sleep. There was a sense of calm and innocence about him when he was asleep that helped soothe her raw nerves. In the end, Bridgette decided that she would put aside her fears and be happy.

There was so much to live for and be content within her life. Ryan had given her family a gift with his letters. He had encouraged them all to live fully and happily no matter what storms came their way.

This was a perfect example of honoring that sentiment. After doing her morning routine Bridgette was showered and dressed. She leaned down to kiss her husband softly and quietly worked her way down the stairs to the kitchen.

There was an instant sense of dread as she saw a letter on their table that had not been there before they went to sleep. Looking toward the back door she gasped in horror as she saw blood all over the glass door. In a complete state of both shock and adrenaline, she decided it would be best to look throughout the house.

This way she could ensure that the person was gone. Also, she wanted to see if there was any other evidence of violence in her home. Everything was eerily quiet and she was thankful she could find nobody in their home.

That sense of relief was quickly replaced with horror as she noticed a box under the tree. She slowly walked toward the box and noticed her name on the tag. Bridgette opened it with careful movements as if it were a snake about to strike her at any moment.

The motion to open the box almost seemed to be in slow motion, but she pushed herself forward trying to move beyond her fear and keep calm. That was until she saw what was inside the box. At the sight, she dropped it and screamed the most blood-curdling scream she had ever uttered in her life.

Bridgette screamed for her husband and started to shake. The next few moments felt like they happened for her in slow motion. She heard a fuss upstairs and then her husband's feet on their stairs as he raced to her.

As soon as he arrived he took in the scene and took her into his arms and rocked her. His hands soothingly raked through her hair, and he murmured words of comfort to her until she could stop crying and breathe again. It was in that brief moment of calm that she managed to say, "T..the... box!"

James carried her to the couch and wrapped a blanket over her as she was shivering. Then he said, "I'm going to go call Devante and have him contact everyone okay? I'm going to get my phone and call our security team. Then I am going to look at the box, okay, kitten?"

She shook her head and said, "No... no please don't leave me! The security may be dead... blood on the door. Just like Ryan... and the letter. Please stay with me!"

James took a second to take in her information and looked into her eyes and said, "I need my phone. I'm going to call help. But, I will come back as soon as I can. We will leave the box for someone else to see. Okay, kitten?"

Bridgette nodded and burrowed deeper into the blanket and trying to make herself small. The moment he found his phone he was waiting for the call to connect him to Devante. Racing back to Bridgette he curled up next to her.

He said into the phone, "Dev we need you. Call the others. It is bad and I can't leave my wife." There was a brief moment where he listened and Bridgette noticed he was nodding. "See you soon, Dev.", he said.

Twenty minutes later Devante, Chris, and Decon rushed into the house and took in the scene. A discarded note on the kitchen table which Chris went to handle (look at with gloves on as to note add more prints to it), blood on the glass door to the backyard which Deacon went to look at without touching it, and Devante went to the living room to check out what seems like a package on its side beneath the Christmas tree.

James was so busy cradling Bridgette in his arms that he had missed some of his brothers' carefully executed maneuvers. He looked up and his eyes met Devante's and he knew the situation was grim. Devante looked pale as he inspected the box with gloves on.

This meant at some point they needed to discuss things privately. Chris returned from the kitchen and sat in a comfortable and puff chair in the living room. He met

Devante's and they exchanged grim nods. This was a very bad situation indeed. Decon came back in and said, "We need a forensic team here, the police to inspect the backyard. I have a feeling we have some bodies on the property from the security team."

Devante stood and turned to his family and said, "First, we need someone to take Bridgette to my house. Cassidy and Elise can care for her and make sure she is comforted. We will have extra security there so everyone is safe and protected. My house has become a fortress for we know they will all be safe."

James looked into Bridgette's eyes and saw she was in shock and not herself. He kissed her gently and squeezed her hand. She seemed to come out of her haze a little.

"Kitten?", he asked. She looked at him and said, "Yes?" He smiled softly and said, "Chris is going to drive you over to Cass' house. That way you can love Jackson and plan the menu for Christmas Eve. Does that sound okay?"

Bridgette nodded at her husband and started to rise to grab her socks and shoes. After she had them on and grabbed her jack Chris guided her out of the house and they were on their way. The moment the door closed Deacon said, "We need to call in extra security for here. But, we need to meet with them first to brief them on what has happened and what they need to do to be safe. But, first, we need to call the police so they can process the scene and it is on paper that this has all taken place. It will help to build a case once we catch the fucker."

James simply nodded processing. Devante said, "The box has small body parts in it. Real ones. This is a clear threat for you both. Let's call the police and tell them that you found Bridgette in a state of shock and cared for her first. You were so concerned with her condition you called us. We have her safe at my home being cared for now. And that it was after we arrived that we all discovered the letter, the box, and the blood on the glass door. It is all the truth just keeping some aspects back."

Chapter Twenty

Everyone agreed with the plan and James called the police office and explained what had happened and asked for them to come to the house. The dispatcher said they would send some police officers and a forensic team to process the scene and not to touch things anymore or go out to the backyard before they arrived. James agreed and told them a thank you for their help.

Devante sat on the couch and said, "This is bad. This house is going to need a new overhaul in terms of your security. Major upgrades. But, more importantly, you will need to hire more men. Better trained men. This is more than any of us anticipated." Decon sat down and ran his hand over his face in frustration.

"I'm having my best men make this their sole priority. We will find this asshole and bring him to justice. I've already texted them to meet with me at our offices this afternoon. After we finish with the police I will head on ours. Chris will meet me there. He is staying to help with Bridgette."

The men waited until the police arrived and greeted them kindly. The police swept in and took their statements. The forensic team started working the scene and looking for prints. Some detectives went out to the backyard and found two dead security men.

Homicide was called in and the house/backyard became a crime scene. Devante told James that he and Bridgette could stay at his house while the house was considered a crime scene. James thanked him and they listened to the police promise to get all of the evidence processed and keep an eye out for the stalker.

They promised to look into it. But, the men had taken photos before they arrived and would do their own private investigation.

~~

The next few days passed in a flash for everyone. Bridgette was feeling more herself and trying to remain positive. James had convinced her to take some time off from work to relax and spend time with Cassidy. Jackson and Elise.

Cassidy took some time off of work and stayed with her. In the meantime, the men worked at their jobs and made it their personal mission to find Bridgette's stalker. Chris and Deacon's men were able to find some new information that took their men to New York State to check out the leads.

If the leads check out there may be a real chance that they'd find the stalker. Until the men returned Chris and Decon tried to focus on their other projects and cases. James was working hard to make his business soar and it was difficult without Bridgette by his side.

But, having her at Devante's place made him feel more secure that she was safe. And that allowed him to better focus on work. At least as much as he could until they found the fucker who entered their home and threatened his wife.

It felt as if time were standing still. The police had no leads or suspects. The funerals for the fallen security men had come and gone.

James had paid for their services himself and offered to assist their families as much as he could. But, none of that would ever bring back those brave men who worked for him. It was nearly midnight by the time James arrived at his house.

He had been staying there alone ever since the police cleared the house. There was no way he would hide from the disturbed man who was stalking the love of his life. As long as she was safe he would fight anyone who dared take that peace from her.

There was nothing in this world that he would not do for Bridgette. Sitting in his living room with a scotch in his hand he drank slowly. The flavor is something to savor on his tongue.

He willed the man to enter his home again and face him. He would fight that man until he had nothing left to defend their home, their family... and nothing would change that. There was a knock on his door around twelve thirty-seven.

He looked from the clock toward the door and steeled himself. It could be anyone at this point, and he was prepared. Taking a big and deep breath before opening the door. Waiting expectantly for him was his wife.

Bridgette stood there wringing her hands. She looked up into his eyes and said, "Hey baby. We need to talk." The look on her face made him worried, but he waited for her to explain.

They moved into the living room and took a seat next to each other. James took her hands into his own and waited for her to say whatever was on her mind.

"I know that everything is in flux right now because of the break-in, the stalker, and everything. But, I needed to talk to you and I couldn't wait. I also didn't want to discuss this at Cassidy and Devante's home. I wanted to discuss it here in our home.", she said.

James was starting to worry and he said in a rush of emotion, "You are starting to scare me here, kitten. Are you sick? Has the stalker found you? Did something happen?" She shook her head and said, "I've been having a hard time sleeping at night and being exhausted all day. Cassidy thought I should see my doctor. So, we went the other day while Elise watched Jackson. We discovered the root of all of my issues. I'm pregnant."

The look on James' face was priceless. He was stunned at the news.

"That is wonderful news, kitten! But, we need to solve this stalker thing now more than ever. If he realizes that you are pregnant it will put you even more in danger. We need to keep it close to our vests. Only close family can know okay?", he said.

She nodded and looked into his eyes and said, "Isn't this the best Christmas gift ever?" James agreed, and they started to talk about their plans and how excited they were. It would be a few months before they would know the sex of their baby.

Bridgette explained her symptoms and how she was coping with them. James shared his ideas for the nursery, and they planned together. It was sunrise when they realized so much time had passed.

James kissed his wife and picked her up and carried her to the car. She was giggling the entire way. He drove his wife back to their friends' home.

After tucking her into bed he went into the office. It was hard not to shout it from the rooftops that he was about to become a father. But, the safety of his wife and child was more important.

The happiness that James was feeling carried into his work. The meetings that happened went more smoothly. Things were looking great for him until two in the afternoon when Deacon called.

"The men arrived we sent to New York have discovered the name of the man stalking Bridgette. They searched his apartment and pictures of Bridgette were everywhere. He even framed some of them. But, he had a lock of her hair for some reason and a vision board of their life together."

James growled at the news and said, "Have they found the asshole yet?"

There was a pause and Deacon said, "Not yet. He seems to be in the wind ever since he arrived in Nevada. We are pulling strings and working around the clock to locate him. We've forwarded the information we do have for the Nevada authorities and New York authorities. Everyone is looking for him right now."

The men discussed things a little more, and then they hung up. Devante called him later on and gave him an update on Bridgette. He said she seemed pretty tired but otherwise healthy and happy.

Cassidy was going to spoil her with her favorite foods for the entire day. They were watching movies and having a dance party too. James tried to keep his emotions under control but it was proving difficult. He was happy and excited about the baby.

He was glad Bridgette was having a good day and being pampered. But, he was worried about her and their growing family. Their home was no longer safe and it would take a few weeks if not longer to change that.

They were in flux and it was really messing with his head. So, he called up his best friend and asked him for help. They came up with a plan to make the time before their home was ready a little easier on them.

After making several phone calls James had the plan in place and was already setting it into motion. By Friday he and his love would be feeling more relaxed and able to better cope with what was happening. The day was shaping up to be wonderful.

He couldn't wait to leave work, drive to see his wife and have family dinner, and then get back to their house and pack some things.

The thing he wasn't prepared for was a strange phone call where all he heard was breathing. He'd made a note of it on his work computer, on a sticky note, in an email to his staff, and then in a call to the police and his brothers. This way if anything happened to him it was recorded.

For the next hour, James sat at his desk and worked through some paperwork and made some notes on what to get done the rest of the week to get ahead. The moment his work was finished he said goodnight to his staff as he walked past them. James was even whistling as he made it to the parking garage.

Things felt hopeful and less dire. Perhaps it was the holiday season or the fact that he was about to become a father in several months. Who knew? And who cared? He was happy!

The walk to his car felt shorter and he went through the motions of placing his briefcase in the passenger seat and starting the car. The drive was going to take him about twenty-five minutes but he knew that wasn't very long. In the end, he would get to hug his wife, share a meal with family, and be uplifted before going home.

He was about five minutes from Devante and Cassidy's home when he heard a weird sound and felt this painful impact. It took him a few minutes to realize that someone had run into his car. Everything hurt, and he could feel blood trickling down his face.

There were screams of horror coming from somewhere in the distance. It was hard to tell the details because it felt and sounded like he was underwater. James knew that somehow he was in an accident but it didn't make sense.

The light was green, and he was driving the speed limit. Did someone run their light? Then the hurt in his head began with fury and he had a hard time thinking.

His eyes wanted to close to try to combat the pain. But, he heard footsteps getting closer to him and knew that it was the stalker posing as a concerned citizen. He had to be alert and awake.

The man approaching him stopped at the car and all James could see were his legs and feet. But, then the man crouched down and looked into his eyes and said, "How does it feel?"

Despite the pain, James decided to remember his face and fight his injuries and listen carefully to what he says. But, he stayed silent. The man leaned in so that James could smell some whiskey on his breath.

He sneered in a low voice only for James to hear and said, "It is a shame I couldn't kill you this time. Next time I will make sure it happens. Enjoy the time you have left."

The man stood and looked toward the crowd around the car and said in a high-pitched voice, "Call 911! This guy is really hurt. This is so sad! How could someone do this?!" The crowd believed him and the sirens were closer and closer.

There was help on the way, and he knew he could ask the EMTs to call his brothers. They would take care of his wife. He just needed to be sure to stay conscious. It felt like it was ages before the ambulance got there but in reality, it was only a few moments.

The EMTs pulled him from the car that was on its side. They placed him on the stretcher and started to work on him. He made eye contact with one of them and said, "Please call Devante Salazar. His number is on my phone. He is my brother and I need him to let my wife know what is happening and inform my family. Please. I can't close my eyes until you do."

The EMT looked alarmed and said, "I'll call. But, Sir... please stay awake!" James blinked his eyes and met the worried gaze of the EMT and said, 'My name is James. And I have tried to stay awake. So hard."

Then his entire world went black. The EMT panicked and looked at her partner, and she said, "You keep this man alive! I'm calling his people."

The partner went straight to work on James. Meanwhile, the female EMT whose name was Trisha picked up James' cell and called Devante Salazar.

"James! We are expecting you. Running late?", Devante said cheerfully. Taking a breath Trisha said, "This is Trisha Smith. I am an EMT in the ambulance with James. There was a car accident and we are taking him straight to the hospital. Please meet us there. Before he blacked out he said that you would tell the family and his wife."

Devante said, "Yes, thank you, Trisha. Please save him! He is our brother." She said she would do her best and hung up the phone. As the ambulance was racing to the hospital and the hospital staff waited to start their part of the process James was out cold.

Across town, in his home, Devante swallowed and held his emotions in check before walking into the dining room where his wife, Elise, his son Jackson and Bridgette were seated waiting for James. He looked at his wife and shook his head giving her a look that said bad news was coming.

She braced herself and looked at him worried. He said, "Bridgette, I need you to listen to me and stay calm okay?" The silence in the room was intense and Bridgette looked at her brother and said, "What has happened to James?"

The way in which her voice cracked almost made everyone come undone. Devante looked her in the eye and said, "He has been in an accident. I will call our contact at the station and get more information after I call Chris and Decon. The person who informed me was an EMT named Trisha Smith. She said they are taking good care of him. We need to stay calm and make our way to the hospital to hear more. Okay?"

Bridgette stood calmly and picked up her purse and started walking toward the garage. Devante followed her while telling his wife that he loved her and would call with the news. The driver to the hospital found Bridgette quietly seated in the passenger seat.

Devante called Chris and Decon and asked them to look into things. Then he called the police station and was told it was an ongoing investigation but it looked like a hit and run situation. The moment the car stopped Bridgette was briskly walking into the Emergency Department of the hospital.

At the desk, she asked calmly for a status update on her husband. The person behind the desk asked for some details and then sent someone to gather the information requested.

Devante sat with her and it wasn't until she looked up at him that she spoke.

"These are the same seats we sat in to wait for news about Ryan. I can't lose James. It would be too much for my soul to take." Devante held her close and said, "James will survive this. I know he will. There is no other option." Bridgette simply nodded and looked at the tile flooring waiting for news.

Ten minutes later a man came and told her that they were still working on him in this department but then he would be moved. At the time they moved him they would inform the family which waiting room to go to. According to the man James was in and out of consciousness and had a concussion due to an impact with the side door.

His arm was broken and some ribs were also broken. They are going to look for internal bleeding and would update them as news became available. Bridgette thanked the man. The second the man left Devante pulled out his phone and called everyone in their family with the update.

Declan said he was leaving Chris in charge at work and coming there to wait with them. It only took him fifteen minutes to arrive and sit with his family. Declan was on one side of Bridgette and Devante sat on the other side.

They were her two pillars of strength as she waited to hear about her husband. It was about two hours later when someone came to discuss James' condition with them. They were told that he had some internal bleeding in his abdomen and they would be doing surgery to repair the damage.

Decon, Devante, and Bridgette made their way to the next waiting room they were taken to. In the waiting room Declan sat down with a magazine on one side of her and Devante was on the other side reading texts from his phone. Bridgette sat in between them hoping the doctors could fix the internal bleeding. She had seen enough Grey's Anatomy to know that it could go either way in the end.

The hope was that they would fix him and he would make a full recovery. As the hours went by Bridgette remembered all of her memories of James. The first moment she saw him she felt her entire body respond to him. It was as if her soul had found its mate.

Their relationship has become so dear to her and they have been through so much in such a short time. They had come so far and now they were going to be parents and raise a family together. After around four hours someone came out to speak to their family.

"The surgery went and we were able to repair the damage. He will need to stay in the hospital for a few days to heal from his injuries. We are keeping an eye on his concussion. He is slowly waking up right now. If you would like to see him you can. Just go two at a time.", she said. Bridgette fought her urge to hug the woman and simply offered her a weak smile.

Devante and Bridgette went to visit with James. The second Bridgette saw her husband laying in the hospital bed she ran to the seat beside his bed. Taking his hand into her own she looked up at him sleeping soundly.

"Baby, I'm here. Devante is with me and Decon is in the waiting room. We are here for you.", she said warmly. Devante sat on the other side of the bed and looked at James. It was hard to see his brother in this situation.

It was too soon since Ryan was in a similar situation. Bridgette and Devante looked at one another across the bed, and they both shared their mutual understanding. It was so hard to see someone else they love suffering.

At the same time, it sounded like with time that James would heal, and they could all move forward. Devante's phone started to ring, and he left the room to answer it. That left Bridgette alone with her husband. She brushed her fingers over his cheek.

"I love you, James." At her words, his eyes fluttered open and he smiled softly, "I love you too, kitten. And our little one too!" She smiled at him and brushed his hair from his face.

"You scared me! What happened?" At his lack of an answer, she arched her brow. "It was -him- wasn't it?" James licked his lips and asked her for some water. That was around the time Devante came in.

James looked to his friend and said, "Why don't you take my wife out to Declan so she can fill him in. You can stay and chat with me. Then you and Dec can switch roles when they come back. Sounds good?"

Devante smiled and said it was a perfect idea. Bridgette was unhappy with the plan but decided to trust her husband

and his judgment on the matter. Devante came back and James filled him in on the accident, what he could remember, the man, and what he said and looked like. Devante wrote it all down and sent it off to Chris.

They would find this asshole and put an end to this horror. The police arrived along with his wife and Decon. Devante stepped into the waiting room to call Chris once again. Bridgette took a seat at her husband's side and squeezed his hand.

"Tell the police everything. I am here, I am safe and I can handle it.", Bridgette said. Decon took the seat on the other side of James and listened as well. James closed his eyes for a moment and then recounted the phone call and his actions after. The rest of his afternoon from there.

The accident itself and what happened between himself and the man. There was a pause before his wife squeezed his hand tighter. The police took notes and promised that they would investigate this accident and the phone call.

Deacon had been texting Chris all of the details and alerting their team. The team had forwarded their information to the police in New York and Nevada. They hadn't heard a thing since.

The man had been in the wind but now they knew he was in Nevada. They just needed feet on the ground here to find him. They knew the name he was using in New York but it seemed like that was a fake name.

It only went back two years. They needed to find out who he was and the identity he was using in Nevada. Chris and Deacon had their men on the case. They kept coming up empty but they were the very best at this kind of thing.

This asshole would fuck up and they would nail his ass to the wall. He'd broken so many laws he would see the inside of a cell for a very long time. They just needed to find him first.

The police asked a few more questions and then excused themselves from the room. Bridgette leaned down and kissed her husband softly, "Thank you for being so brave, my love. I am so glad that you are alright. I couldn't handle it if I'd lost you too. You are my other half."

There were tears in her eyes and her husband returned her gift with a warm smile. "I would never leave you, kitten. We have too much to live for."

Decon turned back to them and smiled saying, "I think she would have dragged you back to life with her sheer will if you hadn't made it." They all laughed and Devante returned sometime later with food for everyone. James was a little salty that he couldn't have any of the delicious-smelling food.

But, it was worth it to heal as soon as possible. There was security posted outside of the hospital room, a cot was placed in the room for Bridgette at her insistence and Chris arrived to stay in the chair for the night to watch over both James and Bridgette in addition to the guard outside. In the morning Decon would relieve Chris, and they would keep a rotation of brothers until James could be released.

At this rate, they should have had stock in the hospital since they were almost always here for one reason or another. At least the hospital staff were very professional and kind to them. Some of the same nurses who cared for Ryan were caring for James.

It felt comforting to know that familiar faces would be helping them this time around as well. The next morning when Bridgette was awake her best friend was sitting where Chris has been and Declan was leaning against the wall watching them. Cassidy smiled at her and wished her a good morning.

It seemed that Cassidy had come with breakfast and some refreshments. It warmed her heart to see her best friend. James had just woken up as well and grumbled about hospital food and rules.

They all laughed and said that he seemed to be healing well now. Cassidy took Bridgette to the ladies' room with her and said, "How far along are you?"

Bridgette blushed and said, "About eight weeks." The girls started to talk about babies and planning for the nursery. It was like all of the bad things hadn't happened for a few minutes.

They returned to the hospital room looking refreshed and ready to face the day. They finally found a trail that proved the stalker from New York had come to Nevada and the name he'd been using there. But, they still couldn't trace his real identity yet.

It was frustrating for them. But, they were running with their new discoveries and were so close to finding him in Nevada. It seemed like despite the police trying their best their resources were being stretched to the max. Chris and Deacon had more resources and men on the ground to make things happen.

They were so close to catching this man once and for all. James and Bridgette hoped that it was soon. They were tired of living in fear and always ending up in the hospital. It would be good to have peace again and be able to have some boredom in their lives.

Chapter Twenty - One

It took two weeks before James was able to return home. It ended up that he was released on Christmas Eve. As a family, they decided that they would all return to James and Bridgette's home with an army of security.

They would spend Christmas there and then they would all return to their homes. James and Bridgette would go to an undisclosed location until the stalker was caught. James fussed and grumbled the entire way to the house.

It was hard for him to be fussed over and told to take it easy. But, had a big grin on his face the second he was settled on the couch in the living room of his home. Bridgette was hovering over him, and he turned to her with a kiss and said, "My darling kitten… please relax. I will not perish if you go to the kitchen or visit with our family. I'm really okay."

Bridgette was not convinced but respected the space her husband seemed to need. The woman set to baking and cooking. They played with Jackson and talked. It felt like the holiday was going to be a balm for them.

Christmas music sounded throughout the house. The Christmas trees were all lit up and decorated. It was a special time for the family.

The men were really happy to spend time watching movies in the living room. If he had been able James would have wanted a scotch. But, since he was on medication it would be a dry holiday for him.

The company of his brothers was more than enough for him. Then ladies joined them while things were in the oven and so on. James was pleased when his wife took a seat next to him and kissed him.

It was then that he lifted her hand and kissed it and then turned to his family and said, "Bridgette and I are going to have a baby. It is our most precious Christmas gift ever." Everyone erupted into shouts of joyful glee. They were given congratulations and hugs.

The entire scene was filled with nothing but happiness. The day continued to be filled with laughter and love. The meal was delicious and they even fed the security men in shifts so they were all guarded. The men appreciated being included in their celebration and delighted in the delicious variety of food provided.

At about eight in the evening, Bridgette took a seat beside the Christmas tree and announced it was time for gifts. There were gifts for everyone under the tree from everyone else. The tree had so many gifts it looked like an entire store's worth of gifts were waiting to be unwrapped.

Between Cassidy and Bridgette everyone had more than several gifts to open. They all agreed that Jackson should get to have his gifts first. So, Cassidy made a little pile for him while Bridgette started making piles for everyone else.

Jackson started to clap with glee as he saw his gifts. Devante got down on the floor with him and helped him open his gifts. Jackson had a short attention span and just wanted to fuss with the wrapping paper. But, his parents thanked everyone for the gifts.

They left a few in the morning and of course, Santa would come and bring even more. Everyone else opened a few gifts and saved some for the morning. They thanked each other for their thoughtful gifts. Then they all curled up on the sofas and chairs and watched Christmas movies until it was time for bed.

Some of them enjoyed cocoa and snacks on the coffee table. Around eleven everyone agreed they should go to bed. Jackson had fallen asleep an hour earlier.

The adults needed some rest for the next morning. They were having a big breakfast, more gifts, and then relaxing with more Christmas movies and spending time together as a family. The next morning they all gathered in the dining room to share a warm feast for breakfast.

They laughed and shared their childhood memories of Christmas. They played with Jackson and tried to make his Christmas as special as possible. They enjoyed opening the rest of their gifts and seeing Jackson react to what Santa had left for him under the tree.

The wonder on his face as he saw all of the gifts just for him made everyone's heart melt a little. The men enjoyed their meals in shifts and were glad to be on this family's security team. Elise was flirting with one of the men and everyone thought something was sparking between them.

It made them happy because she deserved to be happy after losing her husband. The day was passing with a peaceful happiness. That was until Chris and Deacon's phones started to go wild. They looked at it and gritted their teeth and ran out of the house without a word.

A few minutes later Devante's phone started chiming with rapid messages coming in. Devante kissed his son's head and his wife on the lips and said he had to go attend something at the office. James arched his brow but Devante pointed to his cell. They nodded in understanding and Devante fled.

A few moments later a text came to James' phone and his jaw locked in displeasure. Bridgette and Cassidy said, "What is going on?!" at the same time. If it had not been such a severe scene they would have laughed at their similar thoughts.

Taking a moment to wipe his hand over his face James said, "The stalker tried to blow up my office building. He failed because security caught him. They have him in custody. But, there is something hinky in it because the police say they can't keep him. Chris and Declan have more than enough evidence to connect him to several crimes. There is no way he can be released.

Devante has the lawyers all on their way to the station with him. They are going to ensure that he does not get free. We have double the security coming here to the house so we have to lock down as we did earlier in the year."

The girls simply nodded and felt like their Christmas had been cut short by tragedy. They yearned for days ahead when all of this was behind them. Elise tended to Jackson in his bedroom upstairs while everyone else sat in the living room waiting for a call.

They knew that Devante would call with an update as soon as there was news. They just prayed that the news would be positive. It took several hours before the phone rang. James picked up on the third ring and said, "This is James."

There was silence as he listened to the person on the phone. The expression on his face gave nothing away and that only added to the anxiety in the room. After several minutes he hung up the phone and turned to his wife.

"They say it is the wrong man based on my description, and he won't talk about who hired him." She arched a brow and nodded for him to continue.

"They said they can only charge him with the arson attempt. And those charges won't keep him in jail long. Chris and Decon plan to have him followed once he is released. We are determined to find the stalker, and they are on it. Meanwhile, our lawyers are on call to assist in any way they can."

The family all took in his words and Cassidy said, "I will support you no matter what. This means we all need to stay here and hunker down. As long as it takes to keep everyone safe. We are stronger together."

James said that he agreed and that was what the others had been thinking. An hour later a tired-looking Devante walked into the house. He went straight to his wife and kissed her with passion.

She smiled at him and said, "We will get him. I know we will. And in the meantime, we have each other." He agreed and carried her up to their bedroom. Elise was taking care of their son, and he needed some time with his beautiful wife.

After a few minutes, Decon and Chris came into the house and asked about food. Bridgette laughed and told them they had plenty of leftovers with their name on it. She went into the kitchen and started warming things up. James struggled to get up and walked into the dining room to sit with the guys.

Bridgette took the food into the dining room and asked her husband if he wanted anything. He asked for some coffee and took her seat next to him sipping some cocoa.

"The men set up outside of this man's hotel but they also followed him from the station. He did not go to the hotel. Instead, he went to a warehouse to have a meeting with someone who matches the description that James gave the cops. It seems we were able to get audio, video, and photographs. But, we also have some people following the stalker. Everyone in our office is working from different angles. The computer people are sending the evidence to all the police agencies, and they are also hacking to try to find out who both men are.", Chris said.

Decon simply nodded because he was so into his food. Bridgette laughed at her brothers from another mother and shook her head. Who would have ever thought they could be family?

And now they are together as the closest family she had ever had. Then she said, "Do you think we will be able to have this behind us before Spring?"

Deacon swallowed some mashed potatoes and said, "Well, we are thinking it won't be that long since we are hot on his trail. But, he is slimy so who knows. All you need to focus on is making sure that you are happy and healthy. Our niece is growing up there." James smiled and nodded his agreement.

~~

Two months later the entire family was tucked into two SUVs headed to Colorado. They were on the run from the stalker and his associates. The safety of their family came before all else.

There was a large cabin waiting for them. They had used fake names to not leave a paper trail. Jackson was fast asleep in his car seat. His parents were in the third seat with him.

The little space behind that third seat was filled with his stuff. The rest of the luggage was in the other car. In the second seat was James who had almost recovered entirely. Beside him sat Bridgette and Deacon. Chris was in the passenger seat up front, and they had someone from their security driving.

The rest of their team were behind them in the other car. They were trying hard to arrive before a huge storm was supposed to roll in. Everyone was bundled up into warm clothes.

It was intense in the car because everyone was afraid of being discovered. Thankfully, their security had sent several men ahead to fill the house with groceries and make it ready for them when they arrived. The car is silent except for the wind against the car as they drive down the highway.

Their exit was coming up, and they would be off-road for a while. Cassidy silently prayed her son would remain asleep even when they went off-road. It was their lucky day that he was exhausted from all of their travel. They wondered how Elise was doing in the car behind them.

Their security in the car with them was named Johnny. He told them that they were about two hours from their destination. As they drove their shared dreams for the future. It passed the time and made them think of positive things.

A few hours later they pulled up to the cabin. The first thing that happened was that the security team exited the car and met with the team already in place. They discussed their accommodations and changing shifts.

They also ensured that the location was secure. After all of that was complete they gave the all-clear signal and started to bring in the luggage. The moment the men were all in place to protect them everyone started to exit the cars and enter the cabin.

The men went inside and started to move the luggage to the appropriate rooms. Then everyone met in the living room in front of the fire. Cassidy held her son to her chest and kissed his head as he slept peacefully.

Devante looked at her and told her to take their son to the room made up for them. It had a special crib for him. She smiled and went to put their son to bed and to get comfortable.

He told her that he would join her in a little while. Then his attention went to Chris and asked what the plan was. Chris explained when they needed things from in town the security would send people to fetch it. And that they had to stay in the cabin as much as possible.

Everyone agreed. This was going to be rough, but they would be able to make it work. Chris and Deacon went to their rooms for the night. James and Bridgette stayed in front of the fire talking for a while.

This plan to come to the cabin was hardest on them since she was pregnant. Their medical team would have to travel to her, and they would have to be extra careful that the stalker doesn't discover her condition. Around midnight the couple made their way to bed.

It was hard for everyone to get to sleep in their new beds. But, it would get easier over time. In the morning they planned to have breakfast together before going to their separate rooms to work. This would be their new routine. Meals together, work in their rooms, and hang out before bed.

Especially since it seemed they would be snowed in before morning. As the night progressed the snow fell to the point the roads were closed. They would be snowed in but this also worked in their favor.

It would be harder for someone to find them or reach them in those conditions. It did not take long for their security to get into their routine and to check the surrounding area. Due to the weather they were invited inside and told to use sleeping bags on the living room floor when they slept. And to make sure to guard the two exits.

The next morning Bridgette put on Taylor Swift and the girls sang Cardigan as they made breakfast for their family. Elise was playing with Jackson before breakfast. The men sat in the living room and talked with their heads closed.

Probably more security stuff and discussing the latest news on the stalker. If something serious came up they would share the information with their ladies. A little while later with Folklore still playing in the background, they called the men in for breakfast with TayTay!

The girls giggled at their title for the meal. The men seemed less pleased but put up with it to keep the smiles on the ladies' faces. It was wonderful to share breakfast as a family. It was the perfect way in which to start their day.

The rest of the day passed slowly. Each member of the family was seated somewhere in the cabin with a laptop working on something for work. Elise was keeping Jackson to his schedule and trying to keep him happy despite the fact they couldn't go for their daily walk. Thankfully, a new block set had caught his attention and seemed to be doing the trick.

~~

Several weeks passed and nothing out of the ordinary happened. All of the men were puzzled because the investigation was stalled on the police side of things. On their side of things, they had leads that were not panning out.

It was as if the stalker had vanished into thin air. The only positive thing that could be said was that they knew his two fake names and how he pulled off posing as those dead men. His fake ID pipeline was shut down.

So, now he had to be himself or be so underground that it didn't matter. Chris was starting to think he did go underground. They hadn't gotten any hits from anyone fitting his description anywhere.

At the same time, they would not make assumptions and would continue to exhaust all avenues. Their goal was to find the man and make sure that justice is served. He was taken from his thoughts by Bridgette saying dinner was ready.

Everyone was gathered around the table and eating stuffed peppers. Jackson had a ball getting his rice all over the place and making a mess on his face. Everyone laughed and enjoyed their meals as well. Maybe not as much as Jackson enjoyed his though!

After dinner, they all sat around and watched "A Star Is Born" because nobody had seen it before, and they wanted to share it as a family. Jackson and Elise both retired for the night. Cassie was cuddled up to her husband as they watched the movie.

Chris and Decon sat in the chairs in the room and watched. Bridgette and James were on the love seat all cozy together. It was a cold but peaceful night because they had the fire going to keep them toasty. The night could not have been more routine or perfect.

That was until near the end of the movie. Everyone was focused on the movie when they heard a noise and then smelled smoke. There was a fire! The men jumped up and helped the ladies out of the house and at a safe distance.

Elise and Jackson were the first out the door. Then Bridgette and Cassidy were next. The men were grabbing their computers with evidence on it, and then they ran out. Everyone was at a safe distance from the house as it went up in flames.

The security team were on the phone with the fire department, but they all knew the blaze was too out of control, and they were too far away to get there before it was too late. All they could do was stand there and watch it burn. But, Decon noticed some movement in the woods and signaled Chris.

They both went quietly into the woods after the person. Devante and James stayed with the women and Jackson. The security created a circle around them acting as a shield. There were guns drawn and protective stances.

It was like something out of a movie. But, then they heard shots from the woods where Chris and Deacon went. There was silence before Decon came racing out of the woods covered in blood. He was pulling someone by their arm out with him. Chris followed behind them, his arm hanging with blood trickling down.

Devante was on the phone to try to get an ambulance. They said they were en route and would arrive soon. The police were called next since they had found the guy in the woods who tried to kill them all. Decon dragged him to security who had zip ties to restrain him until the cops came.

The moment he was in front of them Bridgette gasped. Everyone turned to look at her and the man smirked and winked at her. She shook her head as if she couldn't believe it. Then she said, "Johan?"

He beamed and said, "Yes, baby. It has been me all along. I always told you we were meant to be together." She shook her head and said, "We were meant to be together as kids. Puppy love. It ended."

James did not like the fact she knew this man who tried to kill them all several times.

And the fact she voluntarily kissed him as a teenager was even more upsetting to all of them including Bridgette herself. She looked at him with disgust and said, "Please take him away. I feel sick to my stomach just looking at him."

The security team took him to the other side of the vehicle to wait for the police to come. Chris was bleeding from where Johan had shot him. He kept telling everyone it was no big deal but it seemed to be bleeding a great deal.

Devante was sending the name of the man to the police in New York, Nevada, and would inform the police here of the situation. They would all link up and charge him for his crimes in each state. They all waited for the fire department, police, and ambulance to arrive.

The fire department was the first to arrive. They explained what happened, and they worked to control the fire. The cabin was completely destroyed.

The next to arrive were the police. They took the statements of everyone and looked at the evidence on Chris and Deacon's computers they saved from the fire. They also put them in contact with the police from the other two states.

About fifteen minutes after the police arrived the ambulance arrived. Chris was taken to the local hospital to have the bullet removed and be properly bandaged. Decon piled into the ambulance and went with him.

Everyone else went to the hotel in town and checked into their last rooms. They would all leave in the morning. It was going to be a long drive back to Nevada.

~~

The next morning they loaded into the cars and started the drive back to Nevada. Everyone felt like a weight was lifted from their chest. The stalker was in custody, and they knew who he was.

They had more than enough evidence to hold him and put him away for a long time. There would be a trial in every state for the different crimes committed in each one. Starting with the great state of New York!

Thankfully, because there was so much evidence none of them needed to attend his trials. They could send video testimony if need be. But, they didn't think they would need anyone's testimony except for Bridgette and James.

And they said given her condition they could just send a video testimony. They were all finally free of everything weighing them down and putting them in danger. The car was filled with classic rock as they made their way home.

Even little Jackson was dancing in his car seat with glee. Things were looking up for them all. The lockdown was over for them, and they could return to their normal lives. Bridgette was looking forward to returning to work before her maternity leave kicked in.

Chapter Twenty - Two

~~June of that year...~~

B ridgette looked around at all of her family and friends at her baby shower and smiled. It was a happy day for them all. Johan had been convicted of all of his crimes in all three states.

They promised he would serve his time, and she would be safe from him. James had allowed his wife to re-decorate their home to make it more their home. And they both had input on their child's bedroom.

They discovered that they were having a little girl. Cassidy joked that Jackson and their little daughter Diana would end up married someday. Bridgette said that would depend on what made them happy.

It was nice to enjoy the Paris themed baby shower for their daughter. It was all pink, black and white. They had finger sandwiches and fruit and veggie platters.

There was pink lemonade. Everyone was thrilled to share in the feast. They even had some cute little cupcakes with pretty Eiffel towers sticking up out of them.

The music was all of Bridgette's favorite songs and bands. There was a great deal of Taylor Swift and as such Cassidy presented her bestie with an outfit for the baby that said "Swiftie" on it. Everyone gave Bridgette some great gifts that she would need to welcome her baby into the world.

In all honesty, her favorite part of the shower was sharing the experience with her loved ones. After a few hours, the shower turned into a BBQ with all of Bridgette's family and her husband. It made her feel so special and happy to share this time in her life with them.

They ate wonderful food, chatted, and even danced around the backyard. The only thing that would have made the day complete would have been if Ryan were there. At the same time in a way, he was always with them.

James called everyone's attention to him and said, "I love my wife very much. And I feel like she and our daughter deserve a special gift on this special day. And so I got them something special." He presented his wife with two boxes.

She opened the first and it was a tennis bracelet. Then she opened the second and found a matching tennis bracelet in a newborn size. The tears started to pour down her cheeks, and she kissed him with love and devotion. Bridgette smiled at her loved ones in the crowd. Then she looked adoringly at her husband.

"It is with great pleasure that we share with you her name. Our baby will be Saskia Ryan!" Everyone beamed at the news and started writing it into their phones so they could have little gifts made up for her and put her name on cards and things.

There was a new member of the family coming and hearing her name seemed to make her more real for everyone. After all of the guests had left and family were at their homes James carried his wife to their bedroom. She giggled as she landed softly on the bed and looked at him with an arched brow.

He looked at her with the most smoldering gaze she had ever seen. It was as if her husband could not get enough of her and wanted more from her. He started to undress her slowly and paid special attention to her stomach and kissed it with reverence and love.

It melted her heart to watch him. He looked up into her eyes and said, "You have never been more beautiful than you have been carrying our daughter. I love you, Bridgette."

There were tears in her eyes and she couldn't speak so she nodded. Then her husband continued to kiss down her body and parted her thighs. Bridgette had not expected her husband to lick and suckle her most private place. But, he was and his arms wrapped around her thighs lifting her up as if she were chalice he was drinking from. James could not get enough of his wife.

The scent of her, the taste spurred him forward, and he continued to lick and tease her folds before sinking inside of her opening. She squirmed on his tongue and moaned in a way that made him lose his mind. James tasted and enjoyed his wife, and she was arching her back to meet his tongue and thirsted for more of what he was providing her.

Unexpectedly, James pulled away and grinned at his glassy-eyed wife. Then he started to do a little striptease for her. Slowly unbuttoning his shirt, letting it fall to the floor beside him.

Then unbuckling his pants and taking the buckle off. The sound of the buckle hitting the floor sent them both on edge. They had a raw need between them.

The minute his pants were unbuttoned and he started to lower his pants his wife licked her lips. She was looking at him as if the only thing she needed in life was his body moving with her own. Slowly lowering his boxer briefs down his legs he stared into her eyes as she drank his nakedness in.

The heat between them was intense, and he crawled on the bed and lowered himself over Bridgette. They began to kiss with their tongues playfully sliding along each other. She

CARRIE CROSS

arched her body begging him to take her to the heights of pleasure.

James wanted to give his wife every ounce of pleasure that he could and so parting her thighs he sank between her legs and placed his hard cock at her pussy entrance. He looked at her and said "You are mine!" as he sank deep within her body.

She matched his movements and soon they were moving at a slow pace. Soaking in every movement, sound, and smell between them. But, it did not take long until they both needed something more.

James picked up the pace and started to be more forceful with his wife. She wrapped her legs around him and held her hands above her head. Bridgette's gaze never left his as he took her with a fire and passion that they had always shared between them.

"I'm yours, Sir", she whispered against his lips as a moan escaped her lips straight after. Taking it as a sign to move harder and faster James started to take her for his pleasure just as much as hers. The sounds of their union could be heard all over the house.

Neither of them cared that their security could hear them. Bridgette was biting her lip as she felt her climax coming hard and fast. James leaned down and bit her lip for her and moved even deeper and harder inside of her body.

The look in his eyes and the way it felt being taken so brazenly by him sent her over the edge and she screamed her release. James continued to pound his hard cock into his wife until she panted and was close to her second orgasm.

The second her tight little pussy constricted around his hardness he lost his control. Growling with his release James emptied his seed deep within his wife. Then he lowered his forehead to hers and kissed her.

"I love you, kitten." She smiled and nipped at his lips and said, "I love you too."

The couple decided to talk about their day, their future, and their baby as they snuggled close in their bed. They had reached a new level of intimacy, and they could not have imagined anything being any better than it already was. But, they hadn't met their daughter yet or seen how much she would enrich their lives.

~~A random Sunday...~~

The home was warm and everything was calm. Bridgette and Cassidy were in the living room near the fireplace talking about how much pregnancy sucks at the end when James came in with snacks.

"You both look lovely today!", he said. The ladies smiled at him and thanked him for the snacks. They were about to have a Fifty Shades of Grey marathon and James supported it for two reasons.

It made Bridgette calm and happy to spend time with her friend. And it also turned her on so she would be riding him after Cassie went home. James could not wait for his wife to come to him all revved up and ready for some really hot sex.

Bridgette's pregnancy made her so much hornier than either of them had expected before she became pregnant. Neither of them were complaining as their sex life had been amazing before and after. Their relationship, in general, had become stronger after all they had gone through, survived, and shared together.

The ladies were commenting on the story and giggling like schoolgirls, and he just shrugged and leaned down to kiss his wife. He announced he was going to the home office to catch up on some work and would see them later on. They waved him away and went back to talking about how hot a man in a suit was.

They would know since they were both married to businessmen. The women enjoyed popcorn, ice cream, and pizza while they watched all of the Fifty Shades of Grey Trilogy. They had a really good time and were stuffed when Cassidy left.

She felt like she needed to get back home to her husband and son. After closing the door Bridgette grinned and went in search of her husband. It was time to seduce her husband. The second she stood in her husband's office doorway she leaned against the trim and admired him.

James was a sexy man in the prime of his life, and he was also the father of her baby. Somehow sharing this child turned her on, even more, when she saw him. Locking her eyes on him she said in a husky voice, "I think I have developed a fetish for men in their prime who happen to be father's."

At the sound of his wife's voice, he looked up. He couldn't help but arch a brow at her words. Lowering his voice with arousal he said, "I'm glad to oblige my wife in any and all of her fetishes and fantasies. Nobody else gets to make those happen. You. Are. Mine."

The last part of his words were said in a growl. Delicious shivers were racing through her body as she went to where he was seated. Bridgette straddled her husband's lap right there on his office chair. She leaned down and licked his neck nibbling along his collarbone.

"You taste delicious, husband." James placed his hands on her hips and moved her backward so he could look into her eyes and then without warning leaned down to spread kisses and nibbles over her breasts. Bridgette moaned softly in his ear and said, "Mmm. I'm so hot and wet for you."

Bridgette decided to grind on her husband's lap so he could feel for himself. Seconds after she did that he leaned down and pulled off her panties ripping them and sending the cloth flying across the room. Then they kissed their tongues dueling with passion.

She leaned down and unbuckled her husband's belt and pants. He lifted himself up so she could pull them, and then he pulled her down on him. The moment his hard cock was encased inside her hot and wet pussy they both groaned in pleasure. She started to move slowly, working hard hips in a pleasurable fashion.

James placed his hands on her hips and leaned down to pull her breasts from her top with his teeth. His tongue swirls around her nipples and bites to the flesh of her breasts. As the pleasure spiked through her body she pushed her head back and moaned in bliss.

How he held her hips indicated the pace of their fucking. There was always love in their sexual unions, but they were not a couple who loved soft and slow sex. They were ravenous for one another, and they started to fuck each other to the point the chair was creaking with their movements.

The sounds in James' study were filled with flesh meeting flesh and intense sounds of pleasure. Bridgette wrapped her arms around her husband's neck and rode his rock with vigor. The moment their eyes met their movements became more frantic, and she started to say in a rush of words, "Oh yes! I'm so close, baby…!"

Then he started to pump himself up inside her and held her body close to his own. Making sure to hit that spot inside her that made her come undone. And she did.

"James!", she screamed in her pleasure as her cunt walls gripped him tightly, milking his cock. The sensations were too much and his own orgasm took over. Bridgette's name was on his lips in a growl as he spilled himself deep inside his wife.

She laughed softly and rested her head on top of him pushing her breasts in his face lovingly. He nipped at them, and they painted a few moments trying to catch their breath.

~~Later that night...~~

James and Bridgette had just finished dinner and were seated in their living room watching a movie when a call came in for James. Bridgette smiled and encouraged him to go handle his business. She was fine watching something else on her own, and they could finish the movie tomorrow.

That was the beauty of Netflix. It took her a few minutes to settle on watching Miss Americana for the sixth time. It always made her happy to watch anything Taylor Swift-related.

After half the documentary was finished she started to feel kind of funny. So, she went to get herself a glass of water. Bridgette stood at the sink and sipped her water.

All of a sudden she was hit with pain and then a strange sensation. She dropped the glass and it crashed and shattered to the floor with the pain. Then she held the counter for support as she just felt off.

In the next few seconds, her water broke. She stood ramrod still and looked down at the puddle at her feet. Then she screamed for James to come!

She was in full panic mode because she wasn't sure if this was normal labor or if something was wrong. James ran from his office and took in the scene before him. The first thing he did was ensure that Bridgette was moved away from the broken glass.

Then he picked her up and carried her to the car. He belted her in and ran inside for the hospital bag and their phones. In less than three minutes he was in the car, belted and ready to go to the hospital.

As he drove he asked his wife to call Cassidy and let her know they were on their way to the hospital and see if she could spread the word. Bridgette called her friend and Cassie said she was on her way. Elise would stay with Jackson and everyone was on their way.

They were having their first little girl in the family and nobody wanted to miss it! James was growling because it seemed like they were hitting each red light at every stop. Bridgette touched his leg lovingly and told him it would be okay.

But, her face was contorted with pain, and he knew they had to hurry. This baby seemed to have a mind of her own, and she wanted to come early. They couldn't wait to meet her, but they wanted to do it in the safety of the hospital and not on the road.

Arriving at the hospital James parked the car and carried his wife to the emergency entrance not remembering where to go. Bridgette protested that she could walk herself, but he wouldn't hear of it. Once inside the hospital, the nurses provided a wheelchair and allowed him to wheel his wife to labor and delivery.

Bridgette was examined and all of the paperwork was done easily. Then they were waiting for the contractions to become closer together. She was dilating rather rapidly as if this baby was ready to come right now!

It was rare for a first child to have this kind of delivery but nature was what it was. The nurses checked on her and the doctor was on her way. They confirmed that before the end of the day there would be a little girl in their arms.

Cassidy was allowed into the room to film while James focused on being her labor partner. Devante, Chris, and Decon were all pacing the waiting room waiting for their niece to be born. At some point, it was understood that they would buy out anything pink from the gift shop. They were all so excited to have a little girl to dote on.

The entire birthing process was nothing like Bridgette had ever read about. This was pain unlike she ever knew was possible. It was like this baby was trying to destroy her insides on her way out.

James felt like his hand would break from her grip. But, he smiled and encouraged her. He even told her he loved her when she told him to go fuck himself. Cassidy was trying not to giggle at the entire interaction. Doctor Simmons came in and smiled widely.

"We have a little girl ready to enter the world! Let's get this show on the road.", she said.

Bridgette growled at her happiness and the woman simply winked at her. Then she started to give her directions on when to push and encouragement that she really could birth this baby. It took them forty-five more minutes before the head was out. Saskia had a full head of blonde hair.

But, all Bridgette cared about was the pain of her most private place being torn apart. The doctor talked her through getting the shoulders out and that hurt even more than the head for Bridgette. She cursed everyone and then started to cry and asked forgiveness.

She didn't want Saskia's first words in the world to be cuss words. Everyone told her to relax and finish her work in getting that little girl out. Bridgette pushed and after that really big push the baby just slid out!

It was freeing and all fire in her personal lady bits all at once. She had screamed so much during the birthing process. The second she was out Saskia screamed at the top of her little lungs and wiggled in the doctor's arms.

Dr. Simmons said that she was the most beautiful baby she had the privilege to deliver. They cleaned the baby up and did all their tasks to handle her. Once she was in a blanket and had a little hat on she was placed on her mother's chest.

Bridgette looked up into James' eyes and said, "We made the most beautiful little human in history." There were tears in their eyes as they gazed at one another. The love was so complete and unconditional that everyone in the room felt it.

James looked deeply into his wife's eyes and said, "She is as beautiful as her mother. You did so well, kitten. I love you." They kissed and then James placed a kiss on his daughter's head. Cassidy was crying as she filmed these special and private moments in their lives.

Then Bridgette turned to Cassie and said, "Come here, God Mom… meet our baby girl." James took over the filming and Cassidy sat down holding her Goddaughter. She smelled so good and was so small and soft. Cassie said, "Hello Saskia. I'm your auntie, Cass. I love you and will always be here for you. No matter what."

Bridgette burst into tears and said, "I love you so much, Cassie. Thank you for loving her so much." Her best friend smiled at her and then went back to admiring the little bundle in her arms. Then she handed the baby off to James and said, "Enjoy your daughter. She is a little miracle. I am going to go let the boys know and show them the video."

Cassidy made her way to the waiting room beaming and said, "We have a healthy and beautiful little niece! I have the video of it all. But, I will just show you guys the part where she is born, and we are all fussing over her. Then you can go in to visit one by one as soon as she has a room. It should be about twenty minutes or so."

The men watched the video in awe and every single man fell madly in love with that little girl. They would be her protectors, her friend, and her safe place. There was not a man in that waiting room who was not puffing out his chest with pride. These men were her family, and they couldn't be happier than she was finally here.

~~Sometime later...~~

Devante was holding his niece and whispering promises to her. She was cooing and kicking her little feet. This was a wonderful time in his life as it reminded him of when Jackson came into his life.

Their children were so precious, and he loved being an uncle. Especially seeing the pride, happiness, and love in James and Bridgette's eyes as they looked at their precious bundle. James was snapping pictures of them as his life depended on capturing every moment of Saskia's first day.

Bridgette let him fuss in part. After all, she was so tired from giving birth and in part because she loved how excited he was to be a father. There was a knock on the door and then Chris was there grinning at Devante and said, "Time's up bro. It is my turn to hold that babe in my arms!"

Devante scowled at his brother and reluctantly gave Saskia to Chris.

He would go and find his wife and take her home to their son. They will come back tomorrow with gifts! In the meantime, Chris was cooing at the baby, and she grabbed his finger and wouldn't let go of it. He beamed at her and said, "That's right uncle Chris is wrapped around your finger beautifully."

Bridgette had tears in her eyes watching Chris hold her daughter. She knew in her heart all of the men in their family will always be there for her. It made her so pleased with how life had changed in the last several years.

The only regret inside her heart was that Ryan couldn't be here to hold her daughter. She knew he would have fallen in love with the precious girl and spoiled her rotten. In her mind, she can picture it and it made tears race down her cheeks.

After about twenty minutes Chris handed Saskia back to James. He said he would get Decon so he could have his time with her. And then they would split to let the little family have some private time together. Not five minutes later Decon came in with a swagger.

He winked at Bridgette and kissed her head saying, "You've done perfectly! She is stunning." Then he took Saskia into his arms and kissed her precious little face and said, "I'm your uncle Decon gorgeous! I will always be here for you. You'll be our princess forever."

There was a hush that came over the hospital room after Decon left and Bridgette used that time to take a nap. James happily spent the time she was resting to spend with their daughter. He had never felt that kind of love before, but he knew that his life would never be the same. Saskia was everything to him and Bridgette.

There was nothing they wouldn't do for their daughter. As James held the baby he looked into her little face and said, "Heaven help the guy who tries to take you from us. There are four of us standing in his way and your uncle Ryan in heaven. There is not a man on this earth that can get past us. So, prepare for disappointment when it comes to boys."

The baby cooed and blinked sleepily at her father. He winked at her and said, "It's okay baby. Get some sleep." As if she understood his words she joined her mother in slumber.

~~The next day...~~

Bridgette was breastfeeding the baby when her husband came into the room and watched. There was a look of peace and love on his face.

"You never cease to take my breath away, kitten.", he said. Bridgette looked up as she softly stroked Saskia's head. "Isn't she just perfect?", she said. James simply nodded and choked up with emotion. The baby took a little nap after her meal.

While Saskia took a rest her parents lounged and watched some talk show. They were laughing at what people seem to think is important when there was a knock at the door. They quietly said, "Come in!"

Then a head peeked around the door, and they saw Ryan's brother Rory. Bridgette beamed and invited him in. She was so glad he arrived and was here to see the baby.

Deep within her heart, she knew that Ryan would be so pleased that Rory was a part of their family. He hugged James and then bent down to kiss Bridgette's cheek. Then his attention went to the baby cooing in the bassinet beside the bed.

The second that his eyes locked on hers Rory was in love. In Rory's life, he had never felt so strongly for another human being as he did for little Saskia. In very soft and gentle movements he bent down and picked her up.

She felt so warm and soft in his arms. She gripped onto his finger and wouldn't let go. He smiled and said, "Hello Saskia. I'm Rory, and I am so happy to meet you." Then Rory walked around the room and showed her everything.

They stopped in front of the window and he said, "See the clouds? That sky is not even a limit for you. You can be anything and everything that you want." Rory never wanted to put Saskia down. He loved the way she felt in his arms.

They spent the next hour just relaxing, and he fawned over her. It amazed James and Bridgette that such a young man would be so taken with their infant. Reluctantly, he gave Saskia back to her mother as he noticed the time.

He had to get to work and said his goodbyes to his new family.

The next several days went really well. The nurses helped James and Bridgette properly care for their little girl. They had visits from their family and friends. Rory made a point to stop by every single day to see Saskia.

It warmed Bridgette's heart that he has become so close to them as a family. Saskia was a very lucky baby to be so loved.

Chapter Twenty – Three

The moment that the little family arrived at home they felt peaceful. Everyone in the family had made sure there was food in the house, their baby things were all arranged perfectly for the baby and the house was cleaned. It made Bridgette tear up to know that they were all so loved.

The transition from a couple into a family was going fairly smoothly. There were some times when they felt overwhelmed in taking care of Saskia because it was such a big change in their lives. But, they were like every other couple with a newborn. Bridgette and James were finding their routine.

~~A few weeks later...~~

James gazed at his sleeping daughter and kissed her head gently. He hated that he needed to get back to the office. His work had always been an escape for him and his mission in life.

Now, it felt like a job he did to provide for his family and his employees. It was breaking his heart to have to leave his little girl at home. Bridgette made him coffee in a travel mug so he wouldn't be late and kissed him at the door.

She was trying her best to help his transition back to the office be the best it could be. They hadn't decided yet what would happen with her career. The position was always open to her but if she wanted to stay home with Saskia he would never force her to come back to work.

The drive to the office felt long and sad for James. But, the minute he set foot in the office it felt like coming home. He greeted his employees and accepted their congratulations.

Then he set himself up in his office and dove straight into his work. James was walking on air by the time lunch came around. It seemed that fatherhood was working for him because he was on fire at work.

He had three new deals for his company in the works and was feeling ready to move forward with them. His team were on top of all his suggestions and responding to some of the new ideas he had for moving forward with the company. The last few years had changed him in the end for the better.

Despite the fear, pain, and frustrations. It seemed like being on the other side of the nightmare he was stronger. He'd decided to take his lunch in his office and called home while he nibbled his sandwich.

"Hey Kitten! How is our precious girl?", he said. The screen showed his wife looking a little frazzled and his daughter behind her in her playpen squirming and cooing. Bridgette said, "Your daughter has decided to switch from being an angel to being a little demon.

The second you left for work she started screaming and nothing I did seemed to soothe her. Then we finally got to a good place, and we were reading stories between her naps and enjoying our time. But, then she had a blowout all over the place."

It took all of his willpower in order to hold back his laughter. The look on his wife's face and the sweet innocent look his daughter currently had was adorable. Instead of making his wife cross with him, he said, "That is terrible, kitten! Well, she must be going through some sort of growth stage or something. I will help out as much as I can when I get home. I also have some good news to share."

The look of curiosity on his wife's face made him smile. She had always been so interested in the business and helping to make it thrive. It would be nice to have her input.

Perhaps after they put their princess down for the night. Thankfully, Saskia seemed to appreciate her sleep at night and was out around nine or ten and stayed asleep until morning. Bridgette and James finished their conversation, and he blew kisses to both his girls before hanging up.

After his lunch was completed James decided to jump straight back into work. There were resumes on his desk for people to replace Bridgette. But, he did not want to move forward until he spoke with her and figured out what her next moves were.

If she wanted to take maternity leave and then come back he would have someone come in part-time to fill in. But, if she wanted to stay home with Saskia then he needed to find a replacement. Things were taking off, and he would need the extra help either way.

The rest of his workday went really well. The staff were buzzing about having him back and having some new things to look forward to. It was really sweet because his last meeting was actually a welcome back party for him put on by his staff.

There was cake, gifts for Saskia and a lot of happiness. This was indeed his second family, and he could not have been more proud of them. Before leaving work he promised he would have Bridgette come in to visit with Saskia sometime soon.

The drive home seemed to take forever. James was just so excited to get home to his girls. He wanted to sit down and eat dinner with his wife while his daughter stayed in her little bouncer swing thing that was all the rage.

It soothed her and made her happy. Bridgette greeted him at the door with Saskia in tow and kissed him happily.

"Welcome home, baby!", she said with a smile. Saskia cooed with glee at seeing her Daddy. It was a wonderful way to end his first day back to work. He went to change out of his work clothes while Bridgette started making dinner. It amazed him how domestic they both had become.

The second he came downstairs he kissed his wife and then went to Saskia in her bouncer. He picked her up and blew bubbles on her tummy. She giggled for the first time.

Both James and Bridgette stopped and beamed at each other. What a milestone for their daughter!

It seemed like the entire day was wonderful for them. Of course, there were dirty diapers and screaming baby moments. But, that was normal, and they were thrilled about sharing all of these experiences with each other.

It was super nice to finally be a family of three. It was also really nice to have their friends to lean on when they feel overwhelmed or unsure of their next steps. Cassidy and Devante have especially been so kind and helpful. This day was a great first step toward their new normal routine.

At least from his side of things. But, James wanted to discuss things with his wife. Bridgette curled up to his side in bed.

"It sounds like things are going well at work," she said. James smiled and kissed her softly, "Yes. We are moving forward with three new projects.

The thing is that I need to find someone to help out until you either come back to work or find someone to replace you. Do you feel like you know what you want to do moving forward?"

It took Bridgette a few moments to speak, and then she said, "I love our daughter. Becoming Saskia's mother has been the greatest joy in my life so far. I am so happy that I'm sharing this experience with you. You are my soul mate and our family is everything to me. But, at the same time work is important to me, and I am very good at my aspect of the business. I want to work with you and explore where we can take the business. I feel like in a way the company is no longer yours but all of ours. It is our family business. Saskia can be anything she wants to be. But, if she wants to be in the business someday she can. Because it is ours."

James listened to his wife speak and nodded when he agreed with what he was saying. Bridgette went on and said, "I would like to wait until she is a year old until I return to work. This way I can be there for her first special moments. Then once she is a little more settled we can see if she could stay with Elise and Jackson during working hours."

James considered her words and said, "I can agree with that. I think that is best for you and our daughter. I will start looking through resumes for someone to stand in until you come back, my kitten."

They spent some time cuddling and some heavy petting but neither were awake enough to do more. That would come in time. Neither were in a rush to go back to sexual interactions. They would rather it be meaningful and right for both of them.

~~

The next few months went smoothly both at home and at work for James. Bridgette was thrilled to stay home with Saskia. And on weekends they had family events at their home or the home of their family members. Saskia and Jackson were usually the center of attention. And life fell into a nice rhythm.

It wasn't until December that things started to change in their lives. On December first Bridgette was packing while Saskia was in her playpen. This would be her first Christmas, and they wanted to make it special.

So, James had rented a home in Montana for the entire family to go and celebrate Christmas with the snow. Everyone had taken off work so they could spend the entire month in Montana. After work that day James would come home and pick her and Saskia up, and then they would meet everyone at Devante and Cassidy's house.

They would take two cars and drive to Montana. Cassidy and Bridgette planned to start fresh the next day on their shopping journey. They were going to decorate the house in Montana and get gifts and wrap them. It would be nice so they could have a good Christmas.

Elise was going to help them with decorating and cooking. But, primarily she would watch the children. It would be a nice celebration with their family.

The family enjoyed listening to Christmas music as they started their journey to Montana. They planned on making stops along the way and also spending the night along the way when needed. Traveling with children changed the number of hours on the road they could spend.

But, it was fun to have a family adventure like this together. It took them several days, but they eventually arrived and crashed for the night once they settled into the house in Montana. The next day Bridgette and Cassidy went shopping for their gifts, wrap, and decorations!

They had a ball and came home to dive into their decorating. Christmas music was always on and everyone seemed to be pleased. Elise helped them plan their Christmas feast, and she was an angel helping them to decorate.

The days were filled with baking cookies, wrapping gifts, and spending time as a family. Jackson had his first experience playing in the snow. They captured it on video and basked in his innocent wonder at the entire situation.

Every member of the family felt so alive and free-spending time together. It amazed Bridgette that Chris and Decon actually left their laptops inside and enjoyed going snowmobiling. All of the adults took turns going out on the snow in the snowmobiles. There were snowball fights and snow angels.

~~Christmas Eve~~

Bridgette had noticed that her husband was acting a little off in the last week. But, she was so involved in the gift wrapping, decor changes, food/baking prep that she forgot about it. It was harder to do all those things with a baby.

At the same time, she couldn't imagine her life without Saskia. It was such a joy to share this first Christmas with her little girl. Even though it would be more of her watching it back after the fact on video.

The Christmas music was making everyone feel the spirit of the season. The fireplace and cocoa were helping everyone relax as she cooked dinner for them. It was an Italian feast in their rented home.

Bridgette remembered that she needed something from the bedroom so she went to get it. The bedroom door was closed, and she heard her husband's voice.

"Stacey, you know I am with my family in Montana. There is no way I could be there. Don't get all upset with me. You knew I would not be there from the start.", James said in a low voice.

Bridgette frowned. Stacey was his temporary personal assistant. She was keeping Bridgette's job warm while she cared for Saskia. Why would she want James to be with her at Christmas?

That was when the thought "Oh my God! My husband is having an affair with his PA!" raced through her mind. She scurried away from the door and checked on dinner quickly. Then she told Elise she needed to go out for a while but would be back soon.

Elise was thrilled to watch Saskia, and so she told her to have fun. If only Elise knew why she was fleeing their rented home. It was Christmas Eve and her entire world was falling apart.

Bridgette walked to the edge of the woods and sat in the snow against a tree and thought about how much she wished Ryan was there. He would listen to her and hold her as she cried. But, instead, she was alone under a tree crying her heart out.

This was supposed to be a happy night where each member of her family opened one of their gifts. And they ate delicious food and thanked their lucky stars for each other. Instead, she felt broken and betrayed.

The fact of the matter was she would need to pull her husband aside and ruin their family holiday by asking if it was true. Perhaps she should just leave it until after Christmas. This way they could have happy memories on tape for Saskia.

It could be her first and last Christmas with her family together. Pulling her knees up to her chest she rested her cheek on her knees. The sobs were shaking her frame, but she didn't care anymore.

The pain of what was happening could be felt in every fiber of her being. James had been the man of her dreams since the moment they'd met. She tried to be strong and fight it, but they both knew she would never be able to.

He'd been by her side through everything with Nancy and Richard. He held her when Ryan died and helped her family move forward. They got married and had a child together.

How could he turn his back on all of that? Will this affair with Stacey be worth it? Bridgette stood up and dusted the cold snow off her butt and made her way back to the house slowly.

She was unsure how she would pull off happiness about the holiday and make everyone believe that things were normal. But, she would find a way for the sake of the holiday and her family. As she was nearing the house Decon was walking from one of the rental cars.

He caught sight of her and arched his brow at her. She stopped and shook her head at him biting her lip trying hard not to burst into tears. So much for keeping it together and acting normal.

Decon came up to her and grabbed her gently by the elbow and escorted her back toward the tree line where she came from. He motioned for her to take a seat in the snow where she had been seated. She sat and he sat beside her.

They simply sat in silence for a few moments. Then Dec turned to Bridgette and took her hands in his. They made eye contact, and she bit her lip in an attempt not to cry but seeing his eyes she could no longer hold back.

The tears began to flow down her cheeks. Decon moved close to her and took her into his strong arms.

"What's wrong, beautiful?" he murmured against her hair. The tears were flowing so freely she couldn't speak. She could only shake as all of her emotions flowed through her all at once.

After several moments she said, "I was cooking dinner and had just placed it in the oven. I wanted to grab something from the bedroom really quickly. I knew that it would need more time to cook and that Elise would check on it if I were away."

Deacon held her and listened to her words as she went on, "I was about to get to the bedroom when I heard James' voice. I thought it was strange that he would be locked in the bedroom. I listened and he was talking to Stacey. She is filling in until I come back to work. But…" her voice trailed off into a sob. Bridgette took a few minutes to gather herself together.

"He was telling her that she knew he wouldn't be there because he was out of town with his family. And some other things that just sounded off. It didn't sound like an employer speaking to his employee. It sounded like a man making excuses to his lover.", she choked out between sobs.

Decon looked at her as she broke down again sobbing into his chest. He rubbed her back and tried to think of what to say. There were a lot of thoughts racing through Dec's head. He felt enraged that James would speak that way to another woman.

At the same time, he tried to see if perhaps it could have been Bridgette misunderstanding the situation. She was so emotional lately and hearing something like that may have made her see it differently than it was intended. At the same time if she were in Bridgette's shoes he would have assumed the same thing and be just as hurt.

Deacon gently pulled away from Bridgette and looked into her eyes saying, "I think you need to talk to James. But, I know you want to make Saskia's first Christmas special before you make any moves. So, let's get through tonight and tomorrow. Then you can discuss it with him. If you want I will hold your hand through it."

Bridgette shook her head and said, "No. When I speak to him it has to be just the both of us." The two friends stood up and walked back toward the house. She turned to him about halfway to the house and said, "Keep this between us until I talk to him. I... I can't handle anything else. As it is, I'm a mess. I need to dig deep and keep myself together over this next little while."

Decon agreed but told her he would be there if she needed him and that she could always come to him for anything. He told her she was brave and he loved her. Even placing a soft kiss on her forehead. James was sitting on the porch and arched a brow at the two as they climbed the stairs onto the porch.

He said, "Hey James. What have you been up to?" At his words, Bridgette went still beside him, and he hugged her closer to his side.

James looked pissed at the other man holding her so close but simply said, "I was on a work call. What were you up to Decon?"

Dec grinned and said, "Just spending some time with our girl. We are and always will be close. We are family after all. Right, B?"

Bridgette simply nodded and tried not to look at her husband. She was afraid if she looked at him she would break down in tears again. James stood and stretched lazily saying, "Well, I am going to go inside and play with Jackson and Saskia. If you have the time I'd love it if you join me, wife."

The way that James said the word wife made everyone tense with how deep and dark it sounded. Inside the house, Chris arched a brow at Decon. It was strange for him to hover so close to Bridgette.

He probably hadn't been that close to her since she left New York. Decon looked at him and simply gave him a look that said it was all good. Bridgette was looking nervous and upset so Chris figured she was upset and Dec was helping. He didn't miss seeing the look of disapproval on James' face at someone else being so close to his wife.

Chapter Twenty - Four

This Christmas was going to be tense as hell between the men. James sat down on the floor and started playing with blocks along with Jackson. Saskia was in her bouncer near him, and he would sometimes hold up a block for her and tell her what color it was.

Bridgette sat on the couch near him and watched. It was hard for her to reconcile the man he was in that moment, the man he had always been with, and the man he was on the phone with earlier. It was tearing her up inside.

Decon sat in a chair across the room staring at James. He was brooding and trying to sort out how a man so in love with his daughter and wife could potentially be a cheater. At the same time, he knew that what Bridgette heard made it seem as if he was.

It was hard for him to not say something to the man. He wanted to know the truth for Bridgette's sake and try to save her the most pain. It was clear that if James was cheating on Bridgette the men in this family would step in and care for her.

She would be protected, and he would be gone within moments. Saskia and Bridgette deserved better than that kind of man in their lives. Bridgette leaned down and whispered something into her husband's ear.

The next thing everyone knew the two were headed toward their bedroom and the door clicked behind them once they arrived. James looked at his wife with his head cocked to the side and said, "Is something wrong?" She straightened her spine and looked him in the eye and said, "Are you having an affair?"

The silence after her words finished was like a fog between them both. James matched his wife's gaze and said, "What would make you think that, Bridgette?"

Bridgette licked her dry lips and forced the lump in her throat to move. Then she said, "You've been acting off for the last two months. More so since we have been here in Montana. And then I overheard you on the phone a few times."

There was something that flashed in his eyes, and then he said in a low voice, "I'm having some problems at work. I have been handling it. But, it seems to have gotten out of hand." It was Bridgette's turn to arch an eyebrow and wait for him to explain himself.

He cleared his throat and said, "Stacey was working out very well at first. She was getting the job done. But, then she started to act differently and started to become flirty. There was nothing I could call her on though. I ignored it as best as I could until it became more blatant. There is a really big deal happening. They wanted to meet in December. I told her that she could handle the meeting herself or it would have been scheduled for January. However, she did not believe that was fair to her or the deal. She assumed we would have a company Christmas party and I'd be there the entire time."

Bridgette sat on the bed and listened. James went on, "I'm here. I'm with my wife and my daughter. And this is not acceptable to her. She feels like I owe her more. Stacey has felt this way ever since she kissed me and I did not report her to HR."

The moment he said she had kissed him it felt like ice was racing through Bridgette's veins. Looking her husband in the eye Bridgette asked, "Why didn't you report her to HR?"

James signed heavily and said, "Because I didn't push her away. And it was caught on camera. It would have looked like it was mutual, and we could have had a sexual harassment suit against us."

Bridgette balled her hands into fists and never took her gaze off of his as she said, "Let me understand you... you let her kiss you, you did not tell HR, the thoughts on your mind were how to make it not look bad for the company and you did not tell your wife."

The fact he said nothing simply confirmed in her mind that she understood properly. She said, "Why didn't you tell me?"

It took a few minutes before James said, "Because I felt like in not pushing her away from me that I had cheated on you. I felt like an asshole and when I got home that day you were so happy. And things between us were better than ever. We created a family with Saskia. You are the woman of my dreams."

Bridgette stood and said, "If I were the woman of your dreams you would have pushed her away, reported her to HR, and told me the truth."

Before he could say a thing she turned on him and said in a low voice, "We will act as normal tonight, tomorrow, and the next day. We will say we need to race home early the day after Christmas. Business-related. Then we will go back to Nevada. Once we arrive we will let everyone think things are good between us. I'll start packing for Saskia and me. We will leave the house and I'll be in touch with when and where you can see Saskia. I will never keep her from you. You didn't betray her, She deserves to have her father in her life."

James stood there looking at Bridgette like she had taken leave of her senses.

"You can't be serious! We are married, Bridgette. We are a family.", he said. She shook her head, "No, we were a family until you picked some bitch from your office over us. It would have been different if you came clean to me when it happened. I had to find out after hearing you speak to your PA like a lover. This has gone on for far too long and you've made your choice."

Then she walked around him and left the room slamming the door behind her. He sat on their bed and looked at the closed door in shock. He imagined he would eventually have to explain it all to her.

But, he thought she would forgive him. He hadn't kissed her back that first time. He had never kissed her in front of a camera. And nothing had gone beyond kissing. But, his wife was going to leave him.

It took a few minutes for James to collect himself before he went out into the open part of the house. He took a seat on the couch after getting himself a scotch. Devante arched a brow at him but didn't ask what was wrong.

Bridgette was acting as if their conversation hadn't even happened. She was playing with the children and working on getting dinner ready. She even fussed with the gifts under the tree.

There was something she wasn't doing though. Bridgette refused to look his way. She looked and talked at everyone else in the entire house.

This was very bad. He loved his wife and needed to make this right somehow. The first thing he needed to do was speak with HR about either transferring Stacey or getting rid of her from the company.

Then he needed to tell her he had made a mistake in ever kissing her back. And that he was committed to his wife and child. James signed heavily. Deep down in his heart, he knew that he fucked up and that this was not going to end well for his company or him personally.

Decon was giving him daggers and the entire scene on the porch made more sense to him. Declan knew he fucked up and wanted to pound him into the ground. Perfect. Merry Fucking Christmas!

Cassidy came into the living room and said, "Dinner guys! Come and get it." Elise and Cassidy picked up the children and placed them in their high chairs. Then she took their seats at the table.

Everyone was seated except his wife and Decon. In the next few seconds, Decon was seated next to him and Bridgette was in between Deacon and Chris at the table. The dinner was pretty quiet except for Cassidy telling some jokes and stories about their holidays.

Rory shared some more stories of Ryan. It seemed like everyone was having a relaxed Christmas Eve. The food was amazing and everyone credited Bridgette for it.

Dessert was all about Cassidy, and she was appreciated for her efforts. The women started to clean up after dinner was finished. The men all went into the living room. James sat apart from them knowing it was a matter of time before he discovered his mistake and that his wife wanted to leave him as a result.

Decon was giving him daggers. Chris and Decon were simply confused. An hour later the children were in bed having sweet dreams. Bridgette and Cassidy were on the floor in front of the large Christmas tree.

They gave a gift to each adult in the room and stated it was time for their traditional gift on Christmas Eve. They decided to go counterclockwise. That meant that Devante would start them off. The gift he opened was from Chris and Decon.

It was a new watch since his old one had broken a few months ago. Next was Elise who opened her gift to see a new coffee maker that she had wanted. It was from Bridgette and James. (Even though James had no idea about it previously.) He simply nodded and smiled as if he knew that was what they had purchased for the wonderful woman.

Cassidy was next to open a gift and it was from her husband. It was a beautiful heart necklace with his birthstone, her birthstone, and their son's birthstone on it. She loved it and thanked her husband with a kiss.

Chris was the next to open a gift. He laughed when he saw it was board shorts and a gift certificate to a surf shop. It was from Decon who said now he had no excuse to not try to surf.

Decon was next, and he grinned at his gift and thanked Bridgette, ignoring him completely although his name was on the card.

Inside was a bracelet that looked like chains but said his initials on the metal in the front. He hugged her and kissed her cheek. Then he looked smug as he pulled away. James wanted to punch him in the face, but he smiled instead.

Next was James' turn to open a gift next. Taking his time he began to unwrap the gift and looked into the box and saw it was a framed picture collage of Bridgette and himself as co-workers, on their wedding day, the day Saskia was born, and a recent family picture of the three of them.

It was from Bridgette. James turned to his wife with tears in his eyes and in a voice thick with emotion said, "Thank you, kitten. It is perfect. I can't wait to put it in my office."

Bridgette simply muttered a small "Your Welcome" and looked away. It was finally the moment for Bridgette to open her gift. She unwrapped the paper and saw it was a ring.

Engraved in it was J & B Now and Forever. She dropped it and ran out of the room crying. Cassidy got up and raced after her while all of the men looked at him with scowls.

Devante's voice thundered as he said, "What the fuck is going on?!" James took a long sip of his whiskey and sighed. Then after a moment, he explained what had happened, why he did it, and what Bridgette had said in the bedroom.

In the end, he looked down and said, "I love my wife and daughter. I really fucked up. I just felt like my wife was grieving over another man and not sleeping with me. Everything was about our daughter. Then there was someone who seemed to want me. I was weak."

Chris had to hold Decon back because he tried to lunge at James. Decon screamed, "I told you before you married her and Ryan told you! If you fuck with her you deal with us! You stupid motherfucker! How dare you!"

James simply winced and looked at Devante trying to find an ally in him. But, Devante's jaw was hard and his eyes were cold when he said, "We may be holding Dec back but that does not mean we do not share his thoughts or feelings. I think you need to pack and leave. Now."

He stood and looked at the men he considered to be his brothers and said, "I have a lot to make up for with my wife. I will be fighting for my marriage. I respect and love you as my brothers. But, if you stand in the way of my family, my relationship with my wife, my marriage I will not play fair."

James moved to his bedroom with his wife and began to pack his things. Elise was watching over the sleeping children in the nursery. His wife and Cassidy were in the room Cassidy and her husband were sharing.

He did not even try to speak to his wife right now. Instead, he peeked in on his daughter and kissed her gently as she slept. The hope was that he would see her again soon. He would find a way to save his marriage.

Meanwhile, Cassidy was seated on the bed across from her best friend Bridgette. Bridgette was hiccuping through her sobs. Moving forward she started to rub Bridgette's back and said softly, "What happened? Did you not like your gift?"

Bridgette looked at her friend and tried to keep herself together when she said, "I overheard him on the phone with Stacey. She was supposed to fill in for me until Saskia turned one. But, she kissed him, and he let her. I know there was more than one kiss. He was so guilty when I confronted him. But, he says he will fight for us. I told him it was too late. And he gave me my dream ring for Christmas. My ultimate act of love ring. And it is all a lie…"

As Bridgette fell into a fountain of sobs her best friend hugged her tight and said, "Are you sure? Perhaps you are just too emotional and assumed some things? Maybe you should talk to him again."

Cassidy was trying to look on the bright side of things. At the center of her being, she knew that her friend was hurting and that this situation was probably not a misunderstanding. Deep in her heart, she wanted to protect her friend from pain and knee James hard so he cried.

How could a man do this to his wife and his daughter? Bridgette dried her eyes and looked at Cassidy, "It isn't a misunderstanding. He knew what he was doing and chose to do it anyway. He called her on our family Christmas vacation. He touched her, kissed her… he betrayed me. And in a very real way, he betrayed the little family we have built. This will impact our daughter too. Even if she is a baby and can't understand. Her parents created her with love and now it is all falling apart."

Cassidy nodded and held her close saying, "We have your back. We will hire you back in the company. You could take over Ryan's role in the business. You are more than qualified and he would love that. You can keep his legacy moving forward. And as a result, you'll get a company car and a moving bonus so we can get you a nice place. A real home for you and Saskia. And if you work it out with James he can come to you."

The words from her best friend made Bridgette tear up again.

"Thank you for having my back, Cass.", she said. They embraced once more and then went to check on the children before facing the music in the living room. The babies were sound asleep and Elise had retired to her room.

But, she always kept a baby monitor in her room in case they needed her. She was talking about her position as a member of the family and nanny for the children well. The moment the women entered the living room all three men stood.

Cassidy gave a small smile toward her husband and said, "There isn't a need to be so old-fashioned fellas. We are used to you."

Bridgette laughed a little and winked at the guys, "I'm sorry for freaking everyone out. I was just not expecting to be so overcome with emotion. I had asked for that gift and felt like it would prove to be a beautiful symbol."

The men nodded. Devante said, "He told us everything. He claims that he wants to win you back and make it right. However, we told him we wanted him to leave. James said goodbye to Saskia and packed his things. He left."

The news hit Bridgette harder than she expected. She quickly recovered and said, "Well, this will be a more peaceful and less tense holiday tomorrow morning. Thankfully, we took some pictures with him and Saskia today. So, at least she will have some happy memories of her father and her parents together on her first Christmas."

Nobody said a word but Decon stood and came to take her into his arms and just hold her tight. After a few minutes Cassidy smiled and said, "Okay, folks let's have a late dessert and enjoy our time together on this holiday! We have plenty to spare and still have enough for tomorrow."

Everyone agreed. Chris and Decon made Bridgette laugh over pie with whipped cream on top. It felt almost as if everything were back to normal. All of the men in her family were looking after Bridgette, but she knew Decon was being the most clingy. He had always cared deeply for her and she was so appreciative for it.

The moment that the dishes were all put in the dishwasher and it was cleaning their dishes everyone agreed it was time for bed. Devante and his wife went first. They wanted to connect and celebrate their love for each other.

They were both so thankful for each other and their relationship. In the wake of Bridgette's situation, they both felt privileged to have each other. Chris and Decon walked Bridgette to her room. They both hugged her and reminded her that they were just across the hall if she needed them.

She thanked them and kissed each other on the cheek. The second her door shut the men made their way to the room they shared. Each man sat on his separate bed and sighed.

It hurt to see Bridgette in so much pain and to accept what James had done. He may make her even more upset in the future due to his stubborn urge to win her back. The moment the door clicked shut behind her Bridgette walked like a zombie to the bed.

She curled up in a ball and clung to James' pillow as her tears began to fall. Bridgette cried into the pillow and tried to be as quiet as possible. But, everyone heard despite her best efforts.

It seemed like when your heart was breaking you couldn't hold the grief in. The night was filled with tears until she fell asleep exhausted.

~~

The next morning Elise was awake first and once she was dressed she went to the kitchen and started breakfast. It was very important to her that she provided a good meal to the family. She wanted to make Bridgette's favorites to spoil her a little based on all she was going through.

It was Christmas, and she wanted to help bring the spirit back to the house. After the breakfast was cooking she took a second to look in on the children. They were waking up so she tended to them.

Jackson was in his high chair and Saskia was in her bouncer when it sounded like the house was starting to rise. Elise finished up with breakfast and waited for the family to trickle out of their rooms with the scent of delicious food. The first to come out of their room was Cassidy and Devante.

They beamed at the spread of the table and then went to their son. They greeted him and made sure he had his breakfast first. Then the couple took their seats and began enjoying Christmas breakfast. They insisted that Elise take a seat and enjoy the meal as well.

A few moments later Chris came out in his pajamas and sat down straight away to dive into the breakfast feast before him. Decon came out next but only stayed a second. Then he turned and went to check on Bridgette.

He knocked on her door and waited for her to answer. She was still in her clothes from last night, and she looked miserable. He beamed at her and said, "Merry Christmas, beautiful! Come have breakfast." Bridgette looked at Decon and forced a smile she did not feel.

"Merry Christmas, Dec." She took his hand and walked to the kitchen. Everyone was in the middle of eating as she sat down and forced herself to make a plate for herself. She sat in silence and listened to her family talk all around her.

Their happy voices kept her eating and moving forward with her day. It didn't feel like a special holiday anymore. It felt like a bleak day with no hope of sunshine.

It was at that moment that Saskia started to cry and her mother jumped up and picked her up. Bridgette held her daughter and cooed to her and rocked her. She wished she could just curl in a ball and cry too.

But, she knew that her daughter was crying for different reasons. After a few minutes of walking the baby around the house, Saskia calmed down in her mother's arms. She rested her little head on Bridgette's shoulder and sucked on her fingers.

Decon came up to them and hugged them both. He said to Bridgette, "I know it is hard and beautiful. But, we will get through it."

Rory had spent a lot of his time off to the side by himself but suddenly he was in the living room with them. She looked at Saskia and said, "I can take her for a while if you want"

Bridgette said it was alright for him to take the baby. So, she went off to go playing peek a boo with Rory. Then Bridgette sat on the couch next to Decon and held his hand.

"At some point, I need to meet up with him. We have to hash out the details, she said. Decon squeezed her hand and said, "I'll be here every step of the way if you need me."

She appreciated his words, but she knew she needed to be a big girl and handle it on her own. The look that Decon gave her said that he knew what she was thinking, and he didn't approve. If the situation had been different she would have laughed at it. But, she could only try her best not to break down.

The family cleaned up breakfast and found their way into the living room. Everyone seemed eager to open gifts. Jackson was amazed by the gifts Santa had left him.

Saskia was too young to enjoy her gifts yet. But, there was a little bunny from her parents that she seemed to cling to. Bridgette remembered picking it out with James and had to hold back a sob at how sweet their daughter looked clinging to it.

Everyone noticed that Bridgette was just going through the motions and the only thing that seemed to keep her attention was Saskia.

But, sometimes she almost seemed painted to look at her daughter all while loving on her. They knew that Bridgette needed time and understanding, and they offered it to her in spades. It was not the Christmas that any of them had planned but somehow they were making it work.

It was nearly sunset and the children were becoming tired when Bridgette stood up and said, "I need to get back to Nevada. I want to go to the house and pack some things for the baby and me. Then I'll get a hotel before making arrangements somewhere more permanent."

Devante said, "Wait for tomorrow. We can all go back early and help you." She shook her head and said, "I appreciate that you all want to help me. And you have and always will. But, this is something that I have to do on my own,"

The next thing she did was go to the bedroom and start packing for her and Saskia to leave Montana. She called one of their security men who work with Decon and Chris and asked if he would escort her back to Nevada in one of their SUVs. Once that was arranged she made arrangements to fly to New York in two days and stay in Ryan's place until she could purchase her own place.

She set up a meeting with everyone at the firm for the next Monday to discuss taking Ryan's position from New York. And then she tried to steal herself for the battle she was about to fight with James once she reached Nevada. An hour later she was placing Saskia into her car seat and watching the men loading the car.

Bridgette kept the diaper bag in the backseat with her. She smiled at her family and hugged them each. There was so much love flowing through all of them. She told them to stay until the New Year and that she would be in touch.

Declan did not like any of this and tried to convince her to let him come with her. But, she simply kissed his cheek and told him to take care of their family and trust her. Saskia was lulled to sleep in the SUV on the drive but Bridgette was awake and thinking about all that was ahead of her.

She had placed some calls into her lawyer, but he would probably get back to her in the morning. It was a holiday after all. In the end, Bridgette did not want to cause a scene between her and James. She just wanted him to leave her in peace.

He would have access to their daughter whenever they agreed on. He would always have time with Saskia. But, he needed to leave her be. The drive took forever as they switched drivers halfway and decided to drive straight through.

They would stop for bathroom breaks, to get food, and stop for gas. Saskia loved the movement of the car and it seemed to lull her to sleep. It was the middle of the next day when they arrived in Nevada.

Bridgette had been careful to call or text her family to let them know how it was going and that they were safe. As the car stopped in front of the house she had shared with James she took a deep breath. It was going to be hell to pack up the things they needed for the trip.

But, she would make it brief and have movers handle the rest. Steeling herself and thinking "The Queen is tall, straight, rigid and she doesn't cry. Be the Queen." Bridgette had the drivers watch Saskia as they were both fathers and bodyguards as well.

Her daughter would be safe in the car with them. She did not plan to take long. Alone she stepped up the staircase to the front door and opened it.

There was silence in the house as she opened the door and entered. She walked into the living room wrapping her arms around herself. She knew he was in the house somewhere.

That was when he walked into the room with Stacey on his heels. She turned frigid and said, "I will be taking some of my things and some of Saskia's things. Then I will be gone. I'll leave the keys on the island."

Not giving either of them a moment to say a thing to her she turned on her heel and hurried upstairs. Taking some luggage out of the closet she packed some of her work clothes, underthings, and mementos from her life. She left the things that reminded her of James behind.

Let him dispose of their wedding photos. On second thought she slid one into a bag for Saskia. Her daughter deserved to see her parents together in love.

Bridgette made her way to the nursery and packed some things for her daughter. There were mostly clothes, pictures, and special items she had been given by others. She was almost finished when she heard someone enter the room with her.

She went rigid and looked up to see James standing there watching her. She said, "I'll be gone in five minutes. Would you like the keys now?"

James shook his head and said, "It is not what you think it is. I had her try to make her see some reason. I wanted her to see our pictures and our family everywhere so she would realize what she was fracturing."

Bridgette rolled her eyes and said, "That is unprofessional. And you are fracturing it all. Your choices made this happen. Make no mistake about that." She stood and slung her bag over her shoulder and lifted the other.

Coming to the space in front of James she looked him in the eye and said, "The best thing you ever did was create Saskia. I will always be thankful for that." At the moment before she left the room she handed him her keys and her wedding set.

James looked down at them with sadness on his face and tears in his eyes. She walked out without looking back. Stacey was waiting at the bottom and the stairs and sneered, "I'm sure you can see yourself out. The trash always does."

Spine ram-rod straight Bridgette walked past her with her head held high. The moment that James realized her wedding rings were in his hand he yelled, "This is not over Bridgette! We will never be over! I'm going to get you back."

As she heard his screams she kept on walking slamming the door in her wake. She hoped it hit Stacey in her face. The men scurried to put her things in the car and asked where she wanted to go.

She told them that they needed to get to the airport. A friend of hers had called in a favor and his plane was on standby. As they drove away she allowed some tears to fall.

The sound of a text message caught her attention. It was from Rory, and he said he would meet her at Ryan's place in New York. He had a proposition for her and thought she would like it. She told him she couldn't wait to see him and not to tell the others.

Of course, he agreed. The trip to New York seemed like a blur for Bridgette. The drive to the penthouse seemed to pass by in a flash.

The next thing she knew it was night again, and she had settled Saskia down for bed. Then like a zombie Bridgette had made her way to the living room with a glass of wine in her hand. That was when she let all of her emotions out.

All of the loss, fear, and devastation from the past year all poured out of her soul. There were so many questions left unanswered. How would she work out custody with James?

How would she convince him to stop torturing her and leave her alone? What did Rory want? Would she be able to walk in Ryan's professional shoes? Would she ever stop hurting?

A text came into her phone and it said, "I'm coming for you…" from an unknown number. She shivered and held her hand over her mouth so as to not scream and scare her sleeping baby. They had security.

Would they be safe? Somehow, based on the sinking feeling in her stomach she didn't think so. Would she ever be safe again?

The end for now...

Note From The Author

Greetings my darling readers! I am so thrilled with the support and kindness you have shown me through the release of my first book. This series was written in 2021 and worked on until the end of 2023 when I first released Surviving Tomorrow.

The New York Family Series is very special to me. It is so nice that you loved it! This second book in the series means just as much as Surviving Tomorrow. I really enjoyed sharing Bridgette's story. It was heartbreaking and uplifting all at once.

I hope you are excited because later this year I will be releasing the third book in the series! It will be a pleasure to share the next adventure with you all. I hope you continue to love my series as we go along!

Love,
Carrie Cross

Books By Carrie Cross

New York Family Series:
Surviving Tomorrow
Needing Tomorrow

About The Author

Carrie Cross is the author of the New York Family series. She lives in Wisconsin with her understanding fiance who does not judge her writing process. She is a fan of road trips, pizza, Gilmore Girls, books, all things bookish and being creative.

Stalk Ms. Cross

Facebook Group: https://www.facebook.com/groups/66770 3342113695

Instagram: https://www.instagram.com/mscarriecross/

GoodReads: https://www.goodreads.com/user/show/141213 434-carrie-cross

Patreon: www.patreon.com/user?u=80615719

Ream: https://reamstories.com/carriecross